TWILIGHT EMBRACE

"You may be a lady, Miss Ashworth, but all you really know are the outside trappings. I don't think you know the true definition of a lady. Maybe I don't, either, but I don't pretend to. And at least I'm honest with myself."

The tin cup slipped from her fingers to the ground, bouncing with a metallic clink across the rocks. Stephanie stood so that her eyes were level with his.

"I haven't pretended to be something I'm not, Cordell. Your opinion of me doesn't matter. You were hired to find my father, not make social conversation, and I feel no need to defend myself against your accusations."

"No? Then don't." Cordell's hands flashed out to grasp Stephanie by her shoulders and he pulled her hard against him. A small gasp escaped her lips before his mouth was over hers.

Stephanie had been kissed before, of course, but never like this. The purple twilight faded and receded, and there was only awareness of the man who held her, who seemed to be drawing her will from her body with his demanding kiss. Somehow Stephanie's hands were against his hard chest, and she could feel the slow thudding of his heart beneath her fingertips.

For the first time in her adult life, Stephanie Ashworth was unable to take control of a situation . . .

MOONFLOWER
VIRGINIA BROWN

ZEBRA BOOKS
are published by

Kensington Publishing Corp.
475 Park Avenue South
New York, NY 10016

ZEBRA BOOKS
KENSINGTON PUBLISHING CORP.

ZEBRA BOOKS

are published by

Kensington Publishing Corp.
475 Park Avenue South
New York, NY 10016

First printing: August 1987

Printed in the United States of America

To Chuck Bianchi

Chapter One

Julian Ashworth glared at the two men in front of him, struggling for patience.

"You two have gotten me lost twice," he said in a fairly even tone, "and because you *think* you can speak their language, I've been shot at by Indians who normally wouldn't harm a fly. I don't know exactly how badly you insulted that Navajo chief back in Chaco Canyon, but it's a miracle we managed to get out of there alive."

"Mr. Ashworth . . ."

"Huntley, don't try to explain. I'm in no mood for it. You and Bates go back to Fort Defiance and send a telegram to my daughter for me. She doesn't need to join me. There's not enough time, and it's too dangerous anyway. I'll wait here at Hubbell's and see to our supplies." He flashed the pair an exasperated glance. "Do you think you can do that without bungling it?"

"Yessir," Bates chimed in, nodding eagerly. His pudgy face creased in a hopeful grin. "Reckon you could give us a lil' advance on our pay? We might need sumthin'," he added hastily when Huntley dug an elbow in his ribs and Julian Ashworth frowned. "Like . . . like food, or sumthin'."

"Whiskey's more like it," Julian observed drily. "Check with me before you leave . . . look out, man!"

Turning, Bates tripped over Huntley's feet and almost sent them both sprawling in the dust in front of Hubbell's Trading Post. The taller, skinny Huntley caught his short, round companion by the scruff of the neck and jerked him upright.

"Dammit, Alvie, watch where yer goin'!" To Ashworth, Huntley apologized, "Sorry, Mr. Ashworth . . ."

"Just go saddle your horses," Ashworth said. "I'll give you the message I want you to telegraph right before you leave."

Watching as Huntley and Bates made a hasty departure, Julian Ashworth entertained thoughts of canceling his expedition. If there just wasn't a damn time element involved, he would be able to search for decent guides! Julian made a mental note to fire the New York agent who had arranged for Huntley and Bates as guides when he returned.

"Couple of clowns, ain't they?" a voice observed, jerking Julian's attention to the shaded porch of the trading post. A scruffy-looking old man attired in various animal skins leaned against the log wall.

Thinking the old man didn't look too much better, Julian nodded shortly. "Yes, they are." He stepped up into the shade of the porch, flicking at the dust coating his long, perfectly tailored jacket.

"Name's Bingo," the old man said after a moment. "I hear tell those two are yer guides."

Julian waited expectantly. It was obvious the old man had more to say. Bingo spat a stream of tobacco juice to the dusty ground beyond the steps.

"Care for a chaw?" he asked Julian.

"A chaw?"

"Tobaccky. Ya want a chaw of tobaccky? No? Fine. I'll save it fer myself. Hubbell says ya need a decent guide. After seein' those two, I'm purt near inclined ta agree."

Julian slid him a wary glance. He wasn't in any mood to waste more time with incompetence. "Are you by any chance suggesting yourself? Are your qualifications commensurate with your appearance?"

"Quali'cations? Fust of all, lemme tell ya that them four-dollar words ain't gonna help ya out here. Second a all, th' most important quali'cation is a steady gun hand even when yer too liquored-up from th' night a'fore. Ya want quali'cations? Hell, pilgrim, I got cher quali'cations right cher!" Bingo slapped one hand on his rifle. "As fer my fam'ly tree, my momma was half wildcat an' my pa wuz a grizzly b'ar! I'm meaner than enny Injun that's ever been born, an' twice as smart! I kin skin a buffalo, rope a wild mustang, tree a panther, an' shoot th' eye out of a jackrabbit at a hunncrd yards in th' time it takes another man ta put on his pants in th' mornin'. How's them fer quali'cations?"

In spite of himself, Julian grinned. "Pretty damn good, I'd say. But can you read an Indian map?"

Bingo aimed a stream of tobacco juice at a fly

9

buzzing past. "Got 'im! Yeah, I kin read Injun maps and Injun sign, pilgrim. Sometimes, I kin even read 'em right. Ask Hubbell if'n ya wanna good reference. He knows me."

Don Lorenzo Hubbell supplied glowing references for Bingo, and in no time at all Julian had a new guide.

"By th' way, Pilgrim, whar we headed?" Bingo asked.

"To Magic Rock, sacred Indian burial grounds. Are you still game?" Julian removed his immaculate beaver fedora, scraping a hand through his thick blond hair. He fanned himself with his hat while he watched the expression on Bingo's face.

"Hmmph. I heerd of that place. Injun legend claims enny who go near it turn black an' die. S'posed ta have powerful magic. What'cha wanna go there fer?"

"I am a collector. I enjoy collecting rare artifacts and displaying them in my home. The acquisition is all the sweeter if I discover them myself, and I heard a story about this legend from a friend of mine who spent some time out West." Julian shrugged. "It sounded intriguing."

"That it do, Pilgrim, that it do." Bingo hitched up his buckskin trousers and adjusted the floppy felt hat he wore. "What'll ya do 'bout yer other guides? They're liable ta be a mite pissed that ya hired me."

Julian slanted a glance in the direction of the pen where Huntley and Bates were retrieving their mounts. "They can be quite painlessly dismissed when they return to the fort to place a wire for me. I'll send Lieutenant Buckner a note informing him of my plans and instructing him to pay them their wages from the account left for my daughter's use. That should forestall any attempts at reprisal."

Noon of the next day found Bingo and Julian perched atop a rocky ridge, staring at a mounted procession in the arid valley below.

"Shaddup an' git yer fool head down! As fur as I kin tell, them are Kiowas, an' I cain't tell yet if they're wearin' warpaint." The crusty old mountain man hunkered down on his heels behind a towering red rock, and motioned for his neatly dressed companion to do the same.

Rock, chiseled by wind and time and underground springs, had formed fantastic sculptures. This harsh landscape had earned the name *aleh-zon* from the Papago Indians—but it was better known to the white man as the territory of Arizona. It was a land claimed by the Indians, and coveted by white trespassers.

Bingo crouched forward on his knees to squint over the rock's scarred surface. "Yep. Them are Kiowas, all right—an' they's wearin' ceremonial stitches. They're pretty far west, I kin tell ya, but it's yer lucky day, pilgrim. Leastways they ain't after our topknots."

"How fortunate." Julian heaved a sigh of relief and pushed back his beaver fedora as he leaned against a rock. He slanted a glance at Bingo. Bright sunlight glittered from the small gold earring he wore in his left ear, and a gray, sweat-stained Stetson was cocked to one side on his head.

"Yep, Pilgrim—it's yer lucky day, all right." A stream of tobacco juice hissed against the hot rock.

11

"'Cause I got a notion, where they's goin' is near ta where we wanna go."

"Do you think they're going to the Sacred Mountain on my map?"

"Well, they ain't got warpaint on. An' it looks like they's totin' one of their chiefs who's gone to the Happy Hunting Grounds, or the Great Bye-n-Bye, or whatever you wanna call it." Another brown stream arched through the hot, still air and he wiped his mouth with the back of one hand. "I'd bet my best squaw and a barrel of whiskey they's headed fer th' one on yer map."

"Seems a pretty safe bet. Let's hope they are. Not very many white men know about it, according to my sources. Huntley and Bates had never even heard of the region where it's located." Julian shook his head at the proffered plug of tobacco from Bingo. "No, thank you."

Replacing the tobacco in his pouch, Bingo snorted derisively. "I don' know who steered ya ta those two, but ya done yerself a favor in gittin' rid of 'em. They shore don' know too much, those no-good, poor excuses fer guides. Hell, they're both dumber than anvils. Th' way I hears it, they're half drunk all th' time, an' all drunk half th' time. I don' think they kin find their way outa th' fort without askin' at least twice fer direckshuns."

Nodding, Ashworth heaved a disgusted sigh. "I'm certain you're right. I can't imagine how my agent could have recommended them to me. He won't be my agent long when I return to New York. I'm very fortunate to have found you."

"Yeah. I'm th' best ya kin git." Bingo's serene

expression was not the least bit self-conscious, and he hardly seemed aware of Ashworth's amused glance in his direction. "I'd be damned serprised," the old mountain man continued thoughtfully, "ta find out Huntley an' Bates even heard of th' Grand Canyon, Mr. Ashworth. They prob'ly woulda took yer front-money an' hightailed it fer th' border."

A harsh expression creased Ashworth's normally placid features. "If they had, they would have found me a hard man to deal with, Mr. Bingo, I assure you. I'm not as soft as I look."

Bingo cackled. "Good thing fer you that ya ain't, Pilgrim! This is man's country out here, an' not fer th' unwary."

"Yes. It's a shame that I was unaware the area we're going can only be traversed at a certain time of year. If I had known there was a time element, I would have brought Stephanie with me instead of having her wait until I had secured the map showing its location. She had every intention of joining me. Though after seeing the rough terrain, I agree with you that my daughter should stay in New York this trip." Julian added in a low tone, "It's the first expedition in a long time that she will have missed, and I'm positive she will be furious with me."

"T'ain't none of my business, Mr. Ashworth, but whut on earth good would a gal do out here anyway? She'd be 'bout as much use as tits on a boar hog." The old man stopped when Ashworth laughed.

"Stephanie? You wouldn't need to worry about her, Mr. Bingo! She's a very resourceful young lady. She'll be most put out with me when she receives the telegram I had Bates send. I just sent her the original

13

map, while I've kept an accurate copy, but that was before I met you. Now her appetite will be whetted, but she'll be in New York. She was to leave this week."

Julian flicked a speck of dust from his fedora, an action Bingo already recognized as a ploy to gain time while thinking. The tall, blond-haired Easterner smiled, reminding Bingo of a sly, tawny cat. "The telegram was a most useful device to rid ourselves of Huntley and Bates, don't you think, Mr. Bingo?"

"Bingo, Mr. Ashworth, jus' Bingo. Don' hold with no formalities out here."

"Fine, Bingo. Shall we be off?"

While Julian Ashworth and his newly hired guide remounted their horses to follow the little Indian band, Huntley and Bates were riding into Fort Defiance. They dismounted in front of the officer's building that housed what passed for a saloon. Spurs jangled as their booted feet trod the creaking wooden boards of the sidewalk and porch. The long coats they wore flapped against their knees, covering the lethal pistols hanging from gunbelts at their waists. Huntley shoved open the saloon door, and they stepped into the cool interior for a drink.

"I'm ready to wash this damned dust outa my throat," Huntley told his companion. "But don't go drinking too much again, Bates. I didn't like leaving Ashworth back at Hubbell's. We can't leave him alone too long. He might get second thoughts."

"Naw," Bates dismissed that idea. "Who else can he get to guide him now? And besides, I don' intend to let go of that gold so quick. Do you?"

Huntley beckoned to the uniformed bartender. "Whiskey," he ordered, "two of 'em. No, Bates, I don't intend to let easy gold slip through my fingers. That's why I want you to stay sober for a while. Ashworth doesn't have any idea that we know about all that Indian gold. He thinks we bought that dumb story about old ruins full of statues and broken bowls. He don't know I talked to that old Indian he bought his map from, and kinda . . . persuaded . . . him to tell me what Ashworth was looking for. The drunken old coot couldn't tell me anything about the map even though I almost broke my hand against his hard head, but we've got the next best thing— Ashworth." Huntley grinned. "We're gonna be rich, Bates, and we can't afford any slipups."

Two glasses of whiskey were downed, then two more. Turning to Bates, Huntley said, "I'll go across to the telegraph office and send that wire to the old man's daughter, while you give that letter to Lieutenant Buckner and see about us a bed for the night."

Bates nodded. "Too bad his gal ain't comin'. I'm 'bout ready to see a decent-looking woman again." Squaring his shoulders, he tugged at the brim of his hat, turned to leave, and put his foot into a brass spittoon. Stumbling, Bates bumped into the bar then staggered backward, earning cuffs and curses from several soldiers seated at a nearby table as he bumped into them. His hat brim tilted over his eyes, momentarily blinding him as he flopped about aimlessly.

Huntley rescued him before he blundered into another table, jerking Bates upright and kicking the spittoon free of his foot. "You damned idiot . . . !"

"Ho! Huntley! Bates . . . !"

A young lieutenant nimbly dodged them. "What're you two doing back so quick?" he asked. "And where's Ashworth?" The spittoon clattered to a stop and he nudged it upright with his boot.

"Back at Hubbell's gathering up supplies, Lieutenant Buckner," Huntley answered. "We brought you a letter from him. He said it was important . . ."

"What does it say?" Buckner asked, reaching out for the soiled letter Bates was producing from the big pocket of his long coat.

"Now, how in th' hell would we know? We don't go around readin' other people's mail," Bates replied in an injured tone. "'Sides, neither one of us kin read . . . What is it?" He sidled closer, trying to peer over Buckner's shoulder at the letter.

Buckner glanced up at the two men, his face darkening with chagrin. This was not a task he relished. It'd be better to get it over with quickly.

"The letter says to pay you boys off for the little you've done, and let you go," he began. "Ashworth's found another guide . . ."

"What?" Huntley snatched the letter from Buckner's hands. "I don't believe it! Who could the bastard find so quick?" His face grew red with anger as he stared at the incomprehensible words, and he crumpled it in one hand and threw it to the dusty floor. "Damn that fancy-pants dude! He just wants to go on some stupid chase after ghosts instead of what's important, that's all!"

"What do you mean?" the lieutenant asked curiously. "What's Ashworth looking for? He never did tell me anything except he had recently bought an old map . . ."

Bates opened his mouth to answer, but Huntley's boot crashed down on his instep. Huntley coughed to muffle Bates's howl of pain, and smiled ingratiatingly at the lieutenant.

"He wouldn't tell us either, Lieutenant. Just something about old arrowheads from a thousand years ago, and broke pots and stuff. That's all," Huntley said. "Now, about the money Ashworth said to pay us . . ."

"What'd you stomp my foot for?" Bates whined when the lieutenant was out of earshot. "That hurt, dammit!"

"Not half as bad as it'd hurt to get hung," Huntley snarled.

"Hung?" Bates's voice was two octaves higher. "Me?"

"Quiet, big mouth? Yeah, you."

"For what? I hadn't got caught doin' nothing . . ."

"It's not what you have done, but what you're going to do. We can't let Ashworth get away with this, Alvie! I'll think of something, I swear I will!" The expression on Huntley's face made Bates's round mouth droop open.

"Uh, I don' know if I'm ready fer this . . ."

"Shaddup. I've already thought of something." His mouth curved into a smile as Huntley fingered the paper with Julian's printed message to his daughter. "I don't think I'll be sendin' this telegram after all, Alvie. Maybe Ashworth's daughter will like Arizona. And maybe Ashworth might want to part with some of his gold to see her again . . ."

17

Chapter Two

"You simply cannot be serious about this, Stephanie!"

Stephanie Ashworth slammed shut the lid of the expensive leather trunk covered with stickers from France, England, Africa, and China. The heavy lid balanced with at least an inch of clothing-cluttered space between the gaping edges.

"Please help me close this trunk, Claudia," she coaxed. Exasperated, an older woman stood with a dubious expression creasing her face in worried lines as she regarded the tall, slender beauty who had been her charge since she was a child. Now perched upon the leather and brass curve of the trunk lid, the stubborn child had grown into a very determined young woman.

"I think it's a mistake, Miss Stephanie. A dreadful mistake. Whoever heard of a young lady of quality traipsing into the wilderness alone?" Consternation tinged the faint tremor of Claudia Tremayne's voice, and thin, frail hands laced and unlaced in quick,

18

anxious movements. "Your father is doing fine by himself, and doesn't need you along . . ."

Stephanie bent a piercing glance in Claudia's direction. "Of course he's doing fine. But I intend to be with him whether he needs me or not. I've been on every expedition since I was old enough, as you well know. Why should I miss this one?" She reached out to pat Claudia comfortingly on the arm. "Father has hired two competent guides, and all the arrangements have already been made. I was supposed to wait two weeks to give him enough time to persuade a map from that old chief Mr. Jackson told him about, then start west. But today, the morning post brought me a copy of the map he sent home for safekeeping, so I'm already behind schedule."

Stephanie's aristocratically tilted nose wrinkled in perplexity as she shook back a stray wisp of silvery blond hair from her eyes. "He must have sent the package immediately. There was no letter with it, but it says in his last letter that he's been staying at a nearby trading post that is much more comfortable. It seems like Fort Defiance would be much safer. Allen claims that there are dangerous Indian uprisings, and I shouldn't go . . ."

"Oh, Stephanie! Mr. Pinkerton is one of your father's good friends, and should know what he's talking about. After all, he does head a detective agency in Chicago. I think you should do as he suggests and stay here."

"So does Uncle George." Stephanie's shoulders lifted in a brief, silk-clad shrug. "I never did agree with George, the pompous oaf, even if he is my mother's brother. And it's my time and my money, so

I'm going. Father would never arrange for me to join him in the first place if he thought it was too dangerous. And he sent me a map, so he must want me to help him decipher it. Look, Claudia." Stephanie held up a small brittle skin that was yellowed with age, "It must be a thousand years old! There was no explanation beyond a short sentence telling me the animal skin was original, and he has a copy. Oh yes, Claudie, I'm definitely going to Arizona Territory!"

"Oh my." The faint sigh that accompanied these two words made Stephanie smile.

"Oh, Claudie—you don't really have to leave New York. It's rough country out there, and you aren't accustomed to it. I will be perfectly all right by myself. I'm quite capable of handling any sort of problem that may arise. Father always said I have a cool head on my shoulders."

Claudia gave a brief shake of her graying head, and her soft brown eyes twinkled behind the wire-rim spectacles she wore. "I realize that you are far more capable than most young women your age, Stephanie. How many girls have had the unusual upbringing that you have? Trotting all over the globe with Julian Ashworth, searching for rare art objects, going on African safaris and climbing through musty Egyptian tombs—no, I realize that you are quite proficient in caring for yourself, but you knew I'd insist upon going with you. I can come back to New York after you've joined your father." The little woman drew herself up and faced Stephanie with all the appearance of a martyr about to meet the den of lions. "I will travel with you to

Arizona Territory if it kills me," she said, adding in a soft moan, "And I'm sure it will."

Stephanie laughed. "I knew you'd say that—but don't say I didn't warn you! Now do help me shut the lid of this stubborn trunk, Claudie."

The trunk was duly shut and locked, and a servant summoned to carry it downstairs. After assuring Claudia that she would rest, Stephanie ushered her firmly out the door. "You do the same, Claudie, or we will both be too exhausted for words by the time we reach Arizona." She gave the older woman an affectionate hug. "Our train does not leave until seven o'clock tonight. Try not to worry."

The door shut softly behind Claudia, leaving Stephanie alone with a jumble of thoughts. Pushing back the tangle of hair that stubbornly persisted in falling into her eyes, Stephanie sank to the comfort of a plump-cushioned lounge and propped her chin in the cradle of her palms. In spite of her bravado, she felt a vague apprehension. Arizona Territory was in the midst of fierce Indian wars. Only a year before, in 1879, an entire family had been massacred when they separated from their group. The Indians had captured a young girl and boy from the family, who had never been seen again. Stephanie shivered.

Julian Stephen Ashworth was one of the wealthiest and most successful financiers in New York, yet never failed to take the most daring chances with his safety. That was one of the reasons she liked to go with him, to insure that he would be more cautious. He didn't take unnecessary chances when his only child accompanied him.

Though her father did tend to become overly

enthusiastic about the acquisition of new and rare art objects at times, he would observe basic rules of common sense when Stephanie was with him. Since her mother's death when Stephanie was only eight years old, Julian had rarely left her behind. Her education had been broadened by impromptu trips to Chinese temples and the Great Wall, elephant rides over the snow-covered Alps, and jolting camel-back across the hot sands of Egypt. This latest expedition Julian embarked upon had been a spur of the moment decision sparked by an interest in artifacts from an ancient Mayan tribe.

Lord knows, Stephanie thought, their New York mansion contained rooms and rooms full of stone statues carved thousands of years before by vanished tribes. Some of the maids even refused to dust in the room containing African voodoo masks, claiming they were too terrified of the frightening caricatures. Art objects had always fascinated her father, but the ones Julian had gone after held a special interest for him. Somewhere in the dry, arid regions of Arizona rested a collection of artifacts carved thousands of years before by a people long extinct. Julian Ashworth enjoyed the thrill of the hunt as much as he did the satisfaction of acquisition.

Stephanie tucked her feet under her and stared thoughtfully out the velvet-draped window. She shared her father's love of adventure, but it was tinged with more caution than Julian possessed. And she frequently worried that somehow his intrepid nature might endanger his life.

"Miss Stephanie?"

The gentle voice jerked Stephanie's attention to

the uniformed maid standing in the open doorway. She had not even heard the light knock or the opening of the door.

"Yes, Molly? What is it?"

"Mr. Farrington is here to see you. He's waiting in the small parlor."

Oh, dear, she had not yet told Reginald of her plans to leave, and Stephanie knew he would be displeased.

"Tell Mr. Farrington I will be right down, Molly."

Reginald Farrington would be more displeased about her failure to consult him first than her planned absence, Stephanie reflected as she quickly inspected her appearance in the gilt-edged mirror hanging on the wall. Their wedding was set for January, and he already exercised an authority that predicted their marital life. It promised to become a bone of contention between them, because she had never been dictated to in her entire life.

Julian had always made suggestions, and none of her teachers or nurses had ever dared make demands of the wealthy Ashworth heiress. Only Claudia had the temerity to present strong arguments to the young woman who had been in her charge since infancy, but she was more like a foster mother than an employee, so it never occurred to Stephanie to question her. Claudia Tremayne was a mild-mannered little woman with all the appearance of a bright spring robin, yet she had always managed her strong-willed charge with little problem. "Stephanie," she would say, "is not at all rebellious, only determined. She listens well to reason."

Stephanie permitted herself the small hope that

Reginald Farrington would listen to reason also. She licked her forefinger and smoothed a fine-arched brow, then pinched her cheeks to lend them color. This would take more than simple diplomacy. She bit her lips to give them a flush of pink and wished once more that her eyes were a popular cornflower blue instead of a brown so dark it was almost black. Julian insisted the contrast was much more striking and unusual combined with the silvery sheen of her hair, but some small quirk in Stephanie still longed for conventional beauty.

She was too tall, and too thin, and her shoulders were too wide and her legs too long. Most acclaimed beauties were petite with golden blond hair, huge blue eyes, and long, fluttering lashes. Not Stephanie. She'd never felt comfortable with girls her age, not even in the exclusive girls' school she'd attended. Even then she'd been different. While her companions were giggling and chattering about boys and dances and party dresses, Stephanie rode her favorite hunter over wooded hills and neat, white fences. The best times were the times spent with her father on some grueling trek through dense jungles and burning deserts.

Oh, she was accomplished as required of an aristocratic young lady in the year of Our Lord, 1880, but instead of playing the pianoforte or singing, Stephanie enjoyed archery or target practice with the latest rifle. Perhaps that was one reason she was twenty-five years old and still unmarried. Once, there had even been a reference to her in the *New York Tribune*'s society column, as the "matron of the unwed belles." That had stung, though she'd dutifully laughed as was expected. She was accustomed to the title of "Ice Maiden" that one rejected suitor had labeled her. He'd said she was as cold and emotionless as an iceberg. Was that the reason she had accepted Reginald Farrington's proposal of marriage? He didn't expect emotion.

Farrington was wealthy and ambitious. Certainly a marriage to the daughter of one of New York's leading financiers could not harm his ambitions, but Stephanie still wondered at his reasons for choosing her. There were any number of lovely debutantes equally suitable. Perhaps it was because Reginald didn't want or expect any display of emotion from her. He certainly didn't offer any himself.

Stephanie cringed at the memory of a man who *had* expected emotion from her. But that was so long ago, when she was young, and it had been a mistake that Julian had quickly nipped in the bud. Only the most secure or vain man had dared approach Stephanie Ashworth, and Reginald Farrington was a combination of both.

Smoothing the wrinkles from her silk blouse with its high collar edged in exquisite lace, Stephanie flicked a last glance at her reflection and straightened her shoulders. This would not be a pleasant interview, and she wanted it behind her.

When Stephanie entered the small parlor, Reginald rose from the austere chair where he was seated and crossed the room to greet her. Stephanie stifled the sudden wish that her heart would race romantically at the sight of him. Her dark eyes scanned his slight frame. As usual, he was attired impeccably and his dark hair was parted neatly in the middle and combed closely to the sides of his head. His black mustache was full in the style of most men, sweeping out like the handlebars of a big-wheeled velocipede. Reginald stroked it with one finger and smiled at her.

"My dear, you are as lovely as always." They were almost the same height, so that when he leaned forward to place a chaste kiss on her brow, he did not have to bend very much. The small peck was his usual sign of affection, and Stephanie had often wondered if she was being ridiculous to want more.

"Thank you, Reginald," she said. "I apologize for keeping you waiting."

"Quite all right. I was enjoying the view of Central Park. Springtime is such a lovely time of year."

"Yes. It is." Oh, Lord, must their conversations always be so trite and inane? "I understand there's a new obelisk from Egypt being erected in the park. Cleopatra's Needle, I believe. Have you seen it, Reginald?"

"Oh yes. Some sort of Egyptian thing," Reginald dismissed the subject with a wave of one hand. "I must say I don't understand your father's passion for crumbling old statues and dirt-crusted coins. Their value is to be appreciated, of course, but I fail to see the beauty in some of the obscene little figures like those he has in his study."

Stephanie felt a wave of pure dislike tremble through her. "Those 'obscene little figures' in Father's study are very rare Greek bronzes, Reginald. Father and I are the ones who dug them out of ruins of an ancient temple on the isle of Crete. They date from the 1400's B.C. Doesn't that impress you at all?"

"Oh, I suppose their antiquity has a certain value,

Stephanie, but aren't you placing too much importance on old artifacts? The new age is what's important and exciting. There are more modern inventions being created every day, and the world is growing smaller with each passing moment. Why, right now we have a railway system going from the East coast to the West, and more tracks are being laid daily." Reginald's mouth curved into a placating smile, and Stephanie suppressed the urge to plant a fist on the jutting arch of his nose.

"I realize that," she forced herself to say nicely. "Which brings up another topic I must discuss with you. I am leaving tonight for Arizona." She hadn't meant to be quite so blunt, and her irritation gave way to remorse at the expression on her fiancé's face.

Stephanie's abrupt disclosure startled unflappable Reginald, and he stared at her. "You're what?"

"Claudia and I are taking the 7:10 train tonight for Arizona," she said gently. "I must join my father, Reginald."

"Stephanie, we've been through this before," Reginald said in the tone of the long-suffering male who must be patient with a dull-witted female. "Julian Ashworth is more than capable of caring for himself. Allan Pinkerton agrees that Arizona Territory is too treacherous for a woman. Julian has simply gone off on another one of his tangents into the uncharted wilderness of those rocks and deserts looking for new toys. He will be quite all right."

"Oh, will he?" Stephanie's voice was dangerously soft. "And what if he isn't, Reginald? What then? My father has never," she said, punctuating each word with a forefinger stabbing his chest, *"never* gone off without me since I've become an adult. I intend to join him at once."

A frown creased Reginald's thick brows. "I fully understand your desire to join him, my dear," he conceded, "but it's hardly the place for you. That's a man's country and not for women. Besides," he added, "we're supposed to attend an important function at the Vanderbilt's. You need to be with me. It won't look right if you're not there."

"Really? How unfortunate. I didn't realize that a party was so much more important than my father, Reginald. I also didn't realize what an insufferable prig you are!" Stephanie's dark eyes were black with anger. She could not recall ever being quite so furious in her entire life. Few men had ever measured up to her standard of Julian Ashworth in her opinion, but until now she hadn't realized just how far below those standards Reginald Farrington stood.

"Stephanie! I'm absolutely shocked by your language!" Reginald's face was almost purple and his pale eyes seemed even paler than usual.

"Are you shocked? I'm glad, because at least that means you possess some sort of human emotion, Reginald. I was beginning to fear you had none." Stephanie took three steps away then turned. "Good day, Mr. Farrington."

Reginald caught her as she reached the parlor door, one hand curling around her wrist. She repressed a shudder at the touch of his soft, moist fingers coiling like a snake around her arm as he continued. "Stephanie, I'm afraid you have misunderstood my intentions. I only wished for your safety, that is all. If I were the least bit doubtful that your father would be perfectly well, I would have already gone to Arizona myself, I assure you!''

"Would you?" Stephanie's eyes met his. "Then why don't you go with us?" She smiled at his instant recoil and muttered protests of business obligations, family affairs, and did she know that hostile savages still roamed Arizona?

"Never mind, Reginald." She gave him a slight pat on one shoulder. "I was only joking. Of course you can't go with me. It's terribly unsafe."

Reginald Farrington III stared at the closed parlor door for a long time after Stephanie had gone, feeling rather like a fool and very much like a coward.

Chapter Three

It was hot. It was even, Stephanie thought, hotter than the jungles of Africa or the deserts of Egypt, though in a different way. She stared out the open windows of the stage at the flat-topped mesas and buttes lining the horizon. Short, twisted trees called mesquite dotted the hard ground, and there were clumps of bristling cactus thrusting skyward. Claudia made a soft, moaning sound beside her.

"Poor Claudie. Maybe you shouldn't have come," Stephanie murmured, giving the older woman a comforting pat on her knee. "I do wish you had listened to me and worn light-colored clothing and no petticoats, Claudie. You'd be much cooler."

Too weary and hot to do more than make pitiful sounds, Claudia Tremayne closed her eyes. The trip from New York had been almost pleasant for a time, but had turned into a nightmare from which there seemed to be no escape once they had left the Atchison, Topeka and Santa Fe Railway in Gallup, New Mexico. Now they were jolting across Arizona territory in the boxlike interior of a stagecoach on their way to Fort Defiance.

"Stephanie." Claudia's voice was a dry whisper. "Do you suppose we'll ever see a decent-sized town again?"

"In Arizona?" Stephanie laughed as she fanned herself with a wide-brimmed straw hat. "I doubt it. I think Gallup and Fort Wingate were the largest we'll see for a while." Her glance strayed back to the interesting landscape outside the window. Dark eyes widened as Stephanie suddenly leaned forward, pointing a finger and exclaiming, "Claudie! Look at that!"

Claudia turned to look, disinterest fading as she saw what had excited Stephanie. A rocky slope slanted above the dusty road they traveled. Halfway up a surface dotted with small, dry bushes, perched a natural arch of rock curved into a bow-shape. The huge arch was large enough for four full-six coaches to have driven beneath at the same time, and was studded with the twisted shapes of bushes and mesquite. It resembled a crude window carved from rock and placed there by a giant hand.

"My word," Claudia breathed softly. "I have seen the most curious things lately!"

The true adventure for Claudia had begun when they'd left Missouri and crossed into Kansas. In Kansas she'd seen her first real Indian, and had almost fainted with fright. Stephanie, of course, had been slightly disappointed.

"He's not at all like I'd heard Indians looked," she'd complained. "Why, that man is just old and pitiful, wrapped in a dirty blanket and drunk as an

Irishman! I've seen more frightening apparitions in a New York alley."

Claudia was rather comforted by the thought that the Indian did not seem at all bloodthirsty. Stephanie might be more well traveled, but she had obviously not seen everything. It seemed that she needed someone to keep her out of danger also, Claudia decided. What would Stephanie do without her?

The stagecoach rocked over a large stone and threw both occupants about like toys. They bounced twice in a flurry of cotton skirts before ending in tangled heaps on the dirty floor of the coach.

"Oh my," Claudia squeaked as she pushed at the brim of her black hat. It hung over one eye obscuring her vision, and a wisp of veil tickled her nose. "What happened?"

"I believe we hit a bump or rock." Stephanie helped Claudia back to the seat and brushed at her skirts. "It will certainly be a great relief when we finally arrive at Fort Defiance. I don't think I can stand much more of this wretched conveyance!"

It was nearly dark when the lathered horses plodded wearily to the top of a rocky rise. Below them lay the fort, and in the dimming light Stephanie could make out the blurry outlines of wooden and adobe buildings beyond the protective stockade-style fence. A small gathering of uniformed men stood beneath the flagpole while the Stars and Stripes were lowered, and the tinny, plaintive notes of a bugle wafted through the still air.

For a moment, as the coach rattled to the crest of the hill, Stephanie thought she had rarely seen a more moving sight. Magenta and rose streaks painted the sky and buttes in glowing colors, and welcoming lights already flickered in unshuttered windows of the fort. Behind the adobe buildings the flat buttes and mesas stood starkly against the purple sky in majestic splendor, and for the first time, Stephanie realized that even arid desolation had a unique beauty of its own.

Booted feet thunked loudly against the wooden side of the driver's seat above them as the driver and guard urged the horses faster down the rocky road to the fort. Dust billowed behind in huge clouds as they passed through the double gates of Fort Defiance and the coach rolled to a halt. The driver, a crusty old man with dust-grimed clothes and a broad felt hat pulled low over his eyes, leaped to the ground and opened the door for Stephanie and Claudia.

With stiff knees and aching backs, the two women tumbled clumsily from the stage and stood in the thick dust of the open yard. Off-duty soldiers ambled across the area and dogs barked loudly. Evening lamps hanging on the outside walls had been lit, and were throwing welcoming pools of light over unpainted boards and adobe walls of the long building in front of them.

Stephanie jumped slightly as the guard who was still perched atop the stage threw her trunk to the ground not far from where they stood.

"Be careful with that," she said sharply. "There's no need to treat my luggage more roughly than necessary."

Behind them a masculine voice laughed softly. "Better be careful, Shorty. The lady seems a bit irritable."

Stephanie was about to turn and reply that anyone should be irritable if their possessions were being carelessly tossed about, when the man added, "Lord, look at the size of her! Tall as she is, Shorty, I wouldn't try arguing if I were you."

His reference to her height made Stephanie immediately self-conscious and furious at the same time. How dare a complete stranger make disparaging remarks! She turned slowly and looked at the man standing on the top step of the long porch. He was partially hidden in the darkening shadows, leaning casually against a rough wooden post that held up the low roof.

"Sir, perhaps you should be just as careful," she said. "I could be very dangerous."

"I don't doubt that, lady." The man straightened and took two steps down into the fading light. "In fact, I'm willing to bet that you are as dangerous as they come."

For the first time in her adult life, Stephanie experienced a rapid change in her respiratory system because of a man. Her breathing quickened, the air seeming to come more thickly than usual as she stared up at the man towering above her on the wooden stair. He was tall, very tall, and his shoulders and chest were broad and muscular. A thin cotton shirt hugged his frame, and was tucked into the narrow waist of dark cord pants that fit much more snugly than Stephanie thought decent. Hung from his lean hips was a leather holster that cradled a lethal-looking pistol. Most of the men she'd seen since arriving in the West wore guns, Stephanie had noticed, but somehow this man wore his with such an air of casual menace that it was frightening. He was grinning at her, white teeth flashing in the dim light, and the probing glance he raked over her body was more insulting than flattering.

"You could hardly be a qualified judge of ladies, sir," Stephanie said stiffly. "I can't imagine any woman of character associating with you."

Beside her, Claudia had drawn her tiny body into an indignant knot, and her voice quivered as she said, "Oh, do not converse with this . . . this . . . person, Stephanie! Let us find the commander so he can arrange for our room and supper."

Claudia's remark brought another light laugh from the arrogant man on the step. "Did you think you were coming to a hotel, ladies? Think again. You're not in Central Park."

His reference to Central Park startled Stephanie. What did this rough, crude individual know of Central Park? He'd probably never been farther east than St. Louis. She whirled around, quivering with anger, and ignored him.

"Sir," she said to the wide-eyed driver, "will you please take our trunks to the commander's for the moment. Thank you." Stephanie's hand cradled Claudia's elbow in a firm grasp. She steered Claudia past the arrogant man still standing on the steps, ignoring him as if he was no more than one of the yucca plants dotting the arid landscape.

For the first time she noticed that their heated discussion seemed to have drawn a crowd. Several rough-clad men stood watching with amused expressions on their faces, and Stephanie was dimly aware of the comments as she and Claudia sailed past with all the dignity they could muster.

"Tall one, ain't she . . . ?"

"Ain't nevah seed hair that color afore . . ."

"Cain't b'lieve some woman talkin' ta Cordell lak she done . . ."

Cordell must be the arrogant frontiersman who had spoken to her so rudely, Stephanie decided as she coolly ignored the men. She rapped sharply on the unpainted wood door of what appeared to be the commander's office. While she waited for an answer she was uncomfortably aware of the eyes turned in her direction, one pair of eyes in particular. They bored into her back like red-hot fire pokers, and she could visualize the amused twist of the man's mouth as he watched her. Odd, she hadn't been able to discern the color of his eyes beneath the shade of his hat brim, but Stephanie had the distinct impression they were as cold and colorless as ice.

The door swung open, and a blue-uniformed officer admitted the two women. He wore a faint look of surprise on his face as Stephanie and Claudia entered.

"Eh, can I help you ladies?"

"Yes. We are here to see Colonel Pritchett. I sent a wire from New York advising him of our arrival over a week ago. I am Stephanie Ashworth, here to join my father. Could you tell me if he's still here, or is he staying at the trading post?"

The man scratched at his head and stared at them with a bewildered expression creasing his sun-lined face. "Sorry, ma'am, but the colonel didn't say anything to me about it, and I honestly don't know anything about your father."

Impatient, and still stinging over the short exchange of words just outside, Stephanie's voice was sharp and imperative. "Perhaps he didn't see the need to speak to you about it. Advise the colonel we are here, please. I am weary and so is my companion."

"What I'm tryin' to say, ma'am, is that Colonel Pritchett ain't here just now. He won't be back for a few days." His voice was calm and patient in spite of Stephanie's acid tones. "And I don't know nothin' about no women visitors."

"Dear me." Claudia's hands laced in agitation and her brow was puckered with anxiety. "What shall we do? We've come all this way and now have no place to stay . . . Oh, dear, where is your father? I knew this was not a good idea, Stephanie."

Stephanie patted Claudia's shoulder. "Everything will be fine, Claudie. Excuse me," she said to the officer, quickly scanning the insignia on his uniform. "Lieutenant. Would you be so kind as to arrange quarters for us until the colonel's return? I am quite certain he will approve."

"Well . . ." The lieutenant pulled at one ear while he considered. "I'll have to ask someone to give up a room. We're a little full up 'cause of a recent Apache uprising. Bunch of settlers came in to stay for a while. That's why the colonel had to leave the fort. Some of the men ought not to mind giving up their room for you, though. I'll ask."

"That's very kind of you, Lieutenant . . . ?"

"Buckner, ma'am. Lieutenant Charles Buckner."

"Lieutenant Buckner, Miss Tremayne and I will be most grateful for your assistance." Stephanie flashed him a smile. "I apologize for my rudeness earlier, but I had to run the gauntlet of those rough-looking men outside, and I'm afraid I was still angry."

"I understand, ma'am. I'm sorry you had trouble. We get a lot of strangers through here. Drifters, trappers, gunslingers, leftovers from the war—they all seem to pass through the fort at one time or another on their way somewhere." The lieutenant shrugged. "Most of them don't stay long. Our soldiers are always gentlemen, however, so if you have any more problems, just ask any man in uniform for help."

"Thank you, Lieutenant Buckner. I will." Stephanie fumbled in her reticule and brought out a folded sheaf of paper. "Could you please tell me where I will find two men by the name of Huntley and Bates? I believe they are to be my guides." Still looking at the paper, she felt rather than saw Lieutenant Buckner's faint start of surprise.

"Huntley and Bates?" he echoed. "Why, they're here somewhere, ma'am. Did . . . did you hire them?"

"No. My father did. Perhaps you met him—Julian Ashworth?"

"Ahhh." Buckner nodded belated recognition. "Him! Big man with blond hair who always wears a natty suit? Sorry, the name didn't register at first. Yes ma'am, I met your father. Are you *sure* he hired those two as guides for you?"

"Yes. That's what it says right here." Stephanie held up the letter from her father. "Hezikiah Huntley and Alvin Bates."

Lieutenant Buckner shrugged helplessly. "Well, I guess he did, all right. I'll tell 'em you're here after I get you all settled into a room."

Stephanie frowned. "Is there something the matter with these two men, Lieutenant? Aren't they guides?"

"I suppose they've been called that. Though there's some that wouldn't say so. I haven't ever ridden with them, so I can't truthfully say whether they're good ones." Buckner hesitated, and Stephanie began to feel impatient.

"Either they are guides, or they are not. Which is it?" She felt a wave of weariness wash over her, and wished the officer would give her a straight answer, then secure them a room. She wanted little more at that moment than food, a bath, and a clean bed.

"Yes, ma'am. They are guides," the lieutenant admitted finally.

"Good. I'm glad we have that straight. Now our room, please?"

Unfortunately, it was close to an hour before Stephanie and Claudia were able to have their luggage taken to a room. The shortage at the fort had necessitated the removal of someone from their room, and there were no volunteers to sleep in the stables.

"I did finally get someone to agree to bunk in with the horses," Buckner told them, "but it took a while."

"There must be a shortage of chivalrous gentlemen," Stephanie commented, glancing around the crude little room that hardly looked large enough for one person, much less two women with enough luggage to stay several months. "I thank you for all your trouble, Lieutenant."

Claudia gazed dubiously at the iron bed with its thin mattress and even thinner blanket. "At least it's clean," she said when the officer had finally gone and they were alone. "I wondered if we would find all sorts of foreign creatures in our beds."

"That's still a possibility. When Father and I were in an African rain forest, I woke up one morning to find a python cuddled next to me. They do seem to seek body heat at night, and some of the insects were as big as birds." She smiled at Claudia's shudder of horror. "Just don't be complacent yet, Claudie. I understand there are snakes and insects here, too. Stay calm if you should see any."

Claudia sank to the hard comfort of the neatly made bed. Her thin face was laced with tired lines, and Stephanie began to wonder how the little woman would fare on the long trip back to New York alone. She had tried her best to dissuade Claudia after realizing how arduous a trip it would be, but she'd refused to go back to New York, saying she wouldn't leave Stephanie alone with all those cowboys, fur-trappers, and smooth-talking men on the train.

Now they were in the barren territory of Arizona and Claudia had little choice. Stephanie intended to join her father. She'd never given up in her entire life, and discomfort was a small price to pay in order to be with Julian Ashworth when he made his great discovery.

Stephanie reached into her velvet reticule and brought out the folded letter Julian had sent her. The paper crackled as she unfolded it. It didn't sound much like Julian's usual style, but then, he'd been in a hurry. A faint smile tilted the corners of Stephanie's mouth. Julian Ashworth was always in a hurry. He hurtled through life at a breakneck speed, as if he was afraid he might miss something.

Magic Rock. It sounded like a name from one of the dime novels turned out by writers of Western lore. In fact, the reason for her journey to Arizona sounded to Stephanie like an entire plot lifted from one of Erastus Beadle's publications about the Wild West.

An ancient burial ground rich with priceless statues and artifacts that had never been seen by white men? It was simply too good to be true. She hoped that her father had not been the victim of a jest, but his sources were usually impeccable.

Sighing, Stephanie laid the letter and her reticule on the table. Kneeling on the rough wooden floor, she opened one of her trunks. Tucked inside a small pouch was the animal skin Julian had sent her. She took it out, turning it over and over in her hands, staring at the yellowed skin that had been scraped clean of any fur. The black markings on the skin resembled stick figures. Her eyes narrowed slightly as she laid the skin out on the small table in the center of the room. Turning it just a bit, Stephanie was able to make out what appeared to be words as well as drawings of animals and people. Jagged lines seemed to represent mountains, and a huge circle must be a lake.

"Do you suppose these drawings will truly lead us to archaeological treasures, Claudia? It seems so unlikely that this map could have survived the years and ravages of time. I wonder if it's authentic . . ."

"It's possible. But how on earth will you be able to figure out what it means, Stephanie?" Claudia lay back on the flat pillow of the bed and closed her eyes. "I'm so tired right now, I can only think of sleep, I'm afraid."

"I'll wake you when our meal arrives. I'm certain I can make some sense of this if I study it carefully." A pucker creased her forehead as Stephanie pulled the brass lamp closer to the skin and stared at it from different angles. She was soon completely absorbed in the charcoal drawings, trying to recall other maps she had helped Julian read and decipher.

A sharp knock at the door startled Stephanie and jerked Claudia from a light doze.

"It must be our evening meal," Stephanie said. "The lieutenant promised to send us something hot to eat." She smoothed her rumpled, dusty skirts before opening the door.

The visitor was not bearing a tray of food, however. It was the same arrogant man who had embarrassed and infuriated Stephanie on the front steps of the commander's office, the man called Cordell. Stephanie's back stiffened and her voice was immediately wary.

"What do you want?"

"Only my blanket roll, lady." He was grinning, a

slightly mocking, irritating grin that grated on her nerves. "I left it in here when Buckner persuaded me that you ladies needed this room more than I did."

"We have you to thank for our room?" Decency demanded that she express gratitude, but Stephanie found it difficult. She almost choked on the words and Cordell knew it. "I extend my thanks for your hospitality . . ." she began, but it was cut off by a wave of his hand.

"Forget it. Just let me get my blanket roll and get out of here. I don't want to risk offending your sensitive feelings again." Without waiting for an invitation inside, Cordell stepped past Stephanie and into the room.

He seemed to fill the tiny space with his big body, dwarfing the rough furnishings with just his presence. At least he had the good manners to remove his hat, Stephanie thought as the brown felt swept from his head. She studied him surreptitiously as Cordell opened a cabinet door. Thick, dark hair grew too long down his neck, brushing the collar of his blue cotton shirt in curling waves. Broad shoulders flexed as he bent to search the cabinet floor, taut muscles straining the seams of his shirt. Cordell's gunbelt was low on his hip and the holster tied to one thigh by a leather thong. The blue metal of his gun gleamed dully in the light from a brass lantern on the table. He wore boots like all the other men who were called cowboys, high-heeled and dusty. Stephanie's gaze drifted up his lean frame as he stood, and she found herself staring into the face of a man who was unquestionably handsome.

He should have removed his hat earlier, Stephanie was surprised to find herself thinking, then flushed at her own thoughts. But he was attractive, even when he quirked a dark eyebrow in her direction and his eyes crinkled in amusement. She should have turned away, but instead she was noting that eyes she had first thought colorless were a clear, piercing gray. They were so clear and sharp they appeared to be almost silver, with dark pupils that widened as she stared at him. Claudia's light cough jerked Stephanie's attention to the fact that she was rudely staring.

"Did you find your blanket roll?" she asked quickly. Her gaze dropped to the rolled-up Indian blanket he held in his hands. "Oh. I see that you did."

Now Cordell was openly grinning again, obviously aware that she had been assessing and approving his virile masculinity. White teeth flashed in his tanned face. "I found what I was looking for," he said, and his tone implied that she had also.

"Very well." Stephanie darted a glance toward Claudia, and her expression prompted the tired woman to come to the rescue.

"Sir, would you be so kind as to inquire about our evening meal?" Claudia interrupted. "Stephanie and I are so tired from the long journey, and Lieutenant Buckner promised to send us some food."

Gray eyes flicked over Claudia's small frame and he nodded. "Yes. Buckner's probably having a hard time with the army cook. I'll see what I can do for you." His gaze returned to Stephanie. "Are you Stephanie Ashworth?" Cordell asked abruptly,

44

taking her by surprise.

"Why . . . yes. How did you know?" Lieutenant Buckner, she answered her own question immediately, and Cordell verified it.

"Buckner said you're looking for Huntley and Bates. Why?"

Stephanie immediately bristled. "That's really none of your business, sir. Now if you will please leave . . ."

"I met your father," Cordell cut in. "He fired those two. Why would you want to hire them?"

Stephanie hesitated. Had Julian actually fired them? Then why would he have sent her a letter telling her he was using them as guides? She didn't trust this Cordell, and quite plainly told him so.

He shrugged. "Fine with me. It's your neck. Just thought you might want to know."

Cordell jammed his felt hat back on his head and nodded at Stephanie as he stepped toward the still-open door.

"Wait!" She reached out without thinking, her fingers closing over the corded muscles in his forearm. "Did you talk to my father? Can you tell me when he left?"

His eyes moved to Stephanie's slim white fingers curled around the bare skin of his arm where the blue cotton of his shirt was rolled up, then shifted away. "Maybe. I'd have to think about it . . ."

Stephanie's sharp questions drowned out Claudia's softer queries about Julian's health.

"When did you last see him? What did he say? Who was he with? Where was he . . . ?"

"Whoa, lady!" Cordell was looking directly into her face now, and Stephanie noted the amused glints in his eyes and the way they crinkled at the corners when he smiled. "How do I know he wants you to find him? For all I know, you may be chasing down a man who doesn't want to be found . . ."

"Oh, really!" Stephanie was indignant. "Do I look like the sort of woman who would resort to such melodramatic methods for finding my father? Obviously, he wishes for me to join him or he wouldn't have sent me a letter. . . . But you needn't bother helping me since answering questions inconveniences you." Her voice grew hard and determined. "I can find him myself."

The amused glints in his eyes flickered into an expression she couldn't quite read, but was so quickly gone Stephanie wasn't quite sure she'd seen the change.

"By yourself? You're loco," Cordell said with a nasty laugh, dispelling any notion that he might have entertained nicer thoughts. "How do you intend to go about finding him?"

"Huntley and Bates, of course."

"Oh, lady, you *are* asking for trouble . . ."

"And why do you say that?"

"You're just a crazy woman out here, not knowing what the hell you're doing . . ."

"Please watch your language, Cordell . . ."

". . . and when you tangle with those two, you may understand a little bit more. If you don't, that's your problem."

"Well, I never . . . !" Stephanie began furiously.

"I can believe that," Cordell cut in again. "Mean as

you are, no man's liable to want to get close enough."

Claudia moaned softly and buried her head in her hands while Stephanie sputtered with sheer rage. No words would come immediately to mind that would have devastated the rude frontiersman. Stephanie swallowed several choice remarks as beyond his understanding.

Cordell's eyes narrowed on the lamp-lit table as he slung his blanket roll over one shoulder and turned toward the door. He paused with one hand on the latch and asked, "That your map?"

Stephanie would have preferred an acid reply, but Claudia's faint voice murmured affirmation before she could stop her. "Yes . . . Mr. Ashworth sent it. I assure you we wouldn't keep any of your possessions, Mr. Cordell."

"No? Maybe not you, ma'am." Cordell pivoted before Stephanie guessed what he was going to do, swiftly crossing to the table to stare at the map. "Nice map," he commented when Stephanie leaned over and snatched it from the table. "Bet your father sent it to you."

"You've already been told that. You're not very subtle," Stephanie observed caustically. "Why don't you just come right out and ask rude questions instead of trying to beat around the bush? My 'none of your business' answer can save us so much time then."

"You're as prickly as a cholla cactus, lady. And if you'd let me, I could save you a lot more than time . . ."

"I'm certain you think so. We are not interested in your offer, however, only in a decent meal and a good

47

night's sleep. Please leave before I call a soldier to have you forcibly removed, sir!"

"Now, that would be great entertainment," Cordell drawled. "But I'm not sure your companion could stand the excitement. I'll leave . . . for now."

For several long moments after he'd gone Stephanie just stared at the closed door, quivering with indignation. When a sharp rap sounded on its surface, she realized she'd been expecting it. He had returned. Of course he had. Cordell sensed value in her father's map, and he wasn't the type of man who would be willing to give up easily. She had certainly been right in her first assessment of his character, Stephanie was thinking as she pulled open the door.

A large bear of a man stood in the opening, his bearded face shadowed by the brim of his cavalry cap.

"Your dinner, ma'am."

Well, Cordell would be back. She knew that for a fact, she told herself as she took the tray. Claudia's nose wrinkled as Stephanie set the tray on the table and lifted the lid from the metal soup tureen.

"What is that horrendous smell?" asked Claudia.

"A stew, ma'am," the soldier said. "We ran out of meat, and the cook used what he had on hand."

Stephanie peered at the contents of the bowl. She easily recognized onions, peppers, and small bits of cabbage, but the lumps of greasy meat floating on the surface eluded identification.

"What kind of meat is this, soldier?"

"Rattlesnake" was the calm answer, and both Stephanie and Claudia immediately gagged. Not even in Africa had she eaten snake! The metal lid clattered back in place.

48

"Thank you," Stephanie told the soldier politely. "You were very kind to bring our meal." Her forced smile was a bit strained, but much more presentable than Claudia's greenish pallor and convulsing throat.

"This," Claudia said when the soldier had gone, "promises to be a very long trip."

Chapter Four

Ryan Cordell pushed open the door to the long room serving as the officer's recreational hall. It was little more than a crude saloon, with a short bar at one end and several tables scattered across the rough floor. Cordell found what he was looking for leaning against the bar.

"Evenin', Huntley. Bates. Whiskey, Jackson," he said to the bartender. "And a round for these two while you're at it."

"Well now, that's right nice of you, Cordell," the taller of the two men said in surprise. "What's the occasion?"

"Just thought I'd congratulate you two on your job, Huntley. I heard Ashworth's daughter hired you to find him for her."

"Yeah. Buckner told us she wuz here lookin' fer us," Bates cut in. "An' here we thought ole Ashworth had fired us fer some other, no-count guide." He glanced slyly at Huntley and laughed, catching Ryan's attention.

"Now, why would he do that, I wonder?" Cordell's mouth slanted into a mocking smile. "Couldn't be that he heard you two are the crookedest pair this side of the Mississippi, could it?"

"Now wait a minute . . . What d'ya mean by that . . ." they chorused.

"Oh, don't get so touchy, boys. I'm just serious." Cordell's glass tilted up as he drained his whiskey. "Too bad you're going to have to pass up this job."

Behind the bar, Corporal Jackson heard enough of the conversation to figure out it was time to leave. He threw down the rag he was using to wipe the bar top clean, and quietly disappeared.

Huntley was almost as tall as Cordell, and he wore his gun slung low on one hip, businesslike. He backed slightly away from the bar, facing the man leaning so casually against it.

"I don't think we're goin' to be passing up ennything, Cordell. Why're you so interested in us guidin' some city gal to her pa anyway?"

"Let's just say I have taken rather a fancy to the young lady."

"Yeah." Huntley spat a stream of tobacco juice in the general direction of the brass spittoon two yards away. "I'll believe that when mules quote Scripture, Cordell. Ever'body knows you ain't got much use for women. Why, there's some as even say . . " He stopped short, realizing from the sudden flare in Cordell's eyes that he'd overstepped good sense.

"Even say what, Huntley?"

"Nothin' worth repeatin'," Huntley backed down. "But me an' Alvie are . . . uh . . . guidin' . . . that lil' gal, Cordell. We figured out this game, and we're cashin' in on it."

A gold coin flipped through the air and plinked on the bar top, spinning aimlessly before it stopped. "No, I don't think you are" was the soft assertion. "I decided you boys need a little rest from hard work. In fact, Arizona climate may not be good for your continued health." Cold gray eyes skewered Huntley and Bates for a moment. "Nighttime's the best time to travel . . ."

"Hold on, Cordell," Bates interrupted. "We kin cut you in on it . . ."

"No. I don't want a cut. Do you think I don't know how you intend to get it?"

"Wait . . . we're jus' tryin' to make a little honest money by takin' that gal to her pa, Cordell . . ."

"I'm sure you are. Forget it." Cordell pushed away from the bar, facing both of them. His hands hung loosely at his sides, and there was no mistaking the coiled tension in his muscles. He waited, watching the two until Huntley finally moved.

Lantern light glittered across the barrel of Huntley's gun as it flashed upward, but fast as he was, he was too slow. He found himself staring into the deadly black eye of Ryan Cordell's Colt .45. A short-barreled Peacemaker, it had a cutaway trigger guard for split-second timing, and Huntley knew it. He cursed softly and very slowly let his gun barrel drop downward.

"No sense in gittin' all riled up now, Cordell," he said soothingly. "Guidin' that gal ain' worth dying for . . ."

"I thought you might feel that way, Huntley. How 'bout you, Bates?"

"Same. Fact is, I got some kin over New Mex way that I been thinkin' 'bout visitin' . . ."

"Have a good trip, boys. You need a vacation."

As the door banged shut behind Huntley and Bates, Ryan Cordell holstered his pistol and reached for the half-full bottle of whiskey just behind the bar. A brief sense of satisfaction tilted the hard line of his mouth into a smile for a moment. Two more obstacles out of the way; and the third shouldn't be at all difficult . . .

"But what shall I say?" Claudia was wringing her hands in familiar motions as she whispered to Stephanie. "Oh dear, why don't you approach him? He looks so . . . so . . . he looks so forbidding!"

They were standing in the open door of their small room. Stephanie had seen Ryan Cordell across the courtyard, and was urging her companion to speak to him.

"No, Claudie. I think it will be much better if you do it. I've already exchanged words and opinions with Mr. Cordell, and you haven't. Try the direct approach. He seems to be a man who appreciates that."

Especially since he doesn't practice it, Stephanie said silently. Directness would not seem to be Ryan Cordell's strong point, but it did seem as if he had been right about Huntley and Bates. She had spoken with them briefly the evening before, and had not been impressed.

"Your pa, he hired us," the taller one said. He'd glanced over his shoulder for the third time within thirty seconds. It was a habit that seemed to be contagious, because his companion kept doing the same thing.

"So?" Stephanie had prompted irritably. "My father hired you to guide me to him, correct?"

"Yeah, but we got another offer . . ."

"Mr. Huntley, do you mind facing me when you speak?" Stephanie interrupted. "I find it most disconcerting to converse with the back of your head . . ."

"Look, Miss Ashworth, we got another job!" the shorter man cut in. "An' your pa's already took off without you . . . Ouch!" Bates stared reproachfully at Huntley and rubbed his bruised side.

"Left without me?" Stephanie was stunned. "But . . . but he couldn't have! Why—he even sent me a map!"

Her words had seemed to freeze any thought processes the men might have had, and she wondered why her father had hired them. They certainly didn't seem very bright.

"Never mind," Stephanie began, but Huntley had gripped her by one arm.

"You've got a map? How'd you get it?"

She frowned, glancing down at her arm. Huntley released it instantly.

"I told you. My father sent it to me. It arrived the day I left for Arizona, Mr. Huntley. Why?"

"It's just that . . . that we didn't know he'd be sending you a map. That makes a difference, Miss Ashworth. We didn't want to go off half-cocked without being sure we could find him, that's all. Sure, we'll do it. We'll guide you. Uh, can you

54

leave tonight?''

"That's impossible. It will be at least two days before I can leave." For some reason, Stephanie had hesitated. She didn't like Huntley and Bates, but hated agreeing with that horrible barbarian, Cordell. Two days should give her enough time to assess the situation, she'd decided, especially since Julian had already departed.

The two scruffy-looking men had assured her they would check back with her, and that was the last Stephanie had seen of them. Sometime during the night, they had disappeared from Fort Defiance. They were obviously not the sort of men she would trust to guide her across Arizona's mountains and deserts in search of her father. Neither was Ryan Cordell, but unfortunately he was the only man available. Lieutenant Buckner had spent a good hour of his time trying to convince her of that fact before finally succeeding.

"Ma'am," he'd said wearily, "there just ain't nobody else. You can either get Cordell or hire some Indian to take you, but them's your only options. Now I have three big stacks of paperwork to get done before the colonel gets back, and I need to get to it.''

His polite dismissal had infuriated and frustrated Stephanie, but she was left with little choice. And Ryan Cordell, she was told, knew this country like the back of his hand.

"I'll bet," she'd muttered to herself as she stalked across the dusty courtyard to her room with skirts lifted high. And to Claudia she'd acidly observed, "Mr. Cordell appears to be the sort of man more accustomed to jail cells."

But here they were, and if nothing else, Stephanie Ashworth was a determined young woman. So if that meant spending a week or two in the company of a disagreeable—but competent—individual, so be it. As soon as they reached her father, she would send Mr. Ryan Cordell packing.

"Go speak to him, Claudie," she urged.

Claudia capitulated, and her soft pleas must have worked, Stephanie decided moments later, because Cordell was taking her by one arm and striding toward Stephanie.

She stepped out of her room to meet him, somehow not wanting to confront him inside. He just seemed so much . . . larger . . . in a small room.

Cordell stopped in front of Stephanie, and his eyes were almost level with hers and alight with laughter. "So you didn't like Huntley and Bates? Too bad."

"Let's get straight to the point, Mr. Cordell. My offer is five hundred dollars to take me to my father. Half now, and half when we arrive. Are you willing to guide me?" Stephanie was definitely uncomfortable with this man. For some reason, he reminded her of someone, but she couldn't quite think who it might be. Probably some known criminal she'd read about in the *Tribune*. "Well, Mr. Cordell?" she prompted when he didn't answer. "Are you for hire, or aren't you?"

"Maybe yes. Maybe no." Dragging a small cigar from his vest pocket, Cordell took his time lighting it. He squinted thoughtfully at Stephanie through a curl of smoke. "I don't work for women."

A wave of pure dislike washed through Stephanie. "Well, of all the most ridiculous things I've heard!

And what is the matter with working for a woman?"

"Well, for one thing, they keep you standing out in the hot sun talking business when there are cooler places to be. And for another . . ."

"Pardon me," Stephanie managed to say, "won't you step inside where it's cooler, Mr. Cordell? I apologize for my lack of manners." Damn him for making her feel gauche!

"Are you sure I'm safe in your room?"

Stephanie's face flamed with color at his obvious insinuation that he would not be safe with her.

"I'm more positive than I've ever been of anything in my entire life, Mr. Cordell," she answered icily. Her tone should have frozen him on the spot in spite of the heat.

"Just checking. A man can't be too safe these days."

"I wouldn't think that would be a big problem with you!" Stephanie snapped before she could stop herself.

"You'd be surprised then . . ."

"I certainly would . . ."

". . . if I told you how many snakes and scorpions hide inside a building where it's cooler. It's been a big problem this year," Cordell said innocently. Stephanie could have cheerfully strangled him as she heard Claudia's muffled cough of laughter.

"Please spare me the details, Mr. Cordell. Won't you be seated?" Dear God, what an impossible man! "Now, about our agreement . . ."

"Five hundred dollars firm. Up front." Taken aback, Stephanie stared at him as Cordell waved an arm at the room and observed that it already had the homey touches of a woman's hand. "Kinda comforting to see feminine things hanging about . . ."

Claudia scurried to snatch down the stockings she'd washed and hung from the rafters to dry, and Stephanie glared furiously at Cordell as he leaned back in his chair and propped booted feet on the table.

"I know what you're trying to do, and it won't work." She folded her arms across her chest and struggled to keep her temper. "My offer, Mr. Cordell, was five hundred dollars flat; half now, half when the job is done. Firm. And just because I'm a woman and capable of being embarrassed by crudeness, does not mean I will allow you to bully me into an unwise agreement."

"Most admirable, Miss Ashworth." Cigar smoke floated lazily through the air as he puffed silently for a moment. "Four-fifty now, fifty when we find your old man."

"I'd have to be an idiot . . ."

"My personal opinions never interfere with good business . . ."

". . . to even listen to such drivel!" Stephanie closed her eyes for a moment. "Very well. Three hundred now, two hundred when we find my *father*."

A dark brow winged skyward as he considered her offer. "I think you're trying to take advantage of a man down on his luck," he said finally. "You're a hard businesswoman, Miss Ashworth."

"Then you accept?"

"I didn't say that . . ."

"Well, say *something*, for heaven's sake!" she

exploded irritably. "The suspense is becoming more than I can stand, and I'm tired of wasting time."

"Okay. Three hundred now, two-fifty when we find your . . . father." He stood and held out his hand. "Shake on it?"

"Wait a minute, that's not what I said . . ."

"I heard you say three hundred now, Miss Ashworth. You should really pay more attention when you make business deals . . ."

"I said three hundred, but I never said two-fifty. It's two hundred, Mr. Cordell. And a signed agreement."

"Whoa." All the humor faded from Cordell's face. "I don't sign my name to anything, lady. Think again."

"Oh, for heaven's sake, it's only a piece of paper stating that you agree to guide me to my father. You can read it for yourself . . ."

"Forget it. Forget the whole damned thing. I'm not signing any paper . . ."

"Then I'll find someone else . . ."

"Have at it." The cigar dropped to the floor and was crushed under his bootheel. "Good day, Miss Ashworth, Miss Tremayne." He pivoted, and Stepanie realized he was actually leaving.

"Wait! Mr. Cordell, you know that there are no other guides available, and that I'm in a hurry." When he remained quiet and just stared at her politely, she added, "Four hundred now, one hundred when we get there, and a signed agreement."

"What damn good is a piece of paper if we get killed?" he demanded. "My word ought to be good enough for you . . ."

"It's my father . . . he's brought me up to always insist on everything in writing, Mr. Cordell. Surely you understand. Didn't your father ever teach you anything?"

For a moment, just for a moment, Stephanie thought he was going to wheel around and walk out the door without answering. She wondered what she had said to strike a nerve, but then he was nodding coolly.

"Okay. Four-fifty now, one hundred when we get there, and a signed agreement. And that *is* my last offer."

"Done."

When the agreement had been signed and the door closed behind Ryan Cordell, Stephanie sank to the bleak comfort of a cane-bottomed chair.

"That," she told Claudia, "was the most difficult bargain I have ever struck. And somehow, I think I shall regret this very much." Her eyes were wide and thoughtful when she turned to Claudia. "There's something about that man . . ."

Chapter Five

"The hell you will!" Gray eyes like storm clouds narrowed at Stephanie. "This is not a tea party, Miss Ashworth, and I am not dragging a bunch of women's paraphernalia across the damned desert!" He waved a hand at the trunks and boxes he could see stacked outside. "Only as much goes as can be loaded on a pack animal. Got it?"

"Mr. Cordell," she began patiently, "have you forgotten whose 'tea party' this is? It's mine. And I intend to take my things with me."

Cordell's still-lit cigar was thrown to the dirt floor of the officer's drinking quarters as he stood up. He stabbed a forefinger in her direction and said through clenched teeth, "You've got more damn money than you do sense . . ."

"Please stop your cursing . . ."

". . . but I don't intend to get killed because you want to carry fourteen pairs of lace panties with you. And you can count on that."

In spite of the choked laughter coming from the

men seated behind Ryan, Stephanie managed to keep calm. Her icy gaze quieted the officers seated at a long table in the stuffy room where she had finally located Cordell. One by one, they got up and left, leaving her alone with Cordell and a bartender.

"Some of those trunks contain equipment I will need when we find my father, Mr. Cordell. I must take them."

"Fine. Whatever you can pack on a horse or mule. But *my* pack animal is going to have food and water. You decide what's more important for your space. And if you think we can handle a herd of pack animals, cross the desert and go through the mountains without attracting a lot of unwanted attention, you'll be wearing feathers in your hair this time next week. Some Indian buck out there would just love to have an addition to his bed, I'm sure . . ."

"As usual, you know just the right thing to say," Stephanie observed icily. "All right. I will eliminate anything that is not absolutely necessary, and have Claudia help me."

"Smart girl. Be out front about four in the morning, and we'll get started." Lifting his glass, he swallowed the remains then offered Stephanie a drink.

"I don't normally drink with hired help, Mr. Cordell."

"Neither do I. I'll make an exception if you will." Without waiting for her consent, Ryan ordered Stephanie a glass of brandy from the bartender. "A *tall* glass for the lady, Corporal," he said, "and fill it to the top."

"All of that?" She took the over-full glass he

handed her, and briefly wondered why she was letting him test her.

"Do you want to drink, or don't you?" A matching amount of whiskey was poured into Ryan's glass. Stephanie didn't dare look too closely at the cleanliness of her glass, afraid of what she might see. Nothing in Arizona seemed to escape the ever-present dust, but maybe the alcohol would kill any germs.

Ryan lifted his glass. "Here's to it! Bears do it . . ." He stopped suddenly. "Sorry. Forgot myself," he said, but Stephanie had the inescapable feeling he hadn't forgotten himself for a moment. "Care to make a toast, Miss Ashworth?"

"Yes. To a successful—and short—journey." She tilted back her glass and drank, not lowering it until the brandy was gone. "Your turn," she said when Ryan stared first at her, then at the emptied glass. "Oh. I'm sorry—did you want to make a toast?"

"That one was just fine, Miss Ashworth." He drained his whiskey in a smooth motion. "Just fine."

"Good. Then I'll see you at four in the morning, Mr. Cordell. Good evening."

"Corporal Jackson," Cordell said to the wide-eyed bartender after Stephanie's departure, "that is quite a woman. As women go."

"Yep," the bartender agreed, "as wimmin go, she'll do."

Stephanie would have been glad to hear that she'd impressed Ryan and Jackson, but as it was, the brandy hit her halfway across the main yard of the fort. Combined with the heat, its effect was potent. She barely managed to stumble into her room, thoroughly alarming Claudia.

"Stephanie! What is it . . . ? Has something happened to you?"

"Yes," Stephanie moaned, holding tighlty to the doorjamb. "I've contracted an acute case of one-upmanship, I think."

"What do you mean?" Claudia helped her to her bed. "Whatever are you talking about, Stephanie?"

"I tried to show up Cordell by drinking an entire glass of brandy in one swallow." Closing her eyes, Stephanie lay back on her bed. The room began to spin at an alarming pace, and her fingers dug into the coverlet so she would not get thrown to the floor. A satisfied smile slanted her mouth. "But I did it. You should have seen the look on his face, Claudie. You would have been so proud of me . . ."

"Of course, love, of course," Claudia soothed, brushing back the hair from Stephanie's eyes. "You lie right here, dear. I'm going to get some water so I can sponge your face for you." She patted her on the arm. "I'll be right back."

Later Stephanie was to reflect that if she hadn't tried to get the upper hand with Ryan Cordell, Claudia would not have had an accident. It was all her fault.

"Ankle's broke," the doctor said, snapping shut his little black bag. "Can't be moved for at least a month until it heals."

Pressing her fingertips to her temples, Stephanie heard Claudia's protests through waves of dizziness.

"But, Doctor," Claudia wailed, "I am supposed to leave for New York in the morning! Oh, what shall I do?"

"Do?" The doctor frowned darkly. "You'll do

what I just said to do, woman! Unless you prefer being crippled the rest of your life." He rose and strode briskly to the door. "It's your choice." The door slammed behind him.

"Oh, Stephanie, look what I've done . . ."

"No, it's not your fault, Claudie. If you hadn't been going after water for me . . ."

"I never even saw that wretched dog! All of a sudden he was tangled up in my skirts . . . and the bucket was so full of water . . . we went round and round and I couldn't stop . . . it was like Jack and Jill . . ."

"Never mind." Stephanie patted her arm comfortingly, much as Claudia had done for Stephanie earlier. "If we're careful, we can take the train back to New York soon, I'm certain. The doctor will tell us when you can travel . . ."

"But you want to find your father . . ."

"I want you to get well . . ."

". . . and I can stay here until you get back. I'll be perfectly fine, Stephanie. Really I will. We can get someone to look in on me . . ."

"Oh no, Claudie, I couldn't go off and leave you . . . !"

"Why not? What are you going to do here?" Claudia looked up at Stephanie. "You're a perfectly terrible nurse, dear, even though I know you try hard. Do you recall the time I had a cold? I vowed to get well so you would stop hovering over me. Always fluttering about with wet cloths that dripped all over my nightgown and soaked me to the skin, and bringing me dreadful 'cures' that I was certain would kill me. No, I'd much prefer you going on ahead and finding Julian. I'll be fine. Truly I will."

"Well . . . perhaps I *could* find someone who would watch over you while I'm gone . . ."

"Where's your companion?" Ryan Cordell slanted Stephanie a questioning glance in the smoky light provided by a sputtering torch. "Isn't she going to see you off?"

"No. She's in bed with a broken ankle. Is this my horse?" Stephanie took a step toward the sleek black.

"Not on your life, lady. That's my horse. And what do you mean, she's got a broken ankle?"

"Just what I said, Cordell. She had an accident, and is confined to her bed. Now show me which horse is mine."

"Well, aren't *you* sweet! Forget it. Just give me the map and I'll go find your father. You can wait here with your companion." Cordell hid a smile as he turned to the sleepy-eyed calvaryman standing close by. It was working out better than he'd hoped—he wasn't even going to have to start out with her. "Unsaddle that bay gelding and mare," he said to the calvaryman. "We won't need 'em . . ."

"Just a moment, Soldier!" Stephanie stopped the man, then turned back to Ryan. "The agreement was that you guide me to my father. Not that you find my father for me. I must hold you to our original bargain, Mr. Cordell."

"Lady, let's get this straight right off—nowhere in that agreement does it say I have to play maid for some damned woman crossing the desert . . ."

"That's right. And I'm not asking you to do so. I

am perfectly capable of caring for myself . . ."

"Yeah, but will you? Don't ask me to help you the first time or we head back, lady . . ."

"Must I remind you that you *signed* that agreement, Mr. Cordell?"

There was a tense silence as Cordell's mouth thinned to a hard line. "Under pressure . . ." he began, and Stephanie cut him off with, "But you did sign it."

"Damn you, woman," he said at last in a cold tone that was more of a growl. "You better not push me . . ."

"And if you don't keep your agreement, Mr. Cordell, I will see to it that you are hunted throughout the entire territory of Arizona. My father has very influential friends, including a Mr. Allan Pinkerton. Have you ever heard of him or his agency?"

"I have." Ryan's hands curled into tight fists at his sides, then uncurled. He jammed his thumbs into the waist of his dark cord pants and glared at Stephanie. Even in the dim light she could see the dangerous glitter in his eyes, and took one step back.

"All right, Miss Ashworth. I'll keep the bargain. I'll take you to your father even if we have to ride into hell and put out the fires, but I don't think he'll thank me for it."

"Yes, he will."

Stephanie's brief sense of satisfaction as Ryan turned angrily away dissolved as he said over one shoulder, "If you're going with me, you can take off those damn skirts. If you're going to behave like a man, you're going to look like one. I don't need a pack of sex-starved Apaches after my scalp because of you . . ."

It wouldn't take long for Stephanie Ashworth to find out she wasn't going to like traveling in Arizona Territory, Ryan figured. Not long at all. Two days at the most, and she'd be begging him to bring her back to the fort.

A half hour later Stephanie stood shivering in the cool morning air clad in buckskin trousers and one of her oldest shirts. A felt hat that had seen better days had been placed on her head, and her hair was tucked beneath it.

"Ready? About time," Cordell said shortly.

The morning sun was still a pearly mist in the eastern sky, and the black velvet night was peppered with more shimmering stars than Stephanie had ever seen in New York. Faint light sprayed softly over the stableyard, giving it an unearthly glow. Horses' hooves stamped sleepily on the ground, and metal bit rings rattled with a tinkly, musical sound. There was the warm, familiar smell of hay and grain mixed with the pungent odor of horse. Stephanie inhaled deeply, keeping her mind from what Cordell must be considering and her eyes averted from the harsh lines of his face as he sliced her a hard look.

Silver spangles of light dulled and faded as they stood in the quiet yard, then the dark purple outlines of the humped mountains began to glow crimson and orange.

"Sun's almost up." Cordell's eyes flickered as he motioned for a soldier to lead out a horse being held in the dim shadows of the stable. "Mount up, lady. You've delayed us long enough."

Stephanie frowned irritably as she turned to the horse led forward by a blue-uniformed calvaryman. A small bay, it seemed full of high spirits. From the corner of one eye, Stephanie noticed Ryan Cordell watching with a slight smile curving his mouth. Damn him, the horse would undoubtedly be half wild.

She wasn't about to let him get the best of her, so Stephanie took the leather reins and determinedly put one foot into the swinging metal stirrup. Did he think she'd never ridden astride? Ryan Cordell, she thought, I hope you choke on my dust! My first pony had more vinegar than any nag I've seen since arriving in Arizona!

Swinging into the high-spined saddle, Stephanie felt the animal's muscles bunch as it prepared for a leap and twist. The troops had begun to gather in the small, dusty stableyard, and she had a blurred view of blue uniforms as the bay spun on its forefeet. Up and down, around and twist, the horse made several crow hops across the yard, then bounced with a stiff-legged gait that jolted Stephanie all the way down her spine before it settled down to just a lively prance.

"Ready, Cordell?" She checked the bay's dancing with a firm hand on the reins, gazing down at Ryan Cordell.

He stood with booted feet slightly apart, gloved hands resting on slim hips draped with double gunbelts. The brim of a dark felt hat hid the expression in his eyes, but there was a certain twist to his mouth that Stephanie recognized.

"Ready, Ashworth."

The sun was just rising lazily from behind a ridged

mountain, gilding its purple edges with gold, when Stephanie and Ryan rode through the gates and down the rocky trail. Iron horse shoes struck sparks from the hard ground with a sharp sound as they left Fort Defiance behind.

A brisk wind was blowing, and Stephanie inhaled deeply. The air was different here than anywhere she'd ever been before, sharper somehow, with the hint of age-old peoples and ancient mysteries in the dry gusts that blew over rock and sand. Fading purple shadows lent the landscape a softer look, subtly changing the harsh, barren world into a land tinged with gold. The ground was bursting with new summer flowers that spread in a bright yellow carpet over the hard ground with its thrusting mounds of rocks. This was not a gentle land, and Ryan Cordell better know what he was doing. The sooner they found Julian, the better.

In spite of Ryan's suggestion that he carry the map, it was tucked into Stephanie's bulging saddlebags. He'd already traced the route depicted on the animal hide, and muttered that it was very vague.

"There should be," he'd said, "another map to show the location of Magic Rock. That's where your father is headed."

Magic Rock. Stephanie had asked around, and for the price of a bottle of bad whiskey, had found an old mountain man who would tell her more about the area.

"Well, a few thousand years ago," he'd said, "there wuz an ancient tribe that lived in them mountains. T'wuz a bad year fer 'em. Crops died, no deer or buff'lo 'cuz of other tribes, raids on their fam'lies—

ever'thing seemed ta go wrong. A high priest, or shaman, demanded a sacrifice, like they likes ta do. Only this here sacrifice demanded th' chief's only child as paymant ta th' gods. Kinda a bad move on the priest's part, 'cuz th' chief weren't no dummy an' he knew that th' priest, who wuz his brother, would be chief when he died, if there weren't no children. Follow me so far?" When Stephanie nodded, he continued. "Good. Seems like this here chief had an ace up his sleeve in th' way of a back-up priest. This guy argued agin' th' fust priest's decree, an' th' war wuz on. Tribe fought tribe, an' they fought within th' tribe. Th' gods got pis—mad, th' legend goes, and sent a rain of fire down on 'em as punishment. Th' rain didn' soak into th' ground like normal rain, but set grass afire an' killed people and animals. When it wuz over, th' gods had left a huge ball of fire as a reminder whut could happen when people get greedy. This fireball didn' burn like wood burns, but jes' glowed red-hot. Anyone who touched it died immediately, an' anyone who came close, died soon afterward. Th' tribes vanished in time, an' th' sacred area of th' Magic Rock wuz taboo." The mountain man's gruff voice had lowered conspiratorially. "No one is allowed to go there, only special priests, or shamans. It's an ancient burial ground, an' whenever there wuz danger of a raid by th' Spanish, th' Indians would bury their precious statues an' gold near Magic Rock. Th' rock of th' gods would watch over their treasures."

"Fascinating. Does the rock still have magic?" She only half believed the man, and he knew it. He'd grinned, showing broken, tobacco-stained teeth.

71

"I'm not sure about magic, but it does have a hell of a lot of gold buried close by. That's th' attraction . . ."

Gold. Of course. That was the main—possibly only—reason Cordell was helping her, Stephanie realized. Ryan Cordell was more interested in finding the buried gold than he was her father. That must have been the reason he had agreed to find Julian— he wanted the gold. And he needed the map to find both.

Chapter Six

Julian Ashworth guided his mule down a steep incline, picking his way carefully through the litter of loose rocks that might start a rockslide at any moment. He grinned jauntily when the mule paused at the bottom, and glanced back up at the sheer rock cliffs behind him.

"That was a damned tricky ride, Bingo, wouldn't you say?"

Saddle leather creaked as Bingo shifted and wiped his sweating brow with the back of one hand. He crooked a grin that was a parody of Ashworth's. "Yessir, I'd say it wuz . . . we're lucky we're straddlin' these damned mules 'stead of lyin' in a heap of bones."

"I'm not quite as certain of that," Julian responded with a grimace. "At least the trip would have been relatively painless until we hit bottom."

Bingo's weather-seamed face creased into deeper lines. He spat a stream of tobacco juice onto the hot rocks, watching impassively as it sizzled and evaporated in a matter of seconds. "Well now, the mules wuz my idea, an' I gotta say, a good one. They's more surefooted than my mountain ponies, even if the ride's a mite more uncomfortable. But fer a city man, you do right well."

"Coming from you, Bingo, the praise is even more appreciated."

Julian's mule brayed loudly and the sound echoed through the winding corridors of rock, bouncing eerily from reddish surfaces deeply etched by the winds of time.

"You know, Bingo, I believe that we've been looking at that map all wrong," Julian commented with a frown. He pulled his hat from his head and wiped his forehead with the red kerchief he kept tucked inside the hatband. The dapper fedora still looked as if it had just come off a store shelf, and he carefully flicked a speck of dust from its brim with thumb and forefinger. "Are you certain the directions are correct, that north is where the arrow indicates?"

Bingo scratched the back of his head with gnarled fingers twisted from too many years spent in the harsh winters of the Dakotas and said, "Nope. I'm not a-tall sure of the directions bein' right. Why?"

Bright sunlight glinted in Ashworth's blond hair as he tilted his head to squint up at a narrow finger of rock pointing skyward. "Because that particular spire seems to be in the wrong place if we read the map the way we have been. But if we turn it just a little . . ." He pantomimed with both hands and continued, ". . . it says we're on the right track. What do you think?"

"Yeah, I think so. Ya might read it better if'n we tried it that-a-way."

Dismounting, Bingo walked a few steps across the rocks, then stopped. He squatted down and began drawing in the dust with one finger, tracing the map as he remembered it. The fringes of his buckskin shirt flapped in the hot wind, and overhead an eagle pierced the air with its hunting cry.

Julian twisted in the stripped down frontier model of the McClellan saddle that he'd bought from the sutter's store in Fort Defiance, staring up at the tiny speck high in the sky. Ashworth had played hunches all his life, and had amassed a fortune doing it. The sudden idea that came to him was little more than a wild hunch.

"The eagle, Bingo. On the map, there was an eagle in one corner. What if we turned it so that the eagle is at the top—north, and the river south. Where would that put us?"

Bingo shifted position, his moccasins making hazy puffs of dust around his heels as he faced the map he was drawing from another direction. He'd drawn stick figures and rocks in a circle, with a squiggle representing a river in one curve. The frontiersman frowned in perplexity at the incomprehensible figures. "I kin read the sign language easy 'nough. It's the placin' of the river an' cliffs that . . ." He stopped. His brow cleared as he looked up at Julian and said, "Three miles from here, they's a valley in a spot jus' like this one. Three miles north of where we are is a gorge like the one cuttin' acrost the valley. An' there's the river . . ." He traced the dust map with a crooked finger. ". . . an' then, there's a pile of rocks

75

an' big butte jus' like those on the map."

"We're right, then." Julian smiled in satisfaction and covered his blond head with the immaculate fedora. He took two cigars from the pocket of his long coat and felt for the matches he kept in his vest. After lighting one cigar, he handed it to Bingo, then lit the other one for himself. "We are to be congratulated, Bingo. I believe that before the week is out, we will have found Magic Rock. I only wish Stephanie could have been here to share the discovery."

Standing, Bingo scraped the side of his moccasin across the map to obliterate it. "Ya better be glad she ain't, Pilgrim."

"I suppose," Julian said, adding glumly, "She's probably being bored to tears by that blithering idiot she intends to marry at Christmas. I'm certain he's had some social function to attend that required her attendance. For a girl who was brought up like she was, I fail to understand why she would consent to marry that preposterous peacock. Stephanie will probably be tempted to do him in before their first anniversary."

Not quite sure if Ashworth was truly serious, Bingo shook his head. "Meaner than a she-bear, then?"

"Oh no. Just an incredible intolerance for fools. Like her father." A puff of cigar smoke curled away on the wind. "She's safe in New York, and I suppose I should be glad I told her not to come. I just miss her. This is desolate country at times, Bingo, and I admire anyone who . . . What is it?"

Bingo had stretched out flat on the rock and was

staring intently down the steep slope. "Kiowas, agin," he said tersely. "I kin smell 'em."

Julian followed his scout's gaze, but could see nothing for miles except red rock and burning sands studded with cactus and mesquite. "Are you sure?"

"Yep. I kin allus tell when there's Injun near. It's an instinct, I guess you'd call it. Sumthin' clicks inside my head, an' I know they's there."

"Are they the ones we've been following?" Ashworth quickly dismounted and stretched out beside Bingo, heedless of the state of his clothing.

"Naw. They's wearin' Lord's shirts."

"What are Lord's shirts, pray tell?" Julian Ashworth turned his head to stare curiously at the mountain man. Bright sunlight glittered on the gold earring in his left ear as Bingo shot Julian a grin. He pulled at the tattered brim of his gray, sweat-stained Stetson, and cast a disparaging glance at Julian's beaver derby as he answered.

"Well Pilgrim," he drawled, "seems as though this warrior got hisself lost in enemy territory, once'n. Feelin' sorta brain-scorched frum lack of water, he had a vision. A white man wearin' a shirt painted with crosses—you know who I'm talkin' 'bout—this here white man said to this warrior, 'I am the Lord. Do not fear, you will return home and live to be an old man.' So when that Injun got home, he made him a shirt like th' one he seen the so-called Lord wearin' in his vision. Figured it was some sort of big medicine. Ennyway, when they's wearin' these shirts, they figure they cain't even git killed, much less wounded. You know how superstitious these Injuns is."

"They're Christians?" Julian asked in surprise.

77

"Some of 'em be. But they's still Injuns . . ."

"Then . . . this means that somehow we've stumbled onto another band of Kiowas. This is a war party, not a burial party."

In spite of the heat, Julian Ashworth felt a cold chill shiver down his spine when Bingo nodded slowly.

Chapter Seven

Stephanie eased down from the bay, stifling an urge to moan. She had absolutely no desire to let that insufferable Ryan Cordell know how sore she was. All day in the saddle! How could she have gotten out of shape so quickly? Even jolting camel rides had not left her aching like she was now. And Cordell seemed to know it. He slanted her a faintly mocking grin.

"Enjoying the ride, Miss Ashworth?" Ryan slid the heavy saddle from his horse's back and upended it on the rocky ground. The bright-patterned Navajo blanket was spread over the saddle to dry, and he deftly replaced the sweat-stained bridle with a rope halter. When Stephanie still didn't reply, he cocked a dark brow in her direction. "The wind still in your ears, or you just being rude?"

Stephanie was tempted to fling a nasty retort, but instead she asked in a sugary sweet tone, "Do you have an extra brush I can use for my mount, Mr. Cordell? I seem to have forgotten to include one with my supplies."

"I figured you wouldn't know beans about horses, so I brought two." A brush sailed through the air and Stephanie automatically fumbled to catch it. She glared at Ryan when he laughed at her muttered "ouch."

"And in case you plan on askin', Miss Ashworth, I'm not grooming your animal. You wanted to come along, so you take care of your own horse."

"I assure you, I had no intentions of asking you to do anything at all for me, Cordell!" Stephanie glared at his back and was glad she didn't have to ask how to remove her saddle. Even if it was different from any she'd used before, she could figure it out herself. But the wretched thing was very different from those she was accustomed to, and the soldier who had saddled the bay had pulled the straps into some sort of unusual knot. Muttering to herself, Stephanie tugged irritably at the leather and sliced occasional glances at Cordell's back.

It was still hot even with the sun sliding behind flat-topped buttes and ridged mesas and spires. Stephanie was decidedly uncomfortable and sweaty by the time she had her mount unsaddled and brushed. She pushed irritably at damp strands of hair hanging in her eyes and glared in Ryan's direction.

It hadn't taken him long to unsaddle and curry his horse, and he'd already started a fire with small twigs. Stephanie's stomach rumbled at the smell of salted beef sizzling in a pan and the strong, fragrant aroma of coffee.

With her mount settled for the night and his front legs placed in the soft leather hobbles so he wouldn't wander far, Stephanie finally eased down close to the fire. Cordell sat across from her, his long legs folded Indian-style. Still fuming, Stephanie tried to ignore him as she reached out for an empty plate lying near the flames.

"What the hell do you think you're doing?"

Cordell's sharp query jerked her head up. She stared at him for a moment without answering, then shot back, "I'm getting a plate so I can eat, that's what I think I'm doing!"

"Not my plate, lady. Get your own. This plate," he said as he yanked it from her hands, "happens to be mine. As well as this food. I didn't see you cook anything."

"Now wait just a minute!" Stephanie's temper soared dangerously. "Whose money paid for this food? And who hired you as a guide? And . . ."

"Guide, not cook," he interrupted coolly. "You agreed to do your own work, remember? So do it. Cook your own supper. Unless you want to work out a trade, maybe . . ."

Stephanie rose to her feet in a swift, lithe movement. Cordell's glance drifted up her long legs insultingly slow, and her eyebrows drew into a tight knot of fury. "Why, you obnoxious, overbearing, arrogant . . ." She sputtered to a stop as she tried to think of a word that was both ladylike and colorful.

"Muleheaded?" Ryan supplied helpfully. "Or maybe even a jackass? Learn to swear properly if you're going to be just one of the boys, Miss Ashworth. Shall I call you Steve instead of Stephanie?"

Several different words she'd heard at her father's occasional poker games came to mind, but Stephanie controlled herself with an effort. "I hardly think, Mr. Cordell, that I qualify as 'one of the boys.' Nor do I wish to do so. I believe that I can get my point across to even so lacking an intellect as you possess without resorting to foul language." Her nails made half-moons in the palms of her hands as she clenched them into fists. Ryan Cordell was deliberately looking her over from head to toe as if she was a prize mare to be bought.

"Maybe you're right," he agreed as he stood up. He towered over her, and Stephanie was glad the fire was between them. "You're definitely not one of the boys, though with your hair pulled back in that tight little knot, you look kinda masculine." Ryan took another step closer. "I wonder what you'd look like with your hair all loose and free, blowing in the wind or spread across a satin pillow . . ."

It must be the flames that were making her so hot, Stephanie decided, for her face was burning with the heat. She took a wary step back as Cordell stepped even closer.

"That's not really the issue here." A faint tremor of nervousness made her voice quiver slightly. "The issue is simply that you refuse to be courteous enough to share your dinner with me." She edged around the stone-ringed fire and away from Cordell. "But I assure you that I am quite capable of cooking my own meal, Mr. Cordell. I only need to find the supplies . . ." Her voice squeaked to a halt as Ryan Cordell stepped over the fire to brush against her, and she leaped backward as if struck by a rock.

"Jumpy little critter, ain't you?" Ryan observed. He grinned as he squatted beside a half-open pack and pulled out salt beef and a brown packet of beans. "I was only getting your supplies for you. No need to act like a skittish mare covered for the first time . . ."

"I'm not impressed by that. I've heard them all before, and would greatly appreciate it if you would use less colorful metaphors, Mr. Cordell," Stephanie said stiffly. "It's so much more polite."

"And whoever told you I was a polite kinda gentleman, Miss Ashworth?" Ryan's hand reached out to snare her by one arm as he rose in a single, smooth motion. "You assume an awful lot . . ."

"My mistake!" Stephanie snapped. She shook loose his hand, glaring at him with furious lights shining in her dark eyes. "I never hinted that you were a gentleman, of course, but I did think you had enough common sense to be polite to your boss!"

"Boss?" Ryan's dark brows lowered in a frown. "Never. Employer, maybe. Never my boss. You're a woman."

"Then what do you call a woman who hires a man as a guide—misguided?"

"No. I thought that was the term for lady guides. Don't talk down to me, Miss Ashworth. I don't like it."

"Don't worry, Cordell—I won't talk to you at all!" Stephanie whirled to walk away. Her graceful exit was marred, however, by the catching of her bootheel on a rock. She half skidded and fell to one knee, catching herself with outstretched hands against the ground. The beef and beans she held fell and bounced across the ground like the Mexican jumping beans she'd seen in Santa Fe, scattering everywhere. Small pebbles dug painfully into the heels of her palms as she slid to a humiliating halt at Cordell's feet. A taut-muscled arm reached down to circle Stephanie's middle as Ryan lifted her.

"Romantic already? You don't have to throw yourself at me, Miss Ashworth." Stephanie aimed a wild kick at him as she heard the laughter in his voice. "Ah, ah! I'll give in without a fight. I'm just surprised . . . Ouch!" The heel of Stephanie's boot caught him on a shin. "You little wildcat," he muttered, and dropped her like a hot rock.

"Oof!" was Stephanie's reply. She lay stretched on the ground like a sunning tomcat. Brown eyes glared up at him through loose waves of silvery hair with the same icy disdain her favorite Persian cat had always had for the world. "You," Stephanie finally said as she got slowly to her feet, "are the most despicable excuse for a man I have ever had the displeasure of encountering, and if I had been able to get another guide . . ."

"But you weren't. You're lucky you got me," Ryan finished smoothly. "Count your blessings. You could have hired Two Toes."

"Two toes?"

"Two Toes. Meanest redman who ever drew breath. He's had fourteen wives in the past five years. None of them lived longer than a few months for some reason or other." Cordell seated himself back on his folded blanket roll beside the fire. "I

84

don't think old Two Toes likes women, what with all those 'accidents' and stuff. Or maybe he just knows clumsy ones. Not like you, of course. You're as graceful as a deer—or maybe I should say buffalo . . ."

"Shut up!" Stephanie's temper was sorely strained, and she snarled at Cordell, wishing she knew of a way to stuff his entire blanket roll down his throat. Too bad she didn't.

"My, my. You're so touchy." Ryan leaned forward to pour a steaming cup of coffee into his tin cup. "This is the only coffeepot, so we have to share," he said, and handed her the cup.

The fire popped and crackled, sending a spray of sparks heavenward, and the beef began to sizzle in the pan. After a brief hesitation, Stephanie reached out for the cup. Her fingers accidentally brushed against his and she shivered at the tingling sensation that shot up her arm. When her eyes met his she saw his amusement.

Jerking back her arm, she said the first thing that came to mind. "I don't trust you enough to share anything but coffee, Cordell. All I want you to do is get me to my father." Stephanie couldn't look at him. She kept her gaze averted, training it on the rather battered tin cup that was curiously shaking in her fingers.

This was ridiculous. Why should he affect her this way? He was a rough, crude, ill-bred man who had probably never been to a decent-sized city in his entire life, and he had no idea what kind of world he lived in. Ryan Cordell was obviously content with living in the mountains and the wilderness, and making what little money he could by acting as guide. What else had he done to exist? She shuddered to think. He certainly had few—if any—scruples, and very probably had never seen the inside of a church.

"You are a snobbish bitch, aren't you?" Cordell commented as casually as if he'd complimented her. "And you aren't even honest with yourself."

Stephanie's head jerked up. "What . . ."

"You may be a lady, Miss Ashworth, but all you really know are the outside trappings. I don't think you know the true definition of a lady. Maybe I don't, either, but I don't pretend to. And at least I'm honest with myself." His face in the fading light was hard, and his eyes were cold as he stood up and stared down at Stephanie.

The tin cup slipped from her fingers to the ground, bouncing with a metallic clink across the rocks. Stephanie stood so that her eyes were almost level with his, and her tone was much more calm than she felt on the inside.

"I haven't pretended to be something I'm not, Cordell. Your opinion of me doesn't matter. You were hired to find my father, not make social conversation, and I feel no need to defend myself against your accusations."

"No? Then don't." Ryan's hands flashed out to grasp Stephanie by her shoulders and he pulled her hard against him. His movement was so quick she had no chance to react, and only a small gasp escaped her lips before his mouth was over hers.

Stephanie had been kissed before, of course, but

never like this. This was more an invasion than a kiss, a harsh, oddly exciting encroachment of her senses. Ryan was forcing her lips apart with the insistent pressure of his tongue, teasing shivers of reaction from her. The purple twilight faded and receded, and there was only awareness of the man who held her, who seemed to be drawing her will from her body with his demanding kiss. Somehow Stephanie's hands were against his hard chest, and she could feel the slow thudding of his heart beneath her fingertips. Why was his heartbeat still regular when hers was pounding like the native drums she'd heard in Africa? This was insane, and she had to stop it, yet she couldn't. For the first time in her adult life, Stephanie Ashworth was unable to take control of a situation.

Her release was abrupt. Ryan's mouth left hers and he relaxed his grip on her arms as he took a step backward. "I was right, Miss Ashworth," he said in a mocking tone that made her want to slap his face. "You are definitely no lady, and I have to say that ain't bad."

"You degenerate!" Stephanie's hand was caught in an iron grip before it crashed against his cheek. "I should shoot you!"

"You may be a fair shot, but I'm better. Remember that." Cordell let go of her hand. "That's your dinner that's burning, Miss Ashworth."

Stephanie watched with helpless rage and embarrassment as Cordell walked away from the fire into the deeper shadows. She wanted to stamp her feet and throw rocks at him, maybe even really shoot him. He had kissed her and she had let him, and the worst of it was that he knew it. Stephanie stared down at the frying pan and the burned slab of beef without really seeing it.

"Damn, damn, damn," she muttered under her breath. If this was the first night of their trip, what would the rest of the journey be like?

Chapter Eight

Stephanie shifted uncomfortably on the thick mounds of Indian blanket she had spread on the hard ground close to the fire. The flames had died to glowing red embers winking sullenly among smoky ashes. It seemed like she'd been staring at the fire all night. How could it have been only a few hours?

Futilely, she once more willed her tense muscles to relax. What's the matter with me? she thought crossly. It would have been gratifying to know that Ryan Cordell was unable to sleep, but to her chagrin, soft snores had been drifting to her ears for at least an hour. And she couldn't sleep! Cordell was too much on her mind. How could he sleep so soundly when she couldn't? Each time he moved in his sleep he drew her attention like a moth to the flame.

For some reason, it was hard to keep her eyes from straying to his lean, half-covered body. The tiny glow from fire and full moon lit his tanned chest where the blanket had slipped to one side. Stephanie squeezed her eyes tightly shut for a moment. It wasn't as if she hadn't seen half-clothed or even unclothed males before. After all, she had traveled extensively in the wilds of Africa where clothing was considered an oddity. So why did Ryan Cordell's bare skin unnerve her? And how could he sleep without a shirt when the night air was so cool?

Lifting one hand, she lightly touched her lips. They were still strangely tingling, as if they had been bruised. Oddly enough, it felt as if he had just kissed her. Oh really . . . she shouldn't even be thinking about it. It was ridiculous, truly ludicrous. He was simply a crude frontiersman with very little regard for proper social behavior. She would be glad to reach Julian and be rid of Ryan Cordell.

A night breeze whispered softly over Stephanie's upturned nose. It smelled different somehow, as if the land conspired to trick her into liking this arid region of dust and hot winds, sparse trees, and towering red buttes. Arizona. Even for Julian this was an unusual adventure, Stephanie reflected. He'd always favored more foreign lands where danger abounded and the wildlife was exotic. Arizona seemed tame in comparison. The most dangerous creature she'd seen since arriving in the West was Ryan Cordell, and she seriously doubted whether her father would find him as dangerous as she did.

A coyote howled close by, its shivering wail hanging in the air for a moment before fading away. It was immediately answered with several short yips and one long, mournful note that quivered tremulously. Coyotes must communicate with each other like wolves did, Stephanie decided. Wolves mated for life, and she wondered if their coyote kin did also.

Coyotes fled Stephanie's mind as she suddenly became aware of Cordell kneeling beside her. She gasped aloud, and a hand quickly covered her mouth. Where had he come from? She hadn't even heard him move from his bed . . .

"Don't make a sound," Cordell said against her ear. She felt more than heard him because his lips were pressed close and his voice was a low, vibrating rasp. Stephanie nodded silently, much too aware of his bare chest in such close proximity. Speak? Not if her life depended upon it right now. Cordell's forearm was nudging her breasts, something he didn't seem at all aware of, but she was very conscious of it. He was bent over her, his face shadowed but so near she could have touched the strong line of his jaw with her lips if she'd wanted to. Now why had *that* occurred to her? It must have been the strong coffee that had caused hallucinations . . .

Then he was releasing her and moving away, and Stephanie could finally breathe more easily as he stood up and motioned to her. She stared up at him for an instant as he stood outlined against the night sky. Her eyes warily traveled his lean frame in one long sweep. Ryan's every muscle seemed to be taut and waiting, and she was filled with a sense of danger and urgency.

Ryan was making quick gestures with his hands that she could barely see, impatiently urging Stephanie from her cocoon of blankets and to her feet. She was shaking all over, but managed to follow his hand signs as she trailed him to a shadowed hump of rocks. She scrambled across gritty rocks and slid to a pitch-black void between them, huddling next to

Cordell. What was the matter? she wanted to ask, but didn't dare utter a sound.

The tails of her blouse flapped loosely in the slight breeze as Stephanie tried vainly to tuck them back into the waist of her trousers. She had unbuttoned her blouse and buckskin trousers while ensconced in the scratchy folds of her blanket. Now the buttons defied her best efforts to force them into the tiny holes, and Stephanie clenched her teeth in exasperation. Good thing she hadn't removed the bulky trousers as she'd thought about doing. They at least covered the necessities, though Ryan Cordell didn't appear in the least interested in her attire—or lack of it.

Stephanie hunkered close to Ryan on her stockinged heels, cupping both elbows in her palms as she squinted into the dark beyond their camp. The vast area beyond them seemed to be holding Cordell's attention, and she had a sudden premonition that the coyotes she'd heard were not coyotes. Good God, she'd read enough of those terrible dime novels about the West on the long train ride from New York, hadn't she? It was beginning to seem as if there might be a little truth in what she had considered highly improbable and completely fabricated tales.

"Apache," Ryan murmured after several long moments, confirming Stephanie's premonition. "Wonder what they're doing in Navajo territory. It might be a raiding party. They're signaling each other."

"About us?"

"They ain't talkin' about the moon, lady." Cordell's white teeth flashed in the dark. "They know we're here, and they're curious."

"Does that mean they'll . . ." Stephanie couldn't finish the thought. Had it been only a short time before that she had been thinking how tame Arizona seemed? Talk about tempting the hand of fate . . .

Cordell's shrug was felt rather than seen. "We'll find out soon enough what they intend to do. I like knowing the odds, so we'll wait up here in this pile of rocks and just watch."

Stephanie's mouth was dry and her palms wet, and even though her hands shook like leaves in a fall wind, her feet were lumps of lead that couldn't have moved if set afire. Oh Lord, she felt the need to excuse herself or be forever embarrassed, and now wasn't the time!

Gritting her teeth, Stephanie hunched her shoulders and peered over the jagged edges of the rock in front of her. Moonlight flooded the flat ground between the buttes. Squat bushes and long-armed saguaro cactus threw sharp shadows that seemed to waver, but there was no other sign of life that she could see.

Beside her, Ryan Cordell remained silent and tense. Stephanie could feel the tautness of his body even though they weren't touching. She slanted a glance at him, and as her eyes became more accustomed to the dark she could make out his features. Cordell's shock of dark hair fell over his forehead and almost into his eyes, and occasionally he would comb through it with spread fingers. In the blanketing silence Stephanie could almost hear his heart beat. She'd never been more aware of a man in her entire life, and her rampant imagination supplied the details the night hid.

Impatient with herself, Stephanie squeezed her eyes tightly shut to close out Ryan Cordell. But the memory of his sleeping form stayed with her; she could almost see the firelight playing over his bare chest and the muscle-corded arms folded behind his head. He'd lain looking up at the star-peppered sky for a short time before falling asleep, and Stephanie had watched him.

It wasn't just curiosity that had kept her attention on him. After their earlier confrontation, she'd struggled for the right thing to say. For once in her life Stephanie hadn't been able to think of a thing, and resented being at a loss for words. This had never happened to her before. Growing up as she had, she'd always known the proper thing to say and do at any given time. Ryan Cordell left her at a complete loss without even saying a word. Like now. Here she sat crouched among a pile of boulders waiting for some unknown disaster, and all she could think about was the man beside her. It was ridiculous. She wanted time to pass quickly, for something, *anything*, to happen.

Miserable, she sat as still as possible for what seemed to be an eternity. Finally she could stand it no longer.

"I don't see anything, Cordell. Are you certain those were not actual coyotes that we heard?"

An irritated snort was her only answer for a moment. Then Cordell's drawl floated through inky shrouds of night as he cordially invited her to take a little stroll in the moonlight and find out for herself.

"Mebbe you can hand-feed 'em, lady, and make

'em into pets. 'Course, the two-legged kind of coyote ain't quite as tame as the four-legged kind . . ."

"I realize that I have offended you, Mr. Cordell . . ."

"You can be pretty offensive . . ."

". . . but it seems like they would have done something by now if they wished to harm us."

"Why? Apaches have all the time in the world, Miss Ashworth. They don't have any socials to attend, or trains to catch, and they're not too worried about mending fences or feeding chickens. All they've got to do is watch us. We might be able to provide them with something to ride, something to eat, and if they're so inclined, a woman to bed . . ."

"Mr. Cordell!"

". . . for a night or two before they get tired of her," he continued calmly. "If you feel obliging, step right on out there. If not, I'd advise you to sit still and keep your mouth shut."

"You are the most abominable man I've ever had the displeasure of meeting," Stephanie muttered through clenched teeth, "and I regret the necessity of having to hire you as a guide!"

"Well, I can't say I'm real thrilled with you, either," Cordell retorted in a low voice that was somehow amused as well as irritated. "You can't seem to make up your mind whether to be competent or a female."

"Can't I be both? Are only men capable of being competent!"

"Oh, God!" Ryan's words were more of a groan. "This ain't the time or place for this kind of conversation, lady. Those Apaches don't care how damn competent you are! And neither do I."

Stephanie's mouth clamped shut. It would be beneath her dignity to continue the argument, and besides, Cordell might be right. There could be Apaches out there watching and waiting, deciding whether to attack or leave them alone.

After what seemed to Stephanie to be hours, Cordell rose from his crouched position and stretched his cramped muscles. "They're gone," he announced to the world at large.

Blinking, Stephanie wondered how he knew they were gone when she'd never seen them in the first place, and said so.

"Instinct. I've been out here long enough. I can tell. You'll just have to trust me, Miss Ashworth, but isn't that why you hired me?"

"It wasn't because I thought you were trustworthy!" she retorted instantly. Standing, Stephanie stamped her feet crossly, wincing as shooting pains raced up her legs. Her feet had gone to sleep, and she was cold and in a nasty humor. "I only hired you because no one else was available, Mr. Cordell, and you know that very well. I'm certain Lieutenant Buckner has already told you I tried others . . ."

"Yeah, he did mention that fact. Too bad. Old Two Toes would have been a great guide if you had enough whiskey. And time." Cordell's tall frame was briefly silhouetted against the moonlight as he stepped to the crest of a large rock.

"You'd make a perfect target if you happen to be wrong about the Apaches' departure," Stephanie observed caustically, almost hoping an arrow would whiz past his ear. It would serve him right to be proven wrong.

"And then you'd be all alone. You better hope I'm right." Ryan half turned, and in the silvery sheen of moonlight streaming over his face, Stephanie saw his mocking grin.

"I'm not paying you to be wrong, Mr. Cordell. I like to get my money's worth from hirelings." She strolled past Cordell, noting with satisfaction that his grin had disappeared. There. That should effectively put Ryan Cordell in his place, for a short time at least.

It was the kiss that had done it. That kiss should never have happened. And it must have been the unexpected reaction to his kiss that had thrown her into such a turmoil. No matter. It wouldn't happen again. From now on, she would revert to the "ice maiden" and not risk such tumultuous emotion.

The tension and fright of the night faded with the bright rays of the morning sun. The world didn't hold the same sinister shadows that hid unknown terrors, and Stephanie was determined to forget all that had transpired the night before—including the kiss. But not Ryan.

Not far from their camp Cordell stopped and dismounted. He held up bent leaves of sparse, dust-covered grass. "Do you see this?" he asked, adding when she nodded with a puzzled look in her eyes, "Our *coyote* friends from last night were riding ponies. Unshod hooves made these tracks in the last few hours. There were about six or seven of them, I'd say young braves out looking for game. We weren't worth the trouble, apparently."

"What color horses were they riding?" Stephanie smiled at the irritated expression on Ryan's face. "I mean, you can tell so much from just a few bent sprigs of grass, I'm certain you have more ways to impress me . . ."

"I sure do, but I'm not at all sure you can handle 'em. You seem to have trouble with just a kiss." The sprigs of grass fell to the ground. "You're a sarcastic bitch, Princess. Do you always hire men you don't think can do the job you hired them for? Satisfy my curiosity . . ."

"I know you can guide me, Mr. Cordell, and I'm quite certain you can follow a decent trail. I just want you to know that I'm not as gullible as you seem to think." She nudged her horse into a walk. "All I want you to do is find my father. Quickly."

Cordell swung onto his horse with a smooth motion Stephanie reluctantly admired, though she would have choked before telling him. She instinctively ducked as the lead lines to the pack horse were tossed in her direction, and Ryan told her curtly that it was her turn to lead for a while. Clouds of dust billowed upward as his mount was kicked into a brisk trot.

For the next few miles Stephanie swallowed dust from the black stallion before finally pulling her kerchief up over her nose to keep out the worst. She was fuming and her arms ached from tugging at the slower pack horse. The sun seared the top of her head even with the protective hat she wore, and her eyes burned from the glare. There was no wind today. Nothing else seemed to move. She was sure they were the only creatures moving across the parched land for miles.

As they rode in silence, Stephanie slowly began to notice the abundant life in the desert. Spiny strongholds and prickly pantries of cactus attracted the desert's feathered homesteaders. A hawk built its nest in the U of a saguaro cactus. Cradled high in the thorny branches, the nest of sticks protected eggs and young from becoming meals for other predators. Pugnacious woodpeckers drilled fist-sized holes in living cactuses, providing comfortable homes that were almost impregnable. Once, she saw a leggy bird sprinting across the flat land at an unbelievable speed to surprise a succulent meal of lizard. Seeing her wide eyes, Ryan identified it as a roadrunner, and pointed out its nest in a cholla cactus.

Even the cactus seemed to come alive at times. They were riding through a thickly infested area of spiny plants, when Stephanie's gelding snorted and squealed. She held tight to the reins to calm the plunging animal, and tried to see what had caused his fright. Moving swiftly forward, Ryan pried a clump of cactus from the toe of Stephanie's boot where it was scraping against the horse.

"How'd that get there?" she asked, bewildered.

"Jumping cholla. It sticks at the slightest touch of man or animal," Ryan answered. "Breaks off at the joint, then eventually falls to the ground to root and grow."

Stephanie just shook her head, feeling as if she'd stepped into the pages of a novel depicting a fantasy land.

They finally stopped for water at a slow-moving

stream Ryan claimed was a clear spring. To Stephanie, there was nothing clear about it, but it did provide cool water. She splashed a small amount on her neck and face, tilting her head back to let rivulets wet her blouse. It might keep her a little cooler for a time. The dust-covered kerchief was dipped into the creek and wrung out for her to use as a cloth, then rinsed again. God, she was filthy. A bath would be a wonderful luxury, but Ryan was already telling her to hurry.

"This is the only water for miles. I don't intend to be caught off guard. Come on."

"Can't we rest for a little while? We've been riding all day, and I'm hot and tired. The horses would benefit, too. Look at them . . ."

"I told you to stay at the fort if you couldn't handle it, didn't I? You should have listened for a change. Now I'm ready to ride, and you can come or you can stay here and float like a rock for all I care."

Ryan swung his horse around and kicked him into a trot, pulling the packhorse with him. Damn. He didn't think he could sit and watch her without forgetting all restraint. Surely she realized that her blouse was transparent when wet, yet she still sat there wetting down her front like she didn't. Whatever happened to all those frilly things women were supposed to wear under their outer clothes? It seemed that Stephanie Ashworth didn't care for undergarments . . . Any relief from the heat that he might have been beginning to feel was rapidly evaporating in a different kind of heat . . .

Grimly, Stephanie pulled her hat back on and tied the damp kerchief around her neck. It was almost dry already, and she stifled a groan. If she dared, she would take off her shirt and ride in just a sleeveless chemise and the buckskin trousers. It would be so much cooler. Slowly, wearily, she checked the girth on her saddle and put one foot into the dangling stirrup to mount. Her horse snorted, rolling his eyes, and Stephanie frowned. She tightened her grip on the reins.

"Whoa, boy. Hold steady now. What's the matter with you?"

There was a strange sound, a whirring noise that was spooking the gelding. Half turning, Stephanie discovered the source of the rattle at the same time as her mount. A large coil of snake was only a few feet away, lethal and threatening. She swallowed hard. The horse was shying away in short, choppy steps, tossing his head and blowing, and she tried to keep her foot in the stirrup. She tightened her grip on the reins and saddle horn and tried to pull up, but he was half rearing. Stephanie held on with grim determination as the gelding bolted forward in a mad dash away from the lunging rattlesnake.

Clinging tightly, she hung on one side of the frightened animal like a banner, not quite able to pull up but afraid to let go. She was bumped and jarred against the leather saddle skirts as she tried to lift her free leg over his back. But she was off balance, and her foot would occasionally drag and hit against the ground or a rock as the panicky gelding skimmed across the prairie. Stephanie had no breath to waste in calling out for help, and just hoped that Cordell would somehow notice that she was in trouble. She wasn't even sure if the horse was going in his direction, or had bolted toward the mountains.

Stinging wisps of blond hair lashed against her cheek and her hat was gone, and Stephanie's fingers were sweaty and slipping from the saddle horn. She'd probably break a bone when she hit the ground, Stephanie thought dimly, realizing that she couldn't hold on much longer. The ground was a blur of dust and clumps of grass, and she prayed that there would be no cactus where she fell. There was a pounding rush in her ears as she prepared to hit the ground, then she felt herself snatched up and backward.

All the air in her lungs left in a "whoosh" as Stephanie was yanked from her horse and banged against another horse's side. Ryan's arm circled her waist and her legs dangled against his stallion like a rag doll's. She was half sobbing from fright and reaction as he slowed his mount to a stop.

Clawing wind-whipped tangles of hair from her eyes, Stephanie gulped for breath as Ryan lowered her gently to the ground. Normally quite dependable legs buckled as her knees gave way, and she crumpled like a heap of old rags. Shaking fingers covered her face, and she realized she'd bitten her tongue somehow. Slowly, Stephanie became aware of Ryan hovering over her like a thundercloud.

"What the hell did you do that for?" Ryan circled his stallion and stared down at her impatiently. A wave of anger ripped through Stephanie, but she was still quivering with reaction, her tongue hurt, and there were several clumps of sharp-needled cactus clinging to her pants legs.

"Snake . . ." The one word was all she could manage, but it produced quick results. Ryan was off his horse in an instant and kneeling beside her, a frown creasing his face.

"Did it get you?" Stephanie was almost upended as he grabbed her ankles and yanked her legs from under her. Flint-gray eyes skimmed quickly over dust-caked buckskin trousers studded with cholla, and the expensive leather boots she wore.

"No. Just scared my horse, not to mention me."

Ryan's brow smoothed and he dropped her legs, sitting back on his heels Indian-style. "Some horses spook at a rattler. Old Cutter here," he waved a hand at his stallion, "cuts 'em to pieces with his hooves. You all right?"

She nodded weakly. Aside from being short of breath, unable to stand, and completely unnerved, she was in splendid shape, Stephanie decided.

"Good. I'll catch that worthless gelding and we can ride on. You've wasted enough time. Pick off your cactus and watch the packhorse."

Stephanie stared wordlessly as Ryan swung onto his stallion and rode after her horse. Strands of silvery hair hung in her eyes and she combed at it with shaking hands. My, my. She *had* wasted time, hadn't she? Just who was supposed to be in a hurry anyway? It was her father they were trying to find. Did Cordell think he was fooling her with his charade about being guide? He was after the rumored gold. Not that it mattered. He would meet his match when they caught up with Julian . . .

Chapter Nine

Dusk again, and with it a fresh breeze. It drifted in light whispers across Stephanie's face and neck, bringing relief from the energy-draining heat. Soon they would stop and she could rest. The sun was just sinking behind the purple and blue haze of the moutains, and they rode in the shadows of the valley. The most brilliant colors Stephanie could ever recall seeing painted the sky in hues of rose, magenta, and peach. Earthbound sunbeams that Ryan called Mexican poppies grew in wild abandon across the plain, and she was awed by the beauty surrounding her. Eye-stopping swatches of riotous color bathed the slopes and gullies in shades of pink, orange, and bluish-purple.

Just ahead of her, Cordell was reining his tired mount to a halt, and she breathed a sigh of relief. Finally. But when she saw that Ryan had picked a spot among the rocks again, Stephanie protested.

"Really, Cordell, can't we camp under those trees?" She pointed to a graceful canopy of mesquite not far away. "They'd provide shelter and shade, and the ground wouldn't be so rocky and hard . . ."

"I thought you were supposed to be tough . . ."

". . . that I get stiff every time I lie down."

"Look, anytime you want to lead this little expedition and make all the decisions, you're welcome to it. If I'm doing it, we'll camp where I say . . ." Leather saddlebags hit the ground with a thud. Exasperated, Ryan stood with his feet apart and fists planted on his hips, staring at her from beneath the brim of his hat.

"I was just making a suggestion, Mr. Cordell. There's no need to get so perturbed. Your authority and masculinity are not being questioned." Out loud anyway, Stephanie thought. She did her best to ignore him as she swung down from her bay gelding with her back turned to him.

It would be too much to expect Ryan to help her. He was too busy being irritated, so Stephanie immediately began unsaddling her horse and the pack animal.

"Your turn to take care of the pack horse tonight," Ryan had informed her earlier. "You can take care of things as well as a man, remember?"

Cordell had picked out a spot nestled against towering red rocks for their campsite, and she groaned at the countless stones scattered on the ground. He was going out of his way to make her miserable, Stephanie decided. It would have suited Cordell if she had been foolish enough to stay behind and let him bring Julian to her. Then he would have taken the map to find her father—and the gold. She'd had enough sense to stop that!

Stephanie swallowed a laugh as it occurred to her that she was now far away from any other human being—civilized, anyway—with no idea where she was. Her life was in Ryan Cordell's hands. Oh, she'd blatantly bribed him by agreeing to pay that exorbitant amount of money for his services, but might very well have leaped blindly into danger by doing so. After all, what did she really know about Ryan Cordell except what Lieutenant Buckner had told her? She could disappear forever; remain an unsolved mystery—"Millionaire Financier's Daughter Disappears In Arizona Territory" the *Tribune* headlines would read: "No Sign of the New York Ice Maiden." Gloom. Only Claudia would have a vague idea what had happened to her. And all Claudie knew was the man's name—fictitious, probably. Who knew if Ryan Cordell was his real name?

Stephanie slid a wary glance in Ryan's direction. She should really try to find out a little bit more about him, maybe just ask an innocent question or two. And if worse came to worse and Cordell was dangerous, she wouldn't hesitate to use Julian's old army pistol. It was in her saddlebags now, but should feel quite at home in a holster on her hip . . .

By the time she'd finished unsaddling her gelding and the pack horse, brushed them down and fed them, Stephanie ached in every muscle of her body. She was bruised from her encounter with the rattlesnake, having bounced all over the side of her horse, and even more tired than she'd been the day before. She sank wearily to the ground and buried her sweating face in her palms. Only yesterday it hadn't seemed possible to feel more tired, or ache in more muscles. What would she feel like tomorrow? Stephanie couldn't help a soft moan as she stretched out her long legs and leaned back on both elbows.

"Through already?"

Stephanie flicked a dark glance to Ryan. A small fire popped and crackled, and the soot-blackened coffeepot sat on a stone in the middle of the flames. The evening breeze gently wafted the delicious odor of fresh-perked coffee in her direction.

"Yes. I'm 'through already'," Stephanie mimicked. She licked her lips as she eyed the slab of salted beef sizzling in an iron skillet close to the coffeepot. Her stomach rumbled ominously, prompting her to a decision. Well, it wouldn't hurt to make a suggestion, would it? All he could say was no.

"Mr. Cordell, since we are—at your insistence— trading off duties, allow me to make a suggestion. I will cook our dinner on the nights you tend both horses, and you cook on the nights *I* tend both horses. Is that agreeable?"

"Beginning tonight, I suppose?"

Stephanie was too tired and hungry to waste time in argument. Clenching her teeth against a hasty reply, she nodded, and was surprised—and pleased— when Ryan agreed.

"Fine with me—as long as you know how to cook. I haven't eaten any of your cooking yet. The deal may be off if you cook like you ride . . ."

"Trust me! I won't poison you—in spite of great temptation." Stephanie managed a too-sweet smile. "In fact, you may grow so fond of my cooking that you'll beg for it every night. I have a King Charles spaniel who absolutely adores my muffins."

A grin tugged at the corners of Ryan's mouth for a moment before he surrendered to it. "That's an interesting notion. Would I have to sit up and beg like your pet spaniel? Or just wag my tail and roll over . . . ?"

"Do you fetch the paper?"

"Would you rather I play dead, maybe?"

"You tempt me, Mr. Cordell . . ."

"I'm trying, lady," he shot back with a wicked leer. "But you keep playing hard to get."

Suddenly the conversation had turned to innuendos that startled and flustered Stephanie. She shifted uneasily and tried to edge away. But it was hard when Ryan was leaning close and looking at her from beneath his thick fringe of dark lashes like she was his next meal . . .

Stephanie cleared her throat and changed the subject. "So . . . what's on the menu for tonight?" Uh oh. Judging from his widening grin, she shouldn't have asked that particular question. Ryan's gaze strayed slowly and deliberately over her body.

"Umm, glad you asked, Princess. We have tender white breasts—of chicken, firm juicy legs—of lamb . . ."

Her forced smile vanished instantly. Why this sudden change in attitude? At least she knew what to expect when Ryan was behaving like a boor. She stood up abruptly.

"You think you're very funny," she said stiffly, "but I don't appreciate your sense of humor." Stephanie yanked the iron skillet from the fire and poked viciously at the slab of browning beef.

"I get the feeling you don't appreciate much of anything, Miss Ashworth. Why is that?"

"Don't be ridiculous. I appreciate a great many things . . ."

"Yeah? Like what?" he challenged. "I'd be interested in knowing what sparks your fire."

Stephanie rocked back on her heels and glared at him while the beef sizzled. Stabbing the fork she held in his direction, she said, "I enjoy beautiful music, paintings by the masters, fine wine, excellent food . . ."

Ryan gave a derisive snort. "Lady, you haven't learned anything about life! All those things are nice, but have you ever stopped to listen to really beautiful music? Nothing man has ever composed compares with the soft sound of wind blowing through pine branches, or the song of a sparrow in springtime. You like paintings by the masters?" One hand swept out, drawing Stephanie's reluctant attention to the sky. The sun was setting behind sculptured mountains, bathing the peaks in glowing colors of saffron and amber. Low-lying clouds drifted in varying colors of gold, seemingly speared by smoky spires of cactus jutting from the desert floor. "Can Da Vinci really compete with God's paintbrush? And I'm willing to bet when we stopped at that cold spring early today, you wouldn't have traded one drop of water for an entire bottle of the finest wine."

"All right, all right," Stephanie conceded with a shrug, "you have made an excellent point." She pushed the iron skillet back into the fire. "But that still doesn't mean I have to endure your tasteless humor and crude jokes."

"Touché. 'A jest's prosperity lies in the ear of him that hears it,'" Ryan began quoting, "'never in the tongue of him that makes it.' Shakespeare. *Love's Labor's Lost.*"

"Well. I am impressed at last, Mr. Cordell. Shakespeare is one of my favorites. You are—in spite of your appearance—an educated man, it seems."

"Did I ever claim not to be?" Ryan flicked her with a mocking glance. "I'm surprised that you like Shakespeare—who wrote some of the most fiendish plots imaginable, complete with murder and adultery—yet are offended by innuendos." He shook his head. "That's a contradiction."

Stephanie was even more curious about Ryan now. Who was he? She had to find out. Her attention wandered to his hands as he leaned forward to take the skillet from her. They were strong hands, like her father's, with blunt, square-tipped fingers. Claudia had always claimed one could tell a lot about a man from his hands. Ryan's were lean, and tanned as brown as the skin stretched over his high cheekbones. Capable hands.

Sitting this close to him, Stephanie could easily see the tiny sun lines fanning out from the corners of his eyes. Character lines, her father called them. When Ryan smiled—and he was devastatingly handsome when he did—his eyes crinkled at the corners.

"Where did you learn Shakespeare?" she asked when the silence stretched too long. "Did you go to school in the East, perhaps?"

Ryan's glance was faintly assessing, as if he was wondering whether or not to answer. Squinting,

110

Stephanie tried to imagine him dressed in a proper suit with a vest, beaver fedora, and shoes buffed to a mirror polish. Hmmm. Not bad. Even with his dark hair too long and windblown, he would be considered very handsome.

Ryan silently handed her a plate heaped with food, and Stephanie decided the conversation could wait until she'd eaten. What was it about desert air that made everything taste so much better? Even salted beef and beans were good.

"You didn't answer me, Mr. Cordell," she said after scraping up her last bits of beef and beans with the remainder of a flat corn cake, "were you brought up in the West?" Stephanie sat with her legs bent and elbows resting on her knees, and regarded Ryan with a frank stare.

"Why do you ask?" He slanted her a curious glance, and she met his direct gaze with one of her own.

"I just wondered. There are times when you seem more . . . well, more civilized . . . than at others. I thought perhaps you had been born in the East and moved out West as a young man."

Firelight played over his face as Ryan lifted a tin mug of coffee to his mouth. A beard shadowed his jawline and upper lip, giving him a harder look, and Stephanie felt suddenly uneasy at having asked a personal question.

"Pardon me. I let my curiosity get the best of me . . ."

"I don't mind answering. I was just surprised by your observation that I'm 'more civilized' sometimes." Even in the dim light he could see her cheeks

111

flush pink, and Ryan laughed. "You put it quite nicely, princess. To answer your question, yes, I was born out here. I have been East, but that was a long time ago and I didn't like it. I prefer open spaces and a sky that has stars at night. There are no stars in the city."

"No stars? Of course there are! I see the stars all the time, and even observe the different constellations . . ." Stephanie paused. He was right. City lights somehow drowned out the stars. She'd discovered that fact at a young age, the first time Julian had allowed her to accompany him on an expedition into some uncharted wildnerness. Lying on the ground at night, she'd seen more stars than she'd ever know existed. How had she forgotten?

"You're right, Cordell. But I hadn't thought about it in ages. Even the moon seems brighter and lower to the earth out here . . ."

"Maybe it is." Ryan set his tin mug on a nearby rock and leaned back on his elbows to light a thin cigar. Gray eyes narrowed, watching her through drifting curls of smoke. "The Indians probably have a myth that explains it."

"What kind of myth?"

Stephanie's interest was caught as Ryan began repeating myths and legends he'd learned from various Indian tribes.

"There's even a Cheyenne legend about a woman with yellow hair," he said with a wicked grin. "Better not get close to any Cheyennes, princess. They might get ideas."

"My hair's too pale to be called yellow. What kind of legend? Was she good or evil?"

112

"Good. She gave the gift of buffalo to the Cheyenne. In ancient times, according to the legend, the tribe had to subsist on fish, geese, and ducks instead of large food animals. They became so hungry the chiefs sent out two young men to search for food. They weren't to return unless they succeeded. After various mishaps, they stumbled into the company of an old couple. The old man and his wife had a fair-haired daughter, Yellow Haired Woman. At the old man's suggestion, one of the young men took her as his wife. As wedding gifts, the old man gave them a knowledge of corn planting and the use of the buffalo for food; but he cautioned his daughter she must never express pity for any suffering animal."

"Why?" Stephanie interrupted curiously.

Ryan shrugged. "The legend doesn't explain. Maybe it's because animals would lose their usefulness if people thought of them in terms of human sympathy. Anyway, the Cheyennes were happy when the two young men returned with Yellow Haired Woman, because afterward they were surrounded by buffalo and were able to get all the meat they needed. But one day some boys dragged a buffalo-calf into camp and threw dust in its eyes. Yellow Haired Woman said, 'My poor calf!' then realized she'd broken the taboo imposed by her father. That day all the buffalo disappeared, and she had to go back to her parents. Her husband and the other young man went with her, and the three were never seen again."

"Is that the end?" Stephanie asked when Ryan finished. "What happened about the buffalo?"

"According to legend, other mythical figures

113

restored the buffalo much later, and brought back tribal fortunes."

"That's an interesting story. Do you know any more?"

For the next hour, Cordell told her legends and myths of the Apache, Navajo, and Comanche nations. Stephanie listened in fascination, almost mesmerized by Ryan's deep, resonant voice as he repeated stories that had been told around countless Indian campfires.

"I wonder why I never heard any of them before," she remarked softly. She gazed at Ryan across the dying fire. "They should be written down and preserved."

He shrugged. "Who'd be interested in reading them? Sentiments against Indians are running high right now." Ryan stretched his long legs closer to the fire and turned on one side, propping his head in the palm of a broad hand as he took the last drag from his cigar. "Even you think it's more exciting to go to foreign countries and listen to their customs than it is stepping outside your own back door."

"Arizona Territory is hardly just outside my door, Mr. Cordell." Stephanie poured herself another mug of coffee and sipped at it cautiously. "We don't have an entire reservation full of Indians in Central Park, you know. After all, they are rather hostile . . ."

"Hostile?" Ryan's brows lifted. "Did you ever stop to wonder why they might be hostile? Or is it inconvenient to think about hungry Indian babies when you sit down at your dinner table every night?" Ryan's cigar stub flipped into the air in a graceful arc before plummeting into the fire.

"Don't be belligerent . . . I happen to know that the United States government provides for the Indians. Why, my Uncle George is on a committee . . ."

"Ah, your Uncle George! I should have known your family would somehow be involved in the Bureau of Indian Affairs." Ryan's eyes glittered coldly. "Has he ever come West to inspect the conditions on any of the reservations? No? Now, why did I expect that answer . . ."

"Mr. Cordell, I don't think that you understand all the political . . ."

"Don't talk down to me, Stephanie Ashworth! I understand a lot more than you do right now. The government provides for dishonest Indian agents, lady, that's who they provide for. The Navajos are starving, as well as the Apache, Comanche, and any other tribe unfortunate enough to be under the 'protection' of the government. Congress may vote 'em enough to eat—barely—but they don't make sure they get it."

"Well, if you can prove any of these allegations, why don't . . ."

"Sweet Jesus!" Ryan exploded. "Go look at the little kids with swollen bellies. Isn't that proof enough? And while you're at it, take a good look at the well-lined pockets of some of the agents the government sent."

"You're making it sound as if I'm personally responsible," Stephanie accused. "How would I know any of this?"

"Ah, I guess you couldn't. I just get angry thinking about it, that's all. Someone should take the responsibility of seeing how their tax money is being spent—right? What do you think your father would say?" Ryan took a deep breath and smiled sheepishly. "That's the end of my speech about injustice. Sorry if I bored you."

"I wasn't bored. I just feel rather helpless. When I return to New York, I intend to speak to my Uncle George about the situation. Perhaps he can help . . ."

"Why did you come out here?" Ryan surprised her by asking brusquely. "For adventure and excitement? Was New York beginning to bore you? You don't fit into this style of life—think of all the dinner parties and operas you may have missed . . ."

Ryan's obvious assessment of her as an idle, easily bored heiress rankled. Why should she spoil his delusion? Let him think what he pleased.

"New York in June *is* rather boring, and Father is always planning new diversions. I usually accompany him on his expeditions, and I enjoy them. We're very close."

"Really? How touching."

"Yes, it is, isn't it?" Stephanie's lips curved in a sugary smile. "Now it's my turn to ask some questions, Mr. Cordell, since we're baring our souls. Why do you persist in being antagonistic when I have done nothing to deserve such treatment? Do you dislike women?"

"Some," Ryan answered shortly. He glanced at her, and Stephanie was startled by the expression of unguarded pain in his eyes. It was quickly masked by his familiar, mocking smile and the acid remark that a man could never really know a woman.

Stephanie propped her chin in her palms and

leveled a searching gaze at him. "While in Vienna last year, I met a most interesting young man. He was studying at the University of Vienna, and also worked in the Vienna General Hospital. Herr Freud has some very novel theories about man's inner self . . ."

"Is this a lecture, Miss Ashworth? I have the inescapable feeling that I am about to be delivered some ludicrous theory . . ."

"I was merely going to suggest that perhaps you are transferring your animosity against one woman to all . . ."

"Dammit!" Ryan gave her a hard look. "I don't need you or some Austrian doctor telling me what I'm thinking, or why I'm thinking it! You need to mind your own business. But most of all," he added when Stephanie opened her mouth to reply, "you need to shut up!"

"Well!" An indignant retort died on her lips as she noted the harsh expression on Ryan's face. When the tense silence grew too much to endure, she decided to go to sleep. Their pleasant interlude of intelligent conversation had—as usual—degenerated into an argument.

"It's getting late and I'm tired. I think I'll make my bed now, Mr. Cordell," she said quietly.

"Good idea." Cool gray eyes glittered as Ryan's gaze skimmed over her face, and a slightly mocking smile twisted his mouth. "Retreat from the line of fire before you get hurt . . ."

"What do you mean by that?"

"You know what I mean." He bent and scooped up his mug, and the dregs of his coffee were flung into

117

the fire, hissing against hot stones. "Little girls who pry into someone else's business usually regret it. Even big girls like you, Stephanie Ashworth."

"Really, your point is quite moot, Mr. Cordell. I have no intention of prying again, I assure you. Good night."

"'Night."

Fully aware that he was watching her like a hawk watches its next meal, Stephanie rose to her feet. She brushed the dirt from her trousers and tried her best to ignore Ryan Cordell. Why must he keep staring at her? It was unnerving. Stephanie whirled to walk away. Her new leather boots had treacherously slick soles, and both feet slid as if she had stepped into a puddle of oatmeal.

Skidding on loose stones, Stephanie's arms waved like windmills as she struggled to remain upright. Her body bent forward, then back like an out-of-control puppet as she lost the struggle. Gritting her teeth, Stephanie steeled herself for a painful landing.

Ryan's hand flashed out and caught her by an elbow, spinning her around. Stephanie barely had time to wonder how he had moved so fast before he was jerking her close. Her fingers instinctively closed around his arms. Ryan's face was only inches from hers, and in spite of her height, Stephanie felt more intimidated than any man had ever made her feel. She still had to look up to make eye contact, and found it a definite disadvantage. Stephanie let go of his arms as if burned and tried to pull away.

"Thank you," she murmured, adding when he didn't release her, "You can let go now. I'm able to stand."

She was pressed close against him, half leaning into his chest so that she could feel his muscles flex when he moved. Why didn't he release her? It actually felt as if his hands had tightened around her arms.

"Mr. Cordell, you are hurting my arm," she said coldly, and was surprised that her voice didn't quiver.

Still holding her tightly, Ryan gave her a slight shake. "Am I? You're a big girl, Stephanie Ashworth. You can handle it."

"I never doubted that. However, I find it unnecessary to 'handle it' at all. Release me at once," she said in her most imperative tone. It was wasted on Ryan Cordell. If anything, it prompted him to hold her even more tightly. Stephanie tried to tug away, but couldn't. It made her angry that he would dare hold her, and one hand slashed quickly upward.

Ryan was quicker, and caught her wrist in his free hand. "Violence again, Princess? You seem to be fond of slapping at men. How provincial. Flay me with your sharp tongue instead. You're so much better at it."

"How would you know what I'm fond of? You don't even know me at all! And for your information, you are the first man I've ever *had* to slap. Most of the men I know are gentlemen." She stressed the word "gentlemen," and was rewarded with a frowning glare from Ryan. Stephanie's heart was pounding so loudly she was positive he could hear it, and she struggled for composure. "You are stretching the boundaries of my good nature with this ridiculous ploy. What do you hope to prove?"

Ryan held her so close that her breasts brushed lightly against his chest. His shirt was halfway open, baring tanned skin and a thick mat of darkly curling hair. It was crazy, but it was almost as if she wore no blouse at all, for she could have sworn she felt every crisp hair on Ryan's chest pressed next to bare breasts. She resisted the impulse to look down and be certain her blouse was still covering her. Of course it was . . .

Stephanie shivered. Her skin tingled as if she was in a thunderstorm with lightning crackling and popping all around her. Stray tendrils of silvery hair had fallen into her eyes, and she shook them back as she stared at him coolly.

An ivory princess, Ryan thought to himself as he saw the snapping anger in her dark eyes. She was furious, and had every right to be. Why had he grabbed her like this? Was it her beauty, or simply the impulse to make her react to him as a man? It didn't really matter. Very little mattered but the gold at the end of this rainbow journey he was taking. He'd known women like Stephanie Ashworth before, all cool and correct, paragons of virtue as long as things went their way. He'd even been a helpless victim at the soft, pale hand of a society belle, and the memory still rankled . . .

"What do I hope to prove, Miss Ashworth?" he mocked. "I'm no gentleman, remember? I have only animal instincts. I don't have to prove anything. I just react."

Stephanie anticipated Ryan's next move by the slight increase of pressure in the fingers gripping her elbow, but could do nothing to halt it. She was pulled forward so that her breasts were crushed against his unyielding chest and her head was tilted back.

"Let me go . . . !" For the first time a trace of panic quivered in her voice, but it was smothered by Ryan's mouth covering hers. There were different ways to kiss, Stephanie was learning, and Ryan Cordell seemed to know them all. This kiss was harsh and frightening, as if he was trying to punish her. There was no passion in the hard pressure of his lips on hers, but only a fierce anger.

She refused to close her eyes but kept them open, glaring at Ryan. It was a battle of wills, and he was determined to win. But so was she. Stephanie was all too conscious of the steely tautness of his long body pressed so close to her, of his arms like iron bands circling her squirming body so tightly her ribs were in danger of snapping. Damn him!

Stephanie squinted through her lashes at him. Gray eyes glittered coldly at her through thick lashes too long to belong to a man, and she felt a chill quiver down the curve of her spine. He was deliberately prolonging the kiss to intimidate her. Well, it wasn't going to work!

Stephanie's reaction was instinctive and un-planned, but quite effective. She quickly lifted one leg to slam her foot down hard on Ryan's instep.

A guttural grunt of pain sounded just above her head, and she ducked under Cordell's loosened grasp and away. Stephanie skittered quickly out of reach before glancing back, and was surprised to see him bent over and dropping to one knee on the ground. Ryan's face was a mask of pain, more than she'd anticipated, and she hesitated uncertainly. Should she see if he was hurt badly?

Stephanie's indecision was cleared, however, when Ryan shot her a baleful glare and said, "You have a wicked knee, lady. I should have known you'd try that dirty trick."

Her cheeks reddened as Stephanie realized what had happened, but she icily replied, "Whatever it takes, Mr. Cordell."

Stephanie retreated, staying well away from him. There wasn't a single word exchanged as she rolled out her blankets close to the fire and chose a clean blouse for the next day. She washed her face with the small amount of water allotted for each day's cleaning and raked wet fingers through her dust-caked hair. It really needed a good washing, and so did she, Stephanie thought with a deep sigh. Arizona dust had a way of seeping into everything. She was quite sure that her throat was coated with a thick layer of red dust, as well as all her internal organs.

Especially her brain, she thought with a trace of disgust. Surely, clogging dust was the cause of her muddled thinking earlier. Just when she'd been thinking that Ryan Cordell might be a presentable human being, he had changed colors like a chameleon. And like that charming little reptile he resembled, he was likely to switch again.

But this would be a good lesson for her. Nothing in Arizona Territory was what it seemed. A small rock lying on a larger one frequently turned out to be a quite lovely lizard; and those beautifully delicate blossoms rising in puffy spires toward the sky were guarded by painfully sharp, spiny leaves of the yucca plant. Even coyotes were not members of the *Canis latrans* family in the order of the animal world, but were actually savage Apaches if Ryan was to be believed.

Stephanie stretched out on one blanket and pulled another one over her to keep out the chill. She tugged the brightly patterned Navajo blanket up to her chin. It had been purchased at Hubbell's Trading Post, when they'd stopped to inquire about Julian earlier in the day. The Navajo nation lived on a reservation close to the fort, and their women wove the blankets and traded them for food and supplies. She frowned, thinking of the Indian situation as Ryan had described it earlier.

Were the Indians really going hungry? Certainly Uncle George and other important government officials would know about it if they were. Stephanie was puzzled. Nothing had been written in the *New York Tribune* about it, and the papers usually reported every little thing about the "Wild West" and hostile savages. Easterners were avidly curious about their western countrymen, yet glad to be safely in civilization. Perhaps some officials were too complacent, Stephanie thought, as Ryan sardonically suggested.

Sparks shot up from the fire as a branch of mesquite snapped, capturing her attention for a moment. Turning her head, Stephanie gazed dreamily at the dying flames through half-closed eyes. Fitful light cast odd shadows around the little camp, briefly illuminating her surroundings. Across the small ring of stones circling the fire she could see Ryan's long shape folded into his blankets. Was he still awake? She hoped so. Maybe his conscience would prick him and he'd be ashamed of the way he'd behaved, but that was too much to hope for.

Shifting, Stephanie turned her gaze away from Ryan. She tilted back her head and stared up at the night sky. It was so vast and immense, and she was just a small speck in the universe, a minute particle lost in infinity. She felt oddly overwhelmed. Why did she let him get to her?

Stephanie would have been surprised to find that Ryan Cordell was having an attack of conscience.

He slid a glance toward Stephanie. She was lying on her back looking up at the heavens, her face half lit by the fire's glow. Damn. Silvery blond hair and big, innocent brown eyes that seemed to hold mysterious shadows in their velvety depths were too tempting. He must be crazy. Only two days from the fort, and he'd kissed her not once, but twice. But there was something about this woman . . .

She was maddening, as irritating as a bee in his ear, but he found his gaze straying to her again and again. In a way he admired her. It wasn't just her determination to keep up with him. Lord, she certainly had the physical capabilities. The woman was as tall or taller than most men, and she packed a pistol at her side like she knew how to use it. He'd hate to test Stephanie's accuracy with a Colt. And why did he always seem to be down a point or two in verbal debate?

Yeah, she was maddening all right, but it wasn't just her cool air of indifference that got to him. Maybe it was the way she'd look at him sometimes; over her shoulder, with a hint of something she didn't even recognize glowing in her eyes. That got to him.

Chapter Ten

There was little conversation between them the next few days. Most of Ryan's time was spent in studying the trail, while Stephanie concentrated on staying on her horse in spite of the intense heat. Moments of shade beside a cool, running stream were pleasant idylls to be dreamed about, while stark reality was a burning sun and miles of rough terrain. How could mountains be so hot? She'd always thought of mountainous regions as cool, with grassy slopes and inclines. Apparently Arizona had never heard of those kind. These mountains were flat mesas and ridged buttes that rose like jagged teeth from the earth, and the grassy slopes she dreamed about were actually sparse clumps of tough grass.

A purplish haze hung like clouds over the land, and Stephanie shook her head. Oh, Lord—it had finally happened. Her brain had been baked by the sun so that she was seeing things. The rocks all around her were in an entire spectrum of colors. Bright sunlight glittered in shades of red, brown, purple, and gray, and the sandstone humps shaped like turtle backs actually seemed to change colors as they rode along. Erosion had worn away part of the land, and there were places the ground abruptly dropped away from beneath their horses' hooves. To Stephanie, it looked as if the Creator had dumped the remains of his paintbox on this dreary stretch to give it some redeeming features.

"I hate to sound foolish," she finally ventured when she rode close to Ryan, "but . . . what's the matter with the rocks?"

"This is called the Painted Desert." Ryan's mouth twitched with amusement. "Goes for about a hundred miles along the Little Colorado River valley, almost to New Mexico."

Reining her mount to a halt, Stephanie tugged on the brim of her hat to shade her eyes and leaned forward. How unexpected. Beauty could be found anywhere, even in a remote, barren desert.

In the next few days Arizona had more surprises for Stephanie. They rode through an area where signs of ancient Indian ruins were barely visible. Ryan veered from the trail long enough to show her a huge, smooth slab of rock etched with petroglyphs that had to be thousands of years old.

"These must have been scratched on the surface throughout the years," Stephanie observed, running the tips of her fingers over the drawings. There were crude pictures of human figures, deer, bison, and other animals, as well as images that probably represented important events.

"On what do you base your opinion, Professor?" Ryan asked in a tone that was only half-mocking.

"They could have all been scratched on there last year, from the looks of it."

"Oh no . . . see this one?" Stephanie pointed to a figure. "This is in the style of Neolithic man, while this one," she pointed to another, "is much more modern. I'd say this was done only a few hundred years ago. For one thing, this drawing shows horses, which we know did not come to the North American continent until sometime after 1540, when the Spanish brought them. Now this one . . ."

"Enough, Professor. I get the picture, if you'll pardon the pun." He took off his hat to rake his fingers through his hair. "I know you're enjoying yourself, but do you suppose we could push on? There's a certain missing millionaire that one of us is in a big hurry to find."

"Of course." Stephanie followed Ryan from the rock, observing that its natural overhang must have helped to preserve the petroglyphs from the elements. "See, it's large enough to keep wind, rain, and sand from eroding the slab."

"I wonder if you're as single-minded in other areas as well," Ryan muttered more to himself than to Stephanie.

"At least we've found a conversational topic that isn't controversial," she shot back. "That should make you happy."

"I'll be happy when we find your father and I get my money. Until then, I'll make do."

The short distance to the horses was crossed in silence. Stephanie mentally counted to ten—a promise she had made to herself to keep from arguing with Cordell—and managed a tight smile when he handed her the lead rope to the pack horse.

"Why yes, Mr. Cordell, I'll be happy to lead for a while. No, of course I don't mind. I'm not in the least bit tired."

A flicker of amusement skimmed over Ryan's features for a moment, but he only gave a slight shake of his head. Stephanie was tempted to revert to childhood and put out her tongue at him when he turned his back, but she resisted. Nudging her gelding forward, she felt a brief sense of satisfaction. Satisfaction would help her endure the shimmering hot days filled with dust and the constant plodding of horses. God, would she always be hot and thirsty?

Just when Stephanie was beginning to think that Arizona had exhausted its source of redeeming features, they rode over a ridge and she looked down into one of the most beautiful valleys she had ever seen.

"Paradise! The Garden of Eden," she murmured in awe. "Complete with bathing facilities."

Oak and young cottonwood trees lined a rushing creek that tumbled over smooth stones, and the clear water reflected the brilliant blue of the cloudless sky. Tall red spires of sandstone flanked the creek, providing a backdrop that Stephanie thought starkly beautiful.

"Keep back until I check it out, Miss Ashworth."

Ryan's terse order burst Stephanie's dream of immersing herself chin-deep in cool water.

"Check it out for what? You can see for miles from this point, and the only things moving are those birds."

"I thought you didn't care for arguments?"

"Right." Stephanie clamped her mouth shut, mentally counting to ten again. She *had* said she would no longer argue, but she'd been hot for so long, even a few minutes' wait seemed an eternity.

The few minutes turned out to be almost two hours by the time the horses picked their way carefully down the mountain trail. Because of steep drops and the ragged edges of the terrain that Ryan referred to as "hogbacks," they had to wind their way down in a zigzag. The land was cut with juniper-choked gorges and humped with hogbacks covered with fir trees. Deep canyons were a tangle of manzanita, the small trees or shrubs that Cordell said were sometimes called bearberry. Thick grass was sparse, but so tall in places that it tickled the horses' bellies as they made their way along.

They finally reached flatter ground and the creek, and Stephanie slid gratefully from her mount. She unbuckled her gunbelt and hung it from the saddle horn, then tied the gelding to a low-hanging tree branch. Her legs wobbled as she made her way to a large stone at the creek's edge.

"Is it safe for me to sit here?" she flung over her shoulder at Ryan, hoping he would say yes. She didn't think she could move another inch without some relief from the heat. Even while she waited for an answer, Stephanie was tugging off her boots and rolling her pants up and her stockings down. Looking over one shoulder, she slid Ryan a questioning glance.

"Go ahead." He was already dismounting, and his boots crunched against the rocky sand as he tied his stallion and the pack horse next to Stephanie's. He grinned as she stepped to the edge of the stream and balanced on one leg, touching the water's surface with a bare toe. "Don't be squeamish. Do you want to get cool, or don't you?"

Stephanie loudly sucked in her breath as she waded into the water. It was colder than she'd thought it would be, but oh, Lord, it felt so delicious on her baked skin!

Stephanie resembled a long-legged water nymph, Ryan thought as she waded farther out. She stepped high, skirting as many stones as possible, pausing when the water level reached the rolled-up cuff of her pants.

"It's not deep," Ryan couldn't resist calling, "go on out a little further." He propped his booted foot on the top of a smooth stone half-buried in the mud of the sloping bank and watched as Stephanie waded in up to her knees. Sunlight glinted from tangled strands of her hair as she bent forward to scoop up handfuls of water, and she almost lost the battered hat perched on the back of her head in the process. Clutching at it, Stephanie straightened and took another step nearer the middle.

There was a loud squeal as she plunged in up to her neck, and Ryan exploded with laughter.

"Cool enough now?" he mocked, and was delivered a glare that should have shriveled him where he stood.

"You did that on purpose . . . !"

"What? I didn't tell you to go *that* far out, did I? I said a little bit farther . . ."

"Ryan Cordell, I swear . . . !" Her words were punctuated by angry slaps of flat hands against the water, spewing it high, and he laughed again. "I wish I never had to lay eyes on you again!" she sputtered furiously. Water dripped from her hair into her eyes and slid down her nose in tiny rivulets.

"I can arrange that easily enough," Ryan answered coolly. He was rewarded with another icy glare.

Muttering under her breath, Stephanie found her footing into shallower water. She took a deep breath and grabbed for her hat as it floated past on a swirl of current. The brim was soaked. Dust still coated the crown, and she contemplated the hat for a moment before flinging it carelessly toward the muddy banks. She didn't even give it a glance when it caught in the branches of a cottonwood tree that slanted almost to the water.

Taking a deep breath, Stephanie turned her back toward Ryan and dove under the water's surface, moving downstream with the current. The creek was surprisingly clear. When she came up for breath, crystal droplets clung like diamonds to her lashes, and she wiped them away with her fingers. Maybe Ryan had done her a favor after all. This was much cooler than simply wading along. Why not ruin his little trick by not getting angry? Stephanie found her footing in more shallow water and stood up, letting her toes squish into the soft mud of the creek bed.

"It feels great, Cordell! You should try it."

"Maybe."

Ryan shifted his rifle and watched as Stephanie shook back her hair with the same jerky motions a dog would use. She slanted him a smile, raking her fingers through the twisted strands of darkened hair that hung like ropes down her back. Stephanie was well aware of Ryan's intent gaze as she made a show of braiding her hair. She was also aware of her wet blouse clinging revealingly to her curves. Not glancing in his direction again, Stephanie stepped back out into the middle to float on her back.

"Bet you didn't know I could swim," she called out. "I learned when I was a little girl." Her long legs kicked high, her bare feet sending geysers of water skyward.

A tight smile slanted the hard line of his mouth as Ryan repositioned his rifle to hold it across his body. Damn. She had to know that her blouse when wet was as transparent as glass. It clung like a second skin to the firm mounds of her breasts, and he could even see the darker area of her nipples through the thin material. His little joke had backfired, it seemed. Stephanie had no intention of getting out of the water for a while, and he wasn't quite sure how long he could stand and watch as she splashed about like a mermaid.

Ryan sliced a quick look upstream. Nothing moved but a hawk lazily circling in the sky. Cold water sure would feel good right now. He was hot and caked with dust, and if he stood there much longer, his temperature was going to rise even higher. Ryan wavered for a moment, then turned to go. Stephanie Ashworth's invitation to swim was too tempting, but he refused to give her the satisfaction.

The rushing sound of water was all that Stephanie heard as it swirled around her ears. Silvery hair was dark and heavy as it fanned out around her in snaking coils, and her buckskin trousers had grown full and heavy with the water. Her body dipped and

133

she could hardly lift her water-soaked legs, but few things she could recall had ever felt better. Cool, running water, and it was wonderful!

Stephanie's cupped hands sliced through the tumbling froth and she kicked again, still floating with the current. Her eyes were closed against the bright glare of the sun, but now the heated rays felt almost good. The day had grown so enjoyable, she felt generous. Cordell should take it easy for a little while instead of playing at being the great Indian fighter and explorer. Maybe his mood would lighten and he would become almost human.

Drifting and bobbing, Stephanie let her mind drift, too. Until now, she hadn't realized how tense she'd been. The constant tension between Ryan and herself was wearying. This was almost too pleasant, too relaxing. It would be too easy to yield to the impulse to float like a random piece of driftwood, spinning in the current to the creek's end. This creek probably ended in some distant canyon or arroyo, diminishing to a mere trickle of water before disappearing into the earth's crust. It would be interesting to follow it along its bends and twists.

"Cordell?" Stephanie didn't open her eyes to look for him. They felt as if they were weighted down with water, and she didn't need to see him to talk to him. "Cordell, where does this creek go? To a river?"

There was no answer. She didn't hear anything but the rush of water in her ears. Maybe she couldn't hear him over the noise of the creek. Stephanie briefly considered opening her eyes and standing up, but it felt so lazy to just float along that she didn't. The question wasn't that important, and who knew when she'd get another chance like this?

Minutes passed in a pleasant blur of water and sun, of floating as free as a hawk in the air, circling and spinning with a delicious sense of weightlessness. Then her buckskin began to grow heavier and heavier, pulling her down until Stephanie gave a sigh of resignation. The idyll had to end eventually, of course. Oh well. She was feeling a little hungry anyway, and her skin was beginning to wrinkle from the water so that she probably looked like a prune.

Stephanie let her feet drift down to the muddy bottom of the creek bed as she tried to balance herself with her hands and arms against the current. The pull of the water carried her a few feet away before she began to make her way back upstream.

The horses were tiny specks on the banks, and she felt a brief twinge of alarm that she'd drifted so far away. That was probably the reason Cordell hadn't answered her, but why hadn't he stopped her? She could have ended up floating to Mexico, but maybe that was what he had in mind.

Stephanie continued to wade through the creek, wondering where Ryan could be. She didn't see him anywhere. He wasn't on the bank—either side—and he wasn't with the horses still tethered to the branches of a tree. There was no sign of him upstream or down. A frown creased her forehead as Stephanie turned in a slow circle, scanning rocks and brush.

It was quiet. There was only the sound of water rushing over the rocks. Where was he? Nothing could be seen of Ryan; only the vast emptiness of the Arizona wilderness stretched around her. Overhead a hawk's cry pierced the air, and Stephanie jumped. It had sounded so much like a human cry that she shivered.

"Cordell . . . ! Ryan Cordell . . ." Her voice bounced from the towering sandstone spires looming like sentinels above the creek. "Ryan?" She struggled to keep her voice calm. Had he abandoned her? No, he wouldn't have left his horse . . . what if someone had crept up on him while he watched her swim? . . . what if she'd been left alone . . . what if . . .

Enough, she told herself sternly. The what-if game could be played all afternoon with very unsatisfying results. She stumbled forward in the water, lurching toward the reddish banks of the creek with clumsy steps. Wet hair fell into her eyes and she clawed at it impatiently. Her heartbeat was a rapid drumming now.

Instead of serene and peaceful, the creek banks took on a sinister aura. Shadows of trees and bushes loomed like monsters, and the whisper of the wind sounded more like a mocking hiss. Stephanie's legs were shaking when she half fell on the creek bank, sinking to one knee in the red mud. She stared in disgust at the mud oozing between her splayed fingers.

"Keep calm, Stephanie," she muttered to herself, and the sound of her voice seemed too loud and alien in the eerie silence. Stephanie sank to a sitting position and wiped her hands on the soggy, probably ruined buckskins. "Nothing was ever gained by panic. Cordell has more than likely just stepped over the ridge to find firewood," she said aloud. "Or maybe a fat rabbit for our dinner. Or even to answer a call of nature . . ."

That solution made sense, and Stephanie felt better. Of course. She was being ridiculous. In a few minutes he would appear over the crest of the nearest ridge, mocking her for being worried.

Shadows lengthened and wavered as she waited, and Stephanie scuttled closer to the calmly munching horses. She crouched close to the ground behind a thick stand of bushes, hidden, she hoped, from unfriendly eyes. Where was he? Cordell would not have just gone off without telling her, would he? Pressing muddy fingers to her temples, Stephanie closed her eyes. She hated waiting. Worse than anything, she hated waiting. Claudie had always told her she had no patience, and that was true.

Claudie. Was her ankle mending? Did she think often of Stephanie, and wonder if she'd found Julian yet? And it was Julian, damn his impetuosity, who had triggered this escapade by being too impatient to wait! Where *was* he?

The stars were sharp and clear in the sky as Julian and Bingo snaked their way through tall grass toward a water hole. They had to be careful. Scouting parties had been seen earlier, and Bingo was "spittin' sure they ain't friendly-like." The water hole was a small spring, easily seen from certain points.

Slowly, carefully, they inched along where the overflow from the spring kept the ground soggy and overgrown with weeds and dank-smelling grass. There was little possibility that a lookout would be watching from that wet piece of ground, and the wet grasses wouldn't rustle and give them away. They slid belly-down toward the pool's edge and lowered hide-bound canteens into the water. Neither man spoke as they concentrated on filling their canteens.

When they were through and had satisfied their immediate thirst, Bingo gave a short nod of his grizzled head. Taking great care, they backed slowly away from the spring until they had worked their way out of sight.

Julian stood. His shirt front was wet and muddy. With the wind against him, he felt almost cold. It was a relief from the grinding heat of the long days when they rode almost without stopping, swallowing dust until he was sure there was more of Arizona inside him than around him.

"What now, Bingo?" He stretched, tilting back his head to look up at the bright stars peppering the night sky. Bingo bit off a chunk of tobacco, then offered some to him. When Julian shook his head, Bingo chewed reflectively for a moment before answering.

"Sleep, I reckon," the old mountain man finally answered. Somewhere in the distance a coyote yipped, and nearby a cougar gave his rasping cough. "Come light, we'll see who our friends are."

"And then?"

"An' then we'll know which way ta ride," Bingo said gruffly. "I ain't in no hurry to have my scalp wavin' from some buck's coup stick." He raked a hand through the sparse strands of gray sticking up from his head like porcupine quills. "Already lost enuf ta some damned griz—grizzly bear ta you, Pilgrim. Like as not, I'd lose a sight more skin than hair."

"Like as not," Julian agreed with a grin. It wasn't long before they were bedded down in thick clumps of manzanita just below an outcropping of rock. The horses and pack mules were hidden farther down the ridge in one of the rocky canyons that ran like jagged scars from the hogback where they lay. A thick blanket of brush covered the terrain, hiding men and animals.

Folding his arms behind his head, Julian peered through a tangle of branches at the night sky. They should reach the general area he sought tomorrow if his calculations were correct. He felt a sense of satisfaction and excitement. Even Bingo had given him grudging respect, and that was worth almost as much as what lay at the end of his journey. He may be an "Eastern dude," but Julian Ashworth had shown himself to be a "man of right proper wit an' adventurous heart," Bingo had allowed in a brief moment of acceptance. "Not ta say you ain't a little uneducated in how ta deal at times."

It was a supreme compliment as far as Julian was concerned.

The shadow of a night hawk flitted across his face, and in just seconds there was the shrill scream of its prey. The cry was cut off abruptly. Survival was the law of the mountains and desert, Julian reflected. He was glad he'd sent Stephanie a telegram telling her to stay in New York. This was different than the other expeditions they'd undertaken together. For one thing, they'd always traveled in a caravan, with native bearers and pack animals loaded with supplies. This was more primitive, and as far as he was concerned, more exciting. But Stephanie was too soft for this kind of journey, and if he'd known it would be this arduous, he never would have suggested she join him. It was somewhat comforting to know that she was safely in New York, even if she was still with that dimwit she intended to marry. And he would do something about *that* as soon as he got back to the city . . .

Chapter Eleven

Deep purple shadows shrouded the high ridges above the creek before Ryan Cordell came strolling casually back. By that time Stephanie was so relieved to see him, that she threw herself into his arms with a glad cry.

"You're back!" Her face was pressed against his neck, and she was shivering with relief.

"I've heard of joyous homecomings before, but if I'd known they could feel this good . . ."

"Where have you been? I missed you . . ."

"I'm flattered . . ."

". . . when I got through swimming." Suddenly Stephanie realized that Ryan wore no shirt, and his dark hair was still dripping wet, "You've been swimming!" she accused hotly. She pushed away, entirely too conscious of his partial nudity.

"Congratulations. Your powers of observation are—as usual—excellent." Amusement crinkled his eyes at the corners as Ryan raked her with a sharp glance. "Did you lose your cake of soap, Miss

Ashworth? You don't look very clean for someone who was splashing about like a tadpole when I left."

"Why didn't you tell me where you were going?" Stephanie folded her arms and glared at him in the dying light, trying to work herself into righteous anger. Then, sighing, she gave up. It was hopeless. She was simply too relieved to see him again. "I thought you'd been abducted or something!"

"Abducted? Kidnapped? Stolen by gypsies? How melodramatic." Ryan propped his rifle against a large stone and shrugged into his shirt. "What sort of literature are you accustomed to reading, Miss Ashworth?"

"Never mind that. You still should have told me where you were going."

"I did. But you had your head underwater at the time." He gave her an innocent grin before turning his attention to his shirt buttons. "Didn't you say earlier you wish I'd disappear? I thought I was doing you a favor . . ."

"You know perfectly well I didn't mean a word of it," Stephanie said defensively. "I was angry." Her toes tapped irritably against red dirt and rocks. Why hadn't he dressed before coming back to camp? It was very distracting trying to talk to him while he tucked his shirttail into the waistband of his snug-fitting cords. Stephanie stared down at her toes scuffing little trails in the dirt. It must be his close proximity, that was all.

"Do you always say what you don't mean when you're angry?" Ryan had knelt and scooped out a hole in the red dirt and was busily stacking small limbs of mesquite for a fire. He glanced up at

Stephanie. "Do you?" he prompted.

"Not always, no." She shifted uncomfortably and looked at him, fully aware of the calculating expression in his eyes. Damn those eyes, she thought, they saw too much sometimes! And why should a man have lashes so long and thick, and eyes that could be gun-metal gray at one moment, then change to the sheen of silver the next? They were so clear and penetrating, that she found it difficult to meet his gaze.

"Then you did or didn't mean it when you said you hated me?" Ryan asked. He fed dry leaves into the barely flickering flames then sat back on his heels.

"I never said I hated you," Stephanie protested without looking at him.

"Not out loud."

"Oh, so now you read minds as well as Indian sign? I never realized the extent of your talents, Mr. Cordell."

"Lady, you ain't seen nothin' yet. I have talents you could only guess at."

Stephanie looked directly at him. "Since we seem to be baring our souls again, perhaps you can tell me why you sometimes lapse into the vernacular of an uneducated backwoodsman? I'd be interested in knowing . . ."

"Uneducated? I'm hurt. Educated backwoodsman, maybe . . ."

". . . in learning why you feel you must put on such a good masquerade. What are you hiding, Mr. Cordell?"

"What are *you* hiding, Miss Ashworth?" Ryan opened one of the packs and pulled out the iron skillet. He shoved it toward Stephanie. "Cook and talk at the same time. I'm hungry. What are you hiding?"

"I asked you first. You answer me, and I'll answer you." Stephanie fumbled for a sharp knife in the food pack and began hacking slices from the hunk of salted beef. "Well?"

"Everybody puts on a front sometimes . . ."

"Let's not speak in generalities, please. I expect specifics . . ."

". . . but it's necessary to know when to be honest. What exactly do you want to know? Why I talk one way one moment, another the next? No big mystery there. I only went to school in the East. I live in the West."

"Oh, dammit!" Stephanie exclaimed suddenly, dropping the knife.

"What's the matter with that?" Ryan began, but she waved an impatient hand at him.

"Nothing. I cut myself with this knife . . ."

"Let me see." Leaning forward, Ryan examined the cut on Stephanie's finger. "It's just a little scratch, but I don't want you bleeding all over my dinner. I'll bandage it for you."

"Your concern is overwhelming," Stephanie said dryly as Ryan pulled out clean strips of cloth and a small bottle from his pack. Blood dripped steadily from the cut, and she squeezed her finger to staunch the flow. It was beginning to throb, and when Ryan poured some of the brown bottle's contents over her finger, Stephanie caught her breath in a sharp hiss and tried to jerk away. "What is that stuff?"

"Whiskey. It's good for lots of things, including

144

cuts. Hold still." He wrapped her finger in quick, deft movements with a strip of cloth, then tied the ends. "Now you'll live."

"I'm not certain the cure wasn't worse than the cut," Stephanie observed with a frown. Her finger still burned from the whiskey.

"Try some of this. It'll make it stop hurting soon enough." Ryan held out the bottle, grinning when Stephanie made a face. "Don't be snooty. It was a vintage year for rotgut, Miss Ashworth. I'll even pour some in a cup for you." He splashed a liberal amount in one of the battered tin cups and gave it to Stephanie. "Here. Drink *this* and go walk your dog."

Stephanie bit her bottom lip as she recalled the last time Ryan had bluffed her into drinking with him. Her gaze locked with his as she considered, then she answered the challenge in his eyes by taking the cup and tilting it bottom up. The whiskey burned a path down her throat and into her stomach, and she fought the urge to choke. Somehow, the nights she'd spent drinking wine or brandy with Julian still hadn't prepared her for this. Stephanie's eyes and nose burned and began to water. God, she was on fire . . .

A glance at Ryan's interested expression stopped her from giving in to the desire to gasp for air. Uh huh. No amount of money or a flaming throat would induce her to give Ryan Cordell the satisfaction of seeing her cough. But it took grit and a great deal of self-control to keep from it.

"Thank you," she finally managed to say calmly, and was rewarded by Ryan's faint expression of approval.

145

"Anytime, princess." Ryan poured himself a drink and tossed it down. "More?" He held out the bottle.

"Not now. Maybe later. What do you want with your salted beef? We have beans. And more beans." Stephanie slapped a chunk of beef into the skillet and positioned it carefully in the flames, then poured a handful of beans in the skillet to fry with the meat. Even that small amount of whiskey was making her head spin, and she concentrated on cooking.

Folding his arms, Ryan propped them behind his head and leaned back against a sandstone rock. He watched Stephanie flip the browning chunks of beef and stir the beans, and wondered how a girl accustomed to velvet cushions and satin pillows could seem right at home in the Arizona Territory. It was easy to visualize her in a diamond-studded evening gown and glittering with jewels, yet she was here beside the rushing banks of the Little Colorado River frying salted beef in an iron skillet. It had never occurred to Ryan that she would make it this far. He'd fully expected to be taking her back to the fort by the end of the first day. What made her so tough? It wasn't as if she was a girl in the first blush of youth; she was a full-grown woman. Had she ever been married? Or was she engaged? That thought was oddly unsettling. He'd never considered the fact that she might have a future husband somewhere.

Ryan pulled a thin cigar from his shirt pocket and lit it with a smoldering twig from the fire. He squinted against the curl of smoke and let his gaze drift back to Stephanie. He was suddenly curious. The only way of finding out if she had a prospective husband was to ask. There were times for subtlety and times for bluntness. Subtlety wasted time.

"You ever been married, Miss Ashworth? Or planned to be?"

Startled, Stephanie jerked her attention from the frying pan to Ryan. "Why would you ask that?"

"Fencing again? You're an expert at answering a question with another question, Princess. Does this particular question call for you to hedge?"

"I'm not hedging, just curious about your reason for asking." Damn. She'd forgotten all about Reginald. And it had been so easy. A quick comparison between Reginald and Ryan left her fiancé sorely lacking in the scorecard of masculine attributes. Of course, Reginald *did* have wealth and position, where Cordell did not.

"Miss Ashworth?" Ryan's voice jerked her head up. "You're burning our dinner," he said politely. "I prefer my meat a little less well done. Did my question upset you?"

"Upset me?" Stephanie laughed. "Why, of course not! I was just thinking of my . . . fiancé . . . since you insist upon prying."

"Lucky man," Ryan said shortly.

She stared at him with something close to dismay in her dark eyes. Fiancé . . . Why was it so hard to say that word? "His name's Reginald. And our dinner is not burned yet. Just a little too done." She deftly flipped two very brown pieces of beef onto a metal plate and gave Ryan a bright smile. "How do you like your beans?"

"Does it matter? I thought you said you could cook . . ."

"I *can* cook! I'm just tired tonight, and . . ."

"Yeah? If this is an example of your cooking, you get horse detail again . . ."

". . . if you hadn't gone off and left me for so long, I could have started the meal earlier," Stephanie finished stubbornly. "I really resent your deranged sense of humor, Mr. Cordell. Did you think it was funny to frighten me?"

"Are we back to that again? You'll do anything but give me decent answers to my questions, won't you, Princess?"

"No, I answered—and don't call me 'Princess'! You may call me Miss Ashworth . . ."

"And you may call me gone," Ryan shot back in a growling tone. "I've never met such a damned touchy woman in all my life! Personal questions are fine as long as you're doing the asking, right?" He rose to his feet in a swift, smooth motion. "You're a snobby, bossy hypocrite, *Miss Ashworth!* Enjoy your solitude, and your lousy meal."

Rocking back on her bare heels, Stephanie stared after him. She wasn't quite sure what had happened. All that really registered was the fact that he was leaving her alone again. No, he couldn't do that, by God! She'd paid him good money to guide and protect her, and he would do it whether he wanted to or not! An agreement was an agreement, and he'd better live up to his end of it.

"Come back here, Cordell! You cannot walk out on me. Cordell!" Her temper flared when he paid her no attention. "Cordell, you signed an agreement . . ."

Spinning on his heels, Ryan took two menacing steps in her direction. "Look, *Ashworth*, you can take that damn piece of paper and stick . . ." He broke off suddenly, but Stephanie was in little doubt as to what he wanted her to do with the agreement. Muttering under his breath, Ryan ground the cigar between his teeth, wheeled around, and stalked out of their camp.

This time Stephanie didn't wait. She leaped to her feet without stopping to think about it and went after him. Ryan's rifle was still propped on the rock he had been leaning against, and Stephanie instinctively grabbed it as she passed. Afterward, she was to realize she'd behaved rashly, but at the time she was so angry Stephanie only reacted.

She'd been shooting since she was a child, and it seemed natural to swing the rifle to her shoulder. The lever action clicked loudly as she pumped it. Just ahead of her, Cordell froze.

"Mr. Cordell, I asked you to stop."

He swung to face her. Even in the dim light Stephanie could see the furious glitter in his quickly narrowed eyes. In a slow, smooth motion, Ryan took the cigar stub from his mouth and dropped it. His booted heel ground the stub into the dirt, and his voice was cold and hard.

"Put that damn rifle down before it goes off, you idiot."

"Idiot? Me? This rifle won't go off unless I intend for it to, Mr. Cordell. Ah ah—stay right where you are."

"I thought you wanted me in camp alive," he answered smoothly. "Give me the rifle before someone gets hurt . . ."

"Don't be condescending, Cordell. And I said stay

right there. I don't trust you not to try something stupid just because you don't think I can shoot." Her insides were quaking as she wondered wildly how to get herself out of the situation without either losing face or having to shoot him. Whatever had happened to her normally cool reactions? They all seemed to have disappeared since meeting Ryan Cordell . . .

"Okay," he was saying, "don't get nervous. I'll stay right here." He very slowly crouched down on his heels. "See? I'm relaxed. Now you relax. And lower the rifle. That's a Winchester, .44-.40, Miss Ashworth, and very accurate even if you're only half good. I would very much appreciate it if you would aim it elsewhere. Please?"

The last word was more of a growl, and Stephanie stared with dismay at Ryan's furious expression. This was not good, she decided.

Chapter Twelve

She might have given in, however ungracefully, and lowered the rifle, but Ryan didn't wait. He moved with a swiftness that reminded Stephanie of the rattlesnake that had spooked her horse, uncoiling his long body from a crouch as he lunged.

Reflex action took over. The Winchester barked loudly and Ryan Cordell wore a small, neat hole in the crown of his hat. Even if she'd wanted to, Stephanie had no time to shoot again. She was slammed hard against the rocky ground as Cordell reached her, and the rifle was wrenched from her hands and flung a few feet away.

"You crazy bitch, you could have killed me!" His face, only two or three inches from hers, was creased with an expression of utter disbelief. "I ought to stake you out and leave you for the damned coyotes and buzzards to find!"

"I only aimed for your hat, Cordell," Stephanie began, but he cut her off with a harsh laugh.

"Sure you did! *If* you aimed at all, I'm sure it

wasn't at my hat." He gave her a vicious shake that threatened to dislodge most of her teeth. When Stephanie tried to move from under his heavy weight, Ryan tightened his grip and threw a leg over her squirming body. "Don't be in a hurry to go anywhere, Princess. You wanted me back here, remember? Well, here I am. What did you want to say to me that was important enough to shoot me?"

"A mistake . . ." she gasped out as his elbow dug into her, "you're making . . . a . . . mistake . . ."

"Am I? You're probably right. The first mistake I made was in agreeing to be your guide, the second was in allowing you along. Julian Ashworth will do just fine by himself. He doesn't need more than one nursemaid."

Before Stephanie could question that confusing comment, Ryan was raking his fingers through her hair to hold her head still. He tightened his grip, pulling her hair, and she winced.

"Does that hurt, Princess? Sorry. I was just trying to get your attention—but at least I don't use a rifle."

The pressure of his body against hers was more unnerving than the dangerous glint in his eyes, and Stephanie struggled to free herself. Sharp-edged rocks dug painfully into the tender skin on her back and hips. Not even the thick buckskins she wore protected her enough, and when she tried to shift her legs from under his, Stephanie felt rocks tear into her thighs.

"Get off, Cordell. You're hurting me."

"Not as much as I'd like to. I'm trying to decide whether to just strangle you, or go to all the trouble of staking you out. Would you care to voice your opinion on that?"

"Very funny. Look, I apologize for shooting at you. Is that better?"

"Oh yes, Miss Ashworth. Why, that even mends the hole in my hat." Ryan tugged her head back so that she had to look into his eyes. "Don't you ever stop and think of the consequences? Or are you too accustomed to just buying your way out if you make a mistake?"

"I don't know what you're talking about . . ."

"I'll bet you do. What happens if your maid breaks an ankle? Why, you just pay someone else to watch over her while you go ahead and do what you want to do. It doesn't matter if she's old and frightened, and doesn't want to be in Arizona Territory anyway, does it?"

"You don't know all the circumstances," Stephanie began defensively. "Claudie *wanted* to come to Arizona . . ."

"Did she? I'll bet she did."

"You make me sound like some sort of . . . of . . . ogre or something, and I'm not!" In spite of her words, Stephanie felt a twinge of guilt. Had she really done that? Had she been coldhearted and unfeeling when Claudia was hurt? Should she have stayed until her ankle mended? Unfortunately, he made it look that way. God, she'd never have been so deliberately unfeeling . . .

"Do I see a light dawning?" Ryan mocked, and in that moment Stephanie hated him. Her eyes danced with dark fire as she glared at him.

"Maybe I didn't stay with Claudie when she was injured, but I didn't *make* her come to Arizona with me. And I would never do anything to intentionally harm her . . ."

"Ah, good intentions. Isn't there an old saw about the road to hell being paved with good intentions?"

"You're horrible!"

"Yes. But I don't pretend to be otherwise. Ah ah. No kicking. Be a good girl and lie still while I consider what I want to do with you."

"Cordell . . ."

"And be quiet."

There was no mistaking the thread of genuine anger in his tone. Stephanie swallowed the hot words on the tip of her tongue. There was no point in deliberately baiting him when she had already provoked him enough by shooting at him. Her position was too vulnerable. Stephanie lay quietly, listening to the sound of her own heart beat and slowly becoming aware of Ryan's.

Damn, he was close—much too close, and in such an intimate position. She could only imagine how it would look to anyone passing by . . . What if Julian saw her now? Stephanie almost smiled at the thought. Her father would never believe that his coolly emotionless daughter—the "ice maiden"— would allow herself to be maneuvered into such a predicament. But she had.

And she was uncomfortably aware that she was definitely not reacting as an ice maiden. Her breathing was shallow for more than the obvious reason of Ryan's weight on her, and her fingers were coiled around the tensed muscles of his arms as far as they could reach. To hold him off, of course, but why this sudden impulse to touch the strands of dark hair

154

that fell over his collar? This close, even in the fitful light from the fire, she could see tiny scars on his face that she'd never noticed before.

There, where his eyebrow winged down, was evidence of a cut from long before. Knife? Maybe a bullet crease, or even an arrow? Anything was possible with a man who lived like Ryan Cordell, she supposed. And on his left cheek above the dark shadow of his unshaven beard there was another small scar. How was it that the scars didn't detract from his appearance? Somehow, they only added reckless flair to a handsome face.

Stephanie admitted the inevitable signs of physical attraction at last, and sighed to herself. After all these years, why a man like Ryan Cordell? There had been only one man in her life who had attracted her, and she'd been so young then, and so foolish. She'd been positive that she would never feel that way again in spite of Julian's assurances that she would find another man one day who attracted her. God, she hadn't thought of him in years, hadn't *let* herself think of him. And now the same, treacherous emotions were threatening to abolish her common sense. It was more terrifying than anything she had ever faced.

Ryan sensed Stephanie's distress, but wasn't certain of the cause. Was she afraid of him? Somehow, he didn't think so. She probably should be, because he'd come very close to hurting her. It had taken a great deal of willpower not to use more force than necessary in getting his rifle away. Damn, but he'd never had a woman shoot at him like that! And he still wasn't sure if she was a good shot or just lucky. Whichever, he didn't intend to test it again.

Stephanie's lips were slightly trembling, and he could feel the rapid pounding of her heart beneath the full breasts that were pressed against his chest. Damn, he hadn't known her hair would feel so silky to the touch, falling in soft waves between his fingers. Or that her curves would be so sensuous and provocative beneath him.

Ryan's eyes skimmed over her face, following the straight line of her nose and the high cheekbones that reminded him of a Greek sculpture. It surprised him that she was so lovely. Why did she try to disguise it with an unflattering bun of hair pulled tightly at her neck? Even in a dress, she hadn't accentuated her femininity but tried to conceal it with wide, bulky skirts and high-necked gowns. And she pretended to be unaware of him as a man, when she wasn't. Did she know that her eyes dilated whenever she looked at him? He could see dark shadows hiding beneath her thick fringe of lashes. How incongruous. Stephanie's eyes were huge and velvety soft, reminding him of the gentle eyes of a doe. But she wasn't gentle. She was hard and calculating, reminding Ryan of those bitchy New York society women. Stephanie—a spoiled little rich girl who would always demand—and usually get—her own way. Too bad for her she'd left New York. Out here she would discover that there were people who didn't care if she got her own way.

"What's the matter, Princess?" he taunted. "You worried I won't let you go? Or maybe you're worried that you've run into a situation you can't handle . . ."

Anger loosened Stephanie's tongue. "Cordell, it's difficult for me to imagine not being able to 'handle' a man of your stature. At home, someone like you walks the dog and tends the lawn . . ."

"Is that right? Well you're not at home now, and this is *my* lawn, Miss Ashworth. So—what'cha gonna do?"

Staring up into gray eyes like thunderclouds, Stephanie was just beginning to wonder that herself. What was she going to do? Ryan obviously had the upper hand. Nothing else had worked, perhaps pure feminine reaction would—no, it was ridiculous to think it would. And anyway, she would not lower herself to such an extreme action. Tears would be humiliating.

"Do? It appears that I have very little choice, Cordell. I'm going to lie here under your crushing weight until you come to your senses, I suppose. What do you expect me to do?"

"Ah, a sensible answer. I didn't expect it." Ryan shifted to one side, still holding her down with his leg across her body, and released his grip on her hair. "This is your lucky day, Stephanie Ashworth. You gave the right answer and now you win your freedom. Don't push it, though," he added when she tried to shove him away. "My good mood may not last."

Propping herself up on her elbows, Stephanie gave a sigh of exasperation. "This is such a silly conversation to be having. Why don't we just get up and eat what's left of our dinner—which has quite probably burned beyond recognition by now? I will admit that perhaps I overreacted to your stomping out of camp like a sulky child, but I'm not accustomed to being left behind as if I was an unwanted puppy, Mr. Cordell."

"And I'm not accustomed to being talked to like a dog, Miss Ashworth. You may have hired me, but you didn't buy me. Remember that." Ryan swung to a sitting position and rose to his feet. He held out a hand to help Stephanie up.

After the briefest of hesitations, she took his hand and rose as gracefully as she could. Feeling slightly awkward, Stephanie brushed at her now-grimy clothes and wished she could think of something quite scathing to say. Nothing came to mind, however, that would not have begun the argument again. She contented herself with a dark glance in his direction and utter silence as she pivoted and returned to their fire with her head held high.

Stephanie managed to choke down her burned beef and beans while Ryan drank his dinner from the brown bottle of whiskey. An equitable enough arrangement, Stephanie thought, as long as he left her alone. With luck, maybe he would fall peacefully into a drunken sleep.

But for once, it was Stephanie who fell quickly asleep and Ryan who was left awake to stare up at the stars. Too many memories were crowding him. It had been too long since he had let himself recall things that had been buried for years. Now, because of Stephanie Ashworth, all the old wounds were being reopened. He should have seen it coming, he supposed, should have known that he couldn't forget it forever.

Shrugging to himself, Ryan tilted the almost empty bottle again. Whiskey didn't erase those memories, but it sure helped bury them again. He didn't need to remember. Not now. Not ever.

Hazy images swam in front of him whenever he closed his eyes, and one of them was a woman with blond hair the silvery sheen of moonlight. Damn. When he opened his eyes she was still there, just across a short space of red dirt. She was asleep, with long strands of light hair spilling across the brightly woven blanket under her, and her eyes were closed. But he knew how she would look at him when her eyes were open—with the same distant expression that could freeze a man's soul to the very depths. He'd seen it too many times before. Not from Stephanie maybe, but he'd seen it. And he knew it well.

The amber bottle tilted again, draining the last of the whiskey. Now he could sleep. Now he could forget those cold blue—no, these were brown, not blue. The other's eyes were blue; icy, wintry blue that left him shivering as if from an Arctic blast. Stephanie's eyes . . . he'd seen them light with laughter, and they were warmer. Like cinnamon. Sometimes they were as dark as the fragrant coffee brewed on a winter morning, and just as inviting. Maybe that was the difference. Stephanie's eyes were softer, warmer . . . it was Emma's eyes that haunted him; still left him with a chill even under the searing Arizona sun. Emma Cordell . . .

Chapter Thirteen

Dark thunderheads rolled over the horizon like nothing Stephanie had ever seen before. The huge towering masses of clouds were accompanied by blistering flashes of lightning that forked across the sky in flickering snake tongues. It was a show of power on an immense celestial scale, awesome and frightening.

The approaching storm left Stephanie feeling oddly unsettled and edgy. Her nerves had been frayed enough by the past few days' events, but now every little thing seemed to set her even more on edge. And it was irritating that Ryan seemed to welcome the storm as a diversion.

"Beats the hot sun, I guess," he remarked casually, and Stephanie's tautly leashed control snapped.

"You guess? It would seem to me that you'd know rain would be much more welcome than that horrible, blinding sun!"

Ryan paused in saddling his horse and turned to look at her. His eyes narrowed on the pinched, white lines around Stephanie's mouth. Her hands were clenched so tightly around the reins of her gelding that her knuckles were white, and she held herself stiffly erect. She looked, he thought, like an incongruously dressed porcelain doll, with just as much animation in her face.

"Yeah. Well, the sun may be hot and bright, but have you ever seen a flash flood out here—the way the small streams and creeks swell into destructive rivers? This nice quiet river can become a wall of water, Princess. And it takes everything in its path with it when it rolls along."

Stephanie's skeptical glance was accompanied by a shrug. "So when do we get there, Mr. Cordell? I am weary of traveling with you. Are you certain you're taking me straight to my father?"

The freshening wind whipped Ryan's hair back from his forehead, and he squinted against tiny grains of sand blown into his face.

"Believe me, Princess, I'm taking you to your father as quickly as I can. I'm enjoying this little trip about as much as you are, and I hope somebody hogties and brands me with a big 'F' for fool if I ever agree to this kind of thing again!"

Turning back to his stallion, Ryan yanked savagely on the leather strap to his saddle, deftly knotting it with quick motions.

"Finish saddling, and get on your horse, Miss Ashworth, before we get caught here," he said without turning back around. "The rain'll come down pretty quick . . ."

As if summoned by his words, fat raindrops began to spatter against Stephanie's hat. The sky grew dark

161

so that it almost seemed like night, and the wind blew hard. Leaves on the trees turned backside up, and the horses nickered nervously. It was going to be a downpour.

Stephanie couldn't quite believe how swiftly the rain came down, turning the red dirt banks into quagmires that sucked at the horses' hooves. She hurriedly knotted the leather straps holding her saddlebags, blinking against the rain, then mounted to follow Ryan. They climbed the banks, slipping and sliding as they scrambled for good footing, finally reaching the rockier crest where they paused for breath. Stephanie was already soaked to the skin, and could hardly see Ryan who was only a few feet from her.

"Is this what you meant?" she yelled over the rattle of rain and thunder. "Now I understand . . ."

But she hadn't known that the breaking of the storm would be so exhilarating. Her tension was released in a flood similar to the muddy torrents that were beginning to rage through shallow arroyos and deeper canyons, spurring them into action.

They raced against the torrential waters tearing through the gullies, barely managing to stay just ahead as they climbed higher and higher. A few times, Stephanie was certain her gelding would slide backward into the raging waters and she would be swept away on the swift-moving current.

Finally reaching a rocky ledge safely above the water, they paused. Stephanie pulled the battered felt Stetson lower over her face, shielding it from the pelting raindrops that stung her cheeks, then changed her mind. Flinging back her head, she yanked off the hat and shook her long hair free. She closed her eyes against the sting of rain, putting out her tongue to taste the rivulets that slid from her cheeks into her mouth. She wanted to run against the wind and feel the rain in her hair, to stand atop a ridged crest and defy the elements. It was a strange feeling, a freedom she had never felt before, and she wondered at it.

When Ryan nudged his stallion closer she was almost embarrassed by her abandon, but oddly enough, he understood what she was feeling.

"Awesome, isn't it? Enjoy it. Believe it or not, this will pass quickly."

"I feel so . . . alive." Stephanie stared at him through the slashing gray rain. He was holding his hat, and Ryan's dark hair was plastered close to his skull. Water droplets clung to his stubble of beard, gleaming like a spray of tiny diamonds. She glanced up at the sky.

"It's getting lighter in places . . ."

"Yeah. But the worst isn't over yet. Come on." Ryan pulled the black's head around and kicked him into a slow trot along the edge of the hogback. He was leading the pack horse, and Stephanie followed closely.

They pushed higher and higher, following a trail she could barely see, riding into thick brush and sparse stands of spruce, fir, and cedar. Frightened of the height, Stephanie didn't dare look back or down. She wasn't about to give Cordell the satisfaction of knowing how the high altitude frightened her.

Now she was cold. Her clothes were soaked through, and even though the rain had stopped, it was much cooler in the higher altitude. Stephanie shivered, and she was quite sure her lips were as blue as the patches of sky she spotted between tangles of tree-limbs and gray clouds.

Ryan stopped when the horses were blowing and flecked with lather, glancing back at Stephanie. His dark brows rose as he saw her pale face and chattering teeth.

"What's the matter with you—cold?"

She threw him a bleak look. "No, my lips are always this purple . . ."

"Well, why didn't you say so?"

"You didn't ask . . ."

"Oh, for Chrissake . . . take my jacket." Ryan flung her his light jacket, and Stephanie wrinkled her nose with disgust.

"It smells terrible . . ."

"Are you cold or not?" He nudged his stallion forward again. "There's an abandoned hut not far ahead. Used to belong to an old hermit. We can use it if the roof didn't fall in during the winter snows."

Stephanie shrugged into the jacket. A light shudder quivered through her at the strong odor of wet fur, but it was better than being cold. She clubbed her hair into a wet braid and let it hang down her back, then tugged on the wet Stetson. A wry smile twisted her mouth at the hat's disreputable appearance. Before too long she would look just like a fur-trapper or mountaineer. All she needed to complete the picture was a string of pelts hanging from her horse's side and a big wad of tobacco in one cheek.

"Is that it?" Stephanie asked when she saw the hut

Ryan had mentioned. Her dark eyes widened at the tiny structure built with logs and mud chinking. It did have a roof, such as it was, but there were no windows and the door hung ajar. "You want me to stay in that?"

"Can't ride on right now because of flash floods. We need to stay on higher ground. Aw hell, it's not the Savoy, but we're not in London. I know you're more accustomed to crystal chandeliers and velvet couches, Miss Ashworth, but all the other rooms are occupied at the moment. At least this one's empty . . ."

A thrashing from inside the hut jerked both their heads around.

"Did you say empty, Mr. Cordell . . . ?"

"Sweet Jesus!" Ryan exploded as a huge white bear rocketed through the doorway and into the small clearing in front of the cabin. All three horses screamed and reared, bucking in terror as the bear lumbered forward with mouth open wide. His lips were drawn back in a snarl and white froth flew from razor-sharp teeth as he charged.

Stephanie was frozen into her saddle, fighting to just stay atop her gelding. Things passed in a blur then. There were roars and grunts, tree limbs snapping, and muffled growls as she saw heaven and earth whirr past. Her feet came out of the stirrups and she clung tightly to the saddle horn. A feeling of panic rose as Stephanie realized she hadn't heard Ryan make a sound beyond his initial exclamation. Surely the bear hadn't . . . no, that was too horrible to even think about . . . where was the bear? And Ryan?

165

A loud explosion sounded so close Stephanie was certain her hearing was gone forever. This time her gelding bolted and she lost her tenuous grip on the saddle horn. She had a brief glimpse of pine trees and sky before hitting the ground with a bone-jarring thud.

Birds. She'd never heard so many birds before. They sounded like the Sunday morning soprano choir of Calvary Methodist Church . . .

"You all right?"

A face swam into view. Ryan. He sounded like he was in a tunnel and she shook her head to clear it. The birds were still there.

"No-o-o, I'm not all right . . . birds . . . so many birds . . ."

"Yeah, they're roosting in the tops of the trees. I musta scared 'em when I shot the bear."

"You . . . shot . . . the bear?" Oh, why wouldn't the sky stop twirling? And those damned birds . . . "My horse . . ."

"He'll come back." Ryan's hands dug into Stephanie's armpits as he lifted her to her feet. "Think you can stand up all right?"

Stephanie reeled like a drunken sailor and Ryan caught her before she pitched forward onto her face.

"No, guess you can't," he sighed. "Damn, but you're a big woman. Not really heavy," he puffed as he lifted her into his arms, "just kinda awkward to carry. Anybody ever tell you you've got longer legs than most men?"

"No insults, please. I've got a terrible headache . . ."

"Don't bother with the excuses, Princess. We're

not married."

"Thank God. Where are you taking me?" She frowned, squinting at the wooden door of the hut as Ryan tried to angle her arms and legs through without scraping her against the door frame. "Where's the bear?"

"Inside the hut—no, the bear's dead," he assured her when she shrieked loudly. "I'm taking *you* inside the hut. Quiet down before Mrs. Bear comes to check on Mr. Bear." He placed her a little less than gently on a rough cot that was probably alive with all kinds of vermin.

Stephanie quite willingly shut her eyes and her mouth simultaneously. It was easier. And she was too weak to argue with Cordell, no matter what he did, she thought.

"What are you doing, Ryan Cordell?" she demanded in as strong a tone as possible. "Kindly get your hands off my body!" She clutched wildly at his hands as they fumbled with the buttons on her jacket.

"Look, you're wet and cold, and it'll take a while to find dry firewood. Besides that, you stink in this wet fur jacket . . ."

"It's *your* jacket, and if you'll remember, I'm the one who told you how bad it smelled . . ."

"Thanks. You're right." He firmly put her hands down at her sides. "Can you undress without help? Fine. Then why don't you take off your wet clothes and get under a blanket while I get some wood."

Stephanie glared at him with as much energy as she could muster when he added from the doorway, "If you aren't under a blanket when I get back—without your clothes—I'll take them off for you,

Miss Ashworth."

That threat worked. Stephanie was shivering under two of the Navajo blankets when Ryan returned. Her drenched clothes lay in a heap not far away.

"Any warmer?" Ryan asked as he dropped an armload of tree limbs.

Stephanie's answer caught in her throat as Ryan shrugged out of his shirt and dropped it in the pile with her clothes. He didn't seem to care that she was lying not four feet from him as he unbuckled his gunbelt and prepared to shuck his pants.

"Mr. Cordell!" She found her voice at last, and her tone was so scandalized Ryan's head jerked up in surprise.

"You didn't expect me to freeze, did you?" He sounded aggrieved. "That's not a Christian attitude, Miss Ashworth."

"And what would you know about Christian attitudes? Oh, never mind! Just kindly . . . don't do that!"

"Don't look. Nobody's holding your eyes open. I've got to dry my clothes out, too."

Stephanie's eyes clamped tightly shut. With her eyes closed, she couldn't see Ryan's amused smile, or the way his gaze drifted lazily over the rounded curves barely visible beneath her blankets. This, he decided, could be a very interesting situation. Very interesting.

Chapter Fourteen

"What's that?" Stephanie eyed Ryan warily as he held out a large chunk of hot roasted meat. "It doesn't look like salted beef . . ." One hand snaked from under the blankets to take the stick of charred meat.

"It's not," he said cheerfully. "It's bear—now, what'd you do that for?"

Shuddering, Stephanie had immediately let go of the stick.

"I don't want to eat bear meat! It's not . . . it's not sanitary."

"Sanitary?" Ryan's brows rose. "It was sanitary before you dropped it on the floor, lady. But that's fine with me. You know, you just wallow in a rut of conventionality, Stephanie. I've never seen anything like it . . ."

"I do not! I just . . . just don't want to eat bear meat, that's all!" She glared at him, uncomfortably aware that he might be right.

"Look, I don't care if you starve to death, and we

happen to be fresh out of beefsteak. If I'd known you were coming, I'd have slaughtered the fatted calf . . ." He jackknifed his long legs to sit on the floor in front of the stone fireplace. Large chunks of meat roasted on a crude spit he'd rigged, spattering grease into the fire.

"Please. Just give me some dried beef and I'll eat that."

"Ain't no more."

"Do you mean we are out of salted beef?"

"Out of everything." Ryan tore off a chunk of meat and stuffed it into his mouth, licking the grease from his fingers as he gazed at Stephanie. "When the pack horse ran off, it lost a few things . . ."

"What?"

"I told you to tie double knots when you loaded the pack horse, not those fancy embroidery knots you use . . ."

"Mr. Cordell . . . !" Stephanie's mouth snapped shut. It was absolutely no use arguing with Ryan Cordell, and she *had* been the one to load the pack horse this time. Her stomach rumbled a protest at the odor of roasted meat. She was starved, but there was no way she could even think of eating bear meat.

"I'm hungry, Cordell. What do we do now?"

"Order from the corner deli? Grow up, Princess. This isn't New York, and you'll either eat what's available or not eat at all."

"What about our supplies?"

"We'll stop at the next town and buy more. You do have money, don't you?"

"In my saddlebags . . . What's the matter? You said you found my horse."

Ryan groaned and shook his head. "Darlin', you are one hell of a trail hand is all I've got to say. Your saddlebags kind of fell off your gelding when he spooked. I'll go back and look for 'em again, but if they fell where I think they did, forget it."

"Oh no-o-! That's all the money I had with me!" Big tears welled in Stephanie's eyes for the first time since she had come to Arizona, threatening to spill down her cheeks and ruin the stoic expression she was struggling to keep. "What . . . what . . . will we do now? All our money's gone."

"All of it? What about my money? You lost the rest of *my* money? Aw, dammit, lady! Can't you do anything right?" Ryan slapped his fists against his knees, then paused at the sight of Stephanie's stricken face. "Ah, don't worry about it. I've still got my rifle to shoot game, and nothing fell off *my* horse . . . What's the matter now?"

Stephanie's muffled snort of anger came to him from between the fingers she hastily pressed over her mouth.

"Cordell, I would greatly appreciate it if you would not mention my untied knots again. All right? I find myself weary of listening to Mr. Perfect boasting. And if you were really a great guide as you pretend to be, you would have known that bear was in here and I wouldn't have lost my saddlebags . . ."

"Now how in the hell could I have known a bear was in here without looking? Besides, I'm glad it was in here. And you better be glad, too."

"I fail to see your logic." Stephanie struggled for control of her temper. Ryan sat cross-legged in front of the fire, lighting a cigar with a small pine limb

171

he'd pulled from the flames. He flung the limb back into the fire and puffed on his cigar for a moment.

"Logic's not a term you're closely acquainted with anyway, Princess, but I'll try to explain," he said between puffs. "You may not have noticed in all the excitement, but that was a white bear we scared out of here . . ."

"So?"

"A white bear, or albino, is worth a lot of money. Or its skin is anyway. So, all we have to do is sell it in the next town, and we've got money. See how easy it is?"

"Oh. Yes." Stephanie kindly failed to mention that her saddlebags would still be with them if the white bear hadn't spooked her horse in the first place. It was odd, but she did begin to feel better. She should have known a man like Ryan would figure out how to survive, but at the thought of being without money she'd panicked. She'd never been without money in her entire life, and would not know how to cope if she didn't have it. Maybe a man like Ryan Cordell was accustomed to it, and had learned how to swindle his way through life, but she hadn't.

Stephanie snuggled deeper beneath the blankets, pulling them up to her chin. It had begun to rain again, and she could hear large raindrops spatter against the roof. At least she was warm and reasonably safe, and this was the first time in almost two weeks that she'd slept on anything but the hard ground. Life wasn't so bad right now, even if she was hungry. And oddly enough, she felt secure with Ryan nearby.

He might be irritating and hateful, but he was a man who knew how to take care of himself and her. In some ways, Stephanie thought drowsily, he reminded her of Julian . . .

"Stand real still, Pilgrim, lest ya make 'em nervous-like. They's 'paches, an' liable ta take offense easy."

Julian Ashworth did as Bingo suggested, though he wasn't quite certain he could have moved anyway. A half-circle of Indian braves stood in front of them. Some had arrows notched in their bows, while others leveled rifles at the two men.

"What do they want?" Julian asked from the corner of his mouth.

"Whatever they kin take. Don' worry none. I'll parley with 'em."

Making short gestures with his hands, Bingo spoke a few words in a strange, guttural language to the tallest of the Indians. They were rather a handsome people, Julian decided, and the first Apaches he had seen up close. Of course, the Navajos were distant cousins of the Apaches, and he had dealt with Navajos at Hubbell's.

Julian shifted cautiously to his other foot, watching as Bingo conversed with the leader. The old mountain man seemed to be enjoying himself, and whatever he said must have been amusing, because the Apaches laughed.

"What'd you say?" Julian asked Bingo without taking his eyes from the rifles leveled at his chest.

"What's so funny?"

"Me. I tole 'em as how yer a great Indian fighter, an' ya have this big string of Comanche scalps back at yer lodgepole. Yer big medicine, an' yer wantin' ta add more Comanche scalps ta yer colleckshun . . ."

"That's funny?"

"It's all in th' tellin', Pilgrim. Ya gotta know how ta tell it."

Julian slanted him a suspicious glance, but said nothing. He had the inescapable feeling he was the butt of Bingo's little joke, but it didn't matter as long as they got out of this alive.

"So what now?" he asked as the Apaches motioned for them to follow. "Where are they taking us?"

"They wants us ta share a bite ta eat with 'em. Us providin' th' bite, o' course."

"They're hungry?"

"Hell yes, they're hungry. 'Paches is allus hungry, whether fer food or whatever."

Julian coughed at the cloud of dust kicked up by the Apaches' ponies. Damn, they were so near their destination and now this . . . Surely the Apaches didn't know what they were after. He certainly hoped not. To disturb a sacred burial ground would be fatal, even if it didn't belong to the Apaches.

An hour later they were sitting around an Apache campfire smoking pipes.

"Smoke fust, talk later," Bingo said. "It's Injun etiquette." He squinted through the swirls of smoke. "An' then we'll eat afore we talk business."

"Right."

Bingo and the Apaches talked in a mixture of sign

language and the Apache tongue while Julian sat silently watching and listening. He understood a few of the more simple signs. None of the Apache words sounded familiar, though the dialect did remind him of the Athapascan tongue. The name Apache he knew was derived from the Zuni word *apachu,* or enemy. The Apaches were formidable foes, Julian reflected, and quite dangerous.

"They admire yer topknot, Pilgrim," Bingo murmured at one point. "Spotted Tail says they ain't never seed hair quite that color afore."

"I hope they didn't mention wanting to keep it as a souvenir?" Julian eyed the Apaches warily. "I've grown fond of it right where it is."

"Yer a great Indian fighter, 'member? They respects that, as long as it's Comanche hair yer takin', an' that's whut we'll use ta parley."

"When?"

"Right now. Ol' Red Shirt there—he's th' one in th' red shirt—seems ready to talk."

An hour later Julian and Bingo waved a relieved farewell to the pleased Apache braves; also bidding farewell to Julian's Spanish silver bridle, a Remington rifle, and two bottles of good French brandy.

"I hope they enjoy the brandy," Julian remarked gloomily when they were out of sight and earshot. "I'd have given two Remington rifles to keep the brandy. Seventy-six was a pretty good year."

"Ah, Pilgrim, leastways ya kept yer topknot." Bingo spat a stream of tobacco juice at a lizard sunning on a flat rock. "An' they sure liked that bright hair o' yorn. Yep. Sure did."

"Family trait. My daughter's hair is even lighter."

Stephanie Ashworth's light blond hair was fanned across a blanket-covered saddle, drying in the heat from the fire. She'd decided to move from the cot after discovering it was already occupied with crawling creatures she didn't dare investigate too closely. She shifted slightly, every few minutes opening her eyes to watch Ryan and surreptitiously scratch.

The blankets were itchy, tickling her bare skin wherever they touched—which happened to be all over. Ryan had very kindly offered to remove them for her when she complained of their itching, and her refusal had been less than polite.

"I'd rather die of a rat bite, thank you, Cordell!"

"Whatever makes you happy, Princess."

"Really . . . ?"

". . . within reason."

What would have made her happy was for Ryan to put on more clothes, but she refused to even suggest it. He was only trying to irritate her, as he'd been doing since they'd ridden out of Fort Defiance. It was too late for him to escort her back to the fort and be rid of her, and now his purpose eluded Stephanie. What did he hope to gain by it?

Stephanie's eyes slid to Ryan's lean body draped casually over a rickety chair. He was fiddling with some sort of musical instrument he'd discovered lying in a filthy corner of the cabin. After evicting the spiders and insects, he was attempting to tune it.

"Damn," he muttered, "these strings are rustier

than those old iron skillets hanging on the wall." A harsh twang verified his words, and Stephanie cringed.

It was a hopeless task and an unwarranted assault on her ears, Stephanie had almost decided, when a remotely recognizable chord squawked loudly.

"Cordell, is that a guitar—or are you strangling a cat?"

"Have more respect for a professional, Princess. I may entertain you yet." More chords rolled from the guitar.

"I hope to live so long."

But in spite of herself, Stephanie was slightly impressed. While he didn't have the musical skills of some she'd heard, Ryan was pretty good. He made some final adjustments, then flashed her a cocky grin.

"Curtain, please. The show is about to begin."

Snuggling deeper into her blankets, Stephanie unobtrusively scratched while listening. Her attention strayed again and again from the lively melody Ryan was playing, dark eyes lingering on his half-nude body. He should really put his clothes back on instead of wearing only a blanket knotted around his lean waist.

An uncomfortably warm feeling washed through Stephanie that had nothing to do with her proximity to the fire. If only his clothes would hurry and dry—if only *her* clothes would hurry and dry—then she'd feel much more comfortable about the situation. It was hard for her to think of anything else, and he was casually strumming the battered guitar as if they

177

were both completely dressed from ankle to eyebrow.

Ryan stood up, propping one bare foot on the vacated chair seat as he slung the guitar across his body. Stephanie briefly closed her eyes as his blanket parted and bared one long leg to just above the knee.

"What do you want to hear, Princess?"

He was talking to her, and she couldn't even look at him.

"Anything . . ." Good-bye, for instance. Or the welcome sound of a troop of calvarymen coming to her rescue. Or Julian. Even the bear. She had to get her mind off Ryan Cordell before she went mad. This has not been a good idea, and she knew it would not get any better before they finally reached her father.

"How about 'When Johnny Comes Marching Home?' Not very romantic, but pretty good. No? Not in the mood for sad songs, huh? Do you like 'Drink To Me Only With Thine Eyes?' Oh. Too romantic, huh?" Ryan strummed a tentative chord. "Let's see if I can remember . . . a G chord . . . yeah, that's right." He glanced up and winked at Stephanie. "Tonight, for your ears alone, I'm going to play one of my own compositions, madam."

"You're only doing this because you have a captive audience," Stephanie complained, but she couldn't hide the smile tugging at the corners of her mouth. Ryan was hard to resist when he was being audacious. And after the first few chords, she was pleasantly surprised by how well he played the guitar.

The melody drifted through the tiny cabin in light, airy notes, soft and soothing, lulling Stephanie into a pleasant reverie.

"No words?" she asked when he finished. "The tune is beautiful, but it should have words put to it . . ."

"Yeah, there are words. Didn't think you'd be interested in hearing them."

"Please. I'd be most interested." Stephanie's eyes widened as Ryan began singing in a deep, rich baritone, and she wondered at the feelings that must hide behind his careless facade. How had he ever written such beautiful lyrics?

> "I've been searchin' all my sunsets,
> but the colors are just a haze.
> 'Til it seems like all my tomorrows
> Just slip into yesterdays.
>
> And every fool's been told
> You got to reap what'cha sow,
>
> But only heaven knows,
> I guess only heaven knows,
> Lord, I got to know . . .
> Where the fair wind blows.
>
> Yeah, been searchin' all my dawnin's,
> Not knowin' what I'd find.
> Some too cruel to remember,
> Some way too kind.
>
> And any fool can see
> Which way the river flows;
>
> But I guess only heaven knows,
> I guess only heaven knows,

179

Lord, I gotta know . . .
Where the fair wind blows.

Some men search for silver,
Some men search for gold,

But I just wanna know,
Lord, I gotta know,
Where the fair wind blows . . ."

The final notes faded and died, but the plaintive melody lingered in Stephanie's mind as she stared at Ryan without speaking. Was this the man she had considered shallow and cold? It didn't seem possible that a man who could write a song like that could ever be cruel or unfeeling. She swallowed the sudden lump in her throat.

"Ryan, that was beautiful," she said quietly.

A half smile curved Ryan's mouth for a moment as he stared into the orange and crimson flames of the fire.

"I wrote it a long time ago," he said softly. "On one of those nights when a man can't sleep, can't hear anything but the howling of coyotes . . ."

"And did you ever find which way the fair wind blows, Ryan?"

Ryan's head turned in Stephanie's direction, and his gaze locked with hers. Her breath caught in her throat as she stared into his eyes, wondering at the emotions she saw in the clear, gray depths.

A feeling of panic tore at her for a moment as she saw her own feelings expressed in Ryan's eyes, like a mirror image. How had that happened?

She could not recall later if she'd somehow known,

or only sensed what would happen. Stephanie pushed to a half-sitting position on her pallet of blankets, and the rosy firelight played in warm trickles over her bare back and shoulders. She was vaguely conscious of the fragrant popping of pine branches in the fireplace and the slight patter of rain against the log walls of the cabin, but Ryan Cordell filled her world. And Stephanie knew that she'd been waiting for this moment since the first day she'd met him . . .

The scratching of the blankets against her bare body became sensuous instead of irritating as Ryan knelt beside her. His hands were in her hair, tugging gently, thumbs pushing her chin upward so that she had to look at him. Stephanie tried to still the sudden lurching of her heart.

"Ryan—I wish—do we always have to quarrel? Why can't we just talk sometimes—?"

"There's a time for talking, love, and a time for . . . other things." His mouth brushed softly against her parted lips, tasting, teasing, making Stephanie's pulse race madly. She must be insane . . . why else would she be responding to his kisses and caresses? "Keep kissing me that way and I'm going to make love to you. You know that, don't you?" Ryan was saying in her ear.

But he was so close—too close—and she couldn't think properly, couldn't do anything but hold more tightly to him, her fingers digging into his shoulders as he trailed kisses along her arched neck to the wild throbbing in the hollow of her throat.

It was warm and shadowy in the cabin, and as

quiet as if they were the only ones in the world. Stephanie's body felt stiff and unyielding as Ryan lay down beside her, stretching out so that his chest brushed against her bare breasts and his legs pressed against the long length of hers. She thought that surely she would break and splinter into a thousand pieces if he touched her again, but then he was pulling her into the warm circle of his arms, holding her close. And after a short time, because he did nothing else, Stephanie began to relax. The dark hairs on his chest tickled her nose as she pressed her face against him, and Ryan's breath was warm against her cheek.

"Ryan . . . I . . . I don't . . ."

"Hush, love. I'm only going to kiss you now. That's all."

His lips moved softly over her mouth, gently instead of passionately, giving instead of taking, until finally she began to kiss him back again. Ryan's hands tunneled into the still-damp weight of her hair, caressing and soft, raking his fingers through the long strands.

"It's the color of moonlight," he murmured. "And all soft like the finest silk."

While they kissed, his hands drifted from her hair along the curving line of her jaw, lightly, whispering over her skin like a fresh spring breeze, over the curve of her throat and down to her breasts. Stephanie tensed at the stirring in him and her, but it was too late for protests. He was exploring the hollows and curves of her body with impatient hands, finding her secrets and pushing her to the edge. She trembled, but could not have stopped him any more than he could

182

have stopped himself. And God help her—she didn't want to.

Stephanie's body arched closer as Ryan shifted slightly away, and she murmured a light protest.

"Be still, love. I'm right here . . ."

Patiently now, yet insistent, Ryan teased her with his mouth and tongue and hands, driving her over the edge of self-control until she was writhing beneath him. He kissed her eyes, her nose, and the tiny, barely visible cleft in her chin; his lips were warm against her skin as he pressed them into the small hollow just below her ear, then his tongue flicked against the delicate whorls in her ear. Stephanie shivered and held him more tightly as Ryan seared a path of kisses from her ear to the taut peak of her breast.

She moaned softly as he teased her breast with lips and tongue, and her eyes opened wide as his hands moved lower.

"Don't, love . . . don't hold my hands back. You're beautiful, and I want to love you . . ."

Now he kissed her fears away with quick, hard kisses, holding her head between his hands as his mouth ravaged hers, until Stephanie could think of nothing but Ryan Cordell. Her body was flushed and shaking with the same wild responses that it had the first time he'd held her and kissed her, only this time it was different. This time she wanted him to hold her, to fit his hard man's body to her softer curves and take her.

Still, Stephanie couldn't hold back the small cry that escaped when Ryan's hands moved to the soft skin inside her thighs, moving upward with gentle but firm strokes. He muttered words of reassurance in her ear, and his voice was thick with passion.

"It'll be all right, love. Let me show you . . ."

"I know. I know . . ."

But she hadn't known how sweet it could be, how completely satisfying it would be to make love with him. She wanted to prolong it, for this wild, sweet feeling to last forever. Ryan lay beside her, still kissing her, his fingers moving slightly over Stephanie's back to the slender curve of her waist, trailing over rounded hips to the backs of her thighs.

When Stephanie could breathe again, she began her own explorations, letting her long fingers investigate Ryan's body as thoroughly as he was investigating hers. She rubbed his unshaven jaw, tracing the hard line from ear to chin, the pads of her fingers scratching against his beard. He had a deep cleft in his chin where hers was more of a dimple, and Stephanie's forefinger dipped into it on its way down. Fascinating, how his neck was so thick and his shoulders so wide, the muscles like small, smooth ridges under his tanned skin. And he was brown all over, not just on his neck and arms, though there was a much whiter strip around his middle. Stephanie paused in her explorations, her fingers resting on a small, puckered scar, and flashed Ryan a curious glance.

"Knife fight. Bullets, arrows, knife wounds, cuts," he answered her unspoken question. Ryan's mouth twisted with amusement. "I've got lots of those kind of scars, Princess. Even claw marks from a wildcat."

She'd almost forgotten what kind of life he led, that he wasn't like most of the men she knew. Stephanie paused, and Ryan recognized the shadows in her dark eyes.

"Worried, Princess? Don't be. This particular wildcat was animal, not human."

Ryan's mouth muffled her indignant exclamation. When his lips released hers at last, she was breathless with wanting. Stephanie could feel his hard impatience, and was suddenly weary of the waiting.

"Ryan . . ." All her longing was in the one word, and he understood. He shifted his body over hers, holding her thighs apart with his knees. His hands tangled in Stephanie's hair as he held her head still for his kisses. She felt him rest against her for a moment before he lifted, poised, then entered her. A soft cry trembled in the air as he penetrated deeply, and her arms tightened around him.

All her earlier concerns faded as Ryan began moving inside her, taking her from awareness to forgetfulness. He was the only reality. Instinctively, she matched her rhythm to his, meeting his thrusts with the supple arching of her body, letting her hands slide down the corded muscles in his back and up again, feeling them tense and relax as he moved against her. Now her fingers tangled in the dark hair that lay thick and long on the back of his neck.

Gradually, Stephanie felt the tempo of his breathing and movements quicken. Her own breathing came more quickly, and her pulses beat a rapid tattoo that drummed loudly in her ears. She was on fire, hot yet shivering as if with a chill, her mouth pressing against his shoulder to still her cries. Twisting and turning under him, seeking release, she whimpered and Ryan's mouth was over hers, muffling her moans as he drove into her endlessly, hard and demanding, until Stephanie heard a crashing in her ears like the foamy breakers of the sea. The roaring melded with her body as she arched high, rising and falling as she plummeted back to reality.

They were both dotted with a mist of perspiration that gleamed in the firelight like rosy pearls, and Ryan reached for his blanket lying close by. He drew it across Stephanie's body, drying her breasts, belly, and thighs, then kissed her gently and tenderly.

Drowsy and replete with satisfaction, Stephanie couldn't even murmur a protest when Ryan folded her once more in her scratchy Navajo blankets. She wanted him to lie beside her for a bit more, and when he slipped under her blankets, she smiled. It was hard to believe that this was the same man she'd battled so hard for the past weeks, had alternately hated and . . . well, tolerated. She'd never really liked him until tonight, and that's what made the entire situation unbelievable.

Ryan pulled her close and kissed her on the top of her head.

"Better go to sleep, Princess. We need to get an early start in the morning so we can make it to a town by late afternoon."

"A town . . . God, how wonderful! A bathtub, and a proper bed—without crawling things in it—and even a decent meal! I can hardly wait, Ryan." She snuggled closer to him and closed her eyes.

186

Long after Stephanie had drifted into sleep, Ryan lay awake. He shouldn't have made love to her. That hadn't been part of the plan, and she was the type of woman who would take it too much to heart. It was all wrong. Dammit, any woman was wrong for him! He didn't need the involvement, the commitment that a relationship with a woman like Stephanie Ashworth would demand. And he certainly wasn't ready for marriage. God. That was a joke. He'd never fit into her world, didn't *want* to fit into her world. And she was too worldly to fit into his.

Ryan squinted against the curls of his cigar smoke, staring at the half-rotted ceiling of the cabin. This was the kind of life that suited him, not parading along busy city streets all puffed up with self-importance. Out here a man was free, was what he made himself, not what people tried to make him. He'd suffocate in a crowded town.

He slanted Stephanie a glance. But damn if she wasn't the finest woman he'd met. She wasn't just beautiful, but intelligent and self-sufficient. That counted for something when you were miles and miles from a town. Self-sufficiency was a mandatory trait in the West.

Stephanie squirmed in her sleep, sighing softly, and the blanket slipped partly off her body. The dying fire silhouetted her small, firm breasts, and yielding to an impulse, Ryan pulled the blanket all the way off. She was lying on her back with one arm folded so that her hand curled beneath her chin like a little child's. Her right leg was drawn up and her left slightly bent in a posture of complete relaxation, and

187

Ryan admired the slim length of her. She was certainly a tall woman, as he'd said the first time he'd seen her, but, hell, she was *all* woman.

Ryan let the blanket drop. He had the inescapable feeling that his actions tonight would have far-reaching and unavoidable consequences.

Chapter Fifteen

"Is that the town?" Stephanie rose in her stirrups to point at a dark blue blur on the horizon. When they were in flat land, it was hard for her to tell if there was anything ahead or not. She wanted to shout with relief when Ryan nodded.

"Yeah, that's Willow Creek."

"What a pretty name. It must have water and willows close by."

"Water's fairly close, but there are no willows anywhere around."

"Then why . . . ?"

"Somebody must've just liked willows, I guess. Come on."

He nudged his stallion into a brisk trot with the pack horse close behind. Stephanie trailed them, thinking grimly that Ryan had had very little to say to her since the night before. He hadn't been sarcastic or hostile, just cool. Why? She wanted to ask him, but their new relationship was so tenuous she couldn't. Was it her appearance, maybe? She'd never worried about it before, and certainly had never been accused of being in the least bit vain, but that had been before Ryan Cordell. No one would mistake her for a female when she looked like this. Her battered felt hat was pulled low, and a dusty red kerchief hung around her neck so that it could be quickly pulled over her nose and mouth to keep out the dust. Julian's army pistol still hung in its holster at her side, tied down like a gunman's, and with the baggy shirt she wore Stephanie looked more like a weary cowboy than a woman. Maybe that was why Ryan was ignoring her.

Just ahead, Ryan nudged his stallion into a lope. All day they had been followed, and he didn't want to be caught out in the open. Two men were trailing them, and he had a hunch that it was Huntley and Bates. He wouldn't put anything past those two, especially if they smelled easy money. He wanted Stephanie protected as quickly as possible. Even in a town she wouldn't be completely safe. Stephanie was too tempting a prize for them to ignore.

They'd be too easily found in one of the hotels, but Ryan remembered a spot where they would be much safer. And with Stephanie dressed the way she was, and looking like a beardless youth, it would be perfect.

But Stephanie didn't agree. Even the fact that there very probably was not one soul in the entire town of Willow Creek who would recognize her as a woman didn't temper her anger when Ryan stopped at the local bordello.

"What do you think you're doing?" she hissed when he dismounted in front of Fancy Lil's Establishment for Gentlemen. She glared furiously at the gaudy red velvet draperies hung at the front windows, and tried to ignore the young women draped over the balcony railing and gazing into the street. "Do you think I don't know what kind of place this is? I'm not staying here!"

Half-clad girls hung over the railing and called invitations down to Ryan and Stephanie, extolling their charms to prospective customers in graphic terms. Grinding her teeth, Stephanie closed her eyes for a brief moment, hoping that by some miracle they would be well away from this place when she opened them again. No such luck. When she opened her eyes Ryan was standing beside her horse. He pushed back his hat, glaring at her, and the expression on his face was cold and hard.

"Do you want a room for the night or don't you? We're liable to get . . ." He paused, and decided not to alarm her by telling her about Huntley and Bates. ". . . fleabites . . . in any of the other 'decent' hotels," he finished lamely. "And besides—Lil's a good friend of mine."

"I'll just bet she is . . ."

"Look, dammit, I'm not going to stand out here in the heat and dust and argue with you about it. Are you coming in, or aren't you? Hell, *Stevie*, no one's gonna ask or even care who you are," he said loud enough for the girls above them to hear. Ryan lowered his voice. "Now are you satisfied? They think you're a man. Get off your horse and come inside with me . . . now."

He waited impatiently while Stephanie glared at him, but when his hands lifted to drag her from her gelding she hastily dismounted.

191

"You'll pay for this indignity, Cordell," she said tersely. Damn him, he didn't need to write it out for her. It was obvious what he was doing. She had behaved loosely the night before, and this was simply Ryan Cordell's method of showing her what he thought of her now. The night had demanded a high price, to say the least. Tears stung the backs of her eyelids, and Stephanie's throat ached as she blinked them back. It should have occurred to her that Ryan would react this way.

Stephanie pulled her hat brim as low as possible without blocking her vision completely, straightened her shoulders to look even taller, and followed Ryan up the wooden steps and into Lil's. She cringed at the sight of women in various stages of undress walking about the main parlor. When one of them—who obviously knew Ryan well—attached herself to him like a cocklebur on wool, Stephanie was vaguely surprised at her sudden desire to shoot both of them.

A most interesting reaction, she told herself lightly, considering he had behaved toward her in such a cavalier attitude the entire day. It was hard to keep her mouth shut while Ryan was talking to the girl, but even harder once Lil of the Fancy Lil's fame swept into the room.

"Ryan Cordell, you rascal! Where have you been? We've been missing you in these parts, and Lord knows, real men are scarce as hen's teeth anyway!"

Stephanie found it difficult to keep her mouth from drooping open as the buxom blond woman planted a long, wet kiss flat on Ryan's mouth. And it didn't help that after rolling his eyes toward Stephanie, he seemed to enjoy it immensely. The kiss went on for so long that Stephanie thought Ryan and Lil should both pass out from lack of air. It was disgusting, and she wished she had never kissed him herself. A wave of fury prompted Stephanie to action.

Putting one hand over her mouth, Stephanie pretended to cough, a loud, racking cough that seemed to shake her entire frame as she stumbled forward. Deliberately, she bumped into a gilt-crusted pedestal table holding a plaster replica of Venus de Milo with fresh flowers blooming from the top of her head. Both table and Venus crashed to the red-carpeted floor in a shower of water and flowers, wetting two nearby occupants of a velvet love seat.

Ryan instantly peeled himself away from Lil, whirling to glare at Stephanie. She gave him an innocent stare, almost daring him to object, and mumbled, "Sorry, ma'am. It's consumption—keeps actin' up on me." Another racking cough left her almost breathless, and Stephanie's curled hand hid a smile at Lil's squeal of alarm.

Ryan's mouth twisted as he recognized the challenge in Stephanie's eyes, and there was a gleam of amusement in his eyes as he tried to calm Lil.

"Lil, Lil, it's just my partner's idea of a little joke," he soothed. "He's real funny that way." Ryan bent a sharp look toward Stephanie that quelled any more coughs. Shaking her head, the blond proprietess stared at her ruined statue in dismay as Ryan continued. "We need a room for the night. Maybe two nights . . ."

"Two rooms, Cordell." Stephanie's pseudomasculine voice was as firm as she could make it.

"Rooms?" Lil said distractedly. She gave Stephanie a doubtful glance. "I don't know, Ryan . . ."

"Ah, Lil, I told you he was just kidding. Stevie's a great practical joker, that's all." Ryan's arm slid around the woman's waist. "If you don't have two rooms, one will be just fine."

Lil heaved a sigh as she picked up Venus's head from the carpet. "All right. You know you're always welcome here, Ryan. I'm just not sure about your clumsy friend."

"I'll pay for the statue," Ryan began, but Lil cut him off with a wave of her hand.

"You'll do nothing of the sort. Think I've forgotten who saved my life and Tommy's back in Deadwood? No, everything's on the house as long as you're here, Ryan. Your pick of the girls who aren't occupied, too."

Stephanie wished it was Ryan's head that had rolled on the carpet instead of the hapless Venus as he slanted her a mocking grin. Damn him! He thought this was funny . . .

"Two rooms?" she asked Lil gruffly.

"Look, don't push it. I've only got one extra room as it is. You two gentlemen can share, sweetie."

Turning, Lil wound her arm through Ryan's.

"Nanette will show you upstairs," she said over her shoulder to Stephanie as she pulled Ryan with her. "I've got . . . business . . . to talk to your partner about."

"Monkey business?" Stephanie shot back, fuming as Lil just laughed archly. She was still fuming as she stomped after the half-clothed Nanette. No other hotel rooms? Ryan Cordell wasn't fooling her for a moment. In a town the size of Willow Creek, it was

194

difficult to believe that there would be no decent hotels.

Stephanie eyed Nanette's swinging hips as she followed her up the stairs. This was Ryan's idea of decent? Her mouth tightened into a straight line, and she tore her gaze from the brunette's swaying bottom. Stephanie shuddered at the garish wallpaper and red lanterns lighting the long hallway and stairs. Everything looked so cheaply ornate and vulgar. Especially Lil.

Stephanie dissected Lil's appearance as well as her establishment. The dress the woman wore had been a horror. No decent woman would wear a dress cut almost to her navel, nor sport those wretched ostrich feathers in such abundance, either. And the hem was cut high to show her legs well above the ankle. But at least it was an improvement on what Nanette was wearing—or not wearing.

"Thees ees your room, m'sieur," Nanette simpered, throwing open a door at the end of the long hall. "Eet ees to your liking, yes?"

"*Oui. Merci*, Nanette. *Au revoir.*" Stephanie smiled at the blank expression on the girl's face. French? The girl had probably never even eaten a croissant, much less been to France. Stephanie firmly pushed Nanette back out the door and closed it behind her.

Oh God, she moaned when she turned around to survey her room, it was even worse than the downstairs parlor. Stephanie closed her eyes and shook her head. There must be a silver lining somewhere in this cloud. Of course. At least she would get a bath, decent food, and a comfortable bed.

195

Her eyes flicked to the huge bed dominating the room.

The dark wood of the headboard was carved with tiny cupids and nude figures reclining on lounges or puffs of cloud. Heavy draperies hung from each side, and gold tassels lined the canopy. Rolling her eyes, Stephanie ignored the smiling cupids watching her and cautiously tested the mattress. Ah, good. Firm, but not too firm.

A smile tilted her mouth as she swept off her hat and flung herself to its surface with a sigh of pleasure. A bed. A real, honest to goodness bed, and all hers. Her eyes widened. Ryan. Well, he would just have to occupy the couch. Or someone else's bed? She cringed from the thought.

This little expedition to find Julian and some lost treasures was turning out to be more trouble and less pleasure than she'd ever dreamed it would. Damn. "Damn," she swore aloud, and was tempted to use some of the more colorful terms she'd heard before. But even as a man, she couldn't be unladylike. Ryan was right. She wallowed in a rut of conventionality.

Sitting up, Stephanie caught a glimpse of her reflection in the cheval mirror across the room. She stared in complete horror. Good God, this was even worse than she'd thought. Slowly, very slowly, she rose from the bed and crossed the floor to gaze at her reflection. This was conventional? She fought a wave of hysterical laughter.

She looked like a bandit with long hair. Stephanie struck a pose, one hand hovering over the butt of her pistol as she'd seen on the covers of countless dime novels about the West. Stevie the Kid, maybe. No, she was too old. Billy the Kid was only nineteen or twenty, and already a legend. Maybe she should emulate one of Beadle's dime-novel heroines like *Bess the Trapper*, or *Mountain Kate*. Now there were real tough women. Stephanie sighed. It was no use. She'd feel better after a good hot bath and something to eat.

But when she'd finished bathing in the high-backed copper tub, Ryan still hadn't returned and Stephanie didn't feel a bit better. Cleaner maybe, but not better. Where was he? Still with that horrid woman? Probably. Or maybe he was drinking in the downstairs parlor with a half-dozen women draped over him.

Stephanie paced the carpeted floor. The feathered hem of the dressing gown she'd found hanging over a folding screen swept the floor with a soft swish as she walked, and she jerked irritably at the gauzy material. Her bare feet padded softly on the carpet as she paused at a window.

It was dark outside and she could hear shouts and muffled laughter through the open shutters. Leaning forward, Stephanie rested her palms on the windowsill and looked out. She was in a front room facing the dusty main street. The windows were dark in glass-fronted buildings that lined the wooden sidewalks, but bright light flooded the areas in front of swinging double doors. This was obviously the end of town where a man went to drink, whore, and gamble. How comforting.

Furious at her situation, Stephanie debated on trying to sneak away from Lil's without encountering Ryan. She didn't intend to argue with him, and she didn't intend to remain in this . . . this whore-house! She should have refused at the very first.

Whirling away from the window, Stephanie resumed her pacing. Part of her rebelled at the humiliation Ryan was inflicting on her, and part of her cringed with despair that he could be so unfeeling. Didn't he care how she felt? The answer was obvious, and Stephanie's resolve strengthened. She would leave Fancy Lil's to Ryan and the rest.

The feathered hem of her dressing gown tickled bare ankles as Stephanie strode to the folding screen in the corner. Lying in a dusty heap were her garments, still crusted with dirt from the trail. Sighing, she scooped them from the floor.

"Going somewhere, Princess?"

Her heart leaped into her throat as Ryan's familiar voice mocked her gently. Turning slowly, Stephanie faced him with dark, bold eyes.

"Yes. I am. How'd you get in?"

She didn't move when Ryan stepped forward and removed the clothes from her loose grasp. His fingers brushed against her arm, sending ripples along fine-tuned nerve ends.

He shrugged carelessly. "I opened the door and came in, that's how. If you want privacy, learn to lock it." Stephanie's trousers and shirt were tossed in a corner, and his glance almost dared her to retrieve them. Stephanie eyed him narrowly. There was a fine shade of difference in his customary stance, and she realized that Ryan had been drinking quite heavily. Recalling her father in his cups, she decided she had a slight advantage.

"You can't keep me prisoner here," Stephanie said coolly.

"What are you talking about?"

"I want to leave . . ."

"In those dirty clothes? Tsk, tsk. Have you no shame, Princess?"

"Ryan Cordell, I don't find this situation at all amusing. I understand your motive for bringing me here, but I still don't . . ."

"You do? Then why all the fuss?" Ryan stepped to the liquor cabinet and poured himself a drink from a tall crystal decanter. "If you understand—cooperate."

Stephanie's hands curled into fists. Cooperate? Oh, the absolute nerve of the man was amazing! Did he think because he brought her to a whorehouse that she would behave like one of the . . . the inmates? A tortoiseshell hairbrush was quickly scooped from the dresser and sailed through the air, striking Ryan in the chest and spilling his drink.

"What the . . . ?"

An ivory box studded with seashells followed the path of the hairbrush, spilling a shimmering shower of loose face powder over Ryan and the floor. While Ryan was cursing and coughing, Stephanie paused in amazement at the change in her personality. Where was the ice maiden who had no emotions?

Stephanie quickly discovered that Ryan in his cups was quite different from Julian in his cups. Too much whiskey did not seem to damper Ryan's reflexes at all. He deftly grabbed her wrists as she reached for another potential missile.

"You're crazy, do you know that?" He gave her a rough shake. "You should be locked up somewhere so you don't endanger innocent folks . . ."

"Innocent?" Stephanie's laugh was shrill. "You can't be suggesting that *you* are innocent? In a pig's eye!" She jerked angrily, but his grip on her wrists was too tight. "Let me go, Cordell . . ."

"I will—when I'm ready." Ryan swung Stephanie around, shoving her toward the bed. "First we're going to have a little casual conversation, Miss Ashworth. Ah ah—no kicking!"

The edge of the mattress caught Stephanie behind her knees and she sprawled across the bed with Ryan still gripping her wrists. She swallowed a gulp of dismay, glaring up at him as he bent across her squirming body. He blinked face powder from his lashes, and tiny sprinkles dotted Stephanie's cheeks.

When she bucked, her long legs thrashing, Ryan threw a leg over her to hold her still. Stephanie writhed and twisted until she was panting breathlessly with her efforts, but as strong as he was, Ryan had the advantage.

"Tired yet?" he inquired in a pleasant tone that was not the least bit winded. "Then let me know when you are," he added as Stephanie renewed her frantic movements.

Dignity demanded an alternate course of action, and her struggles ceased as she recognized the futility.

"Jackass," she said when she could speak without gasping for breath.

Ryan's dark brows rose. "Swearing, Miss Ashworth? I'm shocked! Dammit, I've told you not to swear . . ."

Stephanie's lips tightened into a grim line, and she stared up at him mutely. He was mocking her, of course.

Noting her sudden silence, Ryan's mouth twitched with sardonic amusement. Stephanie Ashworth was not as cool and emotionless as she'd like to pretend. Her passion the night before had surprised him pleasantly, and he'd spent the entire day trying to forget it. He'd deliberately put as much distance between them as possible, but time and again during the long hot ride, he'd found his gaze straying in her direction. He'd remember her long legs wrapped around his waist, or the way her lips had clung to his, and the small, soft noises she'd made . . . It had been enough to drive him crazy. Even now, with an entire houseful of warm, willing women, he'd found himself seeking out Stephanie. He must have leanings toward self-punishment.

"You're awfully quiet," Ryan taunted when Stephanie remained silently glaring at him. Her dark eyes were nearly black as she held his gaze, until Ryan had to look away. "Cat got your tongue, Princess?"

She found her tongue when Ryan's gaze traveled from her mutinous face to the creamy swell of small, firm breasts peeking through the gaping folds of her dressing gown. Shifting his weight, Ryan transferred both Stephanie's wrists to the grip of one hand, while his other began a light exploration in the shadowed valley between the pale globes. When his sardonic expression subtly altered to desire, she tried desperately to forestall him.

"Go ahead. Have your fun. You're bigger than I am, and stronger. I can't stop you . . ."

"Do you want to stop me, Princess?" Ryan's teeth nibbled at her earlobe and Stephanie shivered in spite of herself.

"Yes!"

"Liar . . ."

Ryan's mouth was warm against the hollow in her throat and Stephanie tried to jerk away. A feeling of outrage swelled in her that he would attempt such a thing after his earlier treatment of her, and did he really think she was so easy? She kicked out with one long leg, almost managing to throw him off, but he still held her tight.

Sodden with whiskey, but drunk with passion, Ryan ignored Stephanie's furious protests as he pushed away the flimsy dressing gown with his free hand. He wanted her, and she had wanted him the night before, so why not? His fumbling brain failed to take into account the fact that Stephanie was less than willing.

The grinning cupids and nude nymphs carved into the bed canopy seemed to mock Stephanie as she struggled against Ryan's superior strength. Smoky mirrors glued to the canopy top reflected their tangled bodies as they wrestled across the bedspread. Stephanie's tawny limbs flashed rosy in the soft lamplight as she kicked vainly, and her silvery hair fell in wild snarls across her face.

"Ryan!" She beat at him with her fists, but he seemed impervious to the blows she aimed at his broad back. "No, please don't," she begged in a tearful voice, and her pleas finally penetrated.

Releasing her, Ryan sat up. His gray eyes were like dark, stormy thunderclouds as he gazed at her narrowly.

"Now what?" he demanded.

"I don't want you to touch me." Her chin lifted defensively when he laughed cynically. "Well, I don't!"

"Is that right? You didn't say that last night . . ."

"Forget last night!" She pulled her dressing gown tightly around her body, clutching it at the chin.

"How convenient. Shall I pretend it never happened? Sorry, Miss Ashworth, but you can't wish it away." Ryan slid from the bed and stood staring down at her with an expression Stephanie could only call contempt. "You're not even as honest as a good whore . . ."

"Don't talk to me that way!" She rose to her knees on the bed, glaring at him furiously. "I don't appreciate being brought here, and you know it!"

"Too bad. I intend for you to stay here whether you like it or not."

"I'll leave," she threatened. "You can't keep me here, Cordell!"

"And you can't go on by yourself. You've got no money, and couldn't find your way out of a shopping bag. You're stuck with me, like I'm stuck with you." He unbuckled his pants to tuck in his shirttail, grinning when Stephanie turned her head away. "Don't worry—you're in no danger of rape. I wouldn't take you if you were the *only* woman on earth!" He pivoted and snatched his hat from the small table by the door, jamming it on his head.

"Good!" Stephanie said to the slamming door. She

stared forlornly for a moment, then catapulted from the bed as she heard the unmistakable sound of a key turning in the lock. Damn him! He had locked her in as if she was a naughty child! Her eyes narrowed. He certainly didn't know her very well if he thought *that* would work . . .

Chapter Sixteen

"No, Sheriff, I am not trying to impersonate someone, or rob a bank," Stephanie repeated firmly. "I *am* who I say I am, and I simply wished to send a telegram to New York. See? It's already written on this sheet of paper. It's a very easy matter to explain . . ."

"Then why ain't you explainin' it better?" Sheriff Royce regarded Stephanie from under bushy gray eyebrows. His hands were tucked into the pockets of his long Army-style coat that was pulled away from double gunbelts strapped around his portly frame. "All I know is, my deputy found you sneakin' down some alley dressed up like a cowboy an' followed you. Then you go bangin' on th' door to th' telegraph office, makin' a gen'ral ruckus. Disturbin' th' peace, th' way I sees it."

"Disturbing the peace—with all that noise from the saloons at the other end of town? I thought the office was still open. There was a light in the window and the shades were up . . ."

"I *did* forget to pull the shades, Horace, and the light's always left on," Henry Simms put in. A clerk in the telegraph office, he was a thin man with the nervous habit of pulling at one corner of his limp mustache. Henry had been summoned from his bed to verify that nothing was missing from the telegraph office. He cast admiring glances at Stephanie from time to time. She didn't look half bad when she wasn't wearing that big floppy hat that hid her face, and if he'd known she was a woman he'd never have let the deputy drag Horace Royce into it. A man just couldn't be too careful these days, not with all those desperate outlaws running around the countryside.

"Look, Sheriff, why don't you let Mr. Simms send the telegram for me? You'll find out in a hurry that what I'm telling you is the truth." Stephanie tried to keep the exasperation from her voice. This was too much. She'd never been in jail in her life, and this wretched, hostile sheriff intended to incarcerate her if she couldn't verify her story. How absolutely humiliating.

"Well now . . ." Sheriff Royce scratched his head doubtfully. "Guess it couldn' hurt none. Take a while, though, to get an answer. Meantime, don' you be leavin' town, little gal." He slanted a glance at Henry Simms. "Send the wire, Henry, an' let me know th' answer soon as you get it. Got it?"

"Got it, Sheriff." After a last admiring glance at Stephanie, Henry Simms bustled from the jailhouse with Stephanie's telegraph message clutched in one hand.

"Now where you stayin'?" the sheriff asked. "I'll see that you get back safe."

There was a long pause while Stephanie stood in appalled silence. That would never do. How could she tell him she was staying at Fancy Lil's? He'd never believe that she was an innocent victim of circumstance then.

"I . . . I'm not staying anywhere. I just rode into town, Sheriff. Where do you suggest I stay?"

"Just rode in, huh? Mighty clean for ridin' trail all day, ain't you?" He stared at her suspiciously. "Now, I'll jus' ask you one more time—where you stayin'?"

Rubbing her aching forehead with one hand, Stephanie surrendered. "I know this will be difficult for you to believe," she began, and sighed as Royce lifted skeptical brows, "but I'm staying at Lil's. I had to," she added hastily when Sheriff Royce did a double take. "My . . . my traveling companion insisted . . ."

"Who you travelin' with?"

She hesitated. What if Ryan was wanted by the law? He could be arrested, and she could be considered an accomplice. Stephanie hesitated a fraction too long, and the sheriff was taking her by one arm and saying they were going to take a little walk on down to Lil's.

"I know Miss Lil, an' if she don' know you, little gal, you're in a heap of trouble no matter what those damn wires of Henry's say."

Stephanie felt like an utter fool standing in Lil's parlor beside the sheriff. Especially since the floppy hat that had covered the fashionable bun atop her head had been left in his office, and she was the object of many curious stares. Ryan would be furious with her.

207

When Lil finally swept down the stairs, Stephanie took one step forward.

"Lil, tell the sheriff you know me, please," she began before Royce cut her off.

"Lil, do you know this gal? She says she's stayin' here with you."

"I have never seen the girl before in my life," Lil stated firmly after giving Stephanie the briefest of glances. "Why would I let a woman stay here unless she's working for me? You know me better than that, Horace."

The sheriff chuckled. "Yep, I thought her story 'bout stayin' here with some friend was kinda fishy . . ."

"Wait a minute." A frown creased her forehead as Lil stepped closer to inspect Stephanie. "Stevie? Oh yes—you're Ryan's friend."

"So to speak . . ." Stephanie pulled away from Royce's detaining hand.

"Sorry. Didn't recognize you without the hat. Unusual hair . . . Horace, she is staying here," Lil said to the bemused sheriff.

"Who's her friend, Lil?" Sheriff Royce rocked back on his heels, his eyes scanning the parlor. "I like to know when strangers come into town."

"That's why you make such a good sheriff, Horace." Lil took him by one arm and led him toward an adjoining room. "Your favorite drink still a Stone Fence, Horace? Millie! A shot of rye with a twist of lemon in a glass of cider for the sheriff . . ."

Stephanie stood like a stone. Piano music tinkled merrily in the room opposite the parlor, and muted laughter mingled with the clinking of glasses. Lil's girls were busy at work. She stood alone on the red carpet feeling definitely out of place and wondering if she dared leave. The girl Lil had called Millie paused by her side.

"Lil said to get the hell out of the parlor, honey," Millie advised. "You're liable to get mistaken for a new girl, and put to work. Leave th' sheriff to her. She can handle him real easy." She winked and moved away, leaving Stephanie staring after her.

No fires needed to be lit under her feet, and Stephanie escaped from the parlor to her room with great speed. Sighing unhappily, she found it was unlocked. Obviously, her unorthodox departure out the front window had been discovered. Steeling herself, she swung open the door.

Ryan lounged against the hand-carved liquor cabinet that stood on the far wall, watching her as she entered and reclosed the door.

"Drink?" He held up a half-empty glass in a mocking salute. "You must be thirsty after all your busy little activities tonight."

"Yes. As a matter of fact, I am." Stephanie strolled casually to the liquor cabinet, trying not to look at the nude nymphs that were carved into the light oak. The tall mirror at the back of the cabinet reflected two unclothed women carved into unlikely erotic postures and serving as spindles holding up the small wooden canopy over the cabinet. Stephanie's strained face was flanked by the carved reflections. She could see the pallor of her complexion even in the rosy light afforded by two milk-glass lamps. It was all the nudes, she decided, that put her on edge. The entire house was full of them. Everywhere she

looked men and women were in loving postures that
sometimes strayed over the border of erotic into
obscene. Even the hand-painted dressing screen in
one corner of the room had scenes that should have
made the most hardened harlot blush crimson.

"And what about your 'busy little activities'
tonight, Cordell?" she asked, imitating Ryan's
casual attitude as she poured herself a liberal amount
of port in one of the crystal glasses. "I suppose you
and Lil had a lot of catching up to do on old times?"
Oh Lord, she didn't want to sound jealous. Maybe
Ryan hadn't noticed that acid tinge in her tone. A
ridiculous hope, of course, because he noticed
immediately.

"Jealous of Lil, Princess? She's curious about you,
too. Wanted to know why I'm traveling with such an
energetic young woman . . ."

"I'm certain you enlightened her . . ."

"No. I thought I should mind my own
business . . ."

"Oh, wonderful! Why start now when you never
have before?"

"Now's as good a time as any to start . . ."

"You, Ryan Cordell, are impossible! It's all your
fault that the sheriff is suspicious of me now, and I'm
innocent! While you . . . you are just a . . . a . . ."

"Sheep in wolf's clothing?" Ryan supplied helpfully.

Stephanie waved an impatient hand. "What can
we do about the sheriff? He's down there talking to
Lil now."

"Yeah, what about the sheriff? How did you
manage to come back here with him? And where were

you going in the first place?'' Ryan's empty glass thunked to the gleaming top of the liquor cabinet. "I thought I had you locked in . . .''

"I had different thoughts," Stephanie cut in.

Ryan bent his head slightly. "So you did. What did you have in mind when you brought the sheriff back with you, Stephanie?''

"Do I detect a note of apprehension, Ryan?'' Stephanie folded her arms and watched him over the rim of her glass. "Why should it matter to you if the sheriff is here?''

"That's my business. You take care of yours. Just tell me what brought him to Lil's.''

"And miss the fun of seeing you sweat? No way. For some reason, Ryan, you don't want to run into Sheriff Royce and I'm wondering why. Could it be that you're a 'man on the run'? A gunslinger, perhaps? Or even a bank robber? Are there wanted posters out on you . . . ?''

Ryan's swift lunge was all the warning Stephanie had before he was gripping her by both arms, spilling the remainder of her port down her blouse front and on the carpet.

"You're askin' too damn many questions and answerin' too few, lady. I'd suggest you start talkin' before you begin to regret askin' . . .''

This was a Ryan she'd never seen before, a coldly angry, determined Ryan with eyes like chips of ice. The crystal glass fell from her fingers to thump softly on the carpet as she stared at the tight, hard line of his mouth. Stephanie's chin tilted stubbornly. She would not let him see how he intimidated her, in spite of the fact that she was absolutely quivering with fear.

"If you want to know why he's here, ask him, Mr. Cordell. I'm certain he will be glad to enlighten you." She sucked in a deep breath when Ryan's eyes narrowed dangerously, but plunged on with bravado, "As for me, I intend to remove myself from this . . . this . . . *house* filled with soiled doves, and stay in a decent hotel, fleas, ticks, and bedbugs notwithstanding!"

When she tried to pull away, Ryan would not release her. His fingers dug cruelly into her arms, and Stephanie flinched.

"Let me go, Cordell."

"Not on your life, lady. I told you earlier—you are staying here until we leave—together."

"No. I am dispensing with your services as a guide, Mr. Cordell. If I cannot find anyone else qualified to take me the rest of the way, I will simply wait here until I can. Now release me, and get out of my way!"

Ryan was holding her close to his body, gripping her upper arms with both hands. Infuriated because he still held her tightly, so tightly she was certain she would have large bruises, Stephanie brought her knee up in a swift action intended to gain her release. Half expecting such action, Ryan countered her movement with contemptuous ease.

"Is that the only defense you know? Remind me to show you a few more one day, Princess. You're liable to need 'em if you keep up these kind of tricks. Tempts a man to knock some sense into your head."

"Does it?" Stephanie gasped as he twisted her arm and turned her around, forcing her to the wide bed.

212

"What . . . what are you going to do? Cordell! Don't you dare, you . . . you pervert!" She tried to twist away as he pushed her back on the bed with one hand and began to slide his leather belt off with the other.

"Don't worry. I'm only tying you up so you can't go down the street to sleep in some insect-infested bed." Ryan pulled off his belt and secured one of Stephanie's wrists to a corner bedpost in spite of her wild, futile efforts to evade him, then tied the other one with her own belt. He grinned wickedly. "I assure you I don't have any more designs on that pretty body of yours, Princess. Not right now, anyway." He tested his knots and nodded in satisfaction. "This ought to keep you where I want you."

Ryan slid from the bed and stood looking down at her a moment. Furious, and almost frothing at the mouth like a rabid dog, Stephanie glared up at him, hating him.

"You villain! You damn, adulterous scoundrel!"

"Ah, at least your command of curse words is improving, Princess. You may make it yet. Try to miss me while I'm gone. I'll be back as soon as I can." A dark eyebrow lifted thoughtfully as he swept Stephanie's long body with a considering gaze. "You know, it might be kinda fun to try it that way . . ."

The mattress dipped as Ryan put one knee on the bed and leaned over Stephanie. Ignoring her wild, panting curses and her bucking and heaving, he ran his hands leisurely over the curves and hollows of her body. He unbuttoned her blouse slowly, pulling it aside to bare her breasts.

"Damn you, Cordell! Don't you touch me!"

"You weren't so shy last night, Princess. Why tonight?"

Any answer she might have made drowned in incoherent protests when Ryan's mouth began to tease the taut peak of one breast, his tongue curling around the crest in light, flicking motions. His other hand gently kneaded her other breast, and Stephanie moaned at the betraying rush of desire he'd sparked. The tight knot in her belly burned brighter, glowing hot and high until her breath came so hard and fast she was almost panting.

Sensing imminent surrender, Ryan's mouth moved to the tiny pulse below her ear. His body lowered over hers until Stephanie could feel the evidence of his desire pressing against her belly. Ryan kissed her slowly and lingeringly, forcing her lips apart for his tongue's invasion.

By now Stephanie was almost beyond caring, but not quite. With the last bit of her rational control, she lightly nipped his tongue with her teeth.

Ryan jerked back immediately, glaring down at her with pinpoints of fury blazing in his eyes.

"Bloodthirsty little vixen, aren't you . . ." He touched the tip of his tongue with one finger. "I'll settle with you when I get back, Princess, but I don't have time now." He swung to a sitting position and rebuttoned Stephanie's blouse, stroking her as he did. "Don't worry, sweet, when I get back I'll spend a long time with you. I know that's what you're wanting."

Laughing at her sputtering fury, Ryan buckled on

his gunbelts and left, closing the door softly behind him.

Stephanie's booted heels drummed impotently against the mattress for a moment after the door clicked shut. She hated him, she truly hated him. She should have trusted her instincts and stayed far away from Ryan Cordell, but no; she had ignored those promptings and now look. She was a prisoner in a whorehouse, tied to a bed carved with numerous nudes—oh, Lord. Stephanie's gaze riveted on the ceiling.

It was mirrored and she could see her reflection, but worse than that were the lurid painted figures edging the mirrored tiles. They were in sexual postures that hardly seemed possible, even for trained acrobats. Her interest was piqued for a moment before she recoiled in horror. She was becoming as corrupt as the pitiful soiled doves in Lil's parlor.

She had to get out of here. She wanted to be gone before Ryan returned, and somehow the importance of finding Julian was replaced by the paramount need of escaping Ryan Cordell.

Stephanie pulled herself up on the bed pillows, trying to wrest free of the leather bonds holding her. It was impossible, she decided at last. Her wrists were soon chafed and lightly bleeding, and she'd only exhausted herself. Her only recourse was to involve someone else. Help was certain to come along sooner or later.

When she did finally hear footsteps in the hall and a soft, feminine voice singing a popular melody, Stephanie called out.

"Help! Someone please! Help me!"

The voice halted abruptly.

"Please!" Stephanie called again, hoping whoever it was would not panic and run away. "I'm in here—the room at the end of the hall! Please help me . . . !"

There was a tentative knock at the door and the knob slowly turned. Stephanie could have cried with relief.

"Yes! Here I am . . . in here!"

A face peeped cautiously around the door's edge, eyes widening at the sight of Stephanie bound to the bedposts.

"It was you yelling for help?" the girl asked. Her light brown hair tumbled over her forehead and into her eyes, and she shook it back with an impatient movement as she stepped into the room. "What's the matter—did your customer get drunk and leave you?"

"No! I didn't have a customer . . . wait, please!" Stephanie cried out as the girl backed toward the door. "Where are you going?"

"Are you a man or a woman?" the girl asked uncertainly. "Can't tell much by your clothes. Your voice isn't very deep, and your hair's long—see here, is this some kind of joke?"

"I'm a woman, believe me. Untie these straps, please, while I tell you what happened. Please," Stephanie coaxed when the girl still hesitated.

The girl, who couldn't have been much older than eighteen or nineteen, stepped to the edge of the bed with her hands perched on still-girlish hips. A frown creased her smooth brow, and she chewed on her bottom lip as she gazed at Stephanie.

"Just tell me, is this Lil's idea? I won't buck her . . ."

"No. I had an . . . argument . . . with a gentleman, and he did this as a sort of joke, I guess." Stephanie flexed her arms, showing the girl her bleeding wrists. "Only, I think he's gotten drunk and forgotten me. I can't stay here like this all night—please help me."

"As long as it ain't Lil's doin', I don't mind." The girl leaned forward and quickly undid the leather belts binding Stephanie. "There. Now let me get somethin' for those marks on your wrists, I'll be right back."

By the time the girl returned, Stephanie had washed her wrists in the nearby washbasin and was drying them with an embroidered towel. She sat on the bed and motioned for the girl's help.

"What's your name?" she asked the girl curiously. Except for her attire, this girl could have been any girl she'd known in New York, gone to school with, or even one of her cousins. She wore a dress that was cut very low and edged with lace, and the hem was fashioned so that her skirt parted to show her legs as she walked. It was a whore's dress, designed to be stimulating, and somehow it seemed incongruous on this fresh-faced girl who looked as if she had just left her mother's arms.

"My name's Honey," the girl said as she perched on the edge of the bed to bandage Stephanie's arm. After a moment of silence she glanced up at Stephanie and smiled, a kind of shy, surprisingly innocent smile. "Well, really it's Leah but don't nobody here know that. My ma would burn with

217

shame if she ever found out what I'm really doing to make out. She thinks I'm taking care of children." Honey/Leah smiled impishly. "And takin' care of some of these men *is* just like takin' care of children, I can tell you!"

"I won't argue with that," Stephanie murmured feelingly. The girl's next words stiffened Stephanie's resolve to escape quickly.

"'Course, that guy you're with—th' fancy gunslinger, Cordell?—he'd be a dream to be with for a few hours. All the girls here hope he chooses them sometimes—what's the matter?"

"Nothing! Nothing," Stephanie said more quietly, wishing Honey would finish bandaging her wrists and leave. "I'm just edgy, that's all. And Mr. Cordell will be back soon, and I intend to turn his little joke around on him. Can you help me?" Fancy gunslinger—Ryan? She should have known . . .

"Well . . . I don't know," Honey was saying doubtfully. "Seems like I've done enough . . . what do you want me to do?"

"I need more clothes. My saddlebags were lost in a storm recently, and the stores are closed tonight. I'll be glad to return them tomorrow."

"Oh, that! Sure, I can get you something to wear . . . wait a minute." Honey swept her with an appraising glance. "There ain't nobody here tall as you. The gown wouldn't even cover your knees."

"Surely there's something I can wear . . ."

"Yeah, I just thought . . ." Honey giggled. "It's a sure enough elegant dress, too! But don't you tell where you got it, 'cause it's liable to cost me a hair-pullin' fight if you do, hear?"

218

"Of course I won't tell. Hurry now, before Cordell returns and catches me."

By the time Honey returned with the dress, Stephanie had ransacked Ryan's saddlebags, retrieving most of the money she'd already paid him. He hadn't earned it yet, she rationalized her thievery, and she'd left him part of it as compensation for what he had earned, as well as the bearskin. Though she should probably charge him for the trials he'd put her through. No need to think about that now—there would be time later to embark upon guilt-trips.

Very shortly, Stephanie was attired in a pearl-gray gown of shimmering satin, with a surprisingly high neck edged in exquisite lace. It was a little short, but not so short that it showed too much of the boots she wore. With her hair swept up and a covering of net and lace on her head, she looked very presentable and respectable.

"You look lovely" was Honey's verdict. "And I hope Fawn don't find out it was me that borrowed her dress. She'd be madder than a wet hen, she would! It's her Sunday dress."

"I will have it sent around first thing in the morning, Honey, I assure you," Stephanie promised. "I just need it for tonight. Now, do you have a back door to this . . . establishment . . . that I can reach without bumping into a lot of people?"

In just a short time, Stephanie was being ushered out the kitchen door and into a dark alley.

"Keep your pistol handy," Honey warned in a whisper. "No tellin' what you're liable to run into in th' alleyway. An' be careful passin' the saloon, too. Stray drunks come flyin' outa there a lot."

"Thank you, Honey. I won't forget your help."

"It was nothin'. I don't understand why you're runnin' away from a man like Cordell, but that ain't none of my business unless you wanta tell me, so I ain't askin'. Just be careful, 'cause you seem like a nice lady. And you've got the softest hands . . ." A wistful smile tilted Honey's lips upward. "I always thought it'd be nice to have soft, pretty hands like yours, a lady's hands."

Stephanie was stunned for a moment. The girl was much younger, and more vulnerable than she'd realized.

"Take this for your trouble, Honey." Stephanie pressed a bank note in the girl's hand. "Spend it wisely, and save some for a rainy day."

Honey's eyes widened as she saw the hundred-dollar note, then she laughed delightedly. "That's more money than I'm used to gettin' without earnin'! An' there's always rainy days where I sit!" She gave Stephanie a brief hug, then a quick shove toward the street. "Go now, afore someone sees us!"

Stephanie had no problem checking into one of the numerous hotels in Willow Creek. After a brief survey of the choices, she chose the one that looked cleanest and most expensive.

"Hmmm. Stephanie Ashworth," the desk clerk said reflectively as he read her name scrawled on the ledger. He looked at Stephanie over the top of his wire-rim spectacles. "Do you know we had another Ashworth here not so long ago . . ."

"Julian Ashworth?" Stephanie broke in, hardly able to believe her good fortune. "Was it Mr. Julian Ashworth?"

"Let me check . . . yep. Says so right here. Julian S. Ashworth . . . let's see now . . . that was three—no four—days ago. I take it you know him?"

"No. Never heard of him," Stephanie said cheerfully. She motioned for the boy waiting to take up her bags. Julian! And only four days ago! She wasn't far behind him, then, and he had come this way. Perhaps she could catch up with him in the next few days.

Stephanie made no effort to disguise the fact that she'd checked into a hotel, knowing there would be very little Ryan Cordell could do once she was away from him. The risk involved would be too great, especially if he was wanted by the law.

Luxuriating in a tub full of steaming scented water in the privacy of her room, Stephanie let her thoughts stray to the man she had—asininely it turned out—begun to trust. She wanted to scrub away all traces of his hands and mouth on her. She felt betrayed, though he'd not actually done so. If he was wanted by the authorities, couldn't he have trusted her enough to tell her instead of assuming she'd contacted them in order to betray him? And to take her to a common whorehouse like he'd done, had been humiliating in the extreme! Especially after . . . after . . .

No. She wouldn't think about that now. It was too painful for her to think about.

Lifting one leg, Stephanie carefully studied the mounds of soap bubbles on her toes. They caught the light from a Tiffany lamp burning nearby, reflecting miniature rainbows in the transparent spheres. When the bubbles began to evaporate one by one and the rainbows disappeared, she gave a lengthy sigh.

Rainbows never did last long enough.

Wrapping herself in a fat, fluffy towel, Stephanie sat down in front of the ornately carved dresser and studied her reflection. Her hair was clean and wet, and she braided it atop her head to dry in waves. Leaning forward, she examined her complexion anxiously. The Arizona sun and climate had wrought havoc. Instead of being fashionably pale, she now sported a light tan in spite of the hat she'd worn. And horrors—a small spray of golden freckles dusted the tip of her nose.

Stephanie powdered them furiously with the rice powder the hotel had provided for her use.

Sitting back, she gazed at herself again. She looked so different somehow, and it wasn't just the tan she'd acquired, or the freckles. With her hair pulled back from her forehead like she was accustomed to wearing it, and no grubby hat on her head, she still resembled the familiar Stephanie, yet there was a definite difference. Maybe the eyes. They were still dark brown with thick black lashes, and her eyebrows still winged in delicate curves, but there was something else . . .

Oh, rubbish! she told herself sternly, slamming down the tortoiseshell hairbrush she'd been using. She was just the same. Nothing was different on the outside.

She'd just wrapped herself in a dressing gown borrowed from the hotel proprieter's wife when a knock sounded on her door. Supper at last. Better late than never.

The young man who delivered her meal smiled gratefully when Stephanie tipped him.

"Gracias, señorita, gracias!"

"De nada, Tomás." Stephanie's schoolroom Spanish deserted her for the moment, but with the help of gestures and the few words she remembered, she managed to learn from young Tomás what she wanted to know. It earned the boy another tip, and he left happy.

She hadn't realized until sniffing the delectable odors rising from the silver tray, just how hungry for a real meal she'd been. Stephanie's stomach growled expectantly as she lifted each cover from a dish, finding tender green peas, baby carrots, new boiled potatoes, veal, and fresh, hot rolls right from the oven. Heaven! The wine was chilled to exactly the right temperature, and had been imported from France.

For a rural town almost in the middle of nowhere, Willow Creek certainly did manage to do well, she reflected with a contented sigh. Though the food was not up to standards of New York hotels, it was good, simple fare, and delicious.

After eating until she was certain she would burst if she took another bite, Stephanie took the remainder of the bottle of wine and a clean glass and curled up on the wide bed to read. She'd chosen a book at random from the glass-fronted bookshelves, and when she settled back against the plump pillows and opened it, she froze. Shakespeare. Of all the books on those shelves, she had chosen a play by Shakespeare entitled *Love's Labors Lost*—the same play Ryan Cordell had quoted. The book snapped shut.

Unexpected tears filled her eyes, and Stephanie

was horrified to find herself crying. She couldn't hold back the sobs that tore at her, and with a soft cry, she flung the book to the floor and buried her head in the pillow. Damn him for making her feel like this, for giving to her then taking away.

Curling her hands into fists, Stephanie pummeled the pillow again and again, loosing her frustration and pain. It would be a long time before she could forget Ryan Cordell, she thought painfully.

Chapter Seventeen

Deciding to find Huntley and Bates before they found him, Ryan began making the rounds of the saloons. He pushed open the double doors of the Red Dog Saloon and stepped inside. As usual, it was crowded with men and thick with smoke. A piano plinked a lively melody in one corner, and on stage three women billed as "The Triple Threat" were doing some kind of dance number. Their legs kicked high in a flurry of lace and fishnet stockings, toes pointing to the ceiling.

At one side of the room the tables were crowded with men intent on their card games, while others lined the stage to watch the entertainment. The long, curved bar had its usual collection of drinkers.

Ryan was about to decide he recognized no one there, when a voice hailed him from the far, smoky corner.

"Cordell! Hey, Cordell—over here!"

He tensed, instantly recognizing that demanding youthful voice, then started for the table.

"Hello, Billy." Ryan pulled out a chair and sat down without waiting for an invitation. "Thought you were still hanging around Fort Sumner."

"I am. Got business here, though. What you doing in Arizona?"

"Same. Business."

"Profitable business, Cordell?" Billy Bonney lifted his legs to the tabletop and crossed them at the ankle, laughing a little like he always did. Almost every statement was preceded or followed by a laugh or smile.

"Could be profitable, Billy. Heard you gave Governor Wallace the slip."

"Son of a bitch double-crossed me. Said he'd let me go free if I turned evidence, and I kept my end of the bargain." Billy grinned. "He didn't keep his, so I decided it wasn't too healthy stickin' around."

"Yeah, I heard something like that." Ryan shook his head. "You're going to end up bad, Billy, if you don't stay out of New Mexico. Go west, head for California or Oregon, or Idaho. Get away from here and start all over. They'll get you if you don't."

The ever-present smile on Billy the Kid's face widened to a grin. "They might. But there'll be a lot of 'em in hell with me, Cordell. A lot of 'em."

Ryan poured himself a shot of whiskey from Billy's bottle.

"Look, Billy. I knew you when you and your mother and brother lived in New York, when you were still Henry McCarty, and . . ."

"Henry McCarty's dead, Cordell. Dead." There was no smile or grin on Billy's face now, just a seriously intent expression. "I've been William H.

Bonney since 1873, an' that's how I'll die. Don't ruin a long friendship by makin' me remember things I don't want to."

"Fine, Billy. Hide your head if you want to." Ryan tossed down his drink, still keeping his eyes on the trigger-tempered Billy.

"Not many men can say things like that to me, Cordell," Billy said, and the smile was back on his face.

"Not many men like you well enough to give a damn, Billy. You forget—I knew you before you ever killed your first man. Three years is not a long time to get a reputation like yours. How many have you killed face to face?"

Billy grinned widely. "Fourteen."

"In a pig's eye! You can't even outdraw me, Billy, and I'm pretty damned slow, remember?"

Billy's loud laugh captured the attention of the men sitting at the next table, and they glanced nervously from Billy to Ryan. It was no secret who the young man was, but they weren't certain of the other man's identity. Another gunslinger trying to make a name for himself, maybe? It'd be instant notoriety if he outdrew and killed Billy the Kid in front of a roomful of spectators.

But to Ryan and Billy it was a familiar contest, a game they had played many times. Chairs scraped back from the table as they both sprang to their feet, drawing and shooting simultaneously. Two felt hats flew through the air and men scattered wildly, cards and chips going in every direction as they dove for cover.

"Damn, Cordell," Billy observed with a laugh

when he picked up his hat from the floor, "you came pretty damn close that time."

Ryan stuck his finger through a small, charred hole in the crown of his hat. "You weren't too far off yourself, Billy. It's a good thing I know how loyal you are to old friends."

"Yeah, well, I think we better be gettin' outta here pretty quick, Cordell. The sheriff in this town don't like me too much anyway, and those shots'll bring him runnin' fast enough. Listen, if you're ever over on the Pecos River, stop in Fort Sumner and look me up. I've got a good friend there at Beaver Smith's saloon. He's the bartender, and he'll know where I am. Just ask him—his name's Pat Garrett."

Billy was already heading toward the double doors. "'Bye, Ryan Cordell! Watch your back . . ." He disappeared through the doors and into the night without a single soul opposing him.

"'Bye, Billy. You do the same," Cordell muttered quietly. He put his hat back on, straightened the table and set the chairs back up, then tossed a gold coin to the tabletop to pay for any damages.

Leaving the Red Dog, Ryan stopped just outside the doors, considering his next move. To hell with Huntley and Bates tonight. It was late, and he needed to send a telegram. Then he needed to return to the impetuous Stephanie. She would have had plenty of time to think by now, and get over her anger. Damn, what was the matter with her? He was only trying to protect her, wasn't he?

He wheeled and started down the wooden sidewalk stretching next to the buildings. His boots sounded loud against the boards, and there was an odd echo behind him. Someone was following him. Ryan walked another few yards, then paused to light a cigar. He leaned against a wooden post and reached in his vest pocket, while his other hand surreptitiously drew the pistol hanging at his side. There was a brief flare of light as he struck a match against the post and held it to his cigar, making his face a perfect target.

He was waiting for that telltale burst of orange light from a gun muzzle to pinpoint his ambusher's location, when a pistol cracked loudly. Instantly, Ryan whirled and fired at the brief flare, dropping to one knee. There was a cry and the sound of someone hitting the wooden sidewalk several yards south. Remaining in his crouched position, Ryan kept his pistol drawn. Light from a window behind him splashed across the sidewalk, and he edged further into the dark shadows next to the building. One or two men? he wondered. The echo of bootsteps had sounded more like two men—Huntley and Bates.

Hearing the pistol shots, men poured from the saloon to see the cause, standing in tight knots just outside the doors, uncertain of flying bullets. Ryan didn't move, but remained cautiously against the wall watching.

Finally a man either braver or drunker than the others, advanced cautiously to the fallen man lying on the sidewalk. Kneeling beside him, he rolled the man over.

"Dead," he announced loudly, but the corpse protested.

"I ain't dead, you fool, just bleeding to death!"

"Get the doc . . ." another observer suggested.

"Get the sheriff . . ."

In the resulting confusion, Ryan holstered his gun and emerged from the shadows. He edged to the circle surrounding the wounded man. It was Huntley, all right. Damn that worthless excuse for a scout and bushwhacker . . .

And since Huntley was sprawled in the dust, Bates must be close by. Ryan skimmed the crowd, but didn't see anyone who resembled Bates. He backed away slowly. No point in sticking around for the sheriff, he decided. It would just create more confusion and waste too much time.

Ryan had gone no more than a dozen steps before he was confronted by several men.

"That's him! He's the one who shot my partner . . ."

"And he's the one who's friends with the Kid, Sheriff!" another man blurted.

The men stood in a half circle in front of him, and Ryan easily recognized Bates's pudgy face. He seemed very pleased with himself as he stood there backed by more guns.

The sheriff stood to one side, squinting thoughtfully at Ryan and chewing on a cigar stub.

"Did you shoot him, son? This man claims you did." Sheriff Royce rested one hand on the butt of his pistol in a casually menacing pose. "I wouldn't make any sudden moves if I was you, by the way. I've got a man over there with a rifle, who can pick th' eye out of a buzzard at a hundred yards . . ."

"How many shots did you hear?" Ryan asked. "I only fired one. His partner fired first . . ."

"That's a lie!" Bates shouted. "Poor ole Huntley

could barely get off a shot with yer bullet in him!" He turned to the sheriff. "You goin' to let him git away, Sheriff? Why, he's a dangerous outlaw! I bet there's a dozen posters on him in yer office!"

"Yeah, an' he was with th' Kid in th' Red Dog," another man protested. "They looked pretty friendly-like."

Ryan shifted impatiently. "Look, Sheriff . . ."

"Now you just hold on a minute, mister. Mebbe I ought to check you out."

"This was obviously self-defense. Since when do you lock a man up for protecting himself?" Ryan argued.

"Yeah, he says that after shootin' up the Red Dog with Billy the Kid!" a man shouted.

"Come along with me, son," Sheriff Royce said. "I think we need to talk. An' it'll give me a chance to go through my wanted posters at th' same time."

"Look, Sheriff . . ." Ryan took one step forward, and was immediately jumped by Bates and two other men. It took a pistol shot in the air to break up the fight, and Sheriff Royce gave the two men and Bates a disgusted glare.

"Yer real brave boys, all right, but I see that he still managed ta give you what-for, didn't he? Get out of my way . . . !" He roughly shoved Bates and another man and aimed a half-interested kick in their general direction.

"Now get up out of the street, son, an' we'll take our little walk. Ah, yer pistol, please?" he said to Ryan.

*　　　*　　　*

Groggy with sleep, Stephanie groped for the small bedside clock. Two in the morning, and someone was banging on her door.

"Just a minute, just a minute!" she snapped irritably when the knocking grew louder. "Let me get dressed . . ."

Her eyes widened when Sheriff Royce loomed in her doorway, chewing a cigar stub and smelling strongly of rye whiskey.

"Evenin', ma'am. Disturb your rest?" He briefly lifted his hat then replaced it on his head and squinted at her as he stepped in and shut the door behind him.

"No, of course not, Sheriff. Why would pounding on my door at two in the morning disturb me?"

"You left Lil's without tellin' anyone. Why?"

"Am I under arrest, Sheriff? Was it necessary for me to keep you posted as to my whereabouts every moment? I just understood that I was not to leave town without informing you."

"Yeah." The sweat-stained hat lifted briefly as he scratched his head. "Well, maybe I forgot to tell you. Why'd you leave?"

"Because I was not comfortable staying in a house that caters to men, Sheriff, nor am I comfortable being dragged from my bed at two in the morning to be asked questions that could just as easily be asked in daylight. Do you have a point to make?"

"Kinda. This good wine?" Royce lifted the almost empty bottle and sniffed the mouth.

"Yes. It's excellent wine. The point, Sheriff?" She crossed her arms over her chest.

"Got a man in custody says you hired him as a

guide. Says he's the man who brought you here this afternoon. Name's Ryan Cordell. That right?"

Stephanie was silent for a moment. Here was an excellent opportunity for revenge against Ryan. Maybe some time spent in a jail cell would do him some good.

"Maybe," she said pleasantly. "Why are you holding him?"

"Look. It's either maybe yes, or maybe no, but not just maybe. Which is it?"

"Now, that depends on the man, Sheriff. Anyone can call themselves by that name. Surely you know that." Stephanie took a clean wineglass from the cabinet against one wall. "Wine, Sheriff? Do have some. It was an excellent year."

"Why, thanks. Don't mind if I do."

Stephanie winced as Royce poured the wine down his throat like he would have a shot of rye. Such a waste.

"Now, why did you say you're holding this man, Sheriff?"

"Didn't. But I'm holdin' him 'cause I got a poster that he fits. Big reward, too. Says he was with Billy the Kid and involved in them Lincoln County Wars in Texas a couple of years ago. New Mex Governor Lew Wallace offered the Kid a pardon if he surrendered, but he didn' say nothin' about the guys who rode with him. Cordell fits th' description of a man callin' hisself Jack Robinson, but he says he's been guidin' you the past two weeks. Just got the poster today, and it says Robinson escaped Lincoln County jail two weeks ago. Now, what I need to know is if Cordell is the man who brought you from

233

Fort Defiance."

Stephanie was tempted to tell the truth and free Ryan, but, prompted by vengeance, she didn't. And she wanted Ryan to know it.

"I won't know without seeing him, Sheriff. If you'll pardon me, I'll dress and go take a look at the gentleman in question."

Wearing the pearl-gray dress, Stephanie followed the sheriff to the jailhouse. It was a square brick building heavily fortified with bars.

"Had a lynching a few years back, an' decided to put up bars so it wouldn't be as likely to happen again," Royce explained. "They'd have to use dynamite to get in here now." He swung open a door behind his desk. It led into a darkened hall, and the sheriff grabbed a lantern. "Follow me," he said cheerfully.

Stephanie quelled a shudder as she followed him down the long, dim hall. She wished she'd brought a scented handkerchief to put over her nose. It smelled like . . . no, better not think about that.

"This is the one," he said, stopping so suddenly that Stephanie almost bumped into him. She hastily pressed her hand to her mouth to still a soft cry.

When Sheriff Royce lifted his lantern high, the light sprayed over Ryan sitting on a cot with his back against the wall. He looked as if he had been in a fight with a panther. His face was bruised and scratched, and one eye was swollen almost shut. She swallowed hard.

"Know him?"

Steeling herself as Ryan slowly and painfully rose from the cot to step to the bars, Stephanie began to

234

shake her head in denial.

"No. I . . . I've never seen him before . . ."

"Stephanie! For Christ's sake, I know you're mad, but find some other way to get even," Ryan exploded. "Stephanie!" he yelled when she whirled and ran back down the hallway.

His muffled curses rang in her ears as she fled, and when she reached the steps outside the jailhouse, Stephanie gulped in lungfuls of fresh night air. There was a cold, hard lump in the pit of her stomach, and she felt nauseous. A Judas. She was a Judas, but he hadn't deserved any better. So why did she feel so bad?

"What," she asked the sheriff, "will happen to him?"

"If he's Robinson, he'll hang. If not . . ." Royce shrugged. "Depends on how many other posters I may have on him. If he's got other charges against him somewhere, I'll notify th' marshal. Man like that's liable to be wanted in ten different states."

"And . . . and how long will it take before you know for certain?"

"Oh, th' way th' mail usually runs, couple of weeks, maybe. Maybe longer." Royce rocked back on his heels and gazed up at the stars. "Nice night, isn't it? Sorry to drag you out for nothin', Miss . . . Ashworth, was it? Wonder how this fellow knew your name and all. Oh well." He shook his head. "Some men'll grab at any straw, even hidin' behind a woman's skirts, I guess. Here. I'll walk you back to your hotel . . ."

"No. No, I'll be fine, Sheriff. It's not far, and you can just watch me to the door if you like." Stephanie managed a parody of a smile. "Please inform me the moment you receive an answer to my wire. Good night."

"'Night." Sheriff Royce stared thoughtfully after Stephanie as she crossed the street to the wooden sidewalks. "Mighty peculiar," he muttered. "Wonder why she wouldn't admit ta knowin' him."

Well. Wasn't any of his business if she knew the man or didn't. His business was collecting the rewards.

Chapter Eighteen

The lobby of the Hotel St. Charles was almost deserted when Stephanie entered, which was not surprising considering the fact that it was almost three in the morning. The desk clerk was behind the gleaming desk, nodding sleepily, and there was a young boy halfheartedly swiping at the floors with a carpet sweeper as she crossed to the curving staircase. They didn't appear to even notice Stephanie, so she was startled when a hand suddenly grabbed her arm as she took the first few steps.

"Excuse me, ma'am . . ."

"Oh! You . . . you startled me . . . what do you want?" She shook her arm free and turned to look at the vaguely familiar stranger on the step just below her. He looked like a grubby cowhand, with dust-grimed clothes and a battered felt hat he was holding in his hands. A well-worn gun hung low on one hip like a gunfighter would carry it, she noticed, and his face was unshaven. Stephanie immediately decided she didn't like the way his round little eyes shifted and would not meet hers, and her voice was cold as she demanded again, "What do you want?"

"You . . . you're Stephanie Ashworth, right?"

"And if I am . . . ?"

"Well, ma'am, maybe you don't remember, but back at the fort your pa hired me an' my partner to guide you to him . . ."

"What is your name?"

"Bates, ma'am, Alvin Bates. An' my pardner's name is Huntley. Do you remember?" His voice rose when Stephanie flashed him a look of scorn and turned to go. "Wait, I can see what you're thinkin', an' it's not th' truth of it! Th' reason we left Fort Defiance wuz because of Cordell . . . he waylaid me an' my pardner, told us to git out of th' way or he'd kill us. That's th' truth of it, ma'am, I swear."

Stephanie didn't doubt the veracity of his statement, but she didn't trust Bates, either. He wasn't the kind of man one would trust, and she was usually a pretty good judge of character. Her biggest mistake in judgment had been Ryan Cordell, but maybe it wasn't too late to rectify that.

"So what do you want with me now, Mr. Bates? It's late and I'm very tired . . ."

"Did you know that Cordell shot Huntley a couple of hours ago, Miss Ashworth? It's th' truth . . ."

"I'm aware that Cordell is in jail, yes. Did you come here this late at night to tell me that?"

Bates wiped at his forehead with the back of one hand. Talking to this lady wasn't as easy as he'd thought it would be. She was a lot like her pa, Bates thought disgustedly. He hitched up his trousers and smiled ingratiatingly.

"Well, I thought that . . . seein' as how Cordell won't be goin' ennywhere for a while . . . you'd be needin' another guide. An' since yer pa hired us first . . ."

"I thought your partner was shot?"

"He is. Just in the arm, though. He'll be all right to ride." Bates sidled closer, not noticing the way Stephanie wrinkled her nose at the smell of sweat and whiskey. "What do you say, Miss Ashworth? You need a guide, an' if yer pa hired us, you know he knew we could do the job."

"Let me think on it, Mr. Bates. I will contact you sometime tomorrow. It's late now and I've had a very full day. Leave a message with the desk clerk as to where you can be reached, please. Now, good night."

"'Night." Bates watched with a sullen frown as Stephanie pulled her skirts away and continued up the stairs. She was uppity, in his opinion, just like her old man. Didn't matter, though. Gold was a great equalizer.

Stephanie felt a sense of relief when she'd shut and bolted the door to her room. Bates was definitely not the kind of man she would trust to guide her to the nearest milliner's shop, much less to Julian. Why on earth had her father hired the men? It wasn't like him to be so obtuse. Stephanie shrugged out of the light shawl she wore around her shoulders, and draped it over the back of a chair. Julian had probably hired them by letter, and never met them. That was the only explanation.

She sank to the firm comfort of the bed and buried her face in her hands. Damn. In spite of all he'd done to her, she felt guilty for not admitting she knew

Ryan. He was locked up in jail, and even though he should probably be kept there, she felt responsible. Why should she feel guilty? Ryan *had* shot a man, hadn't he? Sheriff Royce wouldn't be able to keep him in jail indefinitely for a clear case of self-defense. After all, Huntley had just been shot in the arm, not killed.

There was no point in worrying about Ryan. He was a man who could take care of himself, and she should go on to find Julian. Her father had been through Willow Creek recently, and she did have the map . . . the map! A feeling of panic swept through Stephanie. Her saddlebags had been lost in the mountains, and the map had been in her saddlebags! Oh, why hadn't she thought of it before? Now how would she find Julian?

Stephanie collapsed in a forlorn heap of satin. Staring into space, she reflected that the situation had grown hopeless. She would have to admit failure. She'd go back to Fort Defiance for Claudia and return to New York without having done what she set out to do. It was galling, and Ryan would be smug and satisfied when he found out about it. Ryan . . . he hadn't even referred to the map most of the time. He seemed to have committed it to memory. Would he reproduce it for her?

First thing in the morning, Stephanie decided, she would return to that awful jailhouse and ask Ryan if he would draw her a map . . . No, that wouldn't work. After her refusal to help him, he certainly wouldn't help her.

Stephanie rested her chin in her palm and stared gloomily at the rose-patterned wallpaper. There were few alternatives. Either she could catch the next train home, or swallow her pride and tell Sheriff Royce the truth. He would want to know why she'd lied, of course, and it would be very embarrassing. What choices did she have? She had to have Ryan . . .

Oh, her head hurt and she was sleepy, and this was becoming entirely too much to think about. Tomorrow morning would be soon enough to think of something. Daylight would put a fresh perspective on matters, and her usually agile brain would begin to function normally again.

But morning brought no simple solution to her dilemma. Stephanie still couldn't think of another answer to her problem. She paced the thick carpet in her room for nearly an hour before finally conceding defeat.

A short time later she was dressed in a new gown she'd ordered from one of the finer shops, and was on her way to see the sheriff. It would take all her powers of persuasion to manage this, Stephanie told herself grimly as she mounted the shallow wooden stairs to the jailhouse.

"Good morning, Sheriff." Stephanie stood outlined in the open door of his office as he squinted against the sudden shaft of morning light in his eyes.

"Mornin'. Shut th' door, please. All that bright light hurts an old man's eyes." Sheriff Royce swept Stephanie's new gown with an appraising glance. "Got new duds, huh? Expect ta stay in town awhile?"

"Not really, Sheriff. It's just that all my garments were lost in an accident. Have you had a response to my wire?"

She perched on the edge of Royce's desk and drew

off the lace gloves that exactly matched the brilliant blue satin of her dress. Stephanie watched Royce as she tucked the gloves into her matching purse. She knew full well that the color of her dress was the perfect foil for her silvery hair and golden complexion, and that the ebony ostrich plume in her hat was tilted at just the right angle to emphasize the size and brilliance of her eyes. It daintily brushed the high arch of her brows whenever she moved her head. A fashionable hat was more effective than many ploys used on a man, and Stephanie considered it much more ladylike and subtle than a low-cut gown.

"Uhh, answer to yer wire? As a matter of fact," Sheriff Royce said, tearing his eyes away from Stephanie's lovely face, "Henry brought one in a few minutes ago. Hadn' made it over ta yer hotel with it yet." He snuffled a mound of papers on his desk, finally identifying and extracting one. "This is it. Says yer who you say you are, all right, and gives th' bank instructions on a draft for ya some money." He peered at her over the stub of cigar still in his mouth. "You joinin' yer father? Th' clerk at th' St. Charles tells me he was through here a few days ago."

"Yes, I am." Stephanie smiled to mask her surprise at Royce's thoroughness. "I'm really quite capable of 'roughing it', Sheriff. Though dressed as I am now, I know that I look nothing like the cowboy you first met. I enjoy the rigors of the trail, and sleeping outside under the stars. It's a quirk of mine, I suppose. Now, about the gentleman you're holding—Mr. Cordell, I believe you said his name was— I'd like to post his bond, Sheriff. I've . . . recently discovered . . . that he knew my father, and is the only man who can guide me to him."

"Cain't do that, missy. Sorry." The sheriff's tone was adamant. He waved one hand in the air, trailing swirls of gray cigar smoke. "I ain't worried 'bout that shootin' last night, an' he ain't Robinson, but I'm holdin' him until I hear if he's wanted in Texas. An' he was seen with the Kid last night at the Red Dog, so he's got some explainin' to do anyway."

"The Kid?" she echoed, feeling her heart sink. Royce couldn't mean to really keep Ryan in jail!

"Yeah, William H. Bonney, otherwise known as Billy the Kid. Tough little punk, I say. Somebody shoulda killed him a long time ago. Now he's like a rabid dog, goin' around doin' exactly like he wants . . . ah, that's another story. This Cordell fella's gonna stay right here until I hear back. Found an old poster in th' back of my drawer, here, an' I've a feelin' he's still wanted pretty bad somewhere. You can find another guide, missy. You wouldn' want to be followin' this killer around."

Stephanie didn't relish confessing that she'd been doing exactly that for the past two weeks. Damn! She certainly hadn't counted on Royce being so stubborn about his prisoner. So much for the hat being able to work miracles, she sighed to herself, and immediately concentrated on another tactic.

"May I speak to your prisoner for a few moments, Sheriff? Perhaps he can suggest someone capable of being my guide . . ."

Royce narrowed his eyes at Stephanie suspiciously.

"Now see here, young lady, you're not foolin' me one bit with this play-actin'. You know Cordell, an' probably know him pretty well. I don' know why you didn' want ta admit it last night, but now that I seen his description on a poster, it don' matter. He's here, and here he stays until I hear back from Texas."

"You didn't answer my question, Sheriff," Stephanie said coolly, as if his vehement reply didn't matter in the least. "May I please speak to your prisoner?"

Royce's eyebrows raised a fraction, then he slammed both hands down on the table.

"You beat all, missy, you surely do! Yeah, you can talk to my prisoner, but don' get any big ideas." He grinned. "Not that I don' trust you, but . . ."

"That's quite all right. Would you prefer having someone search me?"

"Naw. If you was carryin' a cannon, it wouldn' help Cordell none. He's in there to stay until I let him out."

Stephanie didn't comment as she followed Sheriff Royce down the dim hall. It took several moments for her eyes to adjust to the change in light, and when Royce halted in front of a cell she bumped into him, squashing her nose against the back of his head. Somewhat startled, Royce half turned to peer at her.

"Bit anxious, ain't ya? Well, here he is, missy. Have a nice chat!"

After Royce's footsteps faded away, Stephanie stepped close to the iron bars of Ryan's cell, still rubbing her nose. She could barely see him sitting inside the dark cubicle with his back propped against the wall. Sunlight slanted in through a barred window high over his head, and the striped pattern on the floor provided the only light. She waited a moment, but Ryan said nothing, didn't even move, but sat silently in the shadows.

It was what he didn't say rather than anything he could have said that stung Stephanie's conscience more than she'd thought possible.

"Well," she said at last when the silence was more than she could bear, "*I* didn't know he was going to dig up old posters, did I?"

Silence.

"Ryan, you can hardly blame me for something you must have done before you met me, can you?"

The silence bristled with animosity.

"Oh, Ryan . . . !"

Stephanie was horrified to find herself on the brink of tears, a weakness she despised. She sniffed audibly and pulled a lace hanky from her bodice. Dabbing at her nose with it, she stared unhappily at the dark shadow that was Ryan.

"Oh, Ryan, please forgive me. I tried to make amends with the sheriff. I offered to post your bail; I even told him that you were acquainted with my father, and that I had hired you. But he wouldn't change his mind. He says he's going to wait on an answer from Texas . . . Ryan, you haven't committed any crimes, have you?" Stephanie pressed close to the bars and curled her fingers around them. She stared at Ryan through the slats, resting her forehead against the cold metal and crushing the ostrich feather dangling from her hat in the process.

Ryan shifted, swinging both his long legs over the side of the narrow bunk. His hands rested on the bunk's edge and his broad shoulders hunched forward as he stared at Stephanie. All she could see of

245

his face in the dim light was the silver glitter of his eyes.

"Have you, Ryan?" she asked again when he still didn't answer her.

"A little late to worry about that now, isn't it?" His voice was rough with anger. "You should have thought of that before Royce did, and got me out of here before he checked his posters. Now I'm stuck here, thanks to you, Miss Ashworth."

Stephanie flinched at the familiar, hard edge of sarcasm in Ryan's tone.

"Ryan, I'm so sorry! I didn't think . . ."

"*That's* the understatement of the year . . ."

". . . that you'd be kept very long," she finished with another tearful sniff. "Please say you forgive me."

"Don't be ridiculous."

"Then you forgive me?"

"No. I don't forgive you at all, you hardheaded, pea-brained female!" Rage made his voice almost a growl, and he controlled it with an effort.

"Stephanie," he said more calmly, "why don't you just go back to your hotel room? Please . . . forget that you even know me. You've done enough damage, and I've got to concentrate on getting out of here."

"But what about me? What am I going to do now? *I* can't find my father by myself, and there certainly doesn't seem to be any decent man in this town that I'd trust to guide me." Stephanie stamped her foot in frustration.

Ryan stared at her as if he couldn't quite believe his ears. His solid frame blocked the small square of light slanting through the window as he rose from the bunk and crossed to the bars. He gripped the cold iron and leaned forward, standing so close his nose almost brushed against Stephanie's in spite of the barrier.

"You selfish little beast," he said softly. He should be furious, but instead he was merely amused. It was so in keeping with her character that she would still think only of her goal. "My being in jail is really inconveniencing you, isn't it? You should have told all, Princess, then Royce might have let me go. But no. You had to sull up like a bloated toad . . ."

"Bloated toad!"

". . . and now I'm here for a while. Should have thought about that, shouldn't you?"

"Oh, I am sorry, Ryan, I am! Why, I'll get you an attorney, and . . ."

"Perish the thought!" Ryan gave a mock shudder. "To paraphrase Benjamin Franklin—'Necessity has no law; most attorneys are the same.' No thanks, Princess. You keep any attorney you might meet away from me. I'd rather be in jail." He touched the tip of her nose with his finger. "Go back to New York, Stephanie. This is one expedition with your father that you'll have to miss. There should be a train or stage leaving Willow Creek soon."

"Ryan Cordell," Stephanie said firmly, pushing away from the bars of his cell, "I do *not* intend to miss this expedition. I may be late, but I do intend to finish what I began!" She gave him a sharp glance. "I don't know why, but for some reason, you've been trying to get rid of me since the first day we left the fort. And there seems to be a great deal of interest stirring about my father's discovery. First, you seem a little too interested—don't bother with denials—and now that wretched guide who deserted me at the fort is haunting me."

Ryan's mouth tightened. "Bates? Are you talking about Bates?"

"Yes. Bates—the man you so politely invited to leave Fort Defiance so I'd have to hire you. Bates—the man my father originally suggested I have guide me. Though I'm sure he could never have met him or he wouldn't have," she added thoughtfully. Then, squaring her shoulders: "I do not intend to put up with any more of your stubbornness, Mr. Cordell. I don't know why Lieutenant Buckner suggested you as a guide unless you paid him a great deal, but you signed an agreement . . ."

"That damned piece of paper!"

". . . and I insist that you live up to it. If you try to escape me, I shall wire Allan Pinkerton immediately . . ."

"Ah, the redoubtable Mr. Pinkerton . . ."

". . . and have him find you. He's the best, you know."

"So I've heard." A mocking smile tilted Ryan's lips, deepening the grooves on each side of his mouth. "It'd be a waste of time and money, Princess. I'm stuck in jail, remember? I can't escape Royce, much less you."

"Oh yes. I remember that fact quite well." Frowning, Stephanie chewed her bottom lip for a moment. "I'll do what I can about that. Perhaps Uncle George can help. After all, he's very influential in Washington . . ."

A FREE ZEBRA
HISTORICAL
ROMANCE
WORTH

$3.95

BUSINESS REPLY MAIL
FIRST CLASS   PERMIT NO. 276   CLIFTON, NJ

POSTAGE WILL BE PAID BY ADDRESSEE

ZEBRA HOME SUBSCRIPTION SERVICE
P.O. Box 5214
120 Brighton Road
Clifton, New Jersey 07015

Ryan groaned. "God save us all from beauties and bureaucrats! Stephanie, don't you dare wire your uncle, do you hear me? Stephanie!"

She pulled out of his reach just as he grabbed for her, and Ryan was left with a fistful of ebony ostrich plume. He glared ominously as Stephanie waggled her fingers from a safe distance and bid him farewell.

"I'll be back soon," she promised, ignoring the strangled oaths that followed her down the hall.

Chapter Nineteen

But Stephanie did not return to the jail in quite the way she had in mind. She was sitting glumly in her hotel room pondering any and all viable solutions, when opportunity knocked lightly on her door.

At first, the slight young man with the ready smile did not impress her in the least. Until he solemnly told her his name, and that he was a friend of Ryan's.

"My name's Billy, ma'am. Billy Bonney, an' Cordell an' me have known each other for too long to count. Seems like he's in a bit of trouble that's partly my fault, an' I plan to get him out of it. You game to help me?"

Stunned, and somewhat nervous, Stephanie hesitated. It was only when the young man handed her his pistol butt-end first and vowed sincerity that she nodded and gestured for him to come in.

"Why do you come to me, Mr. Bonney?"

Stephanie watched him in the mirror over the liquor cabinet as she poured them both a drink. Billy had politely removed his hat, and she was surprised at how young he seemed. He wore a smile as he answered.

"Well, me an' Lil have been friends for a long time, an' she suggested you might want to help. She'd help, but she has to live here and Royce could make it mighty uncomfortable for working girls. Thanks," he said, taking the drink Stephanie offered. "You didn't answer me. You interested in helping get Cordell out?"

"Yes. How do you propose to do so?"

Billy's constant smile widened into a grin. "Robbin' a bank."

Stephanie stared blankly for a moment. "Robbing a bank?" she echoed. "How will that help him?"

"Simple. While I'm creating a diversion at one end of the town, you're springing Cordell at the other end. See how it works?"

"I suppose you have all the necessary details worked out?"

"Of course. All you need to do is find where Royce keeps the keys to the cells. From there on out, it's easy."

"But there's always someone at the jailhouse, even if you are creating a diversion elsewhere. Sheriff Royce will simply leave a deputy in charge while he investigates," Stephanie argued. "What do I do about that?"

"Now, I'd say shootin' the deputy would be the thing to do, but I can tell that you wouldn't like that idea." Billy laughed softly at Stephanie's horrified expression. "Don't like it, huh? Didn't think you would. Let's try this, then . . ."

Scudding clouds masked the moon, a fact for which Stephanie was infinitely grateful. With her back pressed close to the walls, she crept along in the deepest shadows, stealthily making her way along the wooden sides of the buildings not far from the adobe jailhouse. Billy's plan seemed foolproof—a fact which should be like a red flag of warning. Foolproof plans never were. So, why was she doing this?

Simple answer, of course. She had to free Ryan. And she had to free him quickly, before Royce discovered some terrible crime in his past and sent him back to Texas. Stephanie blinked at the thought. Why was she anxious to free a man who might have committed terrible crimes? And why, in heaven's name, was she joining forces with a known criminal like Billy the Kid in order to do so? This had to be— bar none—the most insane act she had ever committed. She should probably be thrown into jail. Stephanie amended that to probably *would* be thrown into jail, if plans went awry.

Shifting slightly away from a wall, she peered at the squat adobe building crouched at the end of the street. Everything was peaceful and quiet. Only the occasional barking of a sleepy dog broke the silence. Even the saloons were deserted.

Dressed once more in trousers and shirt, she had slipped out the back exit of the St. Charles Hotel. Who would think much of a scruffy cowboy emerging from an alley? If anyone thought about it at all, they would simply think she was another drunken cowhand who'd lost his way.

Well. Now she was here, and all she could do was cross her fingers and hope things went off as planned. Holding her breath, Stephanie gathered her courage and ran in a crouch across the dusty street to the jailhouse. Her legs were shaking badly when she finally reached it, and she flattened herself against one wall of the jailhouse and took several deep gulps of air. Her heart was racing madly, and she waited for a moment before easing up the steps. When her boots clattered too loud against the wooden porch, she whipped back against the mud wall and hoped no one had heard.

Several minutes ticked slowly past, and nothing inside stirred. Light shone through the window and from beneath the door, and Stephanie edged cautiously forward. Bars covered the one window, and she squinted through them to peer inside.

A man sat behind the desk with his feet propped on its paper-littered surface. His hat was pulled over his eyes and his arms were crossed over his chest as he leaned back in the chair and slept. It wasn't the sheriff, Stephanie decided. It must be the deputy. Where was Royce?

That question was answered a moment later when she heard a shattering explosion. The noise brought the deputy surging to his feet amidst a shower of papers from the desk while Royce stumbled sleepily from a back room. Steeling herself, Stephanie remained at the window as Royce buckled on his guns and grabbed his hat. She had to see where he kept the keys to Ryan's cell.

Narrowing her eyes, she murmured a brief prayer they would both investigate the cause of the explosion. She was disappointed when Royce ordered the deputy to remain.

"Stay here, Campbell! An' keep yer eyes open!" Royce told the deputy. He crossed to the door, and Stephanie poised for flight, tensing her muscles as she waited until the last possible moment to move away. Her efforts were rewarded as Royce paused, fumbled in a coat pocket, then tossed a small ring of keys in Campbell's direction. "An' hold on ta these," Royce ordered as he yanked open the door.

Stephanie dove for the shadows as Royce emerged. She waited until he'd puffed halfway down the street before edging back to the still-open door. Taking a deep breath, Stephanie pulled her kerchief up over her nose and mouth and stepped around the door.

For a moment the deputy didn't notice her. He was picking up the papers scattered across the floor when he'd leaped to his feet. As he straightened, he saw the slim figure standing with feet apart and gun drawn, the muzzle aiming directly at his chest.

"What th' hell . . . ?"

"Don't move," Stephanie said gruffly. She gestured with her Colt and the deputy halted the instinctive reach for his gun. "Now, Deputy, go real slow and easy, one step at a time, and stand in the middle of the room," she ordered. "That's right. No quick move, or it might be your last . . . drop your gun to the floor, very slowly . . ."

God, Stephanie thought, I should have been an actress! She was beginning to sound just like a character in a dime novel, and the dialogue could have been lifted from any of the publications.

"What do you want, mister?" Campbell asked nervously. His unbuckled gunbelt slid to the floor with a thunk, and he kicked it slightly away when Stephanie's gun waggled directions. Licking his lips, he eyed the barrel of the Colt pointing at his midsection.

"The keys. Hand me those keys." Stephanie waggled her gun when Campbell hesitated. "Now! Just throw them on the floor . . . gently, Deputy . . ."

The keys clinked to the floor, and the Colt motioned for the deputy to turn around.

"Slowly," Stephanie said, "and put your hands behind your head. That's right, Campbell. You're doing good. Now this next part is kinda tricky, because I'm probably as nervous as you are, so pay attention." She edged around him to the door leading to the hall and Ryan's cell. There was no sound, nothing to indicate another deputy's presence, and she breathed a sigh of relief. One was more than she could handle . . .

"Keep looking at that wall, Deputy," she told him as she moved behind him once again. Stephanie deftly scooped up the keys and slid the steel ring over her wrist, then repositioned the kerchief which had begun to slip. She was sweating, yet her hands were cold and clammy. Nerves, not heat, she decided. "Now down the hall, Deputy, all the way to the end."

Hopefully, Ryan would still be in the same cell. God, it was impossible to see anything in the dark hallway. The only light was the glow from the outer office and gauzy rays of fitful moonlight through the barred windows.

"Ryan?" Stephanie's gruffly disguised voice quivered through the dark shadows as she peered anxiously into the cells. "Where are you?"

"Here . . ." His voice cut off abruptly, but she'd recognized it. "Last cell. Who is it?"

The muted clank of chains rattled in the inky shrouds of night, ghostly and eerie, and the hair on the back of Stephanie's neck stood on end. Chains? Oh, nooo . . .

"A friend," she answered tersely, hoping Ryan wouldn't recognize her and say her name aloud. The plan centered around her remaining unidentified and returning to the hotel as if she'd never left. The deputy slowed, and she poked him with the long barrel of her Colt. "Keep moving, Deputy. Is the prisoner wearing chains?"

"Yeah."

His answer made Stephanie groan softly. Another time-eating obstacle—just what they needed. It would only take Billy a short time to carry out his part, then the sheriff would figure out the explosion must be a ruse. She had to hurry . . .

"Faster!" The Colt's barrel shoved into the deputy again. The keys on Stephanie's arm rattled as she shook them from her wrist to her hand and held them out to the deputy. "Open the door, then his chains."

"Can't . . ."

"Don't tell me that!" Anxiety made her voice even lower and gruffer, and there was no mistaking the harsh bite of fear in her tone. "You better get them open now, Deputy, if you have to chew through them yourself . . ."

"All right, all right! Only quit pokin' me with that damned gun! I've likely got dents in my back now from it . . ."

"Better dents than holes . . ."

Stephanie was more serious than she'd ever been, and her tenseness made the deputy's hands shake as he took the keys. He was sweating and the keys slipped slightly, earning him another poke from the gun barrel, but he got the door unlocked.

"Now the chains."

The terse reminder had Campbell bending quickly to unlock the manacles fastened around Cordell's ankles. His fingers were trembling so that it took him precious minutes, but finally the chains clanked to the hard floor. Before he could stand, an iron fist slammed into his temple and he slumped unconscious to the floor.

"Why'd you do that?" Stephanie whispered in her gruff voice. "I was going to lock him in the cell . . ."

"We still are. I just don't need him yelling for help any time soon. Where are the horses?"

Ryan was all business, dragging Campbell into the cell and tying his hands behind him with his own belt, then stuffing the hapless deputy's handkerchief in his mouth.

"The horses? Oh, they're behind the North Church, all saddled and ready. Lil saw to that . . ."

"Good for Lil." Ryan paused, and in the fuzzy light Stephanie could see him staring at her. "Stephanie?"

257

"Yes."

"Good God! You idiot!" Harsh hands gripped her by the shoulders and began to shake her so hard her head snapped back and forth like a rag doll's. She bit her tongue, and the sharp pain made her cry out.

Ryan released her instantly, at the same time snatching her Colt from her hand.

"What made you do this?" he demanded furiously, whirling her around and pushing her toward the end of the hall. "Not only could you have gotten yourself killed, but now your lovely little face is going to be on every wanted poster within five hundred miles."

Stephanie jerked away, breathing hard and fast as she glared at him in the dim light.

"I'm wearing a mask, see?" she defended herself, then grew angry at his snort of derision. "Look, damn you, you ungrateful beast, I was only trying to help . . ."

"How? By getting yourself killed? Great idea, but I don't want *that* on my conscience . . ."

"Since when have you had anything remotely resembling a conscience, Ryan Cordell?"

"Oh, for Chrissake! Why did I ever have to get tangled up with a New York society belle? Every man you meet is lacking in something . . ."

"Perhaps because I found you under a rock, I underestimated you," Stephanie began. Her words were cut short by the sound of confusion in the streets.

Pistol and rifle shots rang out, capturing their attention. Stephanie's eyes widened.

"Those sounded close . . ."

"They are!" Ryan retorted. "I hope those long legs

of yours are good for something besides looks, because you're going to need 'em . . ."

He yanked her with him into the brightly lit office. A row of gunbelts hung from wooden pegs, and he quickly located his and grabbed them from the wall. Tossing Stephanie her Colt, Ryan blew out the desk lantern, plunging the office into darkness.

"This way," he said, taking Stephanie by the arm and shoving her toward the door. "Go to the left, and back behind the building . . . Keep down, dammit!"

Stephanie ducked down, running in a crouch across the porch. She leaped to the dusty street and began running close to the side of the jailhouse, keeping to the shadows as far as she could. Behind her she could hear Ryan's spurs jingle as he kept pace.

A shot rang out, and something that felt like a honeybee whizzed past her ear. Where was her hat? It was gone somehow, and the kerchief slipped from her nose to hang loosely around her neck. That didn't matter. Nothing mattered but fleeing the bullets that seemed to fly as thick as a swarm of bees over their heads. Ryan was right behind her, one hand pressed against her back as a guide.

"This way!" he hissed. "The North Church is right over there . . ."

Blindly, terrified and feeling as if her legs would refuse to move at any moment, Stephanie ran. The Colt was still gripped in her fingers, but she could not have used it if a tiger had suddenly leaped in front of her.

By the time they reached the horses, Billy was already there, grinning jauntily at them as he flung them their reins.

"Took you long enough, Cordell! Bet you didn't expect to see me . . ."

"I didn't expect to see either one of you," Ryan replied grimly. "Dammit, Billy, why'd you involve her?"

Ryan half flung Stephanie to the top of her horse, then stepped into his saddle and pivoted his stallion. The three riders raced from town with a half-dozen mounted men close behind.

Because of the darkness, it was much easier to escape. They doubled back once, then cut across their own trail in order to confuse the posse in the daylight. To Stephanie, it was all a blur, and she hardly knew what was happening. She just followed their instructions, riding up rocky slopes and along crests, hiding in clumps of brush and holding her horse's nose to keep it from nickering—anything they told her to do. It was easier than thinking, because if she started thinking she would probably sit down and cry.

By dawn, she was exhausted. She sat numbly as Ryan and Billy spoke quietly just out of earshot, too tired to even wonder what they were talking about. It didn't matter now. She was a criminal. Ryan was right. Her face would be on wanted posters all over Arizona Territory. How much reward would they offer? Stephanie wondered dazedly. Would they use her real name, or make up some romantic title? Oh, God, she must be delirious to even be thinking this! She should be planning a way out of her predicament instead of wondering if her portrait on a poster would be flattering.

"Ma'am?" Billy Bonney reined his horse next to Stephanie's. The early morning light caught in the soft waves of his light brown hair, reminding Stephanie of a young cousin in New York. Billy's gaze was clear and direct, and the ever-present smile curved his mouth. "I want to tell you how sorry I am that our plan messed up. Ryan's called me every kind of an idiot, and I guess he's right. But don't you worry none. If anybody can get you out of this, Cordell's your man. I'm back to the Pecos River now that my business is done. It's been a pleasure meetin' you, Miss Ashworth. You're a real lady."

"Thank you," Stephanie managed to say. "And it's not your fault things didn't work out. I knew the risk."

His smile deepened into a wicked grin, and Billy leaned forward to place a quick kiss on Stephanie's cheek.

"Top that, Cordell!" he crowed, laughing. Billy slapped his hat against his thigh and pivoted his horse in a half rear, waving a cheerful farewell before he cantered in the opposite direction.

"It's hard to believe he's earned a reputation as a brutal killer," Stephanie murmured. She didn't realize she'd spoken aloud until Ryan answered.

"Believe it. I've seen him shoot a man in the back and laugh while he did it. Billy's loyal in a fashion, but more loyal to himself than anyone else."

Ryan nudged his stallion close, so close his leg brushed Stephanie's.

"So, Miss Ashworth—what'cha gonna do?"

261

Stephanie gave him a blank stare. "What?"

"I thought you had this escape all planned. What now?"

She blinked. Her head hurt. Her hat was gone, her hands were torn and bleeding from the leather reins and prickly bushes they'd ridden through, and she was tired. Stephanie was in no mood for Ryan's bizarre sense of humor and said so.

"*My* bizarre sense of humor? Who thought it would be amusing to see me languish in jail, Princess?"

"Ah, it's pay-up time now, is that it? Later, Ryan, please. I just want to lie down somewhere and sleep. Possibly for a week, maybe longer." Stephanie wet dry lips with the tip of her equally dry tongue. "And I want a nice cool drink."

"Cognac? Champagne?"

"Water will do."

"You only provided enough for one, Princess. Where's the pack horse?"

Stephanie sighed wearily and cradled her forehead in the palm of one hand. Her mare stomped tiredly and nickered, and Ryan's stallion answered.

"As you know, Ryan, I had not planned on joining you right now. The plan was to meet you later with the rest of our belongings. We don't even have all our gear . . ." She couldn't help the tears that began to trickle down her cheeks, and kept one hand over her eyes so she didn't have to meet Ryan's critical gaze. "We still have *some* supplies . . ."

"Most of yours went over the side of a canyon, remember? I still have mine." Ryan leaned forward, resting one arm on his saddle horn. "Okay. I see you've had enough, Princess. Fortunately, Lil made sure all my supplies are here. That ought to carry us awhile."

"Wonderful." Stephanie peeped at him over the edge of her palm. "I broke you out of jail. Isn't that proper restitution for my sin against you?"

"Almost. We'll discuss the rest of your penance later." Ryan wheeled his stallion and beckoned for Stephanie to follow.

part to find people at Ryan's wanna arry's cabinet.
```
soman'd not get lines, not been I am right to care, to
of the…
```
```
took little Chilliam, a peach, in hire the two the
```
```
…you, a Mama, I was, you up to with her glad…
```
```
of the, set and to say the with I was set.
```
```
When ware if it asks the create book even mine
```
```
him… sammer, was his half, In a calls… ast, for
```
```
bright into willing it…
```

Chapter Twenty

For several days they hid from the inevitable posse in a cave tucked into the side of a steep cliff. A clear creek snaked past the base of the slope, and Ryan would wait for the concealment of dark to bring up water. The horses were tied at the mouth of the cave, and their sharp hearing served as a warning if anyone came near.

Evenings became the times Stephanie spent learning some of the more elemental rules for survival in the desert. One of the most important, Ryan told her, was to check her boots for scorpions before she put them on in the mornings.

"Scorpions?" Stephanie shuddered.

"Yeah, they live alone in holes or other hiding places, and come out at night to hunt. They seem to love hiding in boots. The sting is always painful, and sometimes fatal."

Stephanie shot a suspicious glance at her boots lying innocently close to the fire, then turned her attention back to Ryan. He seemed determined to teach her how to survive in case they were separated, and that thought half-frightened her.

"Water can be found in cactus," Ryan was saying. "Just find a barrel cactus and slice off the top to get at the small reservoir inside. And the flowers of the yucca are a real tasty treat if you cook 'em right." Cooking a varied menu over an open fire was another feat she had mastered under his tutelage.

"Wouldn't I make a good squaw?" Stephanie teased while she patted out a flat cake made of bluish cornmeal. This corn had been raised by Hopi Indians, and instead of the familiar white or yellow, had a distinctive blue color. Stephanie liked it, telling Ryan it tasted like a cross between hominy and popcorn. She'd even learned to bake paper-thin *piki* bread on a grill, rolling it while it was still soft. Now blue corncakes sizzled on a smooth, round stone heated in the fire Ryan had built against one wall of the cave.

"Squaw is a white man's word, Moonflower. Indians say woman." Ryan shifted position on his saddle blanket as Stephanie slanted him a curious glance.

"Moonflower? Why did you call me that?"

He shrugged. "I don't know. Maybe because you remind me of one, all pale and sweet-smelling."

"I don't believe I've ever seen a Moonflower. Where do they grow?"

"In the tropics. They only blossom at night, and the vines go up to about twenty feet high sometimes. It'll grow in the north, but has to be replanted every year because it can't stand frost. Kinda like you . . ."

"What do you mean by that?"

265

"You're a sheltered, hothouse beauty, aren't you?" His tone was mocking.

She put out her tongue at him. "No. Don't you think I would make a good squaw—I mean Indian wife?"

"Maybe. If you learned to watch your tongue. An Apache husband might beat you for insolence."

"Hah! He'd have a fight on his hands," Stephanie retorted.

Ryan stretched lazily, grinning at her. "A big enough stick would cure your manners," he commented.

"Do I detect a desire to try it?" Stephanie slanted him a teasing glance, and a smile tugged at the corners of her mouth. "Your bruises are just now fading. Are you in a hurry to risk more?" She patted the moistened cornmeal into another flat cake and flipped it onto the heated rock to cook. It sizzled briefly, and small bubbles popped to the surface as it began to darken at the edges. When Stephanie's gaze moved questioningly from the corn cake to Ryan, she completely forgot about their evening meal.

Sparks of desire glowed in his eyes, taking her breath away. He'd avoided looking at her the past few days, and Stephanie had accepted their new situation gratefully. She didn't want another near rape or rejection. But now Ryan was staring at her as he had that evening in the tumble-down hut, and it was both frightening and exciting.

Why had he turned so cool after that night? She'd wanted to ask him countless times, but was afraid of his answer. Necessity threw them together, but she could not make another mistake and leave herself vulnerable again.

A wisp of long hair strayed over her forehead and Stephanie pushed at it, smearing cornmeal across her face. She was quivering inside, and her hands were cold while her face was hot. She was glad that she was sitting with her legs folded beneath her, because she didn't think her knees would have supported her when Ryan looked at her like he was doing now.

She felt much like a rabbit must feel when fixed with a snake's predatory stare, vulnerable and waiting and knowing the outcome. Why had she ever thought she could resist Ryan? She couldn't. She couldn't even look away from the gray eyes that had haunted her sleep every night.

Why didn't he stop? And why did he have the power to make her heart beat fast and her lungs cease to function? She was getting light-headed from the lack of air, and she dragged in a deep breath.

Immediately she began to cough. Thick smoke billowed up from the burning corncake and she automatically reached out to scoop it from the stone.

"Ahhh!" she screamed. Stephanie dropped the hot corncake that she'd picked up with her bare fingers, and flung her hands in the air. Steaming bits of corncake flew from her fingers to spatter over Ryan and, unfortunately, the horses tied a short distance away.

Ryan cursed and the horses screamed and snorted, jerking at the ropes tying them to a dead tree stump. Leaping up, Ryan lunged for the animals and managed to catch his stallion's trailing rope just as the animal bolted. Stephanie watched in dismay as Ryan's heels disappeared over the rocky lip of the cave's entrance.

"Oh dear," she said softly, wiping her burned fingers on her trousers. "I hope he isn't mad."

Her hope was banished when Ryan returned some fifteen minutes later, leading the stallion and wearing huge clumps of cholla cactus. Scratches crisscrossed his face and arms, and he looked as if he'd been dragged through thorns. He threw her a baleful stare as he retied the animal to the tree stump beside the mare.

"Coffee?" Stephanie asked brightly. "It's fresh . . ."

"No."

Ryan stomped toward the back of the cave, and she could hear him snarling unintelligible comments that she had no desire to interpret as he removed the cactus ornaments. Stephanie sighed. She should be grateful that she'd burned her fingers and provided a distraction from a potentially explosive situation, but somehow she couldn't muster up the emotion. A sense of disappointment hovered over her instead.

"Would an apology help?" she asked when Ryan returned to his blanket by the fire. "I didn't realize the cake would be so hot . . ."

"No," he answered shortly, jacknifing his long legs to sit down. "I have been dragged over rocks, through bushes, and been impaled by small clumps of cactus. Nothing short of your dismemberment would satisfy me right now."

"Oh Ryan, it was an accident . . ."

"Everything you do is an accident, Stephanie!" His voice rose and he controlled it with an effort. "Look, I admit that there have been times when I've provoked you, but you have more than gotten even." He began ticking off her acts of vengeance on his fingers, "There was the time you hit me, the time you shot at me, the time you had me locked up in jail, and now you've burned me with hot cornmeal and gotten me dragged through cactus!"

"You're forgetting the time I tried to embarrass you to death by rescuing you from jail!" Stephanie snapped. Her vulnerable feelings were smarting from his acid comments.

"Yeah, that's right. I forgot." He lit a cigar and sat back against his tilted saddle, blowing smoke in the air. "Go to sleep, Stephanie. We'll be leaving here early in the morning."

"I hope," Stephanie said slowly and distinctly, "that you drop from the face of the earth after we find my father."

Ryan stared at her sardonically. "Why?"

"Oh, no reason. I enjoy being made to feel like a . . . a . . . a dishonored woman!" Stephanie was near tears, and damned herself and Ryan Cordell heartily. She hadn't meant to let him provoke her into displaying emotion again, but it seemed as if her composure had vanished.

"What are you talking about?" Ryan was sitting up again. "Dishonored? When? Who—me?" He began shaking his head. "Oh no, little lady! You're not pinning that on me!"

"I'm not trying to pin anything on you." Stephanie stared at him with icy disdain. "But my father will. And don't forget my fiancé," she added, only just recalling Reginald herself.

"Ah yes, the absentee fiancé. Funny that you

269

should think of him now—what was his name, Reginald? You haven't thought about him in weeks. Especially that night in the old cabin," he added deliberately.

Stephanie's cheeks flushed and her head whirled. He *would* mention that, trying to make her seem capricious and disloyal as well as immoral. Her conscience gave a hearty twinge. She *had* been disloyal to Reginald. But she didn't love Reginald, Stephanie realized, and she did—no, love was too strong a word—she'd been infatuated with Ryan, that was all. She'd yielded to the impulse of the moment, because she could *not* love Ryan Cordell. It was an absurd notion to think she could. Maybe it was the smoke, Stephanie thought then, that was making her so light-headed. She frowned, trying to concentrate on their argument.

"Don't change the subject, Cordell."

"I was under the impression Reginald *was* the subject," Ryan pointed out dryly.

"No, Reginald isn't the subject. The subject is you, and your treatment of me." She stared directly into Ryan's eyes and took a deep breath. "I haven't asked, but frankly, I'm curious and have to know—why?"

"Why?" Ryan didn't pretend he didn't know what she was referring to, but he hedged for an answer. He didn't want to tell her the truth, but he didn't want to lie. Damn, the situation had become so complicated. Shrugging, Ryan stalled for time by lighting another thin cigar. Stephanie waited expectantly, and he knew he owed her some kind of a decent explanation for his coolness after their night in that cabin. After all, she had given herself freely, asking for nothing from him, and maybe she had a right to honesty.

"Stephanie, it's not your fault," he began slowly. "I just can't quite believe that a woman who has grown up in the life-style you have would fit in out here. I made a mistake back there in the hut, and I'm sorry."

"So you've decided to punish me for growing up in a mansion in New York? That makes sense!" Stephanie's tone was bitterly quiet. "What about how I feel, Ryan? Have you bothered to ask me how I feel?"

"Ah, you don't understand . . ."

"No, I don't. Do you think you're the only person who's ever taken a chance?" Her short laugh was tinged with remembered pain. "Don't be a fool. We all have if we've dared try to live life at all, Ryan. You're being unfair, when you know I care . . ." She choked on the words, stumbling to a halt. She hadn't wanted to admit aloud how she felt, that she cared so deeply for him, and now she had. Now she was more vulnerable than she'd ever been. Hot tears stung her eyelids, and Stephanie bent her head to stare down at her clenched hands, struggling for composure.

A touch on her shoulder startled her, and she jerked up her head to see Ryan beside her. A slight smile crooked his mouth at one side, and his eyes were soft. Ryan hooked a finger beneath her chin to tilt her face up, and his other hand cradled the back of her head.

"I just don't want to be some rich girl's new toy, Stephanie. I never thought you cared."

271

"Oh, Ryan . . . !"

"Well, we haven't exactly been best friends, you know."

"No, I guess we haven't."

Stephanie couldn't quite meet his gaze. Her long lashes lowered, hiding the confusion she knew must be showing in her dark eyes. A warm flush stained her cheeks, and she hoped they weren't as red as they felt. How ridiculous, she thought in dismay. She was a grown woman, not some awkward schoolgirl, so why was Ryan able to do this to her so easily?

When his hands cradled her face and his head lowered so that his mouth brushed lightly across her lips, Stephanie could not move. She didn't want to move. She wanted him to kiss her, and she realized that she'd only been denying herself. What she felt for Ryan was much more than mere infatuation.

Ryan's hands were warm and familiar, lightly caressing the soft contours of her face, exploring the tiny ridges inside her ear, then swooping back the thick waves of her hair to imprison her head in his palms. He held her while his lips traced the same path his hands had traveled, along the curve of her cheek to her ear, his tongue making her shiver when it flicked inside. Stephanie was quivering with longing for him, shy yet bold.

Deftly undoing his buttons, Stephanie pushed his shirt aside and slid her hands over his bare chest. Her fingers skimmed over the tiny hairs curling across taut muscles, caressing and touching. He had a magnificent body, she thought, like a sleek panther, well muscled and perfectly proportioned. She felt clumsy and shy with him, not knowing exactly how or where to touch, wanting and afraid at the same time. Ryan solved her dilemma.

"Here, love, my beautiful moonflower . . ." His fingers curled around her hands and moved them. "Touch me like that . . . yes."

Somehow Stephanie's trousers and shirt were gone, and Ryan's clothes lay with hers. A thick blanket cushioned Stephanie's hips and shoulders as she reached out again for Ryan, and he lay down beside her.

Firelight flickered warm shadows across them, weaving a canopy of magic that Stephanie was to never forget. In spite of the driving urgency of his desire, Ryan took his time, wanting Stephanie to respond fully. He held her tenderly, and without attempting to disguise his hunger, he began to lightly caress Stephanie's slim curves and hollows. Almost hypnotized by the glow of passion in Ryan's smoke-gray eyes, Stephanie made no move to slow him, her body arching up as she mutely pleaded for the touch of his sun-dark hand against her paler skin.

But Ryan didn't hurry. Instead, he let his eyes caress the slender form beside him, her small firm breasts with hardened peaks aching for his touch, the sweet curve of her slim waist, and the pale golden skin of her flat belly and slender thighs. She was magic, a sorceress who had cast a spell on him, and Ryan felt himself growing tight with the delicious desire to lose himself in her.

Bending his head at last, his warm, moist mouth found and teased a taut rosy peak, his tongue curling in a sweet caress around it, his teeth gently nipping at the hardening bud while his hand found her other

273

breast. Dragging his thumb across it, Ryan heard Stephanie's quickly drawn gasp of pleasure. A soft sigh quivered in the air as she reached for him, her fingers tangling in the thick waves of his dark hair to hold his head as she pressed closer. And when Ryan's mouth moved from her breast to her lips, his tongue ravaging her mouth, Stephanie's hands slid from his head to his shoulders, and she held him as if she were drowning.

She was drowning, drowning in ever-increasing waves of sensuality and passion, sinking deeper and deeper so that she felt as if she'd never come up. There was only the incredibly sweet sensations that surrounded her, holding her in silken embraces.

Wanting him to feel the same, heady pleasure, Stephanie boldly slid the pads of her fingers down Ryan's back in light, feathery touches, exploring the contours of his ribs, then his lean waist, sliding over his hips to slip her hands between their bodies. He shifted to one side, still holding her, his mouth moving to that tiny hollow at the base of her throat, then nipping lightly at her neck.

Ryan's body tightened when she found and held him, and he muffled a groan in silvery strands of Stephanie's hair fanning across the bright Navajo blanket. The size and heat of him brought a soft little gasp of surprise from Stephanie, and her fingers tightened automatically. His hands curved over her buttocks, pulling her closer, and his lips pressed another feverish assault on her mouth.

"Here," he muttered thickly, his lips still against hers, "hold me like this. Yes, that's right, love." His hand guided hers, and they were both shaking with fierce intensity.

It excited Stephanie to know she could make him react to her like she reacted to him, could make his pulses race madly and his heart beat faster. She was a changeling, replaced somehow by this passionate creature who only wanted to feel Ryan inside her, to make him a part of her as she felt she was a part of him.

Then Ryan was murmuring hoarsely, "Stop, sweetheart, or I'll hurry what should be slow . . ."

Stephanie paused with her fingers still curling around him, holding him, and marveled at the velvet texture of his body. This was a completely new discovery, much more exciting and dangerous than any expedition she had ever gone on before, a journey into the hazy world of passion. Never had she allowed herself such a leisurely exploration of the senses, and the night spent with Ryan in that tiny cabin could not compare with the sensations sweeping her now.

Ryan's passion-thick voice gave Stephanie a small glow of triumph, arousing her even more as she realized she could make him lose control of himself, that her hands had the power to drive him to the brink as he did her. Arching her body, her heels dug mounds into the blanket as she twisted closer to him, brushing her hardened nipples across his chest in deliberately teasing movements. Her lips were slightly parted and she flicked out her tongue to moisten them, dragging in a deep breath as dark eyes like jet locked with Ryan's desire-clouded gaze.

Dark and light, hot and cold, soft and hard, they were two contradictions entwined together, each striving to please the other. Stephanie was a wanton, boldly touching, caressing, and stroking his hard male body with her hands, mouth, and tongue, arousing Ryan to a fever pitch.

It was growing more difficult for him to hold back, and his tenuous grip on restraint vanished when Stephanie's tongue traced a hot, wet path across the flat muscles of his belly. Tangling his hands in her hair, he half expected it to fade away in his grip like silver moonbeams or the morning mist. She seemed a creature of myth and fantasy, spun from silken moonlight and timeless dreams.

Tugging gently, Ryan pulled Stephanie upward, dragging her across his body in a slow, sensual motion, moving his hands from her hair to cup her firm buttocks. She lay half across him, straddling his waist, her long legs bent and gripping his sides. Leaning forward, Stephanie kissed him long and deeply, letting her tongue explore his mouth with quick, light touches. She cradled his face in her palms, holding him, rubbing her fingers against the abrasive stubble of the beard shadowing his jaw.

When Ryan's hands moved from the firm flesh of her buttocks to the small cleft between her thighs, Stephanie moaned against his lips. Her breath came in short, jerking gasps and her breasts ached for his touch. Somehow sensing what she wanted, Ryan's mouth found a taut nipple, teasing and tasting first one and then another, until shock waves of pleasure exploded through every fiber of Stephanie's body. She sobbed aloud, arching her back as blinding sparks of light seemed to shower her, then collapsed atop Ryan's hard chest, burying her face into the warm hollow of his shoulder.

He held her loosely, his arms circling her back as she struggled for breath, his fingers twisting a long strand of her hair into a silken rope. For several moments Stephanie lay quietly, recovering from the sweeping rush of ecstasy. She'd never expected that. She felt as if she'd shattered into a thousand pieces and was scattered across the sky like tiny stars.

Ryan's lips against her cheek brought her swimming slowly to the surface of reality, and Stephanie managed a tremulous smile.

"Oh my," she breathed softly, "I never knew it could be like that."

"There's more, love, much more."

"Oh Ryan! I don't think I can . . . anymore . . ."

"Yes you can, love. I'll show you . . ."

Suiting action to words, Ryan pushed her gently to her back. He began kissing her again, her mouth, neck, the shallow pulse throbbing in the hollow at the base of her throat, then her breasts. Cupping them in both palms, his fingers teased one taut peak while his mouth nibbled at the other, until Stephanie was once more writhing beneath him. When he finally nudged her thighs apart with his knees, she was aching for him, eagerly arching her hips upward, crying out when he buried himself in her in one smooth thrust.

Moving slowly and leisurely, Ryan enjoyed the satin heat of her around him, only half hearing the small, incoherent cries in his ear. His rhythm increased as Stephanie's hands drifted over his back to the taut muscles of his buttocks and thighs, then her long legs lifted to clasp him around his waist.

Now his body slammed into hers hard and fast, rocking against her until she was sobbing with pleasure. Searing release pulsed from Ryan into Stephanie, and they both shuddered at the throbbing tides of exquisite satisfaction.

Drained, and unwilling to disturb the warm intimacy of the moment, neither moved, but lay in a soft tangle of entwined bodies highlighted by the dying fire. Damp with their efforts, the night air drifting in the mouth of the cave made their flesh prickle, and Ryan reached for another blanket to draw over them.

He hadn't expected the warm rush of tenderess that would envelop him, so that he only wanted to lie with Stephanie in his arms. His infatuation with her he could accept, however ungraciously, but this unfamiliar emotion was harder to deal with. It would be a struggle of pride against passion, love against caution. Shaking his head, Ryan pulled Stephanie's damp body closer. It didn't matter. He'd think of some way to deal with this new emotion.

Chapter Twenty-One

Glowing embers were all that were left of their fire when Stephanie woke with a start. The memory of her sensual abandon a short time before made her tense when Ryan's arms tightened around her. What did he think?

"Be still, love," he muttered sleepily. "There's a few more hours left to sleep . . ." His voice trailed off as he drifted into slumber again.

Stephanie was wide awake, however. Never had she behaved so brazenly! Like a . . . a girl from Fancy Lil's! And she had enjoyed every delicious moment. She sighed softly. Her true nature was finally emerging. Somehow Ryan Cordell had managed to spark a latent streak of sexuality in her that she could not deny. Even now, with traces of their lovemaking still on her body, she wanted him again. She wanted to feel his mouth on hers and hear him call her love again, wanted to feel that sweet surge of passion that he seemed to evoke at will. She was shameless, Stephanie decided, absolutely shameless. And now that she had come to grips with that darker side of herself . . .

"Ryan?" Her mouth pressed against his ear, and strands of tousled black hair tickled her lips and nose. "Ryan? Are you asleep?"

"Not anymore," he grumbled drowsily, opening one eye to squint at her. "What's th' matter?"

"Nothing." Stephanie nestled closer, letting her fingers tickle across his bare flesh. Ryan's eye snapped shut again and she sighed, her breath whispering over his ribs and stirring crisp whorls of hair on his chest. The one arm he had draped across her tightened briefly, then relaxed. Stephanie's toes skimmed down the length of his leg from knee to ankle, then inched back up in tiny pinches. Ryan's leg twitched once, then twice, and was still.

Frowning now, and more determined than ever, Stephanie concentrated on the flat ridges of his belly. The pads of her fingers skipped like frisky puppies over the taut muscles, pausing to investigate his navel, then continuing downward. Ryan's hand caught her fingers at the same time as he flexed the muscles in his arm around her back, pulling her across him.

"What are you doing?" His voice was warm and thick with sleep, and he nuzzled the nape of her neck.

"Oh, nothing."

He felt Stephanie's smile against his chest. "Nothing?" he echoed. "Hmmm. Feels like something to me."

His palm dropped from her back to her hips, smoothing down over the slender curve of her thighs, then back up. Stephanie's lips were busily nipping at

280

his skin, and Ryan surrendered with a soft laugh.

"Greedy wench," he murmured against her hair, rolling over with Stephanie beneath him.

"Yes," she agreed in a breathy little whisper, *"oh yes, Ryan!"*

They left the cave much later than originally planned, following the barest of trails down the steep, rocky slope to the base of the ridged mesa. Ryan was in the lead, and Stephanie was content just to gaze at his back as she followed.

She was in love. Oh yes, there was no denying it. She was hopelessly, helplessly, head over heels in love. It didn't matter that he'd never mentioned love; he would. He had to. She loved him so much he had to return that feeling. And being in love colored the world with such bright, crisp hues, like an artist run mad with a palette.

The sky was so bright a blue it hurt the eyes, and the spires and mesas jutting heavenward were carved in fascinating shades of rose and carmine. Even the blighted trees and bushes were an understated green instead of the drab, dusty color she'd once thought them.

"What kind of hawk is that, Ryan?" she asked, pointing to the lazily circling dot in the sky.

"That's an eagle, not a hawk." Ryan cupped a hand over his eyes, squinting up at the soaring bird. "Probably has a nest near here somewhere." He slid Stephanie a glance. For the last few hours, he'd known they were being followed but did not want to alarm her. He just wasn't certain who it was, friend or enemy. The next time they stopped for a rest, he would investigate.

When they did stop late that afternoon, Ryan climbed the nearest peak, leaving Stephanie with the horses. He lay flat on his belly, eyes scanning the horizon. Nothing behind them now, not even a tiny dust cloud. Ryan frowned and glanced in the opposite direction. His gaze narrowed on two tiny figures riding a far slope and leading a pack animal. Lifting his field glasses, Ryan focused them.

Bingo leaned over in his saddle and aimed a stream of tobacco juice at a lizard. The offended reptile scuttled from the flat rock, tail waving like a banner as it disappeared over the rock's edge.

"Ruined that lizzerd's day, I reckon!" Bingo observed with a laugh. He took off his hat, raked a hand through sparse strands of frizzled hair, then tugged it back in place.

"I would think so," Julian agreed. He dismounted stiffly, rubbing the small of his back as he seated himself on the now-vacated rock. Placing spread hands on his knees, Julian peered at his guide. "We read the map wrong, Bingo. We must have."

"Yep. 'Pears so." Bingo scratched at a flea that had had the temerity to take up residence in his shirt. "Now, why don'cha be patient a while? I kin tell ya what ever' Injun within a hunnerd miles knows. 'Course, if'n ye're still set on goin' off half cocked . . ."

"No, no. I'm ready for alternate suggestions."

"Good." Bingo joined him on the rock, squinting

282

into the sun slowly sliding behind flat-topped mesas and towering spires. "Now, ya jus' need ta learn how ta wait, Pilgrim, that's all there is to it."

Julian listened with raised brows, glancing skeptically at Bingo. Sitting and waiting was plausible, with plenty of room for error, he decided. Lord knows, it certainly seemed as if his map had been in error. A frown knit Julian's light brows as he pondered the authenticity of his map. They had followed it faithfully, yet had met only a solid cliff wall at the spot where the burial ground was supposed to be located. Now they were backtracking in an effort to discover their error.

"Bingo," he cut in, "why don't we simply ask an Indian if our map is right? He could possibly explain it. It might save time and effort."

Blinking in surprise, Bingo considered that idea for a moment. "Wel-l-l," he dragged out, "I s'pose we could at that. But we'd be likely ta git our fool scalps on a pole if'n th' Injun we ast, didn' like our question." Bingo hesitated for a moment, obviously wanting to say more, and Julian pressed him.

"What is it? You have an idea, I can tell."

"Mind, it's jus' a legend now, an' thar's prob'ly no truth at'all in it, but I recollect a story 'bout a stairway ta heaven. Only, ya got ta find th' steps or ya cain't go. Could be, th' story's 'bout this burial ground yer wantin' ta find."

Excitement swept Julian to his feet. "Then the map could be right after all! We just have to find the trail or steps hidden in the cliff face. Bingo, we could have been in exactly the right spot and didn't realize it! Let's go . . ."

"Wait a minute, now. Don't go off half cocked, Pilgrim. We need ta plan better than yer doin'. Yer just following enny false scent like an unschooled hound. Yer idea 'bout askin' ain't a bad one, an' I think I know jus' th' Injun we kin ask, but it's a day's ride away." He peered at Julian. "Don' go a'frownin' at me 'cause I ain't ready ta jump up an' go. We'll git thar. Them Injuns been dead a few thousand years, an' they ain't likely ta git up an' leave now."

"You're right, of course. It's just that so much time seems to have been wasted." Julian heaved a sigh, stretching to loosen his cramped muscles. "I feel as if I'd been sewn to that saddle with rusty wire." Cupping a hand over his eyes, Julian surveyed the area, looking for familiar landmarks. They'd been so close, and he hadn't even known it. His sense of bitter frustration at coming face to face with a sheer rock wall instead of the burial ground still haunted him. He'd been ready to give up for a moment, before determination returned. Julian Stephen Ashworth had never admitted defeat, and he certainly wouldn't embark on such an ignominious path now.

A stairway to heaven, he mused. There would be steps in that rock wall, he just knew it. And when they climbed them to the summit, he would realize his quest.

Ryan slid back down the slope amidst a shower of small rocks and gravel. Stephanie frowned up at him. "Must you always pelt me with disagreeable objects?" She brushed at the light film of dust and tiny rock chips coating her hair and shoulders.

"What were you looking for up there anyway?"

"Oh, anything."

"And did you see anything?"

Shaking his head, Ryan stepped to his horse and slung the field glasses over his saddle horn. "Not a thing, Princess. Not a thing." He didn't feel the slightest inclination to tell her what he'd seen. Once they joined Julian, Stephanie wouldn't need him to guide her anymore. Right now, he wanted time to sort out his own tangled emotions before a decision was thrust upon him too soon. Julian and his guide were far enough away so that she'd never know how close they were.

Stephanie rose from the rock, stretching like a languid cat with arms raised above her head. She slanted Ryan a smile, her eyes glistening with some emotion he couldn't quite name.

"Shall we camp for the night?" She bent over to touch her toes. The battered hat she wore glided to the ground and thick streamers of hair tumbled down in a silvery waterfall. Ryan let his gaze drift from Stephanie's U-shaped posture to her nicely rounded bottom. Her pose accentuated the tightness of the trousers stretching across her hips. "Well, are we?" she asked again, snatching his attention away from her hips and thighs.

"Yeah, we can stop for the night. But not right here. Let's go a little farther. Only over the next ridge," he added when Stephanie groaned a protest. "I can see the tops of some trees we can camp under."

"I thought you said it was safer camping against a

rock cliff," Stephanie pointed out, but Ryan was already turning away and stepping into his saddle. "Contradictions," she muttered to herself, "always contradictions." It took a great deal of determination to coax her cramped muscles into obeying the command to mount, but Stephanie managed it. She turned her mare down the rocky path behind Ryan.

It wasn't long before thin plumes of smoke rose from their campfire, and Stephanie knelt beside the flames to fry their usual beans and dried meat. It was better than nothing, she supposed, but it was a menu that she'd tired of quickly.

"Ryan?"

Ryan was bent over examining his stallion's hooves for splits or possibly crippling rocks, holding a foreleg between his knees. He dug out a small but sharp pebble that had wedged between the shoe and tender part of the hoof.

"Ryan, why don't you get us some other kind of meat?" Stephanie persisted. "Even rabbit would taste good right now."

Ryan dropped his stallion's foreleg and picked up a hind leg to inspect the hoof. He slanted Stephanie an irritated glance over one shoulder.

"I'm busy," he said shortly. "Maybe later."

"Later will be fine. I'm just tired of dried beef and beans." Stephanie pushed at the pan full of sizzling meat with a long knife. "Lately I've been dreaming about filet mignon, fresh Brussels sprouts, asparagus . . ." She sighed deeply.

"You're the one . . ." Ryan began.

". . . who wanted to come on this trip," Stephanie finished for him. "I know, I know. I've heard you say that often enough." She rested her chin in a palm and gazed at Ryan for a long moment. "Somehow," she said slowly, "I have the inescapable feeling that there's more behind this trip than I know about. Why is that, I wonder?"

"How should I know?" Ryan dropped his stallion's hoof and straightened, giving the animal a pat on his gleaming rump. "I've never been able to figure out why women think the things they do."

"Have you ever tried?" Stephanie poked at the browning meat again, glancing at Ryan curiously.

"Yeah, a long time ago. It didn't take me long to find out that the less I know about women, the better off I am."

"That's an odd decision. 'Knowledge is power' my father always says."

"Maybe that works for him. There's some things a man shouldn't know. Especially when it concerns women." Ryan heaved his saddle to a spot near the fire, upending it to dry. The saddle blankets were quickly draped from the low-hanging branches of a mesquite tree close to their bridles, then Ryan picked up his rifle.

"What are you doing?" Stephanie asked as he walked away from their camp.

"Hunting dinner. But save some beef and beans just in case."

Smiling, Stephanie moved the iron skillet from the fire. She had no doubt Ryan would find a fat rabbit, or maybe even a few plump birds. Stretching out on her blanket, she closed her eyes and waited.

Stephanie didn't even realize she'd fallen asleep until she was being nudged awake. A foot prodded her insistently in the ribs, and she frowned up at the shape outlined against the darkening sky. A chill shivered through her as Stephanie's eyes focused. It wasn't Ryan who was towering over her. This was a stranger, a man clothed in only a breechcloth and moccasins. Long dark hair hung about his sharp-featured face, held back with a red cloth circling his forehead. He was holding a lance in one hand, and Stephanie swallowed a gasp as the man knelt and reached out a copper-skinned hand to touch her.

Instinctively, she reached for her Colt that lay by her side, but the Indian was swifter. His moccasined foot slammed down on her wrist, pinning her arm effectively to the ground as he kicked the pistol away. He muttered something she couldn't understand, and lifted a long streamer of her hair. Her throat tightened as he tugged on it painfully, but Stephanie resisted the urge to scream. She'd heard somewhere that one shouldn't show fear. Indians respected courage. Her dark eyes searched for some sign of respect in the Indian's face, but his flat features were expressionless. He muttered something again in his guttural language, and she realized that this Indian was not alone. Fear surged through her as a quick glance beyond him discovered another man at her feet, and at least a half dozen Indians in their camp. Oh, where was Ryan?

Stephanie was pulled roughly to her feet. The brave who was admiring her hair was obviously claiming her as his captive. He pushed her forward, gesturing to first her, then himself. Frowning, the man who'd crouched at her feet spoke as if disagreeing with the claim, and even though she couldn't understand the language, Stephanie understood that there was an argument over her possession.

She immediately took advantage of the dissension to pull away from the Indian gripping her arm.

"No!" she said loudly, pointing to first the brave who'd woken her, then the other. "No!" She held her breath as they began to argue, hoping for enough of a diversion for her to escape. But when she began to back slowly away, she found herself halted by a hard chest and rude voice in her ear.

"Alto, señorita!"

Instead of the unfamiliar tongue they were speaking, this voice spoke Spanish. Not the crisp Castilian dialect she had learned in school, but familiar enough for her to understand. Stephanie blinked in surprise.

"What do you want with me?" she asked in Spanish. "I have done you no harm."

"We want your horses. And Spotted Wolf wants you" was the answer. The brave gestured toward her with one hand, and Stephanie noted the sharp knife he held. "He admires your white hair, señorita. I have seen hair like that."

Stephanie swallowed a faint moan of dismay. Did Spotted Wolf want her hair attached to her head or his war lance? She had already seen the string of scalps hanging from his lance. The brave smiled, and she knew he'd guessed her thoughts.

"He wants you for his wife, señorita. Spotted Wolf says you are big woman; would make fine sons."

"I don't want to make fine sons," Stephanie answered heatedly, then amended, "Not with

Spotted Wolf! I have a man already . . ."

"Bah!" The brave made a quick gesture as if slicing a throat and Stephanie shuddered. "Your man will not matter. He would be glad to trade you for his life . . ."

"Hello, Spotted Tail," a familiar voice drawled from just beyond the shadows, and Stephanie wanted to weep with relief. "Don't be too sure I'd trade this woman. She's mine, and I like to keep what's mine."

Spotted Tail, Spotted Wolf—Stephanie had the bleak thought that she would be seeing spots before too many moments passed.

Ryan stepped into the light, ignoring the rifles thrust toward him.

"Tell your amigos that I'm an old acquaintance, Spotted Tail." When the brave hesitated, Ryan spoke to him in the same guttural tongue Stephanie had heard the others use. He spoke Indian as well as Spanish? Ryan Cordell seemed full of surprises, and Stephanie watched as the rifle muzzles lowered.

Her head swam, and she realized that her knees were shaking and her hands were trembling. This situation could be worse, she supposed, but it was hard to imagine how. She slanted a wary glance toward the brave Ryan had called Spotted Tail. He was still gripping her by one arm, his fingers like steel coils around her wrist, and she tested his hold. Spotted Tail did not relax his grip or even glance in her direction.

"*Hola*, White Bear," Spotted Tail said, switching back to Spanish. "It has been many moons since I have seen you."

"*Sí*, Spotted Tail." Ryan made a sweeping motion

with his hands. "It was the season of Little Eagles when last I rode with the Apache."

"Now it is the time of Big Leaves, and four Ghost Seasons have passed since you were in my father's wickiup," Spotted Tail answered. "He will be glad to see you again."

Stephanie's head whirled. Apache? Dear God, she'd heard many tales of their savagery. Her heart thumped even faster, and tiny beads of perspiration dotted her forehead. But Ryan was obviously friends with the entire family. Did this mean they were free to go? Her brief hope was dashed when Spotted Tail pointed his knife at her and said, "This woman is sought after by Spotted Wolf and Buffalo Horn. She will choose between them."

Well, that was easy enough, Stephanie thought. She'd choose neither. Her lips parted to emphatically refuse both men, but Ryan caught her eye and shook his head. When she frowned, he said tersely in English, "Say nothing. Do nothing. Wait." To Spotted Tail, Ryan spoke in his own language, and Stephanie felt a flash of irritation. She wished she could understand what they were saying, but then Ryan was turning to her again and telling her to keep calm.

"Calm?" Stephanie rolled her eyes. "I'm supposed to choose between this . . . this . . ."

"Stephanie, Spotted Tail speaks a little English . . ."

"Then why isn't he polite enough to use it?" she demanded.

"It's uncivilized," Spotted Tail answered her in English. "The Apache tongue or Spanish is much more lyrical."

A little English? His pronunciation was letter perfect, and Stephanie narrowed her eyes at Ryan. Was this a joke? Was Ryan playing some sort of horrible practical joke on her?

"Ryan Cordell, if this is your bizarre idea of a joke, I'm not laughing," she began, but he shook his head.

"Stephanie, we are going to go with Spotted Tail and his friends. When we . . ."

"Where?" she interrupted.

"To their camp," Ryan answered in a tone that indicated he was rapidly losing patience with her. Spotted Tail broke in to make an observation in his language, and Ryan grinned.

"What did he say?" Stephanie asked. She pushed damp strands of hair from her eyes and glared at Ryan. He actually seemed to be enjoying this! "What did he say—was it about me?"

"Yes. He said you were a viper-tongued female, and if Spotted Wolf wins you, he's going to recommend that he cut out your tongue."

"Ryan—"

"Don't worry. Buffalo Horn is the better fighter."

"You can't be serious! Ryan, you are taking this as a joke, when they're talking about . . . what are you going to do about this?"

"What do you suggest I do? I'm one man, with one rifle, and there are seven of them here as well as those waiting not far away with a captured herd of horses. These men were on a raiding expedition, Princess, and you are part of their loot." He halted her explosive protest with a warning shake of his head. "Let's just see what happens, Stephanie. Who knows? I may decide to fight for you . . ."

Stephanie watched helplessly as the Apaches scattered their belongings, looking for whatever they might take a liking to. Ryan made no argument or even seemed to notice when she found herself lifted to the back of Spotted Tail's horse. Ryan mounted his own stallion and she noticed that her gelding was being herded along with the pack horse.

There was no light now. The sky was a deep purple that was almost black, with only tiny pinpricks of light from the stars. In the distance an eerie howl shivered in the air, then was answered by another.

Spotted Tail vaulted to his horse and reached around Stephanie to take the reins. She wondered how she would be able to stay on when he nudged the horse to a steady gallop, but managed to wind her fingers into the animal's mane. The saddle was only a soft pad stuffed with buffalo hair and grass, and she just knew that at any moment it would slip and deposit both of them on the hard ground whisking beneath their feet. Sensing her precarious grip, Spotted Tail curled an arm around Stephanie's middle and pulled her against his chest. She sat stiffly at first, but as the miles passed, she was able to relax slightly.

Her mind was racing as swiftly as the ground beneath churning hooves, bouncing to first one fear and then another. Occasionally Stephanie would catch a glimpse of Ryan riding not far away. Where were they going? And why?

Somehow, in spite of her discomfort and fear, Stephanie succumbed to exhaustion sometime during the night. She woke just as they crested a rocky ridge that dipped into a small valley.

Spotted Tail's arm tightened painfully across her ribs, jerking her awake, and her head snapped up. Rubbing her eyes, Stephanie's jaw dropped at the sight of hundreds of tipis sprawled on the plain below.

A half moon shone brightly as it hung low in the sky, illuminating the area with pale silver light. There seemed to be no pattern to the placing of the tipis, though they were clustered more thickly by a stand of trees. Plumes of smoke curled from the center of several of the buffalo-hide cones, drifting over the camp like low-lying clouds. It reminded her of a painting by artist George Catlin that she'd seen in a Washington museum, primitive and beautiful.

To Stephanie, brought up to rever ancient cultures, the Apache village was exciting as well as frightening. If it wasn't for her precarious situation, she would be thrilled at the opportunity of investigating their customs.

Stephanie turned her head to glance at the Apache holding her. His face was silvered by the moonlight, and seemed even harder and colder than it had earlier. Maybe he would be disposed to kindness if she treated him as a friend instead of captor.

"This is your home?" she ventured in Spanish, and he nodded shortly. "Are you the . . . chief?" she tried again.

An amused smile curled the Apache's thin lips. "No, woman. I am not the chief. I am the chief's younger son. He is the one who will decide your marriage price, so do not ask more questions of me."

Stephanie took the blunt hint to be quiet. Beyond a

quick glance at Ryan, she kept her eyes forward as they rode down the rocky slope into the village.

While most of the braves herded the captured horses around the fringes, the other Apaches walked their horses slowly into the middle of the village. Dogs barked sleepily as the village awakened, and here and there a tipi flap was opened for curious eyes to watch the small procession. Cottonwood trees towered at one end of the camp, some of them taller than the tallest tipi. A small stream snaked through the trees, and there were several tipis erected on the banks.

Dogs milled among the tipis, searching for discarded meat and bones, and investigating one another. Here and there two dogs would circle stiff-legged and then spring upon each other in a snarling, rolling fight. One woman closest to a battle seized a stick of wood and beat at the dogs, sending them scampering away with loud yelps.

A rich mixture of smells permeated the valley, combining wood smoke, rotting meat thrown on garbage piles, of human wastes behind thick clumps of bushes, of steaming cooking pots, and broiling meat dripping fat onto coals. Stephanie wrinkled her nose at the odors.

Spotted Tail jerked his horse to a halt in front of a tipi decorated with painted figures and slid off with a quick, agile movement. Stephanie stiffened with apprehension when he stepped to his horse's head and motioned for her to dismount. He frowned when she hesitated, and reached up to grab her by one arm.

"No," Stephanie said. "I will get down by myself." She threw one leg over the front of the saddle and slid down in a decent imitation of Spotted Tail. Her eyes were level with his as she gazed back at him steadily and folded her arms across her chest.

For a moment Spotted Tail seemed nonplussed at this white woman who was as tall as he and had hair lighter than the sun. He'd been tempted to stake his own claim to the woman until Buffalo Horn had challenged Spotted Wolf for her. Now he considered it beneath his dignity as the chief's son to bargain for a white woman.

Pivoting, Spotted Tail strode to his tipi and raised the flap.

"You and the woman will stay with me, White Bear. My father will decide when to visit with you."

Stephanie wasn't sure whether she should be relieved or worried, but she was certainly glad she wasn't going to be alone with Spotted Tail. She started forward to enter the tipi, but was rudely pushed back.

"No! Woman enters last," Spotted Tail said harshly. "It is the Apache way."

Though tempted to tell him white women always entered first, Stephanie graciously conceded the point, following behind Spotted Tail and Ryan. It was dark and hazy inside the tipi, but surprisingly spacious once through the low flap. Formed in more of an oval than a circle, it was roughly fifteen feet in diameter at the base. The frame was not a true cone as it first appeared, but slightly tilted. This asymmetry provided more headroom in the rear because of the slant. A tripod of especially strong poles were the main support, with smaller poles serving as the frame.

As her eyes adjusted to the dim light, Stephanie saw that Spotted Tail's possessions were neatly stacked around the edges of the dwelling. Embers glowed in a fire pit just off center, and beds of dried grass covered with blankets were arranged against three sides.

Spotted Tail stepped to the right and Ryan followed, but when Stephanie would have done the same Ryan whispered, "No, women go to the left! It's . . ."

"I know! It's the Apache way," Stephanie hissed. She flung him a condemning glance as she stomped in the opposite direction and sat down on a mat several feet from them, tucking her feet beneath her.

Ryan and Spotted Tail spoke quietly in the Apache language, and Stephanie stifled an irritated groan. She was tired, aching, and hungry, and admittedly scared. Would Ryan be able to convince Spotted Tail to release her? He certainly hadn't been very encouraging earlier. And the Apache seemed indifferent to her fate.

Sounds outside the tipi indicated that the rest of the village was beginning to awaken, and Stephanie heard the laughter of children and muted chatter of women. Cooking odors filled the air, and her empty stomach rumbled so loudly Ryan glanced in her direction. She shrugged, recalling that she'd had no supper the night before. When her stomach growled a second time, Stephanie flashed the men a defiant stare, daring them to object. Ryan had the audacity to laugh, and even Spotted Tail permitted himself a smile at her embarrassment. The Apache rose from his mat and stepped to the open flap and spoke to someone just outside the door.

"Ryan," Stephanie leaned forward to whisper, "let's get out of here! I don't want to be some Apache's wife, and I don't even want to be a breakfast guest! You know them, can't you . . ."

"I'm doing the best I can. This situation calls for diplomacy, especially since I've known Spotted Tail's father for several years. Be patient and keep calm. Trust me, Princess."

Ryan's smile was encouraging, and she began to feel better. She'd have to trust him. He'd managed to keep them alive so far, hadn't he? Stephanie sat back on her mat as Spotted Tail returned.

A few moments later a woman clad in a long dress and soft boots entered the tipi. She was carrying a large bowl which she set in front of Spotted Tail. He spoke to her, and the woman nodded and left. When she returned with more bowls, she dipped into the larger one with a ladle fashioned from a gourd, portioning out what looked and smelled to Stephanie like stew. Recalling her experience with the stew at Fort Defiance, she glanced at Ryan questioningly.

"You're expected to eat all of it," he murmured. "It's an insult if you don't."

"What is it?"

"Just eat it."

Stephanie stared into the bowl the Apache woman gave her, wondering what animal had donated the chunks of meat bobbing among wild onions and prairie turnips. She was handed a spoon made from buffalo horn, and bleakly nodded her thanks. Mentally crossing her fingers that the ingredients didn't contain snake or dog, Stephanie began to eat. Though strongly flavored and a little greasy, the stew was spicy with desert herbs and quite edible. She had no trouble eating it all.

After the meal Ryan and Spotted Tail left the tipi, leaving Stephanie alone with the Apache woman who'd brought their food. Each attempt at conversation was met with a blank stare and hostile silence, and Stephanie soon gave up the effort. It didn't seem worth it when she was so tired. After several long minutes of uncomfortable silence and trying to keep her eyes open, she rose from the hard, thin mat.

"I—am—sleepy," she said slowly when the woman jerked her head to stare at Stephanie with flat black eyes. She gestured to one of the sleeping pallets against the side, and pantomined sleep with folded hands against her cheek. The woman nodded shortly and Stephanie stretched out on the bed of buffalo hides and grass.

Just before she fell into a deep, dreamless sleep, it occurred to Stephanie to wonder if Julian had experienced any trouble with the Apaches.

Chapter Twenty-Two

Julian rested his arms across his saddle horn, staring into the valley below. A village of thatched huts shaped like domes neatly carpeted the arid ground between fields planted with corn.

"Papagos," Bingo said, pointing to the natives tilling their crops. "They eat mesquite beans, but they ain't nasty-tempered. 'Paches now, they eat cactus, an' they's real mean-tempered. If'n I wuz gonna ask a question 'bout sumthin' I wasn' supposed ta find, I'd ask them Papagos, Pilgrim."

"Sounds feasible to me," Julian agreed. "How'd you know this village was here?"

"How? Why, Pilgrim, them Papagos been livin' here since th' Spaniards first came over. An' fer hundreds of years afore that, another tribe built their houses in th' same spot. Th' Pima Injuns called 'em th' Hohokam, meanin' 'those who have gone'. Int'restin', ain't it?" Bingo tugged his hat lower to shade his eyes. He'd exchanged the battered felt he usually wore for a hat made from a wolf's head. "Big

300

medicine," he'd assured Julian. And, looking at the perpetual snarl of bared wolf fangs sitting on the old man's head, Julian agreed that it had to be.

"Bingo," he said, "you would make a most fascinating archaeologist. Have you ever considered it? You already know more than many who have studied in Europe."

"T'ain't never been ta Europe, but I knows 'bout where I live an' hunt. An' if'n I don' know, I try ta find out." He shifted in his saddle to peer closely at Julian, and offered him a plug of tobacco, which was refused. "But that's why I kinda like you, Pilgrim. You like ta find out th' where and th' why of things, but you don' believe in disturbin' 'em. Ya got respect, Mr. Ashworth. That's what makes you different from a lot of others who come out here."

"You do realize that when I find this ancient burial ground, Bingo, I intend to dig up artifacts to take with me?" Julian's light brows rose questioningly.

"Yep, I know well what yer gonna do. Disturbin' th' dead ain't gonna bother th' livin' unless yer plannin' on bringin' in a whole bunch of them arkee . . . arkee . . . whatever ya called 'em. Now, I seen some of them at work, an' *they* can wake up th' dead with all that damn hammerin' an' diggin' they do."

"Well, Bingo, that would be the last thing I would do, 'bringing in a bunch of ar-kees' as you call them to create a scene," Julian said sternly. He hoped they understood each other perfectly. "I work better alone or with my daughter most of the time—with an occasional assistance from a guide of your caliber and stature."

"Well, thankee kindly, sir. We seem ta be seein' a little more eye ta eye now," Bingo grumbled. "It's jus' that I seen a lot of keerless know-it-alls and greenhorns comin' in this country, 'spectin' ta claim it and tame it in the time it'd take any proper mountain man ta clean his rifle. Now don't get me wrong, Mr. Ashworth, I ain't nessecelery talkin' 'bout you, but I seen a lot more gents leavin' this country with a arrow in his ass than a saddlebag full a'gold. No offense intended, sir."

"No offense taken, Bingo." Julian sighed wearily. "I just wish I knew what to do next, that's all. I'm at a stand-still. I've got a map that I can't even read and I . . ."

"My pappy always said that knowin' what ta do next was th' definition of wisdom," Bingo interrupted. "Yep, I'd say the wisest thing ta do here is ta ask ole Chief of th' Papagos jus' whar in th' hell is this ole stairway ta heaven, or whatever th' hell ya call it, on that thar map of yourn." Pausing to scratch one side of his nose, Bingo thought a moment before he continued. "Th' only thing we got ta lose is our scalps—or if'n Mother Luck is a'with us, jus' our horses."

"Hopefully neither!" Julian snorted. He still didn't know whether to take Bingo seriously or not.

The midday sun in the Arizona Territory is not exactly the kind of sun one would find in a North African desert, but the sun that was baking his derby certainly reminded Julian of the Sahara. He mopped his forehead with the linen handkerchief he carried in his breast coat pocket, and squinted at Bingo.

"I'm ready if you are," Julian said, then grinned at

the old man's muffled curse. "These are friendly Indians, remember?"

"I recollect what I said!" Bingo snapped testily. "But I never did trust *no* Injun, no matter how friendly they might 'peer ta be! I'm jus' thinkin' a minute, that's all." Finally he motioned for Julian to follow him, pausing for a moment to issue last warnings. "Now 'member, Pilgrim, lissen up, an' do what I do. Thar's a rule most white men should follow when dealin' with Injuns—observe their customs, an' don' offend 'em! We don' wanna step on any toes . . ."

That's a rule that Ryan Cordell intended to observe also. At the moment, he was seated in an Apache sweathouse, purifying his body. Spotted Tail had not yet taken Ryan to visit the chief, possibly because he was considered unclean until he'd joined the other men in the ritual of cleansing their bodies.

Water from the slow-moving creek was sprinkled over hot stones that had been heated in a fire, and clouds of steam filled the large, dome-shaped hut made of tree limbs and covered with buffalo hides. Ryan crouched at one side with several Apaches who had remained in camp, listening to the solemn chants that told of the recently returned warriors' brave deeds. Sweat trickled down his face and sides as the steam boiled up from the rocks, and he blinked away huge drops that clung to his eyelashes.

Sitting back on his heels, Ryan listened as Spotted Wolf bragged of the capture of the "white woman with hair made of moonlight."

303

"She is tall as a man," Spotted Wolf said loudly, "and will produce many fine sons for a warrior such as myself!"

Ryan listened impassively, recognizing Spotted Wolf's strategy. Buffalo Horn also claimed her, yet she had belonged to Spotted Tail's white friend, whispers informed the Apaches who had remained behind. Who would win the white woman?

Spotted Tail slanted a considering glance at Ryan, noting that he was wisely remaining silent, while Buffalo Horn was becoming angry. A thin smile curled Spotted Tail's mouth. It would be a fine entertainment to see his warriors fight over the white woman. He scratched at a bothersome fleabite and wondered why Ryan Cordell had not yet stated his intention to fight. Beyond his first claim of ownership, there had been no mention of wanting the woman. Perhaps he was tired of her and wished to bargain.

Flicking a long streamer of dark hair back over his shoulder, Spotted Tail considered this new thought for a moment. In spite of the threat to his dignity, he pondered issuing a challenge to the winner of the woman. She had felt good in his arms on the ride to their camp. Even though she was not well endowed like his wife, he had noticed her womanly curves, and how she had been soft and pliant yet as firm as a maiden. This white woman had silver hair like the moon, yet her eyes were the dark color of Earth Mother, and that was good medicine. She was taller than many of his warriors, and had shown little fear when they'd found her asleep in her camp. She was spirited like the feisty, half-wild mare who had produced his best war horse. Spotted Wolf was right—she would make a good wife for the man who won her, Spotted Tail decided.

Somehow Ryan sensed what Spotted Tail was thinking. He saw the flat black eyes swing toward him and narrow as if searching out his strengths and weaknesses, and knew that the chief's son had decided to fight for Stephanie. Damn! Since he was considered the original owner—if he'd been less than a friend to the chief his wishes would have been disregarded—there would be a contest between all the challengers. Ryan already knew what Chief Black Hawk's sense of justice would demand. He could either sell Stephanie or fight for her. As owner, he would be required to fight each of them in hand-to-hand combat. If he won, he would fight the next challenger, and then the next, until there were no more. If he lost to one of them, the winner would then fight the other challengers until there was one victor. That man would claim Stephanie as his wife, and as a consolation, Ryan would receive a few horses for her loss. The occasion would be a holiday for the Apaches, with feasting and games before and after the contest.

Considering the alternatives, Ryan had very little choice. He'd briefly weighed the possibility of bargaining for her, but then the Apaches would think him a coward if he didn't fight. As an honored friend of Black Hawk, it would be more shaming to the chief if he refused to fight than if he lost. An Apache saw no shame in retreat if it meant living to fight another day, but they took dim views of a cowardly warrior.

Stephanie had better appreciate the fact that he hadn't sold her outright, Ryan thought grimly. If he'd taken the horses Spotted Wolf had offered him, he wouldn't be sitting in this Apache sweathouse bleakly contemplating the future. The disagreement would be between the three Apaches then, with him well on the way to—

Ryan sighed disgustedly as he recalled his reason for being in Arizona Territory with Stephanie Ashworth. All a man's troubles could be blamed on either love of money or a woman, he reflected. In this case it was both.

Chapter Twenty-Three

Chief Black Hawk did just as Ryan had thought he would. The contest would be fought between Ryan and each of his challengers, with the winner being decided by the shaman in case of a tie. The rules were simple: each man fought until one of them could not get up or until the women of the village declared him to be too badly wounded to continue fighting.

"You have been gone long from our people," Black Hawk told Ryan. "Are you still a powerful warrior, White Bear?" The Apache name had been give Ryan years before because of the thick mat of hair on his chest, like that of a bear.

"Tomorrow will answer that question," Ryan answered, handing the chief back his pipe. His head was already spinning from the strong tobacco mixed with peyote that the chief favored. The cactus button called peyote produced hallucinations, and was usually reserved by the Apache people for religious ceremonies or special occasions. It had been a long time since Ryan had shared an Apache pipe. This pipe was more intricately decorated than the usual, simple hollow deer bone. Chief Black Hawk had come into the possession of a valuable pipe made of red stone called catlinite. It was carved into the shape of a horse in full gallop, with a pipestem made of cottonwood. From time to time, Black Hawk would dip into a beaded buckskin pouch to refill his pipe bowl, tamping the tobacco with a quilled tamping stick. Now he smiled at Ryan over the thin gray streamers of smoke drifting upward.

"As usual, you are quick with an answer that does not answer," Black Hawk observed. "Let me be specific: Do you think you can outfight my son as well as two other trained Apache warriors?"

Ryan resisted the temptation to shake his head clear of the fuzzy cobwebs that seemed to cloud his brain. Hedging for time, he took the pipe Black Hawk offered and held it in front of his face, squinting through the smoke. The old chief gazed back at him, eye for eye, his noble features creased into a questioning expression. Ryan almost smiled. Black Hawk was as brave and honorable a man as he'd ever met, with a presence as commanding as any Washington senator's. Born into a different world, Black Hawk would have been an illustrious leader known throughout the world. But as an Apache chief, he was simply a redskin destined for extermination, sharing that fate with other Apache leaders like Geronimo, Cochise, and Mangas Coloradas. Of those, only Geronimo was still alive and he was now living on a Federal reservation for Apaches. This renegade band was small, and had somehow avoided being herded onto a similar reservation.

"I believe myself strong enough to fight your best Apache warriors, yes," Ryan finally answered Black Hawk. He handed him back the pipe. They were sitting cross-legged in Black Hawk's tipi. The old chief leaned forward, fixing Ryan with a searching look from eyes that had grown glazed.

"This combat, though friendly, represents your people against mine, White Bear," Black Hawk said in a somber voice. "Things have happened in the past years, many things that have changed the ways of my people forever. We will become like the buffalo, vanquished and forgotten. Soon the plains will no longer thunder with the sound of the buffalo or the Apache."

Ryan couldn't argue. Black Hawk had seen the future as plainly as he had. It was sad, and in some ways unforgivable, but unavoidable.

"Yes, Black Hawk. But perhaps one day your people and mine may live in peace together."

"Perhaps. But now there is the question of the white woman with hair made of moonlight. Three of my best warriors, including my youngest son, want her. There will have to be a contest to decide among them. She is your woman, White Bear?"

Hesitating, Ryan searched for the right answer. Finally he said, "Yes, she is mine now. But the contest will decide whose woman she is tomorrow."

If Stephanie had known that her fate hinged upon Ryan fighting three battle-honed Apache warriors, she would have been much more apprehensive than she was already. As it was, she was only cross that Ryan had found better things to do than keep her informed about his progress.

"Where is he?" she demanded when Spotted Tail returned to his tipi. "I haven't seen him all day!"

"Keep your tongue, woman," Spotted Tail answered shortly. "You will be told what is necessary." He dropped a deerskin bag on the pallet at one end of the tipi and sat down.

Frustration made her voice sharper as Stephanie once more demanded, "Is Ryan still in the village? Why hasn't he come to see me?"

Spotted Tail gazed at Stephanie with narrowed eyes. She certainly wasn't as smart as Apache women, he decided. While Little Bird, his wife, might nag or become angry, she also knew when to be quiet. Still, this one could surely be trained in the ways of the Apache.

"He will be here soon. Now be quiet," Spotted Tail said in a tone that Stephanie immediately recognized as hostile.

Obedient at last, she folded her hands and sat back down on the pallet where she'd been sleeping. Upon waking, she'd first been slightly confused and disoriented, finally recalling the events leading to her presence in a cone-shaped dwelling made of buffalo hides. Spotted Tail's wife had been absolutely no help at all, simply shaking her head and shrugging her shoulders whenever Stephanie asked a question. Curiosity and doubt gnawed at her as she shifted uneasily on the pallet, wondering about Ryan's whereabouts. Surely, he hadn't left her!

It was already afternoon, and the bottom edge of the buffalo hide covering the tipi frame had been lifted for ventilation. A slash of sunlight dancing with dust motes lit the interior, and Stephanie

310

coughed as the dust settled in a fine film. In spite of the heat, it was bearable in the tipi, which surprised her. Maybe it was because Spotted Tail's tipi had been erected beneath the spreading branches of a cottonwood tree, and cooler breezes drifted from the slow-moving water of the little creek winding through their village.

Resting her chin in a cupped palm, Stephanie listened to the laughter and shouts of children playing in the water. She sighed wistfully, wishing she could join them. It had been days since she'd had a proper bath, and there were few things more restful. Right now she needed peace, needed a rest from the frightening events that she couldn't control, that were controlling her.

All her life, Stephanie had been taught to be in control, to master her own fate. Since coming to Arizona Territory, she hadn't been in control of a single thing, it seemed. Especially her own emotions. Ryan Cordell had turned her world upside down. Even her present danger was dulled when she thought about her feelings for Ryan. He would somehow rescue her from this crisis, but who would rescue her from him?

Stephanie's head jerked up as Ryan entered the tipi. Ducking to step through the door flap, he paused just inside the opening. Her eyes widened as Stephanie stared incredulously. Ryan was dressed in a breechcloth, and his dark hair was tied back with a strip of cloth wound around his head. He wore moccasins made of buffalo hide, with high tops stretching to just below his knees. She might not have recognized him as quickly if it hadn't been for the pelt of dark hair on his chest. Few Apaches had any hair at all on their chests or bodies, she'd noticed.

With his dark hair and skin, Ryan resembled an Apache warrior until one looked closely at his face. No Apache had those silver-gray eyes like clear mountain pools, eyes that seemed to see into her soul and know how she felt. Now his crooked smile made her heart leap, and Stephanie didn't realize she was standing until she was folded in Ryan's arms. She pressed her face against his shoulder and wrapped her arms around him, holding tightly.

"Miss me, Princess?" Ryan's teasing tone sparked an impudent answer.

"Like a boil," she replied, rubbing her cheek against his clean-shaven jaw. "Where the devil have you been?"

"Ah, what a welcome! I can always count on you to show me your best side." He held her at arm's length, surveying her with a critical eye. "You look terrible, love."

"Thank you, Sir Galahad! If you have any more compliments, give them to our friendly hosts. I don't need them. And you're avoiding my question—where have you been?"

Ryan laughed. "Parleying with Chief Black Hawk . . ."

"Parleying?"

"Conversing, if you prefer. Discussing our somewhat precarious position in his village . . ."

"But I thought you were supposed to be good friends with the chief," Stephanie interrupted. "Can't you just tell him to let us go in peace? Why do they keep calling you White Bear? And why were we

312

dragged away from our camp and . . ."

"Stephanie, lower your voice." Ryan's fingers curled around her arm and he sat down, tugging her down beside him. "I am friends with Black Hawk, but *you*, Princess, are considered part of the loot from their raid. There are three contenders for your lily-white hand in marriage. One, the warrior who first claimed you, Spotted Wolf; two, Buffalo Horn, who also wants you; and three, Spotted Tail, the chief's youngest son who has decided to risk his dignity by taking you as his second wife. His first wife, Little Bird, is less than thrilled."

"Second wife?" Stephanie's brows rose. "Do you mean second to that sour-faced witch who tries to pinch me when no one's looking? That should be fun. There are only three contenders, Ryan?" She wanted to ask the obvious question, but the remaining shreds of her pride made her pause.

"Oh, did I forget someone?" Ryan's eyes danced with pure deviltry as he grinned at her. "Let me see—" He made a show of counting on his fingers and Stephanie lost her patience.

"Idiot!" She slapped at his hands. "Are you going to bargain for me or not?"

"What if I said not?"

"I'd find some way to hunt you down and shoot you."

"Left with that option, I suppose I will." All traces of humor faded from Ryan's face as he leaned close, his lips almost brushing against Stephanie's ear. "Listen, Princess. It's not a matter of bargaining. I have to fight for you, and I'm not too sure I'll win."

"Ryan . . . !"

"Hush and listen—I'll do my best, but if I lose, don't try anything foolish. Just make the best of it, all right?"

"Ryan, I cannot believe that you are calmly sitting there and advising me to live happily ever after with some Apache brave!" Stephanie stared at him incredulously, unwilling to believe there was even a remote possibility. This had to be a nightmare. But a glance at the grim expression on Ryan's face confirmed her worst fears. "Can't you do something?" Her voice rose on the last word and his fingers tightened around her wrist.

"Look, the white man has pushed these Indians back from their ancestral homes until they're living with their backs against the wall. I'm lucky that Black Hawk and Spotted Tail consider me a friend. They could have just killed me and taken you captive, you know."

"Can't you tell them we're married or something, that I'm already your woman?" Stephanie struggled for control, but her expression was pinched and her face pale.

"I already did, remember? But though the Apache prize fidelity among their own women, they don't look upon whites the same way. Stephanie, whatever they tell you to do—do it. Apache husbands aren't noted for their patience."

"You're talking like the outcome is already settled. Is there a chance you'll lose?"

"There's a slim chance I'll win. I have to fight all three, Princess, and each one of them is going to try his best to beat me. By the third round, I'll be pretty damned tired."

Tears welled in Stephanie's dark eyes and she tried to blink them back. She failed miserably. Wet paths trailed from brimming eyes down her dusty cheeks to drip from her chin, and Ryan smiled tenderly as he wiped them away with his fingers.

"Who are you crying for, Princess? Me or you?"

"Both." Her voice caught on a sob. "You might be killed, and I . . . I . . ." She couldn't finish the thought.

"I might be bruised and bloody, but this isn't a fight to the death, love. We're both survivors, remember? Don't let anyone see you cry. I've got to go now."

"Ryan!" She clutched at his arm as he rose from the mat in a lithe movement. Everything she wanted to say was in her eyes as she looked up at him, but all she could manage was a soft, "Good luck . . ."

He grinned. "You, too, Princess. It'll be all right. Trust me."

Stephanie stared after him. Her future hinged upon the outcome of hand-to-hand combat, and she was terrified.

Chapter Twenty-Four

The early morning sun glinted behind distant hills, then shot rays of light over the Apache camp nestled by the stream. People were already stirring in anticipation of the day's events, including Stephanie.

Spotted Tail's wife had brought her clean garments, insisting with gestures and sharp commands in Apache that she put them on. Balking at first, Stephanie had finally relented when Spotted Tail was summoned.

"You will wear them," he said coldly. "I will hear no argument."

"And if I choose not to wear them?" Stephanie asked defiantly as Spotted Tail turned to leave.

He turned back to stare at her with a disdainful expression. "Then you will suffer the indignity of being dressed by the women. I do not think you would choose such a thing."

He was right. Stephanie quietly let Little Bird dress her in a long gown made of softened deerskin. It had been beautifully decorated with colored beads and shells, and was studded with bits of turquoise. A fringe hung from the hem that reached to just below her knees, and more fringe was sewn into the seams of elbow-length sleeves. Stephanie realized that the dress was for special occasions, as most of the women she'd seen wore skirts and blouses instead of such obvious finery. Her wedding dress? A grim thought.

The long night before had been spent tossing and turning restlessly in spite of her exhaustion. Neither Spotted Tail nor Ryan had returned to the tipi, and she had been left alone with Little Bird as a hostile guard. A thousand different fates had presented themselves in the darkness, until Stephanie had wanted to pull her hair in frustration and fright. She was calmer now, letting her long hair be braided and tied with thin strips of leather, waiting for the inevitable.

When she was led outside, Stephanie saw what she was certain was every man, woman, and child in the entire village gathered around a small clearing. This was the area cleared for battle, and the combatants were already standing at the sides. A steady tattoo was being pounded on wood and hide drums, the tempo beating faster and faster as the men who were to fight stepped forward.

Stephanie's gaze immediately riveted on Ryan. He was standing a little apart from the others, and his body glistened with the same oil the other warriors had used. While the others paraded about like gamecocks, calling out insults and challenges that delighted their audience, Ryan stood quietly with his arms folded across his chest. Like the others, he wore only a brief breechcloth, and his hair had been tied back from his forehead with a strip of rawhide. To Stephanie, it seemed as if he'd become one of them, as feral and savage as any Apache warrior. She stiffened in alarm when she spotted the gleaming knife Ryan held, and her eyes flew to the Apaches who were to fight. Yes, they held knives also, and now she understood that the combat was to be more dangerous than she'd thought.

Her heart raced madly as the drums began to beat slower, then grew quiet. No one in the crowd spoke. It was to begin.

Spotted Wolf was the first challenger. He began to move in a large circle, watching Ryan and taunting him with boasts. Ryan's expression never altered. He moved counter to Spotted Wolf, his muscles taut and ready as he waited for the brave's first move. It came quickly, with a sudden lunge forward. Ryan pivoted at the last possible moment, letting Spotted Wolf rush past him with the force of his momentum. He brought the edge of his hand down on Spotted Wolf's neck as the brave stumbled forward, sending him sprawling into the dry grass.

Leaping to his feet, Spotted Wolf faced Ryan with narrowed eyes. He would not underestimate this white man again. Now he would treat him as a formidable foe.

They circled warily, like two fighting cocks, tensed and ready. Again Spotted Wolf lunged, and this time Ryan met him. They grappled, muscles straining as each sought to throw the other one to the ground, grunting with their efforts. Spotted Wolf wrested free, whirled, then slashed at Ryan with his knife.

The point grazed a thin red trail along Ryan's ribs before he could leap back, and Stephanie stifled a moan of fear for him with fingers pressed against her lips.

The woman beside her tugged sharply on Stephanie's arm and signaled that she was to make no sign of favoritism. Jerking free, Stephanie's chin lifted stubbornly. She might be forced into Apache clothing, and forced to watch this spectacle, but she could not be forced into suppressing her emotions. She was not an Apache, and would not behave like one. Stephanie's braids whipped defiantly as she tossed her head, and the Apache woman threw up her hands and muttered a sharp comment to Little Bird.

When Stephanie turned back to the fight, she was relieved to see Spotted Wolf once more lying on the ground. He tried to rise only to fall back, clutching at one shoulder. Ryan must have cut him, Stephanie realized, and her eyes raked Ryan's lean frame. There appeared to be no more damage inflicted; maybe the fight was over.

When Spotted Wolf lurched to his feet, Stephanie gnashed her teeth in dismay. Her throat ached as the two men closed, fought, pulled apart then closed again, knives flashing in the early morning light. Then just as suddenly as it had begun it was over.

Rolling across the ground amidst clouds of dust, the tangled knot of sweating combatants finally stopped. One man lay stretched upon the ground while the other stumbled to his feet. As the dust cleared, Stephanie closed her eyes and offered a brief prayer of gratitude. Ryan stood with his legs apart and feet braced. Slowly, he lifted one hand to signal that he was the victor.

Apparently few cared who won, because the Apaches laughed and shouted congratulations. Ryan was immediately surrounded and led away.

The next few hours Stephanie spent wondering what had happened, and what would happen. No one seemed the least bit inclined to tell her anything, not that she would have understood them anyway. She was seated beneath the spreading branches of a cottonwood, still guarded by Little Bird and two other women. From time to time she was offered food, which she refused. How could she eat anything?

The second bout took place when the noon sun was high above, glaring down with brutal intensity. Stephanie once more watched with her heart in her mouth as Ryan fought the warrior named Buffalo Horn.

This warrior preferred forcing Ryan into making the first moves, and he cleverly used some of his opponent's own tactics. Feint, draw, lunge, parry—it reminded Stephanie of a fencing match. Only this was real, and she was the trophy.

To her relief, Ryan quickly disposed of Buffalo Horn, luring him into a fake pass that he quickly countered with a chopping blow to his exposed neck. Buffalo Horn tumbled head over heels, dazed, and Ryan was once more declared victor.

Again, there was a time of feasting and games, with Apache children playing with hoops and sticks, and men clad in headdresses dancing about as if in a play. Diminutive figures imitated the costumed braves, much to the merriment of the crowd.

A group of women, including Little Bird and her other guard, began playing a game near Stephanie. She watched with vague interest as a blanket was stretched over the grass. Each position was pegged through the blanket with an awl, a tool which Stephanie had seen the Indian women using on tanned deer hides. Laughing and giggling, each player would throw four sticks at an awl stone in the center. Apparently the sticks had different values as points, because one had a special mark and all were flat on one side and curved on the other. Finally losing interest in a game she didn't understand, Stephanie let her gaze wander.

Naked children ran squealing among the tipis, riding stick horses, chasing each other, pausing at times to stare with wide dark eyes at the white woman with silver hair. Older boys set out on short hunting and exploring expeditions, carrying half-sized spears and bows and arrows. Failing to find birds, prairie dogs, or jackrabbits, they attacked grasshoppers and dragonflies with their fierce weapons. Much larger boys played at war, or rode their shaggy ponies across the plain to show off their riding skills, hanging from the side of a galloping mount, then swinging down to scoop up an object from the ground in the hopes of impressing a pretty girl.

Thick smoke drifted toward her as the green willow branches used in the cook fires were burned to discourage mosquitoes, gnats, and green flies that plagued the camp.

Leaning her head back against the tree trunk behind her, Stephanie's eyes half closed as she listened to the whoops and yells from the men playing a wheel game. The players threw arrows or sticks at a rolling hoop laced with rawhide, shouting and bragging with good-humored gusto.

Fidgeting, Stephanie watched for Ryan, hoping he would come and speak to her. Where was he? She hadn't had an opportunity to speak to him since the day before, and she needed reassurance. A gleam of hope sparked now, where there had been little before, but there was still one more contest to win.

It was late afternoon before the final match began. Once more Stephanie was led to a spot to watch, guarded on each side. She shifted from one foot to another, anxiously scanning the crowd for Ryan until she finally found him. He seemed as fresh as he had early that morning. Spotted Tail stood not far away, a faint smile curving his mouth as he observed his opponent.

Ryan heartily wished that he was as fresh as he'd been earlier. His strained muscles were tight now, and not as limber as they had been, while the cut along his ribs ached with throbbing pain. And to make it worse, Spotted Tail knew his weakness. Ryan gulped in a deep breath of air. The drums had stopped; it was the signal to begin.

Balanced on the balls of his feet like a sleek cat, Ryan carefully watched Spotted Tail. This would be his most formidable adversary. Spotted Tail was no novice to the art of knife fighting, and always kept a cool head. They circled each other like wary cats, assessing size and strength as well as agility. Spotted Tail had had plenty of time to watch Ryan, while Ryan had to depend on his memory.

Spotted Tail made the first move, a quick slice of

his knife and twist of his body that almost caught Ryan off guard. Leaping back, Ryan just barely managed to avoid the glittering blade. Taking advantage of Spotted Tail's foiled thrust that left him slightly off balance, Ryan lunged forward and deliberately gashed the brave's arm. He'd drawn first blood already, and a murmur rippled through the crowd.

Black eyes narrowing, Spotted Tail's mouth thinned to a straight line, and Ryan had the impression of a wild cat with its ears laid back. Retaliation was immediate. Knife raised high, Spotted Tail rushed him and Ryan caught his knife hand in a harsh grip. They grappled, each trying to free his hand from the other, until finally they broke apart, sweat streaming down their oiled bodies. Beads of sweat dotted their faces as well, running into their eyes, and leaving both of them half blinded.

Shaking his head to clear his eyes, Ryan lowered his guard slightly and Spotted Tail took immediate advantage. A burning sensation like liquid fire seared across Ryan's chest, and only a quick twist of his lean frame kept him from being seriously injured. The cut jolted him, made him vicious and less careful, and Ryan concentrated only on his foe.

His street fighting days in the back alleys and docks of New York came to his aid now, and all the little tricks he'd learned came into play. Spotted Tail was quickly winded and confused, not expecting the fancy tricks Ryan was using. Ryan was in front of him, then in back, spinning so that Spotted Tail had to constantly turn to keep his back guarded. Ryan pretended to trip, then, moving swiftly on the balls of his feet, he threw his knife from his right hand to his left and slammed his body into Spotted Tail.

Grunting, Spotted Tail crashed to the ground like a fallen tree and was instantly straddled by Ryan. Quick reflexes made the Apache grip Ryan's knife hand, keeping the blade from slicing into him while his knife hand aimed for Ryan. Fingers like iron bands coiled around Spotted Tail's wrist, straining to keep his knife at bay. Ryan half rose to his toes for leverage, pushing his hand down and down, closer and closer to Spotted Tail.

A thin scream rose behind Ryan, calling his name before the voice cut off abruptly. The distraction was just enough to catch Ryan off guard when Spotted Tail heaved upward, bucking him off. Ryan found himself staring up into Spotted Tail's dark eyes as the brave pinned him to the ground. The Apache's knife pressed coldly against Ryan's throat.

Ryan stared up at Spotted Tail with glittering, fearless eyes, defying him, and the Apache smiled. Deliberately, the knife drew across Ryan's throat in a shallow crease. It stung, but was not a mortal wound. Leaping to his feet, Spotted Tail held his knife high, declaring himself the winner to shouts of praise.

Stephanie, watching, was horrified. She hadn't meant to scream, but hadn't been able to stop herself. Her scream had cost Ryan the fight, and now she was to marry Spotted Tail. Closing her eyes, Stephanie did something she'd never done in her entire life. She fainted.

Chapter Twenty-Five

Moaning, Stephanie struggled awake. She was back in Spotted Tail's tipi. It must be close to dark, for long shadows had deepened into purple, and the air was cooler. Sitting up, Stephanie threw back the light blanket covering her and started to rise.

A quick command in Apache halted her, and her head jerked up to see Little Bird glaring at her. She was obviously none too pleased to have the prospect of another wife in her home. The Apache woman shoved a bowl toward Stephanie, indicating she was to eat. Shaking her head, Stephanie shoved it back.

They faced each other like two weasels fighting for the same den, hostility in every fiber of their bodies. To Little Bird, this was an unforgivable intrusion. Second wives or even a third was not unheard of in Apache tribes, but usually they were sisters to lessen the friction between women. A helping hand was often welcome, but this white woman would be no practical help. She was to be little more than a brood mare because Spotted Tail had no sons, and it shamed Little Bird that her husband had chosen another. She shoved the bowl back toward Stephanie and reached out to viciously tug one of her prized silver braids.

Surprised, Stephanie sucked in a pained gasp, then reacted with a quick slap across the woman's face. The force of the blow rocked Little Bird back on her heels, but she recovered swiftly. Lunging forward, she tackled Stephanie with both arms around her middle, sending them both sprawling backward on the woven grass mat. They rolled across the floor of the tipi, through the ashes of the fire, and over woven baskets and cooking utensils. Possessions scattered as Stephanie and Little Bird wrestled with panting gasps of rage, pummeling each other and clawing like enraged cats.

Too engrossed in their battle to notice, they rolled outside through the opened flap of buffalo hide. The celebrations were at their height, and few noticed them at first, until an old woman called a shrill summons to others to enjoy the fight. A laughing circle formed as Stephanie and Little Bird rolled in a tangle of flying braids and fists.

A shriek of pain mingled with fury when Little Bird sank her teeth into Stephanie's shoulder, and using her long legs as leverage, Stephanie flipped the shorter, stockier Apache woman onto her back. Straddling her, Stephanie gripped a handful of Little Bird's hair in one hand and yanked her head back. Her fingers curled into a fist that slammed against Little Bird's chin repeatedly as Stephanie lost all control. The Apache woman represented all her frustrations and helpless anger.

326

When iron fingers closed around her wrist, holding her arm, Stephanie half turned with a snarl of rage, hitting out at the interloper. She was yanked roughly to her feet and held above the ground by strong arms around her middle while others came to Little Bird's aid. Kicking and bucking against her captor, Stephanie panted with renewed fury.

"Be still!" a harsh male voice growled in her ear, but Stephanie was past hearing. She screamed furiously as she twisted against the arms holding her tighter and tighter until she couldn't breathe, then finally recognized Ryan's voice. "Dammit, Stephanie, I said be still!"

Growing quiet, she stood passively in Ryan's embrace, catching her breath as she watched the Apache woman through narrowed eyes. Wild tangles of hair hung in her eyes, obscuring her vision, but Stephanie could still see Little Bird being helped to her feet. It seemed as if the entire village had turned out to watch them fight. Everywhere Stephanie looked she saw people jostling for a look at the white woman who was to be Spotted Tail's new wife.

Half turning, Stephanie slanted a glance at Ryan's grim face. He was angry with her, muttering in her ear, "I told you not to make any kind of fuss, dammit!"

"She started it . . ."

"That's no excuse!" His hold tightened savagely, forcing the breath from her lungs again as he lifted her from her feet. "You don't understand, Stephanie— Hey . . . !"

Ryan's surprised exclamation warned Stephanie. She jerked her head around as Little Bird lunged

327

forward with a wild whoop of hatred, her fingers curved into clawing talons to rip at the white woman's face. Instinctively, Stephanie brought up her long legs, taking advantage of Ryan's tight hold on her to kick out with both feet, catching the Apache woman square in the stomach. Little Bird flew back with a pained "whoosh," and sprawled on the ground like a dumped sack of cornmeal.

Ready to continue, Stephanie struggled against Ryan's grip. He was stunned. Could this be aristocratic Stephanie Ashworth? Darling of New York society? Beloved daughter of wealthy financier Julian Ashworth? This wild, snarling creature with lips pulled back in a feral snarl as she tried to get at her opponent? Ryan shook his head in amazement.

"You're a barbarian," he told Stephanie, pulling away before Little Bird could recover. He half dragged Stephanie to a distant spot beneath a tree, still holding her tightly. "Do you realize you might have really hurt Little Bird?"

"I wish I'd killed the bitch!" Stephanie spat viciously. She was shaking all over, trembling with anger and reaction. When Ryan released her arms, she pushed at the silky tangle of hair in her eyes, facing him defiantly. She'd had enough. She'd been pushed to her limits and she knew it. Never, in her entire life, had she been reduced to this uncivilized level.

Ryan stared at her as if he'd never seen her before, and this Stephanie *was* unknown to him. Her eyes were huge, dark smudges in her pale face, and her mouth, usually so soft and quick to smile, was thinned into a hard line. The neatly braided hair had loosened into a wild mane that tumbled into her face and down her back almost to her waist. A slow smile tugged at the corners of his mouth as Ryan shook his head again.

"You're dangerous, Stephanie Ashworth," he said softly. "I never knew you had it in you."

"Well, neither did I. So now we both know that I can be just as barbaric as these heathen Apaches." Stephanie's legs, usually quite obedient and dependable, turned traitor. They trembled as if afflicted with a palsy, threatening to deposit her on the ground like a pile of old rags. To keep the remaining shreds of her dignity intact, she promptly sat down.

Hesitating, Ryan debated on the wisdom of joining her. According to Apache law, she now belonged to Spotted Tail and he had no rights. It was a sticky situation that required tactful handling. He had to observe their laws or both he and Stephanie would pay the consequences, but would she understand that? No easy answer came to mind when Stephanie tilted her head to look at him and asked, "What are you going to do, Ryan? Surely you won't leave me here . . ."

Her eyes grew larger, dark velvet pools that stared at him with mounting apprehension when he turned his head and didn't answer.

"Ryan? You . . . you aren't thinking about leaving me with these Apaches, are you?"

His voice was rougher than he intended, but anger and doubt gave it a sharp edge.

"What the hell do you expect me to do? Just politely tell Black Hawk and Spotted Tail that I have no intentions of leaving you here even though I lost the fight?'' His fist smacked into the tree trunk Stephanie leaned against. ''Dammit, I can't fight an entire village of trained warriors, Stephanie!''

''But . . . but there must be some way . . .''

''Yeah? Then give me a solution. I'm willing to listen to any feasible plan.''

She stared at him blankly, feeling as if she'd just stepped into a yawning black void. Stephanie hardly realized when Spotted Tail strode up to them, his gaze darting from her ashen face to Ryan. He spoke to Ryan in Apache. Ryan nodded curtly, glanced at Stephanie, then pivoted and walked away.

Stephanie slowly became aware of Spotted Tail's hand reaching out to help her up. Listlessly, because she had very little choice, Stephanie placed her hand in his. She was his now, and Spotted Tail's brief nod of approval at her compliance was perfunctory. He expected obedience.

''I will treat you well, '' he said quietly. ''Little Bird will bother you no more. She has been chastised for her unseemly jealousy.'' Spotted Tail lifted a hand and let his fingers comb through Stephanie's tangled waves of hair, watching with admiration as the silky strands slipped through his fingers. ''You will learn the Apache way quickly, and will be happy.''

''Spotted Tail, I do not wish to offend you, but my heart is elsewhere.'' Stephanie's chin lifted as she gazed into the eyes level with hers. ''It is not my desire to be your wife.''

''But it is my desire that you be. In time you will forget the man we call White Bear. He will be as the wind,'' he said, making a sweeping gesture with his

330

hands. "You will know he exists but you will not see him."

"No. I will not forget him."

Losing patience with this stubborn white woman, Spotted Tail shook his head angrily.

"I will make you forget him! I want sons, tall, strong sons to go with me into battle, and you will give them to me!"

"No!" Stephanie jerked away. "I will give you no sons, Spotted Tail."

The Apache drew himself to his full height, a scant inch above Stephanie, and glared at her fiercely.

"Because you belonged to a friend of our people, I will be lenient. You will have two suns to make yourself ready before I come to you, but on the third night I will wait no longer. The magic will be stronger if you are willing."

Without waiting for an answer, Spotted Tail took Stephanie's elbow and turned her around, pushing her ahead of him across the dusty grass. His tipi was empty when they arrived.

"Do not think to escape," Spotted Tail said when he noticed Stephanie's quick glance around. "I am not foolish enough to leave you unguarded. Any attempt to leave will be halted, and I will not be pleased that you have tried." He shoved her toward the mat where she usually slept and said, "Sleep, woman, so that you may rise early to bid farewell to White Bear. He will be leaving at first light with the horses I paid him for you."

Stephanie's aloof disdain vanished as she jerked her head around to stare at Spotted Tail.

"You . . . you paid Ryan for me?" She didn't believe him. Ryan wouldn't do that!

"Yes." Spotted Tail smiled cruelly. "I gave him five good horses and a white buffalo robe for you. Your value is more than anyone can remember paying for a woman."

"I don't believe you," Stephanie said flatly. "You're making this up so I'll hate him."

"You do not believe the word of an Apache warrior?" His hands flashed out, tangling in her hair as he drew her close. Spotted Tail's face was only inches from hers, so close Stephanie could count the sun lines fanning from the corners of his eyes. She didn't flinch when his hands tightened harshly in her hair, but narrowed her eyes.

"You are defiant, but you will see what I say is true," Spotted Tail said after a moment. "You will stand with me when White Bear leaves our camp, and see that Spotted Tail speaks straight."

Clenching her hands, Stephanie remained silent. She would not let him taunt her into answering again. It was only after Spotted Tail had released her and left the tipi that she yielded to emotion. Collapsing on the straw mat, Stephanie squeezed her eyes tightly shut. She refused to believe that Ryan would callously sell her to the Apaches.

But when morning came after a long, sleepless night, Stephanie stood beside Spotted Tail and watched Ryan cut his new horses out of the herd. She stood as if carved from a block of marble, tall and straight, glaring at him when he paused in front of them.

Once more dressed in trousers and a shirt, Ryan

332

tugged his hat lower over his eyes.

"I don't suppose you want to talk to me," he said to Stephanie. He shrugged when she remained silent. "Well, enjoy your new family, Princess . . ."

"You bastard!" Stephanie took a furious step forward, her dark eyes blazing with hot lights. "I hope you get trampled to death by your precious new horses!"

A mocking smile tilted Ryan's mouth as he tipped his hat. "You've learned to properly swear, I see. Think about me some night when you hear the wind outside your tipi . . ."

"You'll be in hell a long time before I think about you again, Ryan Cordell!"

Ryan slid Spotted Tail an amused glance. "'Heav'n has no rage like love to hatred turn'd, Nor hell a fury like a woman scorn'd,'" he quoted. "William Congreve, *The Mourning Bride*. Rather fitting, don't you think? 'Bye, Spotted Tail. Hope you survive her. She's a little rough on a man."

Stephanie's eyes were dry as she watched Ryan ride away, and her low voice followed him, carried on the early morning breeze.

"You're a deceiver, Ryan Cordell! You're a liar, and . . . and I hate you!"

She watched until he disappeared over a rocky ridge, then turned to face Spotted Tail. Behind the knowing gleam in his dark eyes there was a spark of pity, and that she could not tolerate.

"I still won't let you touch me," she stated calmly, and wheeled to walk back to the tipi. Spotted Tail's answer was expected.

"I won't need your permission, woman."

Even after reaching the privacy of the tipi that was her new home, no tears would come. Stephanie sat on her mat and stared at the glowing embers of fire in the center of the floor. She was numb, with no emotion left. This was a dream, a nightmare, she thought. It had to be.

Chapter Twenty-Six

Night shadows fell softly on the Apache village. Dusk had a strange way of being heard, Stephanie had discovered. The children's voices were muted somehow, as if heard through a mist, and even the barking of the dogs seemed more quiet. Cooking fires were lit outside, and families gathered to share their meals and gossip.

No one had intruded in Spotted Tail's tipi during the long day. Bowls of food were discreetly left just inside the door flap, but Stephanie had not been tempted. True to his word, Spotted Tail had not bothered her, but Stephanie didn't intend to take any risks. Tucked inside her sleeve was a knife, discarded by some careless soul on the ground outside the tipi. Wary at first, Stephanie had stared for a long time at the sharp knife lying at the bottom edge of the tipi where the cover had been lifted for ventilation. When no one returned to claim it, she had scooted stealthily across the tipi and snatched it up, expecting at any moment to hear a harsh command behind her. But no one seemed to know.

It gave her a more secure feeling to know she had a weapon. Too bad her father's Colt had been confiscated by the Apaches. She would certainly have used it, given the opportunity. Forcing her brain to contemplate escape had been difficult at first. In spite of her best efforts, thoughts of Ryan kept returning to haunt her. It took great determination to exorcise him, but Julian had always claimed Stephanie had great willpower. This should stretch it to the limits.

Dusk deepened into night, and Stephanie had only the glow of smoking embers from the fire pit as light. She poked halfheartedly at the fire for a few moments, then lost interest.

Familiar night sounds filtered in through the still open door flap. The village was quiet for the night as everyone settled wearily to sleep. Only the guards posted at several points remained awake and alert, watching for enemies. Stephanie shifted when she realized her foot had fallen asleep, jerking herself fully awake. She'd been on the brink of dozing, but some alien sound in the night had disturbed her.

She waited, hair on the back of her neck bristling as she strained to hear. There was nothing stirring but her active imagination, Stephanie decided. Spotted Tail had promised he would leave her alone, and his pride would not allow him to do otherwise. She'd been half expecting Little Bird to attempt vengeance, but reasoned that unless she was stupid, the Apache woman would know where suspicion would fall should Stephanie come to harm.

A small limb she'd placed in the fire popped, sending up a spiraling shower of sparks. Curls of smoke drifted out the smoke hole at the top of the tipi. Yawning, Stephanie surrendered at last to the temptation of sleep and stretched out on her mat.

But when she closed her eyes and tried to relax, she found she couldn't. Her muscles were tense and tight, and the back of her neck ached almost unbearably. It was well past midnight before she finally drifted into a restless sleep peopled with frightening dreams.

Though the hours seemed to drag the next day, it was over all too quickly as far as Stephanie was concerned. Only one more day was left in the three Spotted Tail had given her. She watched the sun sink behind western ridges in a blazing ball of fire that lit the entire sky.

Desperation tinged Stephanie's last night alone in the tipi. Tomorrow she would wed Spotted Tail in a brief Apache ceremony. Her throat ached, and she couldn't help thoughts of Ryan.

How could he have left her like that? In spite of herself, she'd entertained the hope that he'd return for her, but even that had faded now. Ryan Cordell had obviously abandoned her to her fate. "Trust me," Ryan had said. And she had.

Sliding sweat-moistened hands down the sides of her beaded dress, Stephanie knelt on the thin mat that was her bed. Two guards stood outside the closed door flap of the tipi, ruining any chance she might have for escape. Stephanie's fingers lightly touched the bone handle of her hidden knife. If worse came to worse, she would use it on herself.

Night shadows curled into the tipi, bringing cooler breezes through the cover lifted at the bottom edge. Dry grasses rustled like the husky whispers of a lover, and in the distance a mountain cat rasped its peculiar cough. It was a warm night. No moon brightened the sky; only a handful of dusty stars twinkled like fireflies.

Stephanie stretched out on her mat staring through the small opening at the bottom of the tipi. The night breezes blew toward the open plain, and she wished she could drift to freedom on them, riding the wind like puffs of thistle.

She closed her eyes to shut out the sudden stab of pain that pierced her like a knife. She'd never be free again, never see her father again, never see . . .

A hand clapped over her mouth and Stephanie's body went rigid with fear. Her first instinct was to grab at the hand to pry loose the hard fingers digging into her lips and jaw. Frantically, she clawed at the hand cutting off her air.

"Stop it!" a voice hissed. "It's me . . . !"

Nothing registered with Stephanie for a moment. All she heard was the sound of fear, and she reacted wildly. The knife she'd found slid into her hand with little effort, and she slashed at the shadow looming over her head. There was a muttered curse in a voice she dimly recognized as the hand was snatched away, and Stephanie twisted to see.

"You idiot," Ryan snarled, "do you want to stay here?"

"No! Oh, no . . ." Stephanie dropped her knife. "What are you doing here?"

"I'd heard there was a church picnic. Did I miss it?" Ryan crouched on his heels beside the ventilation flap. "If you want to leave, you'd better come now. Things are going to get warm shortly . . ."

"What do you mean?" Stephanie didn't hesitate as she followed him through the tall grasses outside Spotted Tail's tipi. A quick glance back satisfied her curiosity about the two guards posted outside her door flap. They were stretched motionless in the grass.

"I mean just what I said," Ryan answered in a whisper, then placed a finger over his mouth to indicate silence. They were among the horses now, crouching down as they mingled with the herd. Ryan pulled Stephanie with him, hoping the horses wouldn't give them away. Any moment now there would be sheer pandemonium, and he had to be ready.

Stephanie noticed a subtle difference in the night air, a sharp, acrid smell that wafted on freshening breezes. A swift glance gave her the answer at the same time as it was discovered by the remaining Apache posted as guard. Fire.

"This is it," Ryan was telling her then, boosting her to the back of a snorting horse. A length of rope trailed from its neck, left there by the owner for ease in capturing it, and he wound it swiftly around the animal's lower jaw in a makeshift bridle.

The dry grass caught fire quickly, spreading across the plains in a crimson tide. Men, women, and children poured from the tipis to fight the blaze, bringing buckets of hide to dip water from the creek. The Apaches didn't attempt to stop the grass fire, but dampened their tipis to prevent damage. Several braves began to cut a fire line around the encampment even though the blaze was spreading in the other direction. The wind had been known to change directions swiftly.

In the confusion, no one paid any attention to the terrified horses running away, or to the two buckskin-clad riders astride one of the animals.

Ryan and Stephanie rode without stopping or speaking. It was near daylight before they paused and turned the Apache mount loose.

"What are we going to do now?" Stephanie asked wearily. Though tired, she was exhilarated. She was free!

"Walk. Or climb, that is." Ryan gestured to the towering sandstone cliff behind them. "Just on the other side of that little mound are our horses and gear."

Stephanie's doubtful gaze rose up the steep sides. "Do I sprout wings, maybe?"

"It'd be easier if you could. Wait here." Ryan rose from the rock where he'd been sitting, and started across the plains at a brisk trot. He ran until he came to the banks of a small stream that was little more than a thin trickle of water. Kneeling, he removed his boots. Wading into the water, he made his way downstream for a distance, then returned to the point where he had entered. Now Ryan slipped on a pair of moccasins, and, turning, ran backward along the faint marks of his earlier footsteps. It wasn't a ruse that would fool anyone for long, but it would possibly cause a short delay.

"Ready?" he said to Stephanie when he returned.

She shook her head, but rose from the humped shadow of a rock where she'd been sitting. It was hard climbing up the face of the cliff, especially in the binding Apache dress, but with Ryan's help she finally managed to make the summit with nothing more than skinned knees and scraped hands.

Collapsing to catch her breath, Stephanie frowningly examined her palms. Tiny pebbles were embedded in the raw skin from sliding against the rough rock surfaces as she'd climbed.

"You'll live," Ryan observed unsympathetically. He crouched down beside her. "Come on. It's almost daylight and we need to be moving."

"Your concern for my welfare is overwhelming," Stephanie commented dryly as Ryan grabbed her wrists and tugged her to her feet. "I'm deeply touched."

"If we stay here much longer, you're going to be more than touched. It's almost daylight, and Spotted Tail and friends may join us at any moment."

Stephanie dusted her hands against the beaded dress, peering at Ryan in the dim light.

"Would he follow us this far?"

"He might. Depends on how mad he is. Watch that hole . . ." Ryan guided Stephanie around a deep crevice in the path hacked into the sandstone. "This is steep, so try to follow me closely. One false step might get you to the bottom before me, but you'd be in as many pieces as an eggshell."

"Thanks for the comforting warning," Stephanie muttered as she clung to Ryan's waist. Going down was much worse than climbing up had been. As the rising sun spread bright fingers of light in the sky, she could see the dangerous path.

By the time they reached bottom, Stephanie was certain she'd never be frightened of anything again. It had been a harrowing climb down, slipping on loose rocks, stepping into crevices, and nearly sliding over a shallow ledge.

Grateful to be on flat land again, she collapsed on a rock and watched as Ryan checked the horses he'd left hobbled.

"I hope I never have to do that again!" She tilted the water pouch Ryan handed her, washing dust and grit down her clogged throat as she swallowed several mouthfuls.

"Did you enjoy your stay with Spotted Tail?" Ryan asked, gazing at her with casual interest as Stephanie choked on the water. He brushed at the spots she sprayed on him.

"I cannot imagine why you would bring that up," Stephanie said sharply. "If you hadn't come back for me, I would have . . . have . . ."

"Given Spotted Tail sons," Ryan supplied helpfully when she faltered. "You knew I'd come back for you."

"No, I didn't! You took those horses . . ."

"Which I turned loose last night . . ."

"You didn't intend to keep them?"

"No. It's too hard trying to feed that many on the trail—hey!" Ryan caught the water pouch Stephanie threw at him. "That's not the only reason. I never intended to trade for you. I just didn't have much choice after losing to Spotted Tail."

"Why did he bother giving you horses after winning the fight?" Pulling the hem of her dress to her knees, Stephanie began massaging her aching calves.

"Hmm. Who knows? His idea of fair, I guess." Ryan slid a speculative glance at Stephanie's bare legs. "He probably figured you were worth it. Of course, he doesn't know you like I do."

Stephanie snorted in a very unladylike manner. "You don't know me at all, Ryan Cordell!"

"I don't?" Ryan grinned at her. "Don't be too sure of that. Here." He tossed her a bridle and horse blanket. "Let's saddle up and get out of here."

Chapter Twenty-Seven

Brown-feathered ducks floated serenely on the calm surface of the spring-fed lake, and bluish-gray coots poked their ivory bills along reed-lined shores. Then, startled by human presence, the ducks took flight in a flurry of feathers and quacking. The slower coots pattered along the surface of the water for a hundred feet or so before taking wing. A Great Horned Owl had built its nest on a rocky ledge of the surrounding cliff and grumpily announced its displeasure with all the unusual activity below.

"This is amazing," Julian said to no one in particular. He stood on the rim of a ridge overlooking the inner lake and ancient ruins. The trail forked, with one path leading down to the water's edge, passing by small cliff ruins and the lake's outlet, and the other path bearing right at the rim to more, larger pueblos.

Following Bingo and a Papago guide, Julian had been brought to the limestone sink that was actually a spring-fed lake placed in a deep round cavity atop a hill. Water flowed through its outlet at an estimated half million gallons a day. Ancient irrigation ditches stretched for at least a mile from the lake's outlet, watering acres of garden plots. The Papagos, Bingo had explained, simply took up where former cultures had left off.

"Th' Hohokam used ta' farm this," Bingo had said, waving an arm to indicate approximately sixty acres. "Nobody knows why they up and left. Mebbe they didn' like th' climate."

Standing on the rim of the lake, Julian estimated it to be four hundred and seventy feet across. Large trees fringed this peaceful oasis tucked into a semiarid, dusty region.

"These pueblos remind me of apartment buildings in New York," he told Bingo, gesturing to the ruins tucked into the face of the cliff. "What amazing people they must have been to carve their homes out of solid rock!"

"Care ta take a look at sumthin' that'll really throw a crick in yer neck?" Bingo asked. "Let's ride a few miles south, an' I'll show ya 'apartment buildin's' like ya ain't never seen!"

A few hours later Julian stood in a thicket of sycamore trees close to Beaver Creek, gazing one hundred feet straight up at a sheer cliff pocked with doors and windows.

"It looks like a European castle," he said in amazement. "I've never seen anything like it! How do we get up there?"

"Hakiwuh has a way," Bingo answered, gesturing to their grinning Papago guide. "I'm stayin' down here an' waitin'. I seen all of them pueblos I keer ta see."

Hakiwuh propped a ladder made from a sycamore trunk with lopped-off branches against the rock wall, firmly planting it into the valley floor. Bingo seated himself in the shade of ruins at the base of the cliff and lit his pipe while Julian prepared to climb.

"Sure you don't want to join us, Bingo? Last call . . ." Julian stood on the lower stubs of the ladder behind Hakiwuh. The Papago guide had been furnished them by the village chief, and though Julian didn't understand a word of his language, there had been no lack of communition. Hakiwuh seemed to understand what interested Julian as well as Bingo did.

"Naw, Pilgrim," Bingo answered, scooting to a prone position on a cushion of dry grass. "I'm happy. 'Sides, I kin keep a good watch frum here." He pulled his wolf-head hat over his eyes, giving the lie to his last comment.

Grinning, Julian eagerly climbed the ladder after Hakiwuh. Halfway up the side of the cliff was a path that joined with another path from the side. At the junction of the paths squatted a small, smoke-blackened room with narrow inner keyhole doorways. Hostile entry was virtually impossible, and Julian decided it must have been a sentry post. While Hakiwuh lounged in the shade of a doorway, Julian explored further.

The castle, as he had dubbed it, was sheltered under a deep overhang in the cliff. It was constructed of small limestone blocks laid in mud mortar and roofed by large sycamore timbers overlaid by poles, sticks, grass, and several inches of mud. He shook his

346

head in awe imagining the labor required to haul those heavy materials up the sheer rock face. The outer room walls of the pueblo were nearly at the edge of the high ledges, and were curved to conform to the arc of the surrounding cave. Craning his neck, Julian estimated the dwelling to be five stories high. He counted seventeen rooms, some still bearing evidence of their former occupants.

Pottery and basket fragments littered the dirt floors, as well as dried berries, wild seeds, and nuts. Julian's attention was caught by an unbroken vessel perched on a nearby stone ledge. It had been designed in the shape of a seated man, wide at the bottom with bare feet jutting from the base. Ceramic arms winged from the sides, and the head formed the vessel's mouth. The potter had possessed a sense of humor, for a large nose curved out to provide a handle in the bearded face. The buff-colored jar had been painted with red squares. Julian sifted through some of the woven baskets, discovering what appeared to be ears of corn and beans. Though primitive, the early inhabitants had apparently mastered the art of cultivating crops. This would be an ideal spot for them, providing protection from enemies while offering a supply of fresh water, arable bottomland for farming, a variety of wild food plants and berries, fish, and game. There was an abundance of raw materials for building, tool manufacture, and pottery making.

Lifting a basket lined with pitch, Julian recognized the same style the Papagos used for their water baskets. The skill had been passed along to others, it seemed. He was fascinated. It was almost as if he could hear echoes from the past and feel the presence of the people who had lived in these rooms. It was an impregnable castle dating back hundreds of years, probably to a time when medieval man in Europe was still wearing a suit of armor and fighting in the Crusades.

Hakiwuh's faint shout of concern brought Julian back to the present, and he regretfully left the musty rooms. Bending, he scooped up the effigy vessel and a basket that was not as deteriorated as the others. He would add them to his collection.

"If I wasn't in Arizona for another purpose," Julian told Bingo when he rejoined him, "I would spend a great deal of time here. Why do you suppose no one knows about it?"

Bingo spat a stream of tobacco juice at a sycamore leaf. "Who told ya no one knew 'bout it? I knew 'bout it. Hakiwuh knew 'bout it, an' so docs most every Injun in these parts." He scratched idly at a bothersome fleabite. "Met a man kinda like you a few years ago, up in Canyon de Chelly. Name was Jackson. William Henry Jackson, an' he rode one of th' finest mules I ever seen. He had this strange-lookin' contraption that'd put on a lil' piece of glass, whatever he pointed it at . . ."

"Jackson? I believe I've seen his photographs of the West! He's very talented. Carries his own darkroom in a tent, I believe."

"Yep. That was him, all right. He'd heard of lots of ruins like this."

Julian tilted back his head to gaze up at the impressive cliff dwellings. "I did see some ruins in Chaco Canyon while searching for my map. But *I* never heard of this place."

"Prob'ly a whole helluva lot ya never heered of, Pilgrim," Bingo cackled. "Same as me. Diff'rence is, I don' keer 'bout it like you do. Yer th' kinda man who's always got ta know th' why of things, while I'm satisfied ta have a full belly, good whiskey, an' a woman—good or bad—ever' now an' then."

Slapping his knee, Julian laughed and Hakiwuh laughed with him. "Does he understand English?" Julian asked Bingo in surprise, glancing at the cheerful, broad face of their Papago guide.

"Naw. He jus' unnerstands laughter. Kinda universal language, ain't it?"

"You have made a very profound statement, Bingo." The old man's comprehension of human nature continually surprised him. Julian's blond eyebrows rose skeptically when Bingo offered him a plug of his tobacco, but this time he took it.

"Stick it in yer mouth like this," Bingo instructed, "an' bite off a lil' chunk. Not too big or you'll choke—that's right. Now let it rest easy-like on one side of yer jaw. Spit ever' now an' then when ya feel like it, but fer Godssake, don' dribble it on yer chin!"

Never having chewed tobacco, Julian rather expected it to be like snuff. Inhaling snuff was a gentleman's pastime that he'd never been overly fond of anyway, but chewing tobacco, he discovered, was a pleasant experience. He'd always considered the art of inhaling snuff faintly effeminate, while spitting was definitely masculine.

"This is quite good," he said around the tobacco quid. "I should have accepted your offer before . . ."

"Yep. It'll grow hair on yer chest, Pilgrim. Jus'

don' swallow yer plug. You'll be sick as a dog an' green as a pine if'n ya do."

Stretching out in the shade provided by leafy sycamore trees, Julian folded his arms behind his head and stared up at the bright patches of blue sky. The urgency of his journey had lessened in the past week with the Papagos. They were a friendly tribe, offering food and shelter as well as a guide.

The Papago chief had invited them to share a pipe in the evenings, and with Bingo as interpreter, had told Julian a great deal about their customs. This particular tribe had wandered far from their original territory farther south, taking advantage of better farming and gathering conditions. Much of their food was still gathered in timeless tradition, consisting of piñon nuts, squawberries, succulent yucca stalks, and mesquite beans. Julian had been surprised at how tasty the unusual diet could be. Their main crops were corn and squash, but as it was only early June, they were still eating dried ears of corn from the year before.

Many members of the tribe wore jewelry fashioned from copper, silver, and turquoise, and he'd been amazed at the quality of the workmanship. They were skilled craftsmen, with crude, clumsy tools. How could he have ever thought them uncivilized?

"Ya know," Bingo remarked lazily, capturing Julian's wandering attention, "I been thinkin', Pilgrim. Chief Pacal made a comment that set me ta wonderin' 'bout sumthin'. He's heard 'bout this place ya got yer heart set on seein', an' he mentioned th' steps as bein' sent from th' gods only at certain times of th' year. Says th' sun god points th' way."

Scratching at stiff, prickly bristles of his beard, Bingo squinted at Julian. "What does that tell ya?"

"Certain times of the year?" Julian echoed. "Why—I don't know what he could mean. Did he say what seasons?"

"Nope. Wouldn' say nuthin' else. Guess he figured we'd have ta do some thinkin' of our own."

"Maybe when we get there we'll see what he means."

"Mebbe. An' mebbe we'll end up with a handful of dust fer all our troubles."

"Somehow, I don't think so, Bingo." A slow smile curved Julian's mouth. "I just don't think so."

Chapter Twenty-Eight

Dust puffed around the heels of Ryan's boots as he stepped from his horse to kneel on the ground. Faint tracks were still visible, and the Papagos he'd spoken to had described Julian. In spite of all the odds, he'd somehow managed to stumble across their trail again. For a while, Ryan had thought it hopeless. He'd heard of the sacred grounds of the ancient tribes, but had always thought it a mere legend. Maybe Julian Ashworth was really on to something . . .

"I think we're getting close to your father, Stephanie." Ryan rose and stepped to where she waited on her horse. Hooking one elbow around her saddle horn, he pushed back his hat to look into her eyes. "It's only fair to tell you that it might get dangerous from here on out. You still game?"

Stephanie stared back at him incredulously. "*Might* get dangerous? What do you call the past weeks—a Sunday school outing? I think I can handle it, Cordell!"

"Fine with me, tough guy." Ryan couldn't help a grin. "Don't you ever give up?"

"No. Should I?"

"There are times when it's smart, Princess. Even the Apache know that there are times to stay, and times to cut and run."

Stephanie shuddered. "Please don't mention the Apache again. For a while, I thought I was going to breed an entire flock of them."

"Blond Apache warriors could be very interesting . . ."

"Oh, shut up," Stephanie said mildly. "You just enjoy provoking me, and I refuse to let you. We're close to my father, and I want to hurry, Ryan."

Swinging on to his stallion, Ryan slid her a mocking glance that was half serious. "Anxious to leave me, lady?"

Stephanie didn't answer. Her mare fell into step beside his stallion, prancing and dancing nervously. The Apache pony she rode was much sturdier than her gelding had been, but the stallion's proximity obviously disturbed her. In all the confusion at the Apache village, Ryan hadn't been able to find the reliable gelding she was accustomed to riding, and Stephanie was having a bit of trouble handling the skittish mare.

"Should I be anxious to leave you?" she finally answered, and he laughed.

"Ah, we're back to answering questions with questions, are we? I swear, for every step forward, we take at least two backward."

"I didn't realize we were trying for any particular goal." Stephanie veered their conversation in another direction. She didn't quite trust Ryan anymore, not after his abandonment of her in the Apache village. There remained shreds of doubt that he hadn't first intended to leave and not return. So he'd had a change of heart—big deal. She'd endured days of torment not knowing.

Stephanie pulled at the hat of Ryan's she wore, tugging it lower over her eyes. It was his oldest, and had seen better days, but at least it shaded her face. She would probably resemble a withered apple by the time she returned to New York. The constant sun and wind on her face should dry it like a prune.

"When are we going to find me some decent clothes, Ryan? I can't continue wearing this Apache dress, and, besides, it isn't decent."

Ryan's gaze skimmed over the long length of her legs stretching from beneath the pushed-up hem of her dress. The Arizona sun had gilded them a light, peachy color that was most becoming, and if the truth were known, he was enjoying the view.

"Soon," he promised. "Soon."

"I find it difficult to believe that you don't have at least one extra pair of trousers in your saddlebags." Stephanie's moccasins nudged her mare into a trot. "Are you certain you checked thoroughly?"

"Look, Princess, if you don't believe me, you're welcome to check yourself. I thought mundane items like food was more important than extra trousers."

Sighing, Stephanie murmured that she believed him. What would her father say when he saw her wearing this dress and riding astride? Even in the jungles of Africa, she had managed to preserve her modesty.

"Oh, look, if you're going to pout," Ryan said in exasperation, "I'll strip the next man I run across and give you his trousers. Will that make you happy?"

Stephanie gave him a frigid stare. "Deliriously happy," she said.

As luck would have it, the next man they ran across was Alvin Bates. He was sitting alone by a small fire while Huntley was beating the brush for their dinner.

Lying on his belly atop a rock ridge, Ryan motioned Stephanie to silence with a finger over his lips. This was too good to be true, and he grinned. Stephanie grinned back as Ryan handed her his Winchester rifle, indicating that she should cover him. Pulling his pistol, Ryan slid down the ledge as quietly as possible.

Bates jerked around in surprise when Ryan stepped up behind him, and one hand froze on his gun as he saw the muzzle of Ryan's Colt leveled at his chest.

"Hullo, Bates. Saw your fire, and thought maybe you'd like a little company."

"Cordell! What . . . what a surprise!" Bates's pudgy jowls quivered nervously as he attempted a smile. "Yeah, company would be right nice." He waved in the general direction of the ground around the fire. "Have a seat, why don'cha?"

"Where's your buddy?"

"Huntley? Oh, he's not here. Nope. Stayed back in Willow Creek." Bates shook his head dolefully. "That lead you threw into him stopped him pretty good." He glanced behind Ryan. "Where's th' girl? You lose her already?"

Ryan ignored his question. "Bates, you've got something I need."

"What . . . what's that?" Bates swallowed a nervous laugh. "You know I'm always glad ta share, Cordell. My ma used ta say I was overgenerous, always givin' away stuff—what'cha need? Can . . . can I put my hands down now?"

"No. Keep 'em up where I can see 'em." Ryan stepped closer and gestured with his gun barrel. "I need your trousers, Bates."

"My . . . my trousers?" Bates's voice rose shrilly. "Why, you can't leave me out here without any pants, Cordell! That's inhuman!" Bates slid his eyes to a spot behind Ryan, then quickly flicked his gaze back.

Ryan had already sensed Huntley's approach, and hoped that Stephanie was still hidden behind a rock watching. He kept still, waiting.

"That's right, Bates. It is inhuman. But I still want your trousers. Shuck 'em." The muzzle of the Colt waggled and Bates reluctantly moved one hand to his belt buckle. Just as the trousers slid to a heap around his ankles, Huntley's voice came from right behind Ryan.

"Drop your gun, Cordell!" There was a click as he cocked his pistol, and Ryan let his Colt fall to the ground. Grinning, Huntley kicked it away and stepped to face Ryan.

"Well, well! Fancy meeting you out here! What brings you this way, Cordell?"

Shrugging, Ryan answered, "The same thing that brings you this way, Huntley. Ashworth."

"Yeah, wonder if Ashworth knows how popular

he is?" Huntley gestured with his pistol. "Move over there by the fire. With your hands over your head, Cordell."

Bates was grinning happily. "Yeah, that's right, Huntley! Let's tie him up and leave him! No, let's shoot him first, then leave him! Or . . ."

"Shut up, Alvie!" Huntley snapped. "I need to think. And pull your pants up, you idiot!"

Walking slowly, Ryan began to wonder irritably if Stephanie had fallen asleep. Dammit, where was she? She had the drop on them, and that Winchester could shoot the eye out of an eagle at a hundred yards. He turned slowly, with his hands still above his head, and faced Huntley and Bates. They stood in whispered conversation for a few moments while Ryan began to plot an alternative plan. Maybe he could rush them, take them by surprise without getting shot first. No, that was too risky. Where in the hell was Stephanie?

Huntley stepped forward, his pistol aimed at Ryan's chest. "We decided what we're gonna do with you, Cordell," he began. "We're gonna give you a fair chance. There's an old Indian method I've been wantin' to try, and now's as good a time as any."

"Yeah? What's that, Huntley?"

"We just happen to have a shovel with us, and we thought we'd let you dig yourself a little hole, say . . . up to your neck? If you dig yourself out, fine. If not . . . we gave you a sportin' chance."

"Right. That's real sporting of you, Huntley. I'll have to remember that when I come after you."

Huntley chuckled and Bates slapped his knees, guffawing loudly.

"That's a good one, Cordell!" Bates said. "When ya come after us, yeah! Glad to see ya kin keep yer sense of humor at a time like this."

"Shut up, Alvie, and get the shovel," Huntley cut in. "We're wastin' time."

"Right . . ."

"Hold it right there, Bates! You touch that shovel or your gun, and you'll be wearing a necklace of hot lead! Both of you—drop your guns now!"

Stephanie was faintly proud of herself as she stood straddling a rock, the deadly muzzle of the Winchester pointing at Huntley and Bates. Their guns were tossed in the dust immediately when she pumped the lever with a loud click.

"Necklace of hot lead?" Ryan echoed as he scooped up their pistols. "You've definitely been reading too many novels, Stephanie!" Jamming his own Colt back in its holster, Ryan shoved the other two pistols into the belt at his waist.

"Well, I thought it sounded pretty good," she muttered. "It worked, didn't it?"

"I think the Winchester might have had something to do with how well it worked," Ryan commented dryly. He turned to Huntley and Bates who stood with their hands in the air.

"You can have these pistols back, boys, when you pick up your horses," he told the pair. "I'm going to give you two a sporting chance." He grinned when Bates whimpered pitifully. "Don't cry 'til you've heard the ground rules, Bates. First, I want your trousers. Then your boots. We'll see how you like walking ten miles in your bare feet. Well?" He lifted an eyebrow at them. "Strip!"

The command was emphasized with his Colt, and Huntley and Bates stripped to their underwear. They looked ridiculous, Stephanie thought, standing on first one foot and then the other, reminding her of flamingos in their faded red longjohns. Why on earth would any man wear those things in this heat? She shook her head.

"What'll I do with these?" she asked Ryan, holding up their trousers and boots.

"Beat the lice out of 'em and try 'em on. Huntley's will probably fit better. Bates is too fat."

"Hey!" Bates protested. "I'm not fat . . ."

"Hell, you could pass for a beach ball, Bates. Now stand with your back to your buddy." Ryan tossed Stephanie a length of rope. "Tie 'em tight, Princess. By the time they get loose, we'll be ten miles down the trail."

"What makes you think they'll get loose?" she asked, winding the rope around the men's wrists. "What if they don't?"

"I've had experience with your knots, remember? They'll get loose."

Stephanie shot him a sour look, but she couldn't argue. She tightened the ropes and knotted them twice while Ryan watched. When she was done, he collected Huntley and Bates's horses as well as their own.

Wheeling his stallion, Ryan gestured for Stephanie to mount, and tossed her the reins to one of the extra horses. He turned and grinned at the consternation on the two faces watching him.

"I'm taking your horses, boys, but you can find 'em down the trail a ways. Don't get blisters on

359

your feet!''

Ryan kicked his stallion into a trot and Stephanie followed. He glanced over at her, noting with a sigh the legs now covered with trousers.

"Satisfied, Princess?"

She smiled. "Yes. But I intend to wash these things at the first stream we find!"

Shaking his head regretfully, Ryan said, "I'm glad you're satisfied, but you sure spoiled one hell of a great view!"

Stephanie wrinkled her nose at him. "You'll get over it."

Ryan wished he was as certain about that as she was. Stephanie Ashworth was a thorn in his side, a job to do, a fortune in gold, but damn if he could keep things in proper perspective. Every time he thought he had his priorities straight, Stephanie scattered them like the wind. He was beginning to suspect that she did it on purpose, that somehow she knew his most vulnerable areas and played on them. How else could he explain the fact that he was falling in love with her?

Chapter Twenty-Nine

Stephanie held up the clean, dry trousers she'd just removed from the spreading branches of a bush, and gave Ryan a smile of satisfaction.

"Don't they look much better?" she asked. "They certainly smell better, and all the little creatures have departed." She glanced around the small lake and sighed contentedly. "I could stay here for a few days . . ."

"Don't homestead this place, Princess. We're too close to waste time now. We leave first thing in the morning."

Propped against a tree stump that had probably been a towering cottonwood at the birth of Christ, Ryan folded his arms behind his head. He was tempted to remain. His days with Stephanie were numbered, and once they found Julian, his services would no longer be required. He hated to admit even to himself that he would miss her. Damn.

"Ryan," Stephanie was saying, "where are we? All

these old ruins just invite exploring, and I certainly never expected to find such a peaceful, lovely lake in the middle of the desert.''

"That's probably the reason all these ruins are around it. Ancient Indian tribes must have been as pleasantly surprised as you are. They even dug about a mile of irrigation ditches from this well to water their crops. Beaver Creek is not far that way, and I stumbled across some ruins there that would make any building in New York look small.''

"I'd love to see them!" Stephanie exclaimed. "I wonder if my father took the time to explore.''

"You can ask him when we find him. If we stop to look at them now, we might miss him.'' Ryan shifted position, lying on his side to watch Stephanie. He much preferred her dressed—or half dressed—in nothing but his shirt. It was too big for her, the sleeves flopping loosely around her wrists and the shirttail reaching to just above her knees. He gave a sigh of regret that her clothes had dried so quickly, and forced his attention back to their conversation. "We'll ride by the ruins if you like, but I don't think we should stop.''

"You're right," she agreed, "maybe I can see them another time." Folding the trousers she'd stolen from Huntley, Stephanie was careful not to look closely at Ryan. She wanted to ask him what would happen when they found her father, if he would stay with them or just take the money he'd earned and leave, but she was half afraid of the answer. She couldn't bear the thought of never seeing Ryan again, even though the logical, cautious side of her nature urged differently. Since when had caution been so desirable? she argued with herself.

But instead of asking the question that was really important to her, Stephanie asked, "What kinds of birds are those, Ryan? Those bluish-gray ones? Watch them when they take flight—they run across the surface of the water for a great distance first."

"Those are coots." Ryan didn't even twist his head to look. He kept his gaze on Stephanie's face as she knelt not far from him. He'd learned to recognize her moods by now, and knew that she had something else on her mind.

"Coots? At home, we have similar birds called rails. Father used to hunt them when I was a child. Now he prefers big game, like tigers and lions. He even has a water buffalo head on the wall of his study. The horns on that animal are amazing! Why, they stretch . . ."

"Stephanie."

The intensity in Ryan's voice caught her attention, and Stephanie turned to look at him with widened eyes. She was afraid. Not so much afraid of Ryan, but afraid of her own reactions and tempestuous emotions. She couldn't let herself be hurt again, she just couldn't! She'd trusted him before, hadn't she? And what had happened?

Ryan watched her expectantly, waiting for her to respond, and Stephanie found herself rattling inanely. She said the first thing that popped into her mind, just like an empty-headed schoolgirl.

"There are no water buffalo in Arizona, are there? I know there are foxes, bobcats, jackrabbits, and bighorn sheep, but the only animals I'm familiar with are rattlesnakes, scorpions, and those pesky coyotes. Oh, and that wretched white bear that had taken up occupancy in the hut . . ."

Her voice trailed off as she recalled the night hours following the discovery of the white bear. Ryan was obviously thinking of the same thing. He twisted to a sitting position and reached out to touch Stephanie lightly on her cheek. His fingers trailed a warm path from cheek to slightly quivering lips as Stephanie met his eyes.

"I've thought often of that night in the hut," he said softly. "And of the nights spent in that cave after we left Willow Creek. Those are nights that will always be special, Stephanie. Don't try to forget them. And don't forget me after we find your father." He smiled at her faint exclamation of denial, and said lightly to mask his sincerity, "I won't forget you, Princess; how could I? No other woman has ever caused me so much trouble . . ."

"Ryan," she blurted, catching his fingers between her hands, "please don't! I . . . I . . . it's going to be difficult enough as it is."

"Difficult enough to what? Forget me? You probably won't have much trouble once you return to New York . . ."

"Oh, you don't understand," she said fretfully. "I'm only an interlude for you while you mean . . . more . . . than that to me. In the few weeks I've spent with you, I've discovered that some things which were once so important, aren't anymore. Don't you see what I'm trying to say?"

Ryan took a deep breath. "Maybe I do, Princess. Are you just trying to say you'll miss me, or . . . ?" He couldn't help the tensing of his muscles as he waited for her answer, yet he wasn't sure why it meant so much. What would he say if she *did* love him? Could he risk loving her back?

Stephanie pushed his hands away and rose to her feet, cupping her elbows in her palms as she paced the reed-lined shore. The water of the lake was deep and mysterious, with a calm, smooth surface that hid centuries of secrets. She felt the same way. Did she dare tell Ryan her most vulnerable secret? Did he know it already in spite of the calm, smooth surface of casual companionship she'd tried so hard to cultivate?

He was still sitting on the ground watching her through narrowed gray eyes. She could feel them boring into her back just like they had that first day she'd met him in Fort Defiance. Had she fallen in love with him before she'd even been introduced? In spite of her choking anger that day, she'd been well aware of Ryan Cordell as a man. Stephanie knew that all her avowals of dislike and animosity had been efforts to disguise her attraction. She'd only been fooling herself, as she was trying to do now. Yes, she was angry and hurt that he'd left her with Spotted Tail in spite of her pleas, but justice demanded that she consider the alternatives he'd faced. It was just so hard to place her trust in him again.

Turning, Stephanie stared hard at Ryan. He hadn't moved, but was still watching her quietly.

"Of course I'll miss you," she said lightly, and the

moment for confidences passed. "In spite of our differences, we've been through a lot together. But why are we discussing this now? We haven't even found Father yet . . ."

It was a middle-of-the-road answer and Stephanie knew it, but she admitted to cowardice. Ryan's intent gaze altered to a slightly cynical expression.

"You're adept at giving noncommittal answers, Princess, and I admire your talent. What are you going to do when I insist upon honesty?" He stood up and grabbed his rifle. "Think I'll just scout around a bit. Use my pistol while I'm gone, if you need it."

"Do you think I will?" Stephanie's dark eyes reflected her sudden panic at being left alone. Would she ever be able to forget being captured by the Apaches?

Ryan's expression softened. "No. You won't need it. These high ridges surrounding the lake are pretty good protection, and, besides, that owl nesting up there goes into a noisy tantrum whenever anyone approaches. You'll have plenty of warning."

Stephanie nodded. "I remember how loud she screeched when we climbed to the rim. I thought someone was being murdered."

A slight smile lifted one corner of Ryan's mouth. "Did sound that way, didn't it? Camouflage isn't confined to just owls, it seems."

Unable to meet his knowing gaze, Stephanie fidgeted silently with her shirt-sleeves. She knew what he meant by his cryptic comment, but couldn't bring herself to discard the security of her own emotion-camouflaging tactics. Lifting her head, she watched

Ryan pivot and walk away. He intended to force an answer from her before they reached Julian. Would she follow her heart or her head?

If only she could talk to her father. He'd always advised her in the past. Julian Ashworth would be able to tell her what to do.

Chapter Thirty

But Julian was beginning to doubt his ability to make intelligent decisions. He stood gazing up a sheer rock wall that was clearly inaccessible. No man could climb the smooth sides from any direction, and it would take weeks to hack steps into the impregnable surface of quartz sand cemented with silica. Chief Pacal had insisted the steps could be seen or mounted only at certain times, and they didn't have weeks to spend cutting toeholds with their crude equipment. The butte rose straight up to a height of at least four hundred and fifty feet.

"What now? This has to be the place. It's the only butte for miles that could have a top large enough to be any kind of burial ground." Julian's spirits drooped. He'd been so certain Hakiwuh would know of a hidden trail to the summit. But the Papago guide had only referred to the map, insisting it was correct. Shaking his head, Julian contemplated admitting failure.

Bingo sat on an outcropping of rock, his gnarled

hands resting on both knees as he considered the butte. He'd already examined the face the last time they'd been here. Even if they meticulously went over every foot of the base searching for the mythical stairway to heaven, it could take weeks.

"Well, Pilgrim," he said at last, "I'm thinkin' our agreeable guide here, don' really want us ta find this ladder ta th' stars. Papagos are as superstitious as th' next Injun, ya know, an' he believes he'll die if'n he disturbs th' sacred burial grounds."

"That's utter nonsense!" Julian snapped irritably, turning to gaze at Bingo and their guide. "Tell him I will give him many valuable presents if he will show us the way, or even tell us how to find it."

Bingo dutifully translated Julian's promise, but Hakiwuh shook his head vigorously. His voice rose shrilly as he refused, staring at the mountain man with wide, frightened eyes.

"Nope," Bingo said. "Hakiwuh claims th' presents won't do him any good once he's dead, an' he ain't ready ta take that final journey to th' sky jus' yet. Cain't say as I blame him, but it does make it a mite harder on us."

"Just a mite," Julian agreed dryly. He sank to the flat rock beside Bingo and stared blankly at the cliff face. "I wonder," he said slowly, "why the Navajo chief who traded me the map said the sacred area of the magic rock could only be seen at certain times of the year. Do you suppose it has something to do with the seasons?"

Bingo shrugged. "Might. Them ancient tribes wuz real parti'clar 'bout markin' th' calendar. Had sumthin' ta do with th' right time ta plant corn,

I guess."

Julian shot to his feet, raking his fingers through the thick strands of his light hair with excitement.

"Bingo, that's it! A calendar! Oh, how could I have been so blind . . . all the ancient tribes had their own methods for marking the days of the year, and they were usually quite accurate. In South America, the Mayans built intricate calenders to signal the winter and summer solstice— Do you know the date today?"

Eyeing Julian warily, Bingo shook his head slowly. "Nope, cain't say that I do. It's th' month of June, but I don't rightly know which day. Somewhar in th' middle, I'd say. But how would knowin' th' right day help find them steps, Pilgrim?"

"Don't you see?" Julian's voice roughened with excitement. "Both chiefs stressed that the timing must be exactly right, which can only mean that the steps are visible at certain times of the year. There must be some sort of sundial around here, and I'm willing to bet the steps will be found close by it . . ."

"Now, that's a bit farfetched fer me ta swaller," Bingo admitted. "But I reckon it wouldn' hurt none ta try." He turned to Hakiwuh, who sat apprehensively watching their conversation, and smiled. "Why don' I jus' ask our lil' friend here 'bout that?"

It took several minutes of explanations and assurances that a method of marking time was all they were asking the Papago guide to reveal before he finally consented. Julian watched in utter astonishment as Hakiwuh immediately turned and sprinted down the rocky slope. He ran across the flat, dusty ground toward the horizon until he was almost out of sight, finally stopping beside a small outcropping of rocks and boulders.

"But . . . how could that lead to anything?" Julian muttered in disappointment. "It's too far away."

"Reckon that's an underground tunnel?" Bingo suggested. "Thar's a lot of weird rock piles aroun' here . . ."

"No, it's too far away. Let's go take a look," Julian said. "Maybe there's something we can't see from here."

When they got to the jumble of rocks where Hakiwuh patiently waited, Julian discovered a crude sundial.

"This is amazing!" he exclaimed, carefully examining the stone slabs and petroglyph. "See, these three stone slabs, which must weigh tons, were slanted against this larger rock at just the right angle. The slabs bracket this spiral petroglyph, guiding rays of sunlight across its surface. This smaller petroglyph must announce spring and fall equinoxes. Now . . ." Julian stared perplexedly at two smaller wedges of rock carefully perched atop the stone slabs. "I'm not certain what function these two rocks perform, but they must mean something. They are intricately carved with figures and ancient pictures. Look!" Julian's attention was captured by something else, and he pointed to the late afternoon shaft of sunlight bisecting the spiral etched into the rock. "See how it's close to the exact center of the petroglyph? When the light bisects that center mark, Bingo, it will announce the summer solstice, or my name's not Julian Stephen Ashworth!"

"That's all very int'restin', but how's that gonna help us find them steps?" Bingo pointed out. A stream of tobacco juice splattered against the dusty ground.

"I don't know. We'll just have to camp here and wait for the summer solstice to find out," Julian answered.

"We're gonna bake our brains fer nothin' is whut *I* think," Bingo grumbled good-naturedly, "but I ain't got th' heart ta say no. Here. Gimme th' map to study fer a while, an' mebbe I kin figger it out usin' this rockpile as a guide. Wasn' thar sum kinda rockpile drawn on it?"

"Yes, yes, I think so," Julian answered distractedly. He was on his hands and knees examining the petroglyph. "The map is in my saddlebag, Bingo. Help yourself."

"Mighta knowed it'd be way back thar," Bingo muttered as he sat down on a rock shaded by the larger boulder. He turned to Hakiwuh and smiled.

Chapter Thirty-One

"How about a swim?" Ryan suggested later that afternoon. The sun was still high over the ridges circling the deep lake, and they'd sought shade in the shadows of the cliff ruins. "I recall that you swim very well," he added slyly.

"Do you? And I recall you leaving me the last time I went for a swim," Stephanie retorted. "Is that what you're planning?"

"I plan on taking a swim to beat this heat. And the last time, you *asked* me to leave. Remember?" Ryan rose in a smooth motion, his hands moving to the buckle of his gunbelt. He smiled at Stephanie's widening eyes when he unbuttoned his shirt and threw it carelessly to the ground. Kicking off his boots, Ryan began unbuckling the leather belt that held up his pants.

"Don't watch then," he chided when Stephanie muttered a protest and turned her head away. "No one's forcing you. But I do recall that you've done more than just look, even though you seem to have forgotten that fact."

"You *would* remind me of that," she said bitterly. "So I've made a mistake . . ."

"Is that the way you look at it? Fine, Princess. We all make mistakes. I'm going for a swim. You can sit here in those hot clothes and watch."

Stephanie waited until she was certain he had left the ruin before turning back around. Resting her chin on her drawn-up knees, she sighed. It was hot, and so were the confining trousers and blouse she wore. Why did it have to be this way? Why couldn't they share the intimacy they once had—the companionship as well as the physical? It had been so sweet and satisfying, and she missed it. Now her faith in him had been shaken, and she couldn't seem to get it back.

Moving to the doorway of the ruin, Stephanie gazed down at the small lake. Ryan stood on the reed-lined banks, obviously searching for a spot without logs or marshy plants. The late afternoon sun glinted from the rocky rim circling the lake, playing in golden streams over the hard angles and planes of his body as he stood outlined against the smooth surface of the water. Rising on his toes, Ryan poised for a moment, then dove, knifing cleanly into the depths.

It wasn't until his dark head popped up in a shimmering spray of water that Stephanie realized she'd been holding her breath, waiting. Ryan shook his hair like a dog, then began swimming toward the opposite side with strong strokes of his arms.

The water *was* inviting, and she was so hot and sticky with perspiration. Stephanie fidgeted irritably, wishing she hadn't been so hasty with her refusal to swim. Now she would have to swallow her words and pride if she joined him. Several minutes ticked past as she watched Ryan swimming in the cool, beckoning water. And what would she wear, anyway, if she yielded to the temptation? Her deerskin dress would be too heavy and bulky in the water, and she hated the thought of wearing wet trousers if they didn't dry overnight.

Stephanie's glance fell on Ryan's shirt. Why not? It covered her fairly well, and would dry much more quickly than the thicker trousers. And she could point out the fact that she didn't have proper garments for swimming if Ryan was rude enough to mock her for capitulating to his suggestion. A smile curved Stephanie's mouth as she began undressing.

Floating on his back, Ryan reflected that it was a shame Stephanie was missing out on such a relaxing respite from the heat. A water spume rose high as he kicked with one foot, then gravity brought shimmering drops down on him in a soft spray like raindrops. He kicked again, moving his arms through the water to propel his body backward.

He was having more trouble than he'd anticipated with Stephanie. It wasn't just her reluctance to trust him again, Ryan thought, it was his own emotions. He hated to admit it, but somehow, in spite of his best intentions, he'd fallen in love with her. His first opinion of her was as a haughty, spoiled heiress accustomed to snapping her fingers for instant catering. Somehow it had altered. He wasn't sure exactly when he'd fallen in love with her, but it had happened. And it complicated matters considerably. Now he didn't know how to even talk to her.

Ryan's arms cut savagely through the water. Not that it really mattered. It was only a matter of days before they caught up with Julian, then he would take his wages from Stephanie and leave. He had to. This had all been decided before he'd even seen her get off that stage in Fort Defiance. Damn. He should have kept heading in the direction of Bonner's Ferry and never agreed to take this job, but he hadn't. Hell, he'd needed the money to make that final payment on his father's ranch in northern Idaho. Jake Cordell had lost his wife, then his life for that land, and his only son didn't intend to let it go without a fight. The money he'd get for this job would more than pay the last note to the bank—that's why he'd agreed to do it.

But that had been before he'd known Stephanie. Then she'd just been one rich man's faceless daughter, a method for earning money. A faint smile curved his mouth as Ryan recalled his stunned surprise when Stephanie had stepped down from the stage. He'd expected her peremptory attitude, but never such a regally tall beauty. Now it was hard to think of being without her. Ryan's jaw clenched in frustration and he closed his eyes. If he ever regained her trust, he'd never do anything to lose it again.

Another strong kick sent him surging backward again. With the water in his ears it was hard to hear, but Ryan recognized the muffled sound of a duck flapping past, its wings beating against the lake surface. His peaceful swim was no longer as peaceful, he thought irritably, though it had more to do with his turbulent thoughts than ducks. He'd just give up and go back to the ruins and sit with Stephanie. Maybe they could resolve their differences.

Before he had a chance to open his eyes or change direction, Ryan felt a powerful tug on his ankles that pulled him underwater. Caught by surprise, his first reaction was to kick free as he clawed his way back to the surface. He wasn't certain if he'd somehow become entangled in weeds or had been snared by a submerged vine. Coughing and sputtering, Ryan surfaced, wiping water from his eyes. Immediately, his eyes narrowed on Stephanie's grinning face.

"Can't you swim?" she mocked. "The idea, I believe, is to stay on *top* of the water . . . Ryan!"

She dodged his diving attack, nimbly skimming across the lake in a maneuver that reminded Ryan of a coot's attempt at flight. As her arms slashed through the water he recognized his shirt and grinned. Vengeance was at hand.

Though Stephanie could swim well, Ryan was a more powerful swimmer. His strong strokes brought him to her side swiftly, and she squealed in alarm as one arm circled her waist. Whipping her head around as she struggled, long wet streamers of her hair struck Ryan's face in stinging slaps. The lake was deep, and Stephanie was treading water as fast as she could in the effort to stay afloat. Half laughing and half choking, she felt Ryan's steady pull tugging her determinedly downward, and managed to catch her breath before she was ducked.

The lake closed over the top of her head as Ryan pulled her under, and Stephanie's long legs wound around his torso like a vise. Still holding her breath, she squeezed tightly. Now we'll see who can hold their breath the longest, she thought, opening her eyes.

Clear water blurred Ryan, but she could still see his lips curve into a wicked smile as one hand reached up to her shirt buttons. Stephanie realized his intention and released him immediately. When she tried to kick free, she discovered that Ryan's free hand was tightly gripping her ankle. The water slowed her frantic efforts to fend off the hand unbuttoning her shirt, and she was rapidly running out of breath. Caught between her need for air and the struggle over her shirt buttons, Stephanie surrendered to the former.

Clawing her way up, she broke through the surface at the exact moment Ryan unfastened the last button. The shirt was neatly peeled away in a quick motion as Ryan's head popped up next to hers.

"Satisfied?" she asked when she could catch her breath enough to speak.

"Almost," he answered with a grin. "I was just reclaiming my shirt, Princess."

His contagious grin made Stephanie's lips quirk in response. "You wretch," she said amicably. "I should have drowned you when I had the chance."

Almost out of breath again, and weary of treading water, Stephanie struck out toward shore. Reaching it at last, she waited in the shallows among concealing reeds.

"Modest?" Ryan asked as he joined her in the waist-deep water. He eyed her efforts at hiding behind slender reeds poking up from the lake bed. "You needn't be. You've got a beautiful body, Stephanie, and shouldn't try to hide it."

"Does that mean I should stroll casually down every main street in Arizona without my clothes?"

Stephanie made a face. "Forget it!"

"This isn't exactly a main street, and there's no one here but you and me," Ryan pointed out with a grin. "And I've seen all of you before . . ." His grin faded as he met Stephanie's gaze. He stepped closer, and water swirled around his lean waist in widening circles. Rivulets streamed over Ryan's sleek, tanned muscles, and the wet, dark hair on his chest curled outward as it dried.

Still holding his clear gaze, Stephanie found herself more breathless than she'd been when underwater. And a part of her acknowledged the fact that she'd come down to the lake knowing this would happen. She'd wanted it to happen, wanted their former intimacy. Nothing had been the same since her capture by the Apaches, and she wanted an end to the constraint.

"So," she finally said when it became clear Ryan was waiting for her to make the first move, "'what'cha gonna do?'"

Hearing her repeat the phrase he'd used so many times, Ryan laughed. "This, Princess," he said softly, and bent to scoop her into his arms. "Have you ever made love in the water?"

"You know I haven't . . ." Her words were breathed against his neck as she held tightly to him. "I've always been stuck in a rut of conventionality, remember?"

Ryan groaned lightly. "Do you have to remember *everything* I say?"

Nuzzling her nose into his neck, Stephanie nodded. "I hang on your every word, Ryan Cordell."

Water dripped from their bodies in tiny waterfalls

as he carried her through the shallows to a spot clear of reeds. The mud made a soft bed, and water swirled gently around them in small pools and eddies as Ryan lowered Stephanie to her back on the bank. Half in and half out of the water, he stretched out beside her. Cushioning her shoulders with one arm, he pushed back wet, tangled strands of hair from her eyes with his other hand.

Stephanie felt deliciously wicked and abandoned. She'd never dreamed she could behave so wantonly and not feel remorse, but there wasn't a shred of repentance in her. In fact, she reveled in Ryan's lingering touch, his slow kiss calculated to summon passionate response. It all felt so right, so natural.

High overhead the sun smiled warm approval, and the wind whispered a blessing as it passed over them. Cool water lapped gently at their entwined bodies, and the reeds surrounding them rustled softly.

Stephanie traced the path of a fat waterdrop as it slid from Ryan's neck to his shoulder. Her chin tilted up and she smiled into his eyes almost shyly, small teeth digging into her bottom lip as he caressed her slowly.

"Not changing your mind, are you, Princess?" Ryan asked, and his exploring fingers walked a fiery trail from her mouth downward, pausing to delightfully tease her small, firm breasts.

"N-n-no," Stephanie half gasped as his mouth closed over a pink bud. Her fingers dug into his arm and she arched her back like a tawny cat. "Why would I want to do that?" Her dark eyes closed, spiky lashes making long shadows on her cheeks as she sighed with pleasure.

A heady, breath-stealing languor stole through her body, leaving her feeling weak all over. The deep, burning ache in her belly curled upward as Ryan's hands worked their magic, and Stephanie responded with sighing moans and sinuous twists of her body, rolling on her side to face him.

Soft urgency replaced the languor, and Stephanie's hands began explorations of their own. She caressed his sides, the hard ridges of his ribs and lean, tight muscles in his belly, then let her fingers skip lightly over the sharp angle of his hip to his buttocks. A smile curved her mouth as Stephanie's hands circled to Ryan's legs, caressing his inner thighs with slow, rhythmic motions that made him groan softly. He caught her hand as it found and held him, burying his face in the hollow of her neck and shoulder.

"Witch," he muttered thickly. "You've got a powerful magic, Stephanie Ashworth."

"Do I?" She turned her head slightly, nibbling at his ear with her teeth, then kissing it. "So do you, Ryan Cordell, so do you."

Words drifted away on the wind, and the bright blue bowl of the sky overhead seemed to fade to nothing as she saw only Ryan. He filled her world with his smoky gray eyes and dark, wet hair that curled endearingly around his ears and over his forehead. Her palms rested on his flat belly and her eyes devoured him hungrily, admiring the smooth bronzed skin that had grown even darker in the Arizona sun the past weeks, and Stephanie forgave him everything. Nothing else mattered now. There was only Ryan and only this special magic between them.

Another delicious shudder brought her even closer to him, then he was throwing one leg over both her long, slender limbs. Water rippled in ever-widening circles around them as Ryan moved between Stephanie's legs, with both his hands digging into the soft bank beneath her head. Bending his dark head, he kissed her long and deeply, inhaling the sweet scent of her, tasting the honeyed depths of her mouth. Stephanie's arms rose to wind around his neck and hold him, and Ryan poised over her for a moment before thrusting forward.

Arching her back like a cat, Stephanie made a small noise in the back of her throat as Ryan entered her, and her fingers tangled in his hair. She matched his hard, rhythmic thrusts with a fierce urgency like someone too long denied. Waves of sheer pleasure coursed through her with the swift pounding of his body against her, and Stephanie couldn't hold back the burst of ecstasy that came too soon. She was barely aware of crying out, clutching at him and half sobbing his name, then he was holding her tenderly and kissing her nose, her closed eyelids, her parted lips.

"Now it's my turn," Ryan murmured against her mouth, and began a slow, sweet rocking until Stephanie was once more quivering beneath him. This time they shared the achingly sweet release, shuddering in each other's arms. Ryan rested his chin against Stephanie, and kissed her lovingly on the top of her head.

"Ryan?" Stephanie pressed her lips against the smooth arch of his throat where the stubble of his half-grown beard melded into the softer mat of curls on his chest.

"Hmmm?"

"I love you," she dared to say softly, and felt his body tense. Oh, God, had she risked too much? Stephanie was alarmed at the quick tears filling her eyes, and tried to blink them away. But when she tried to move from beneath him, Ryan held her fast.

"Ah, babe," Ryan said gruffly, and his arms tightened around her comfortingly. "I love you, too . . ."

Chapter Thirty-Two

A bright fire filled the crumbling ruin with rosy light and flickering shadows that danced like maddened fairies on the stone walls. Stephanie sat close, drying her hair in the heat, and a smile that wouldn't fade was pasted on her face. She was happier than she could ever recall being, and gazed at Ryan with her heart in her eyes.

He smiled back, feeling slightly awkward and a little foolish, but filled with a peace he'd never known. So this was what it was like to be truly in love, he thought. The last woman he'd loved had been his mother, and that had been so long ago . . .

"Ryan, tell me about yourself," Stephanie said as she gazed dreamily into the fire. "I don't know anything about you, where you're from, your upbringing, your family . . ."

"I don't have any family. I'm an orphan. Care to adopt me?" he teased.

"Oh, do be serious!" Stephanie took the roasted duck he offered her. "I know you went to school in the East, but that's all I've managed to learn about you.''

"Does my past matter that much?" Ryan managed to ask lightly. He turned the makeshift spit he'd erected, browning the duck on the opposite side. "It's the future that really matters . . ."

"Are you hiding something? I don't care if you've been in trouble with the authorities before, unless . . . unless you're wanted for murder, or something." Stephanie stared at him with big, dark eyes, recalling the posters Sheriff Royce had mentioned in Willow Creek. "Are you?"

"No. There aren't any current posters out on me . . ."

"Current?"

A rueful smile slanted Ryan's mouth. "You do pick up on every word, don't you?" He sighed. "Yes, there were once posters out on me. Occasionally old posters still cause me some trouble, but not often."

"What did you do? Murder? Kidnapping? Robbery?" Her tone was only half jesting.

Ryan's dark brows rose. "I'm pleased you have such a high opinion of me, Princess! No, I didn't do anything like that . . ."

"Then what?" Puzzled, she stared at him.

"Let's just say . . . there was a little misunderstanding." His mouth tilted in a smile when she shook her head in exasperation. "All right, all right—there was a range war in Texas that I became involved in. Unwillingly, I might add, and to make a long story short, I ended up on the losing side. Bitter words were exchanged, a few rifle shots in the night, and the man I worked for came up dead. A couple of his boys, including myself, decided to take the killers in to the law. Instead, we found ourselves facing charges of murder. No, I didn't kill anyone," he added when Stephanie stared at him questioningly. "But I wanted to."

"So," she prompted when he paused, "what happened? How did you end up with wanted posters out on you? And are you still wanted by the authorities?"

"We escaped from jail, and they put out posters, which are probably the ones Sheriff Royce still has. Eventually, we were able to prove that we didn't kill our boss but that took a while. And no, I'm not still wanted by the law. In fact, there are times I work *with* the law."

"Oh." Stephanie brightened, then realized, "That's why you were so upset when we were in Willow Creek! You were concerned that the situation would jeopardize your career . . ."

"No, that's not the reason. I'm just familiar with how slowly the wheels of justice can grind, and I knew it might take days or even weeks before Royce got an answer. During that length of time, you were liable to do most anything," he added dryly. "I wasn't sure what you'd be up to . . ."

Licking grease from her fingers, Stephanie arched a brow at him. "I would have managed just fine," she assured him. "I always have."

"That's exactly what I was afraid of. I'd had experience with your management, remember." Ryan surveyed the roasted duck with a critical eye, then removed it from the spit to a battered metal plate. "Our dishes have seen better days, Princess."

"We can manage. Tell me about your family. Are your parents still alive?" Stephanie paused at the expression on Ryan's face, and shifted uncomfortably. His features had darkened ominously.

"No. I told you I'm an orphan," he said shortly.

"Ryan, I'm sorry," she said softly. "I thought you were just joking again. I barely recall my mother, but I've always felt her loss . . ." She stared in amazement as Ryan shot to his feet angrily.

"My mother! If it wasn't for her, my father would probably still be alive!" he half snarled, then seemed to catch himself. Taking a deep breath, Ryan struggled for control. "Sorry," he muttered. "You'd think that after all these years I'd forget, but I can't."

Stephanie remained quiet, watching Ryan as he paced the dirt floor of the pueblo ruin. His bronzed face in the shadowy light was hard, as if carved from granite, and when he turned to look at her, Stephanie knew he wasn't seeing her but his past. His gray eyes were cloudy with scenes she couldn't see, and his voice was rough with pain as he said, "I can still see her, my beautifully remote mother, her blond hair perfectly in place, and china-blue eyes so cold and hard." Ryan shrugged helplessly. "I never understood how my father could have been so blind, but God help him, he loved her faithfully. My mother was from New York," he said with a strained smile in Stephanie's direction, "and her family was high society and rich. Her parents were scandalized that she chose to marry a Westerner, even one with twenty-five hundred acres of prime land in northern Idaho. That's where I was born, near a main street with a few stores they call Bonner's Ferry. Naturally,

Emma couldn't stand living in such a remote part of the world for long, far away from opera houses, carriage rides in the park, elite restaurants, and with no social activities to fill her days. When I was still a boy, she left my father, and took me with her. He never recovered from that." Ryan's mouth tightened grimly. "It was hard for a ten-year-old to understand the sudden change in social climate. I was more comfortable in the back alleys of New York than in a drawing room impressing my mother's friends. She sent me to school, of course, hence my 'proper' English and manners. I hated it. I missed my father. I missed the mountains and the early morning mist that smelled of fresh air and pine, not gas lamps and garbage.

"I used to run away a lot, but they'd always find me down in the shipyards, or fighting on the docks. Once my uncle found me living in the back room of a tiny Italian restaurant. I still don't know how he managed to find me, but he did. When I was returned home, my mother was too busy to notice. She was having a dinner party, you see, and couldn't be bothered with her twelve-year-old son. The next day, I said I wanted to go home to my father. She slapped me and said in the coldest tone imaginable that I would be brought up to be a gentleman, not an illiterate backwoods cowboy like my father."

A bleak smile stretched Ryan's mouth as he stared into the flames, and Stephanie could see his remembered hurt and bewilderment. Her heart ached for the young boy who had been a pawn between his parents, and she couldn't help holding out her hand in a conciliatory gesture.

Ryan's expression grew faintly embarrassed, as if he was ashamed of his emotion, the despair he'd felt as a child.

"It doesn't matter anymore," he said stiffly. "I left New York when I was eighteen and went back to Idaho. My father died ten years ago, when I was twenty. You know, in spite of what my mother had said, he was one of the most well read, well informed men I've ever met. He'd come from a wealthy family, and even been to Europe. But he was a broken man when he died, still loving my mother. And now I do my best to hang on to the land that meant so much to him."

"What about your mother?" Stephanie asked after a moment of hesitation, wondering if she should even ask. "What happened to her? Wasn't she upset when you left?"

"It was several months before she even knew I was gone," Ryan said bitterly. "And by then, she had a new project. She never wrote or tried to contact me after that." He shrugged. "Two years later, she died in a carriage accident."

Appalled, Stephanie couldn't think of another thing to say. How could his mother have abandoned him like that? The loss of her own mother had been felt deeply, but at least she'd had the comforting knowledge that her mother had loved her. Stephanie offered up a prayer of gratitude for having Julian in her life. He may have been a little different from a conventional father, but she had never lacked understanding and love.

"Tell me about your land, Ryan. I've never been to Idaho," Stephanie said softly. "Does it compare with

Minnesota, perhaps?''

Welcoming the change of subject, Ryan's tension eased. "Minnesota? Not hardly! Imagine mountains where the snow falls so deep you can lose a house in it, and clear, rushing creeks where the water is icy cold year round, even when the sun makes it hot enough for a beaver to shed its skin. Trees grow so thick there you can't see the sun when you're standing under them. The land rolls in places, then seems to climb straight up toward the stars . . ." Pausing, Ryan flashed her a sheepish glance. "It's beautiful," he ended lamely.

"So it sounds." Stephanie hugged her knees, gazing at Ryan through half-lidded eyes. "You're still looking for that spot where the fair wind blows constantly, aren't you?" She smiled at his puzzled expression. "Your song, the one you sang back in that old hut," she explained.

"Yeah, I suppose I am still looking for that fair wind, Princess—and someone to share it with.''

Stephanie's heart pounded like an Indian drum, but she said coolly, as if his reaction didn't matter in the least, "I'd like to find it with you someday. Maybe in Idaho?''

For a moment Ryan didn't answer. His eyes traveled over Stephanie's damply curling hair and her heart-shaped face with the big, dark eyes that were staring at him so appealingly. In the faint light from the fire, her entire body radiated a golden glow like old Spanish coins, muted and soft, a deep, rich color that contrasted sharply with hair bleached almost white by the sun. Long slender legs were bent at the knees, and her bare toes dug into the hard dirt of the pueblo floor as she waited tensely for his reply. Recognizing the strain in her eyes, Ryan smiled gently and stepped close.

Bending, he crooked one finger under her small, pointed chin, and kissed her lightly on the mouth.

"I can think of nothing I would like better than for you to go with me to Idaho," he said simply. It was all he needed to say for the moment. To Stephanie, it was more of a commitment than she'd dared hope for.

Her arms wound around his neck, holding him, and she returned his kiss. It was an unspoken seal on their alliance of hearts.

Chapter Thirty-Three

It was still cool when they left the limestone lake the next morning, and early mists made the air clear and sharp. Stephanie double-checked the knots on her saddlebags, and retightened them. She didn't want to lose anything else, especially when they were so close behind Julian. Biting her bottom lip, she was concentrating on the stubborn leather straps and didn't hear Ryan's approach.

When his arms circled her waist, Stephanie couldn't help a startled gasp. Half turning, she said reprovingly, "You're as quiet as an Indian, sneaking up on me like that!"

"I should be. I rode with Apaches, didn't I?" His lips smothered Stephanie's next indignant remark, then he was lifting her to the paint mare's broad back. "We need to make as much time as possible today, Princess. With any luck, we should catch up with Julian sometime tomorrow."

"I can't believe we're finally so close," Stephanie said, fitting her feet into the stirrups. "It seems like years instead of months since I've seen Father. You know, he's never before sent for me and not waited upon my arrival. I thought that surely we would have at least gotten a message from him by now, but nothing!" A puzzled frown creased her forehead as Stephanie tugged her felt hat lower. "I can't understand why he didn't send someone back to wait for me. Besides Huntley and Bates, I mean," she added with a grimace.

"Stephanie, has it ever occurred to you that your father may not have wanted you to join him on this expedition?" Ryan asked. He stepped into his saddle and nudged the stallion forward.

"Of course it hasn't. He wouldn't have sent me that map if he didn't intend for me to join him, and if he'd changed his mind for some reason, he would have contacted me."

"Maybe he tried, but the message didn't get delivered like it was supposed to," Ryan said quietly.

Stephanie reined her mare to a halt. "What are you trying to say?" she demanded. "Do you know more than you're telling me?"

"Sort of . . ."

"Sort of? Either you *do* know something, or you don't! Which is it?"

"Do." Ryan's eyes met Stephanie's suspicious gaze. "Wait a minute, *I* didn't do anything. It was Huntley and Bates. They were supposed to send a telegram from your father telling you not to come to Arizona. That's one of the reasons I ran them out of the fort as soon as you got there."

"One of the reasons?" Stephanie's eyes narrowed. "What were the others?"

393

"They had no intentions of guiding you to Julian," Ryan answered with a trace of impatience. "What they really intended, was to hold you for ransom."

His answer checked her quick anger, and Stephanie's gaze softened. And Ryan hadn't wanted her to be harmed, she thought. Maybe he had been attracted to her from the first, after all.

Aloud she said, "I'm doubly grateful to you for running them off, then. And I'm glad we took their trousers, too. Do you think they found their horses?"

He grinned and nudged his stallion into a trot. "Yeah. After a long, hot walk!" Ryan said over his shoulder. "It'd be murder to leave a man afoot in this country, and even Huntley and Bates don't deserve that."

Dust boiled behind the stallion's hooves as Ryan kicked him into a gallop, leaving Stephanie to follow. The paint mare leaped eagerly forward with very little encouragement, and miles of rocky trail were soon behind them.

Damn, he'd almost said too much, Ryan reflected. And Stephanie seemed to listen to every little word he said. This job was almost over, and he didn't need to risk telling her too much now. It'd cost him a big bonus if he did, because confidentiality had been stressed. Besides, what difference would it make if he told her? He'd gotten her safely this far, hadn't he? And knowing wouldn't change anything; not now.

Ryan leaned forward in his saddle, urging his stallion up the side of an arroyo. The land had flattened out more, and huge mesas and red-ridged buttes jutted up from the arid ground dotted with cactus and yucca plants. As far as he could remember from the map Stephanie had lost, they were in the general area of the burial ground Julian was seeking. Ryan eyed the towering mesas that ran like jagged rows of dragon teeth along each side of the flat, open plain between. Which one sheltered the magic rock of ancient myth?

It could be any of them. The sandstone ridges held hundreds of crevices that might lead inward to a plateau or cave. Only the Indians who had lived in this stark region for centuries were familiar with the vast terrain that comprised this part of Arizona Territory. The Mogollon Rim, an escarpment stretching two hundred miles across Arizona and into New Mexico, slashed its way through in a series of encroaching canyons and jumbled mountains. Along most of its length, the rim was a distinct wall of rock that was sometimes white, sometimes blue-gray or red or cream. Erosion had bared great layers of limestone, sandstone, and shale, and had bitten deeply into underlying granite. Along the line of the rim, above its cliffs and down in its shadow, a quiet forest of aspens gleamed against the dark green of Ponderosa pines and Douglas firs. Farther below were broad stands of pine, then the land sloped away toward the desert, where bare buttes and stark peaks gnashed at the southern horizon with serrated teeth. In the fall, bright splotches of color revealed the maples and oaks above the rim and again in the mouths of canyons at the rim's foot.

Not far away, Ryan recalled, was a rock bridge that arched over one hundred eighty feet above a creek, shading a rocky vault below. He remembered riding across it once, and, approaching on a level with the top of the bridge, had not even realized it was only a narrow rock formation spanning the creek until he was at a certain point. His stallion had spooked, and for several moments he had wondered if he'd end up plunging from the bridge to the shallow creek below.

Ryan briefly considered taking a small detour to let Stephanie see it, then changed his mind. As much as he enjoyed showing her things he thought interesting, it would have to wait. Maybe later—if he was still around, or if she would still speak to him . . .

"Ryan," Stephanie was saying excitedly as she rode up beside him, making him slow his stallion, "look!"

He turned in the direction she was pointing, and saw what had stirred her interest. Shimmering as if in moonlight, a shaded slope glowed with lupine and the silvery spines of cholla cactus. The blue and purple flowers of the delicate lupine waved gently among fading yellow blooms of brittlebush, and there were only remnants left of deep-pink owl clover and orange poppies.

"You've seen these before," he chided.

"Yes, but not quite like this. It's daylight, yet somehow on this side of the mountain it looks like night."

"That's not a mountain, Princess. It's a butte. There's a big difference . . ."

"I know," she said crossly. "You've told me before, but they're still mountains to me. Anything bigger than a molehill is a mountain."

"I always knew you thought like that. I just never expected you to admit it," Ryan teased.

Pulling a face, Stephanie tossed back, "It seems to me that *you* are the one who enjoys making mountains out of molehills, Mr. Cordell! I'm always even-tempered."

"We'll see how even-tempered you are when we reach open desert again."

"What? I . . . I thought we were almost there! What do you mean 'desert', Ryan Cordell! Miles and miles of sand and dust and those horrible jumping cactus plants . . . Aren't we almost there?"

"Yeah. I just wanted to see how far your even temper would stretch . . ." Ryan ducked the slap she aimed at him with the loose ends of her leather reins. "Ah ah, you're even-tempered, remember?"

Laughing, Stephanie shrugged. "So I lied. How much farther is it?"

It was Ryan's turn to shrug. "I don't know. We don't have the map, remember? As much as I can tell from their trail, they're only a day's ride ahead. If it doesn't rain, or no windstorm comes up, I can just follow their tracks."

"And if it does rain?"

"Then I'll have to depend on my memory of the map. Don't worry," he comforted at the sight of her crestfallen face, "we'll find 'em. And I'm not expecting any rain." He squinted up at the cloudless blue sky.

Three hours later, storm clouds chased the sun from the sky, shadowing the earth. It was going to be a summer downpour that would swell dry arroyos with torrents of water and turn barren plains verdant. Ryan decided to take shelter beneath a large outcropping of rock high above flat ground.

Stephanie, recalling the last storm and flash flood, urged her mare faster up the rocky slope, closing her eyes at the familiar grip of fear as they clambered higher and higher. Rocks, loosened by Ryan's stallion, skittered haphazardly down the slope past the nervous mare, bouncing from ledge to ledge.

"I feel like I'm part mountain goat," Stephanie muttered under her breath, casting an anxious glance at the sky again. She didn't dare look down at the safe valley floor. "I'm either climbing up or climbing down some kind of precipice."

"You don't want to get caught in a flood, do you?" Ryan asked. He'd slowed his stallion, and was carefully picking his way through a jumble of small and large rocks.

"No-o-o," she answered, but Stephanie's voice didn't carry the ring of conviction. "I'm scared of heights!" she finally snapped when Ryan commented that she was too lazy to get out of the way of a flood. She stared at his surprised face defiantly, giving a half shrug. "I can't help it, but I am."

"Then why haven't you said so before? Good God, woman, we've been up and down hills that'd make a hawk nervous, and now you tell me you're scared of heights?" He whooped with laughter. "You are some woman, Stephanie Ashworth," he said when he stopped laughing for a moment. "You are some woman . . ."

"I know." Her chin lifted in a faint challenge that dared him to retract his backhanded compliment, and he didn't even attempt it. Nodding his head, Ryan agreed.

When they reached the wide ledge beneath an

overhang, they loosened the girths on their mounts and fed the animals a handful of grain. This would probably be the only rest they would take until nightfall. Storms were usually swift and fierce this time of year, sweeping across plains and over mountains with devastating force, but gone as quickly as they'd come.

Stephanie crouched down on the hard shale floor of the shallow cave, staring out over the rocky lip. Thunder boomed so loud it sounded like an avalanche, and lightning cracked from earth to sky, making the hair on the back of her neck stiffen. She shivered suddenly without knowing why.

"Cold, Princess?" Ryan came up quietly behind her, resting one hand on her shoulder.

"No, I'm not cold. The wind is a welcome relief from the heat." Stephanie glanced up at him, then back to the sea of cactus and sage stretching below. Removing her hat, she combed through her tangled hair with splayed fingers, tugging at the snarls.

How could she ever hope to retain his attention when she looked like this? Stephanie wondered with a twinge of despair. Ryan must think she was the most hopelessly homely female he'd ever seen. Vanity had never been one of her faults, but lately she'd been more than aware of her appearance. She looked, Stephanie decided dismally, like a sunbrowned porcupine. Her hair was frizzy, her nose was red, and her fashionably pale skin was now an unfashionable brown. A swift glance in the clear, calm waters of the lake early that morning, had plunged her into misery.

The reflection mirrored on the surface hadn't the

faintest resemblance to the Stephanie that she recalled. What had happened to the hair she'd kept tucked into a neat bun? And her vibrant complexion only made her dark eyes seem darker. Except for that brief respite in Willow Creek, when she had at least been able to wear a decent dress and bathe, she had presented all the refinements of a washerwoman since arriving in Arizona Territory.

It was fortunate that Ryan harbored no illusions about Stephanie. He still thought her a naturally beautiful woman, and wouldn't have understood her sudden descent into the yawning abyss of vanity.

Standing behind her, Ryan stared out over the top of Stephanie's head, watching as blinding sheets of rain rolled across the ground in constant waves like the ocean. The rain would wash away all traces of Julian's tracks on the hard ground. Now he would have to rely on his memory of that damned map, which he'd never thought too accurate anyway. Rubbing a palm across his face, Ryan had the fleeting desire to tell Stephanie it was hopeless. But if they turned back, she'd always think he'd never done his best. No, he'd push on. They were bound to run into Julian once they reached the vicinity of the burial ground.

Chapter Thirty-Four

Wondering if he was even within miles of the burial ground he sought, Julian stared at the butte. The stump-shaped promontory reared abruptly from the canyon floor, rising four hundred fifty feet straight up. This couldn't be it, yet it had to be. If the map was even vaguely correct, this should be the sacred area that cradled the magic rock. It was the only butte of any size within miles.

Glancing at the smaller stones perched atop the larger rocks of the ancient solar observatory, Julian sighed. He knew those rocks had a purpose, but he hadn't yet been able to determine it. Hakiwuh hadn't been much help, mumbling wild excuses and dire predictions about their doom if the spirits were disturbed.

"Nervous kinda fella, ain't he?" Bingo observed with grim humor when Hakiwuh prostrated himself after a particularly loud clap of thunder following a sudden summer storm. The Papago guide seemed certain they would all perish.

"He certainly is," Julian agreed, giving Hakiwuh a sour glance. "Why on earth didn't he protest when Chief Pacal told him to guide us? Why wait until now?"

"Accordin' ta him, th' ole chief never thought we'd want ta really *rummage* aroun' th' magic rock, jus' kinda take a quick peek. Hakiwuh bein' th' greedy kind, he never asked too many questions till now. Now he ain't so sure he wants th' risk."

"It's too late now. We're here, and I don't intend to leave until I find this 'magic rock' that guards priceless artifacts buried with their late owners," Julian answered. "I've come too far and risked my neck for this thrill. I don't plan on quitting now."

Bingo spat at a scorpion scuttling deeper into the shadows of a rock. "Ugly lil' critter, ain't it? Naw, Pilgrim, ya cain't quit now. We'll know fer sure if'n this is th' right place purty soon." He nodded at the carved petroglyph. "Th' ancients, they knew whut they wuz doin' when they made that thing, an' you know whut yer doin'. Jus' have a lil' more faith in yerself, Pilgrim."

"By heavens, Bingo, you're right!" Julian smacked a fist into his palm. "I *do* know what I'm doing. I needed a reminder of that fact. Thank you."

Unrolling his copy of the precious map, Julian studied it again. This butte rising like a grim sentinel from the canyon floor could very well be the sacred mountain indicated on his map. The sacred eagle feather drawn over the peak, named it as the spot, while the shafts of sunlight that streamed from what he'd earlier thought to be a crudely drawn sun in the eastern sky could be this highly sophisticated astronomical device. Tomorrow would be the test.

Julian could barely sleep that night, tossing and turning and wondering what the morrow would bring. He was more excited than he'd ever been about a find. This one had taken more than just perseverence and the ability to withstand harsh conditions; this discovery had demanded courage and intelligence. All in all, Julian was amazed that he had made it this far.

Stephanie would be astonished at her father, he thought with a smile. She'd never believe him when he told her about Arizona and all its wonders, and he wouldn't be able to blame her. After all, if he hadn't experienced it himself, he would never have quite believed how the weather could change at a moment's notice, and how the landscape could meld from harsh red ridges into stands of evergreen trees within the space of a few miles, and then back again. And tomorrow's sun would shine on the pinnacle of his accomplishments, pointing the way to the lost treasures of kings. It would be a discovery to delight archaeologists' hearts and excite their intellects, Julian reflected. He had already decided on which museums would benefit from the pieces he did not want.

The first bright rays of sunlight shot over the horizon, brightening the sky and the flat canyon floor. Julian waited with nervous excitement, staring intently at the petroglyph. He hadn't even stopped for breakfast, and Bingo appeared beside him, holding out a strip of beef jerky and cold corncake.

"Might as well eat, Pilgrim. Starvin' ain't gonna make this enny quicker, ya know."

"Thanks," Julian responded absently, keeping an eye on the dagger of light playing over the slanted stone slabs. "When the sun reaches its zenith, it should bisect the petroglyph and show us the way to Magic Rock."

"Yeah." Bingo sounded unconvinced, scratching at his beard-stubbled jaw and gazing upward.

"You think I'm wrong." Julian bit off a chunk of jerky and stared at the old man through narrowed eyes. "Why?"

"Now, I niver said no such thing. Yer jus' lettin' yer worries run off like a bee-stung horse." He hitched up his tattered trousers, staring thoughtfully at the smaller rocks perched atop the stone slabs. "I wuz jus' wonderin' whut them lil' ones are fer, that's all."

"The smaller rocks?" Julian lifted his gaze to study them.

"See how they stick out taller than those big slabs? They remind me of arrowheads," Bingo said. "An' I keep thinkin' that thar must be a reason fer 'em."

Standing in the shade of the huge slabs leaning against the rounded boulder, Julian contemplated Bingo's statement. "We'll watch those, too," he said finally. "They could be markers of some sort, I suppose."

Waiting impatiently, Julian kept his gaze trained on the dagger of light as it moved at a snail's pace across the petroglyph. Hours dragged past, yet the ray of run did not bisect the exact center of the carved spiral. Finally, Julian was ready to suggest they return the following day.

Glancing at Bingo, who was propped in the shadows of the slabs, Julian said, "I suppose we should give it up for today, Bingo. It's after noon. Maybe we'll have better luck tomorrow."

Bingo squinted up at him, and sunlight glittered from his gold earring. "Mebbe so, Pilgrim—" He paused, then shot to his feet with an agility that surprised Julian. "Looka thar, Julian Ashworth!" A twisted finger pointed to the top of the stone slabs, and Julian turned to look.

A narrow shaft of sunlight climbed the two arrows of rock perched atop the slabs, balancing in a burst of light at the apex. Staring down the sight as if he was looking down the barrel of a rifle, Julian saw a finger of light stream across the face of the sheer rock butte beyond. Illuminated in the bright swathe of light was a dark cleft near the base of the butte—an opening in the closed face.

"Bingo! That's it—it's got to be! An entrance that is hidden by a false front— Come on!"

Bingo was close behind Julian as he raced toward the narrow mouth before the pointing finger of light moved on and it was hidden again. They arrived panting and out of breath, clambering like landed crabs over the jumble of small rocks at the base of the butte.

Julian reached it first, and stood excitedly in the shadow of a twisted rock tunnel. The narrow walls were too close to permit horses. The exploration would have to be done on foot.

"I can't believe it," Julian kept saying over and over, raking a hand through his hair. His fedora slanted sideways on his head, and a smear of dirt streaked his cheek.

"Now calm down, Pilgrim," Bingo advised a little breathlessly. He was getting too old for all this damned sprinting, he thought as he caught his breath. "Look," he wheezed, "why don' we rest first, then explore."

Distracted by curious drawings on the tunnel walls, Julian slid him a quick glance.

"I'll go on ahead. You and Hakiwuh can follow with shovels and picks while I try to decide . . ."

"Whoa, Julian! Ya ain't even found th' burial ground yet! What makes ya so shore this is th' place?" He fanned himself with his wolf-head hat, and sparse strands of gray hair quivered in the breeze. "'Sides, gittin' Hakiwuh ta come in thar is gonna take some doin'."

Impatient to continue, Julian flicked Bingo an exasperated glance. "Well, do what you can." He scrambled up a rocky lip further inside the tunnel, then called back, "I'll need a torch! It's total darkness in here."

A short time later, an unhappy Hakiwuh brought Julian his torches, shovel, and packs. He was still babbling in his own language, and Bingo didn't bother with interpretations. Every now and then, Bingo aimed an irritated stream of tobacco juice in the Papago guide's direction.

"What's he so upset about?" Julian finally asked. "Does he think the gods will kill him for helping us?"

"Well, Pilgrim, I reckon he is a mite upset. But I don' think he'll be too upset ta take enny golden

406

coins ya might bring back down with ya." Bingo squinted disgustedly at Hakiwuh. "He's greedier than he is scared, I think."

"He wouldn't accept my offer of money in exchange for information earlier," Julian pointed out, frowning at the guide. "What changed his mind?"

"Ta my way of thinkin', since the sun dagger pointed th' way, he figgers it'll be all right with th' gods if'n he accepts their bounty. At least, that's whut I git frum all his mutterin' and carryin' on."

"Well, we can always use an extra hand with a shovel, Bingo. And Hakiwuh is younger and stronger than both of us."

"Speak fer yerself, old boy. I got plenty of strength left!" Bingo snorted.

Grinning, Julian motioned them to follow, and started the tortuous climb up the narrow rock tunnel. The walls rose sheerly around them, and were just wide enough for two men to walk abreast. Panting and huffing, the three men walked a path worn smooth by the sandals of men hundreds of years before. The rock floor slanted almost straight up in places, so that they frequently had to stop to rest. There were turns so sharp Julian wondered how the ancient Indians had ever managed to carry a burial litter through them, and in places, the tunnel even dipped sharply downward before rising again.

The flickering torchlight reflected figures carved on the walls, Julian noticed. They seemed to be spaced at exact intervals, almost like some kind of primitive signpost pointing the way. Holding the torch high, Julian pressed on in the lead, leaving the slower Bingo and nervous Hakiwuh to follow.

Occasionally loose rocks would roll from beneath his feet, and the walls would be wet to the touch. Pausing for breath, he leaned against a dry spot on the tunnel wall, and raised the torch to peer ahead. Half turning, he called back to Bingo, "Bring your torch, Bingo! Mine must be growing weaker . . . I think I feel a draft . . ."

Suddenly his feet slipped on loose rocks and he slid forward. The torch fell from his hand as he tried to catch himself, and he landed on a sharp ledge projecting from the wall. A cold chill swept through Julian as the torch fell in a hissing arc, growing smaller and smaller until it was only a tiny speck far below. He scrambled for his footing, feeling himself slip closer and closer to the edge of what must be a chasm that reached to the center of the earth.

"Bingo . . . !"

"I'm comin', I'm comin'," the old man answered testily, and Julian could barely hear him add, "What's yer dadblamed hurry ennyway, Pilgrim? Them Injuns up thar is dead, I tell ya! They ain't liable to go nowhar . . ."

Bingo's voice stopped abruptly, and his face peered over the lip of the chasm to stare at Julian clinging grimly to the ledge.

"Havin' troubles, Pilgrim?" Bingo aimed a stream of tobacco juice into the pit, staring with interest as it disappeared. "Gimme yer hand. That's whut ya git," he grumbled, gripping Julian by the hand, "fer bein' in such a all-fired hurry!"

Bingo jerked, and Julian hit the dust beside him in a shaking ball of relief. Lifting his head from the hard shale floor of the tunnel, he stared at the old man in astonishment. A satisfied smirk curled Bingo's mouth, and he nodded his grizzled head, holding up one arm.

"One-handed," the old man said, and Julian grinned.

Rising, Julian brushed off his clothes and scooped up his fedora from the floor. Slapping it against his thigh, he looked at Bingo and said, "Well, I guess I owe you one more. Put it on your bill, will you?"

"Hell, Pilgrim, that's whut I'm gittin' paid fer, ain't it? An' ta tell th' truth, yer more work than I ever thought you'd be." He grinned. "But at least we're havin' a good time! Ennyway, looks like we took a wrong turn back thar. I been lookin' at them lil' drawin's on th' wall, an' it 'pears ta me like we shoulda gone on that offshoot a couple hundred yards back. What'cha think?"

"Lead on," Julian said firmly. "Lead on." He cleared his throat and glanced at Hakiwuh who stood holding two torches. A slight smile curved his mouth at the Papago's expression of terror. "I don't think he's having a good time, Bingo," Julian said.

"Well, hell, we kin fix that! Here, ole boy, we're gonna let you go first . . ."

A reluctant Hakiwuh held the two torches high, leading them back to the offshot they'd passed earlier. He felt his way along carefully, constantly muttering prayers to his gods.

"See these?" Bingo pointed out, indicating the figures carved on the rock walls. "Seems ta be tellin' us ta go this way, don'cha reckon?"

Squinting at the crude figures representing a man,

Julian agreed. The torches flickered dimly, and he turned with a frown.

"Do we have any more torches?"

"Yeah, but we still got ta come back this way, don' ferget. We kin use one, an' save th' other fer a while longer."

"We don't really have much choice, do we?" Julian observed with a sigh. "Lead on!"

"Mr. Hakiwuh," Bingo said to the guide, "if'n ya will do th' honors . . ." He gestured with one hand and repeated his request in Hakiwuh's tongue. For a moment it appeared that the Papago might refuse, then he extinguished one torch and started forward with the other, carefully feeling his way along.

"You have a way with words," Julian said as he followed them.

The musty tunnel wound up almost in a spiral, rising higher and higher until a tiny speck of light could barely be seen far above. Julian's earlier feeling of exhilaration returned, and he held back the urge to race forward. Caution, he told himself.

Bingo seemed to have no similar impulses, but measured each step carefully as they trudged closer and closer to the light at the end of the tunnel.

A stiff breeze swept fresh air over them when they finally stood near the opening. Shading his eyes with one hand, Julian stumbled forward behind the Papago guide.

Hakiwuh threw down the torch and raced out into the open, throwing his arms wide to embrace the sky and his gods. The bright sunlight nearly blinded him and he faltered, covering his eyes with both hands as he dropped to his knees. Balanced on the edge of a crater, Hakiwuh gradually slid down the slope on his hands and knees in a shower of pebbles and rocks. It was only a slight incline, but Hakiwuh gained momentum as he pitched forward, rolling like a ball until he reached the flat bottom of the crater.

Coming to a rest against a porous rock studded with tiny pits, Hakiwuh was stunned and shaking. Watching, Bingo and Julian remained in the shaded opening of the tunnel, letting their eyes adjust to the brighter light.

"See, Pilgrim?" Bingo remarked, "I knowed thar wuz a good reason fer lettin' him go first . . ."

"Do you suppose he's hurt?" Julian asked.

"Naw, them Papagos got buffalo hides. Pebbles ain' gonna hurt him none."

Julian stood for a moment gazing out at the ancient burial ground with an emotion resembling reverence. It was a perfect spot for a man to meet his maker, he thought, for standing atop the butte was almost like being in heaven. He had a brief understanding of how the Greek gods must have felt staring down from Olympus at the tiny mortals peopling earth. Julian's reason for climbing the butte faded for a moment as he gazed at the magnificent panorama surrounding him.

Before him lay a vast chronicle of time, with the weathered spires that rose sharply in the distance carrying the marks of wind and sand that had carved them into fantastic shapes. The flat canyon floor stretched in a giant imprint of zigzagging gullies and arroyos like a patchwork quilt, and in the distance the blue horizon appeared like an endless sea. It was awesome and impressive, and Julian felt a sudden urge to fall humbly to his knees. He knelt on the flat lip of the crater denting the top of the butte for several long moments.

Bingo's tone was strange as he tugged at Julian's sleeve, muttering, "Reckon our guide hit his head, Pilgrim? He's staggerin' 'round that rock like he's had too much mescal ta drink . . ."

Turning, Julian watched as Hakiwuh stumbled in vague circles around the pitted rock jutting from the crater floor. His arms were held straight out at the sides as he walked toward them with short, jerky steps. Half falling, he attempted to climb back up the rocky slope, sliding backward in a shower of pebbles.

Julian started forward, but Bingo grabbed his arm. "No, Pilgrim. Wait—"

A thin wail rose from Hakiwuh, but the words were unintelligible to Bingo as he strained to hear what sounded like a chant.

"Bingo," Julian said, "shouldn't we help him? What is the matter with him?"

"Don' know, but I ain't in no hurry ta git whatever got him," Bingo answered tersely. "Let's jus' wait a minute an' see." He pointed a finger to the rock in the middle of the crater. "'Pears ta me, that them folks got bit by th' same thing as our guide, here."

Julian followed his gaze, and noticed for the first time several sun-bleached skeletons close to the rock. Had the ancient Indians practiced human sacrifice, perhaps? Or were those burials uncovered by the erosion of time and wind? He slanted Bingo an uncertain glance as Hakiwuh inched his way toward them on hands and knees.

"I'm going to help him," Julian said, starting

toward the fallen guide.

Bingo was close behind, muttering, "Thar's sumthin' wrong here, Pilgrim, very wrong. I jus' can' put my finger on whut it is. That lil' fall wouldn' hurt a child. I cain't understand whut's th' matter. Look—he ain't even bleedin'."

Kneeling beside Hakiwuh, Julian could see no evidence of a cut or even a bruise. The guide was shaking as if with a chill, and his teeth were chattering so badly Bingo couldn't understand what he was trying to say.

"What's he saying, Bingo?" Julian lifted Hakiwuh's arms while Bingo lifted his feet, and they began carrying him to the shade of the tunnel.

"Hell if I know," Bingo muttered. "Sumthin' 'bout bad medicine is all I kin make out."

They lowered Hakiwuh gently to the ground and covered him with a blanket from one of their packs. Hitching up his trousers, Bingo said, "Let's find whut ya came fer, an' git outa here, Pilgrim. I'm thinkin' I don' wanna stay long, 'cause this place is big medicine ta a lot of Injuns. If'n they find out we've been here, let alone took along a bunch of souvenirs from their ancestors, they's gonna be a mite perturbed. I don' want 'em bushwhackin' us afore we kin git down frum here."

Nodding slowly, Julian agreed.

Chapter Thirty-Five

Ryan reined his stallion to a halt, pausing at the sharp edge of a steep arroyo. In the distance, a thin plume of smoke rose from the top of a solitary butte taller than any other for miles, signaling the end of their quest. He was willing to bet Julian Ashworth was atop that butte.

Rising in his stirrups, he silently pointed to the ridged promontory.

"That's it?" Stephanie pushed back the brim of her hat to stare. The sandstone butte thrusting its solitary mass from the canyon floor was large, but it wasn't the mountain she had expected. "Are you certain?"

"Yeah, far as I can remember. There's no other butte within miles that could be it." He urged his stallion forward, half sliding down the sides of the arroyo slashing in front of them. "Come on, Princess. Let's take a look."

Stephanie followed silently. As they grew closer and the butte grew larger, she realized how it could be classified as a mountain. It was much bigger than she'd thought it would be, she thought, standing at last in the shadow. Did the curls of smoke drifting from the top belong to Julian? Surely they hadn't missed him! She scanned the area around the foot of the butte, searching for some sign of life, but saw nothing.

It was Ryan who spotted the first tracks, dug deep into the hard rock and dirt.

"Ponies, lots of 'em," he remarked with a puzzled frown. "I thought your father only had one guide with him, but the signs point to—" He paused, and Stephanie flashed him a sharp look.

"What is it?"

Dismounting, Ryan crouched by the trampled tufts of grass and overturned rocks, carefully examining the tracks. There were many ponies, Indian ponies from the unshod hooves, and he recalled seeing Julian and his guide mounted on mules. He traced the blurred outline of a footprint with one finger, identifying the marks only a moccasin could make. Indians. Friendly, maybe? Ryan grimaced, wondering if he should tell Stephanie.

Straightening, he looked into her worried face and knew he had to tell her.

"Indian sign. They could be friendly," he hastened to add, but knew from the apprehension in her eyes that Stephanie didn't harbor that hope for a moment.

"Do you . . . suppose . . . that Father is all right?"

"I'm sure he can take care of himself, Princess. And I know his guide's reputation as an old Indian fighter and trader well worth his salt. Try not to worry until we have to."

Swinging back into his saddle, Ryan kicked his

stallion into a brisk trot that took him swiftly around the base of the butte. It was late afternoon, and it would soon be too dark to search for Julian. They'd just have to wait until tomorrow, he decided.

"No, I want to look now," Stephanie argued when he told her his decision. "Father may be in trouble, he may need us . . . !"

"Be reasonable, Stephanie. There's nothing we could do if we found him in trouble anyway. We just have to wait and be cautious."

"Since when has caution been in your vocabulary?"

"Since I got surprised by those Apaches when I camped under trees to please you!" Ryan shot back. "I should have trusted my instincts, but I didn't. I am now."

Silenced, Stephanie clamped her lips tightly shut. It wouldn't do any good to argue with that, and she recalled the consequences of unwise camping.

They made their camp among a pile of rocks and boulders, and ate cold corncakes for their dinner. Ryan didn't want a fire.

"It could be seen for miles in this country," he said, "like we saw your father's smoke miles away. Even a small fire would be like a beacon in a lighthouse. We have food, and we'll have plenty of light shortly. It's a half-moon night."

Huddled under two blankets, Stephanie just nodded miserably. She hugged her knees, worrying about Julian. What if he'd been captured by Indians? Or simply murdered for daring to desecrate their burial grounds? The possibilities were endless, and gnawed at her constantly.

Ryan's hand touched her lightly on the shoulder, and Stephanie turned a woeful face up to him.

"I know you're worried, love, but I think your father is all right. Here, drink some of this." He grinned at her surprise. "I've been saving it for a special occasion when we might really need it, and now seems as good a time as any."

"Where on earth did you get French brandy out here?" Stephanie squinted in the dim light, reading the label. "Why, it's '76, my father's favorite—" Stephanie halted.

"I didn't want to worry you before, but seems like Spotted Tail ran across your father before he did us. He traded for brandy and rifles with Julian." A wicked grin slanted his mouth as he added, "This was part of your dowry, love . . ."

"You scoundrel!" she scolded, but Stephanie couldn't help an answering grin. She cradled the bottle of brandy that had belonged to Julian in her palms. "At least you're sharing it with me."

"That's 'cause I'm a good guy." Ryan took the brandy from her unresisting hands and worked at the cork, finally managing to open it. Producing two battered tin cups, he filled them to the brim. "Let's make a toast, love," Ryan suggested. "To the future, and all that it holds . . ."

Meeting his clear gaze, Stephanie echoed, "To the future . . ."

Their cups tilted, and the smooth brandy slid down parched throats, sealing their hopeful toast. Stephanie held her cup between her palms, rolling it slowly back and forth as she gazed at Ryan. It would be too much to hope that he might go back with her to New York, and she wondered fretfully if their relationship would end in the Arizona canyons and plains. Resting her chin on the hump of blanket-covered knees drawn up to her chest, she searched his face for a clue. How could she be sure he loved her enough to return with her? Ryan had made no mention of anything beyond the present, no hint of what he wanted for their future, and the thought was always just below the surface of her conscious mind that he had no intention of prolonging their relationship once her quest was finished. Did his vow of love include a future?

"A penny for your thoughts, Princess," he teased, yanking Stephanie from her gloomy conjecture.

"Only a penny? You expect a bargain, I suppose," she answered with a half smile. "Remember, you always get what you pay for, Ryan."

"So give me a nickel's worth. You worrying about your father again? I told you he's probably all right . . ."

"No. I wasn't thinking about him just now." Stephanie took a deep breath. "I was thinking about us, Ryan. About afterward . . ."

A wary expression creased Ryan's face as he met her steady gaze, and his voice was carefully noncommittal.

"I see."

"Do you? What do you see?"

Shrugging, Ryan skillfully dodged the question. "I see us quite happily helping your father tag all his artifacts, and packing them in bags. After that, the crystal ball grows too cloudy to see much of anything."

418

A faint smile lifted the corners of Stephanie's mouth in a curve that was barely visible in the bright moonlight. "Can't you read tea leaves or something? I was hoping . . ."

"You were hoping for some sort of commitment," Ryan finished for her. "I know. But I can't give that right now. You'll understand soon enough, and then I'll let you make the decision."

Puzzled, Stephanie stared at him in the golden flow of light that brightened rocks and ground. He cupped her chin in his palm and kissed her gently.

"You'll understand," he repeated.

Leaning forward, Stephanie opened her mouth to demand an explanation, but a fist-sized rock rattled noisily down from the stone slab just behind her. Ryan immediately leaped for his rifle, but a voice halted him in midstride.

"I wouldn't, Cordell. Unless you wanna wear a 'lead necklace,'" the voice taunted in a faintly familiar phrase. "Sorry to interrupt such a tender scene," Huntley said, stepping down from the high boulder to the ground, "but it looked like it might get kinda awkward if I didn't." He gestured with his cocked rifle for Ryan to raise his hands.

Bates crowded close behind Huntley, wearing a silly grin that made Stephanie want to smack him in the mouth.

"What do you think you're doing?" she demanded, shooting to her feet. She towered over the much shorter Bates, and he backed away immediately. Huntley wasn't as easily intimidated, however, and he shoved the rifle barrel in her direction.

"We don't think, lady, we know what we're

doing," he said, stressing the difference. "We've eaten yer dust fer too damn many miles not to git what's coming to us, so don't git any big ideas now." Huntley slanted a crafty smile at Ryan. "How 'bout yer big plans now, Cordell? Did you ever tell the lady 'bout them?"

"Shut up!" Ryan growled, taking a menacing step forward. Ryan's hands dropped slightly, and Huntley's rifle muzzle jerked them back up again.

"No, I ain't about to shut up! It's yer turn to lissen now, Cordell! Mebbe this lady should know about yer plans, heh?"

Slicing Stephanie a quick glance, Ryan said, "Don't believe anything he says, Stephanie . . ."

The rifle poked him hard in the ribs, and Ryan winced. "You better lissen, lady," Huntley said. "I seen him down here trying to romance you, and if you fall for any of his lines, you're not as smart as I thought. Did he tell you that he was waiting on yer stage to get into Fort Defiance, and that he had it all planned how he was going to be yer guide when you got here? No? I'm not surprised he didn't tell you. A man can't pluck a pigeon that's on to him, now can he?"

"Huntley . . ."

Ryan's quick step forward was halted by Bates this time, as he brought the barrel of his rifle across the back of Ryan's legs in a crashing blow. Pitching forward, Ryan landed on his hands and knees.

"Stay there," Huntley advised, seating himself on a flat rock. He watched Stephanie's face in the bright moonlight, and knew she'd taken his words to heart. He hid a grin.

"Ryan," she asked, turning to him, "is that true?"

"Partly," he admitted, "but he makes it sound much worse than it is."

Stepping away from the blankets puddled at her feet, Stephanie crossed slowly to face Ryan. He sat back on his heels with his hands on his knees, watching her through narrowed eyes as she searched his face.

"How much worse could it get?" she choked. "I trusted you!"

"Stephanie . . ."

"Don't bother trying to lie anymore, Ryan. The truth answers so many questions that have been bothering me since I first met you. I must have been blind not to see . . ."

"Dammit!" he swore through gritted teeth. "Why are you always so ready to believe the worst? Can't you see you're thinking just what they want you to think?"

"All right, Cordell," Huntley broke in. "That's enough. Let's get down to business now. Me and Bates, we're not greedy men, we just want what we've worked for. We're willing to take our cut, and give you yours. Just tell us how to find Ashworth."

"If I knew that, I'd already have joined him," Ryan answered impatiently. He looked back up at Stephanie, but she turned her head, crossing her arms over her chest. His mouth tightened grimly. So much for her undying faith in him, Ryan thought with a cynical twist of his lips.

Looking back at Huntley, Ryan said coolly, "How much of a cut do I get for leading you to Ashworth?"

"Now we're talkin' business!" Huntley exclaimed. He gestured to Bates, who leaned forward to jerk Ryan's pistol from his holster. "Just in case you change yer mind," Huntley explained. "Since I'm on the business end of a rifle and you ain't, I'd say eighty-twenty was a good cut."

"No. Fifty-fifty."

"Hell, Cordell, that'd only give me and Alvie a quarter share apiece. Nope. How 'bout seventy-thirty of what we steal?"

"Done." Ryan ignored Stephanie's outraged gasp as he took Huntley's proffered handshake on the deal. "Now, how about giving me back my pistol?"

"Oh no, not until we git to Ashworth. Then we'll know yer serious 'bout cuttin' us in, Cordell." Huntley flashed Stephanie a big smile. "See, doll? I told you that yer boyfriend here had other plans, didn't I?"

"Go to hell," Stephanie said tonelessly. Her gaze was riveted on Ryan, but he didn't look at her. Instead, he held up the bottle of French brandy he'd opened only a short time before.

"Let's drink to our partnership, boys," he said to Huntley and Bates. "Seeing as how this was Ashworth's brandy at one time, I think it would be fitting to toast our meeting up with him."

Bates laughed and rubbed his hands together gleefully. "By God, Cordell, you ain't got bad ideas! And pour th' little lady a drink, too . . ."

Before he could finish his statement, Stephanie lunged forward, grabbing Bates's pistol and pointing it at Ryan. She was blindly angry, hurt, and determined that they wouldn't drink any of her father's brandy. Aiming, she fired, and the bullet hit her target exactly dead-center. The bottle exploded into hundreds of tiny splinters, peppering Ryan and Bates with stinging cuts.

Ryan's reaction was swift as he leaped for Stephanie and the pistol. Wrenching it from her hands, he bent one arm behind her back as he wrestled her to the ground. As angry as she was, it took several minutes and a great deal of effort to pin her down, but Ryan finally managed to tie her hands behind her back with his belt. Panting, he sat back on his heels and regarded her gravely.

Furious, Stephanie kicked out at him, and this time Bates laughingly threw Ryan a leather strap for her feet. It was swiftly looped around her ankles, and she was dragged through the dust and propped against a nearby rock.

Tears stung the back of her eyelids as Stephanie watched Ryan drag out a bottle of whiskey from his saddlebag and break it open. The three men sat in a half circle, drinking from tin cups and discussing how they would find Julian and divide the gold.

Gold? Stephanie wondered wearily, letting her head fall back to rest against the rock. Did they mean the art objects, or the rumored gold she'd heard about from the old man back at the fort? What kind of gold would Indians bury with their dead? Her eyes snapped open. Golden statues and vases arrayed an entire shelf in one room of their brownstone mansion in New York, gleaned from the ruins of ancient Grecian temples. That must be the gold these men were talking about. They intended to retrieve those priceless art objects and melt them down into bars to use for barter. It would be a stunning loss from a world already past, and there would be no way to replace them.

Her eyes narrowed on Ryan at the same time as he slid her a glance. There was no mistaking the animosity in her gaze, and his gut tightened. Damn her for always being so willing to believe the worst of him, and just when he'd begun to think she really cared. Well, he'd get this little job over with and get completely out of her life. He'd forget Stephanie Ashworth before he'd ridden ten yards away from her.

Chapter Thirty-Six

The half moon hung for a time on the tip of a distant spire before finally sliding behind a low-lying mesa, and Stephanie glanced again at the three men close by. Ryan was the only one fully awake. Huntley was nodding, and Bates had passed out a short time before, having drunk all of Ryan's whiskey.

A sneer curled Stephanie's lip as Ryan rose to his feet, dusting off the seat of his snug-fitting trousers.

"You can wipe the dirt off your pants much easier than you can remove the stain on your name, Ryan Cordell," she said in a low tone when he stepped close to throw a blanket over her. "There's no soap and water in the world able to clean that."

Pausing, Ryan just stared at her silently. There didn't seem to be any answer he could make to her observation, and he pivoted on his heel and walked away from their camp. Stephanie's head fell back against her rock pillow again. Her throat ached with unshed tears, but she would not give any of them the satisfaction of knowing how deeply she was wounded—especially Ryan.

"Cordell!" Huntley called after him in slurred tones, "whar ya goin'?"

"Not far," he answered. "How far could I get without my horse and gun?"

Satisfied that he was telling the truth, Huntley settled back against a rock, still cradling his rifle.

Footsteps echoed eerily as Ryan's boots crunched on crushed rocks and small pebbles. With Huntley and Bates down for a while, he intended to concentrate on finding the entrance to the burial ground. It had to be here somewhere, because he'd seen that telltale plume of smoke rising from the top of the butte.

But by the time he'd circled half the butte, he still had seen no sign of an entrance and it was almost dawn. Discouraged and disgusted with the entire situation, Ryan walked back toward the camp.

He'd gone no more than a half dozen steps when something a foot above his head caught his eye. It was just a flash of something, like the glitter of moonlight against metal, but it was enough to pique his interest. Turning, he backstepped about three paces, looking up at the shelf of rocks above his head. There—he saw it again. A glimmer of light reflected against stone.

Propping one foot against a hump of granite, Ryan levered his body up, catching at a ledge with his hand. He pulled himself slowly upward until he could see. Odd, a shovel lay on a wide, rocky ledge. A shovel? Julian, of course, it had to be. That meant he was near the entrance to the burial ground. Sparing a swift regret for the whiskey he'd consumed, Ryan finally managed to pull himself to the ledge beside the shovel. It was hard to see in the dark, and he felt his way carefully along the sharp-edged lip of the granite shelf for several feet.

He was about to decide to turn back and try the other direction, when his hand suddenly encountered empty space. Edging around the corner, Ryan stepped into a tunnel. His steps echoed eerily in the blanketing silence. This was it. This was the tunnel leading to the ancient burial ground. So where was Julian Ashworth?

Frowning, Ryan wondered if Julian had remained at the top of the butte for the night. If so, where were his mules and gear? There was no trace of them at the base, and no mule could navigate the climb to this entrance.

He was still puzzling about Julian's apparent disappearance as he scrambled down from the ledge and returned to the camp. On the walk back toward the butte, he devised a plan concerning Huntley and Bates. Now would be the time to rid himself of their unlikely help, and he grinned at the sight of both of them sleeping. Only Stephanie remained awake, glaring at him as if he had two heads. Dammit, he had no intentions of allowing her to get in his way either. Searching for Julian would take time and planning, and he didn't need a woman who obviously trusted him about as much as she did a snake getting in his way. He'd take the time later to explain it all to her, and by then he shouldn't have to.

In only five minutes, Ryan had Huntley and Bates trussed up like turkeys ready for the market. They never even woke to protest, only mumbled drunkenly, and he was glad he'd remembered their habit of drinking themselves into a stupor. It had certainly made it much easier for him.

"Well?" Stephanie demanded when Ryan paused to light a cigar, "aren't you going to untie me?"

He took a deep drag from the cigar and blew it out slowly, then gave her a long, considering look.

"Not on your life, lady."

"What? Ryan Cordell, I demand that you untie me this instant!" Stephanie glared at him. "Do you hear me?" she added when he remained silently staring at her.

"I'm not deaf, of course I hear you. And so does every Indian within a hundred miles. Voices carry at night on the desert, Miss Ashworth, in case you don't recall . . ."

"I recall a lot of things! Like an agreement that you signed, and your promise to keep me safe, and . . ."

"So go fetch a sheriff," he broke in. "I'm sure he'd be interested to learn about your jail-breaking experience in Willow Creek— Ah, your memory's improving! You recall that, too?"

"You bastard!"

"Why is it that you only swear properly when I'm planning to leave? You know how I enjoy a good cuss-fight, yet you wait until I'm in a hurry." Ryan took a puff of his cigar, squinting at Stephanie in the waning light. "Don't worry, Princess. I'm going to look for your daddy. He'll listen to all your complaints, I'm sure."

A disbelieving Stephanie watched while Ryan finished his cigar in silence. He was abandoning her again, and she plotted several fiendish methods of disposing of him the next time she caught up with him. This was the last straw. It was difficult to believe that he'd managed to fool her all these weeks with his pretense of love, and she'd been so damn gullible!

Grinding her teeth in frustration, Stephanie twisted her wrists. They were still securely confined in the leather belt and pulled behind her back. If only she could work free, then she would show Ryan Cordell exactly how vengeful she could really be!

Her head snapped up as Ryan stooped beside her and held a waterskin to her mouth, offering her a drink.

"Better take it," he said when she shook her head furiously, "you won't get another chance until I come down from the butte. That may be several hours."

"I'd rather die of thirst than take one thing from you," Stephanie said, holding his eyes with hers.

Shrugging, Ryan tied the mouth of the waterskin shut again and slung it across his shoulder.

"Suit yourself. I'm going to drag you in the shade so you don't get so sunburned your father doesn't recognize you. I'd hate to get stuck with you if he refuses delivery."

"Fat chance!" Stephanie snapped. She wriggled helplessly as Ryan dragged her across the ground over rocks and sharp edges of shale. He dumped her unceremoniously in the shadow of a stone slab where she would be shaded in the sunlight, and tucked her hat under her head for a pillow.

A faint, pearly mist was already in the sky,

signaling the rising of the run, and Ryan wasted little time gathering what he'd need. He placed Huntley and Bates's guns next to Stephanie, then dragged the pair a short distance away, out of her sight. Not bothering to worry about their thirst, he left them sleeping by a boulder.

Scooping up his saddlebags, Ryan pulled out a clean shirt and tore it into strips while Stephanie watched with feigned indifference. Winding the cloth strips around a thick tangle of sagebrush, he clubbed it together to form one stick for the handle of his torch. Reaching again into his saddlebags, Ryan pulled out a small packet of bear grease saved from the albino grizzly he'd shot. He rubbed the entire packet on the strips of cloth to make it burn longer, then shouldered his makeshift torch.

In spite of everything, Stephanie couldn't help a sudden grip of fear for him as he rose to leave. But she said nothing, even when Ryan halted beside her to say good-bye. Staring at him mutely, she was unable to wish him well, but unable to speak harshly. He seemed to understand her turbulent emotions, because he gave her a faint smile and touched her lightly on the cheek before turning away.

Pausing just long enough to make certain the horses were securely hobbled, Ryan grabbed up his rifle and headed back to the tunnel entrance. At first he was afraid he'd lost it again, then Ryan finally spotted his shirt where he'd left it at the opening like a banner. It was even more difficult climbing up the loose rocks and steep side with his gear, but he finally pulled himself on the ledge leading to the tunnel.

Sun rays shot over a distant peak as Ryan stood on

the ledge, half blinding him as the morning sun flooded the plain with light. Stepping into the tunnel, Ryan lit his torch and started through the winding corridors of rock.

A musty draft permeated the air, and the farther he went into the tunnel the staler it got. It was cool and clammy, and the steep walls were wet to the touch in places. The floor was either slick or rough with loose rocks and pebbles, and he frequently stumbled and had to catch himself with a hand against the wall. Holding the torch high, Ryan made his way carefully along, peering into the inky darkness ahead.

Petroglyphs had been carved into the wall just above his head, and he ran his fingers over the etched figures of men and animals. Not daring to linger too long in case his torch sputtered and died, Ryan pushed on. The path grew so narrow in places he wondered how ancient Indians had been able to bring their dead through the twisting passages.

A feeling of dread welled in him when Ryan recognized petroglyphs he'd passed earlier. What if this was an endless maze hacked into the butte, and he never found his way out? Stranger things had happened. No, he would find the right path, he told himself. Someone else had, or there wouldn't have been smoke rising from the top of the butte the day before. He spared a grim hope that it had been Julian and not Indians.

Ryan put one hand to rest against the damp wall for a moment, and his fingers encountered no resistance. He stopped dead-still and lifted his torch. Just ahead of him a few feet there was a black void. Swallowing, he backed slowly away, praying his feet wouldn't slip and send him hurtling into empty space. When he was far enough away, he bent and picked up a rock to throw into the pit. Time ticked slowly past before he heard a faint sound that could have been his rock hitting the bottom of the pit. It could have even, he decided, struck the side of the chasm and still not reached bottom.

Backing down the way he'd come, Ryan retraced his steps to a tiny indentation in the rock wall. The indentation turned out to be an offshot that grew wider soon after he squeezed through. Trekking on over a path that wound up in a spiral and then down, Ryan wondered at the tenacity and ingenuity of ancient Indians. How had they had the temerity to explore these timeless caverns? And how many had survived the explorations?

By the time he reached a spot in the path where he could see a faint square of light far ahead, Ryan felt as if he'd been cast into eternal darkness. His torch was flickering and dim, and he'd known several moments of fear wondering if it would die before he reached the top. His breathing sounded harsh and rasping as Ryan struggled for air, and when a fresh breeze caressed his face he began to move faster toward the block of light.

When he got close enough to see the flat top of the butte stretching outside the tunnel exit, Ryan slowed his pace cautiously. He had no intention of blundering into a situation that might get him killed. After all, Julian Ashworth didn't know him and might not be in the mood to wait until he could introduce himself.

Edging along with his back to the wall, Ryan

squinted against the bright rays of light that hurt his eyes as he neared the exit. He cupped one hand over his eyes to shield them as he frowned at a sagebrush and stick barricade blocking the tunnel exit. It smelled charred, and was still smoking in places. Taking a deep breath, Ryan stepped out onto the butte.

Chapter Thirty-Seven

Twisting and turning her hands, Stephanie worked feverishly to pull her wrists out of the belt binding them. Rocks bit deeply into her back and thighs as she wriggled on the hard shale surface. Panting, and with her chafed wrists torn and bleeding, she was finally able to loosen the belt enough to tug free. She sucked in a deep breath and rubbed at her sore wrists, then bent to untie her ankles.

A fresh wave of determination spurred her as Stephanie recalled Ryan's final betrayal. He'd admitted it this time, and there would be no second chance. Her jaw clenched as she yanked on the leather straps wound around her ankles, cursing Ryan Cordell and the fates that had brought them to this point.

Why? echoed over and over in her head, until Stephanie was almost sick with grief. She wavered between hatred and despair until she forced back the emotions tearing at her soul. She had to concentrate on finding Julian, then she could yield to the luxury of emotion.

Freeing her ankles, Stephanie rolled to her feet, then paused. Voices . . . Huntley and Bates, she realized with a trace of panic, and they were coming nearer. She could hear the crunch of their boots against rock, and the familiar whining of Bates. Quickly, she resumed her former position and loosely rebound her wrists and ankles. She might have a better chance for escape if they thought her asleep or unconscious.

Huntley and Bates rounded a huge outcropping of rock just as Stephanie's eyes snapped shut, and she watched them beneath the fringe of her lashes. They were arguing as usual, with Bates trying to keep up with Huntley's longer stride.

"But, Huntley," he was saying, his pudgy face creased into a worried frown, "what're we gonna do now that we're loose? Cordell's gone, an' we ain't got no rifles or guns—"

"Shuddup and let me think," Huntley snarled, then came to a stop so quickly Bates bumped into him. "Look—it's the girl, Alvie!"

Rubbing at his squashed nose and straightening the hat tilted on his head, Bates sent Huntley a reproachful glance as he nodded agreement.

"Yep. That's th' girl, all right."

Huntley's voice was impatient as he said, "Do you know what that means, Alvie? The girl? Cordell? Ashworth? Think about it a minute now, and it might come to ya."

Pursing his lips, Bates concentrated while Huntley strode toward Stephanie.

She stifled a groan of dismay and remained as still as possible. Then, belatedly recalling the guns and rifles Ryan had left somewhere under the rock near her, she offered a silent prayer they wouldn't find them.

Crouching down beside her, Huntley gave Stephanie a little poke in the ribs with his finger. She remained still and quiet. He leaned forward, lifting her eyelid with one finger, and Stephanie struggled against the urge to gag at the strong smell of whiskey and sweat. She must have been successful in playing asleep, because Huntley rocked back on his heels, satisfied.

"She's out colder than a mackeral," Huntley observed. "Cordell musta smacked her one when she got too mouthy."

Peering over Huntley's shoulder, Bates said with a note of sympathy in his tone, "Aw, he shouldn'a done that. She's a purty thing, don' ya think?"

"The color of her pa's gold is what's purty, Alvie, and don't you go forgettin' that! We didn't follow her and Cordell all this way 'cause she's 'purty', you idiot! You can buy lots of women—pretty and ugly— once we're rich." Huntley paused, rubbing his beard-stubbled chin thoughtfully. It would be simple enough to use the girl as a hostage, like he'd originally planned. Only this time, he could catch two birds with the same girl. He grinned.

Lying as quietly as possible, Stephanie listened to their conversation with growing dread. It didn't take a genius to realize what Huntley had in mind. He intended to hold her for ransom, forcing Julian to pay for her release with his treasured artifacts.

436

Priceless art objects would be melted down into globs of gold to use as barter.

Stephanie's eyes opened to mere slits as Huntley and Bates moved away a few feet. Slightly twisting her head, she was able to see the faint metallic gleam of a rifle barrel peeking from beneath the rock behind her. Maybe they wouldn't see the hidden weapons, and if she could just ease a bit closer . . .

More rocks dug into her tender skin as Stephanie snaked toward the rifles. She held her breath when a loosened shower of pebbles rolled down the rocky slope toward Huntley and Bates.

"Hey, what's that?" Bates squinted in Stephanie's direction.

"Ah, she must have just rolled over or something, Bates; pay attention to what I'm saying, now," Huntley answered irritably. "You can never keep your mind on what's important."

Inching her way along, Stephanie was finally able to draw within reaching distance of the rifles. Her hands, still bound in front of her, flexed as she prepared to try for the weapons. Sliding her wrists gently from the looped belt, she let one hand flop to the ground. Neither Huntley nor Bates noticed. Now her arm moved slowly out, and her fingers edged toward the smooth oak stock of a Winchester rifle. Turning her head slightly, Stephanie opened her eyes wider as she reached for it.

"Hold it!" A foot crashed down on her arm, pinning it to the ground and bringing a cry of pain from Stephanie. "I thought I saw you wiggling around up here," Huntley said with a short laugh. "Bet you didn't think I was watchin'."

"No," she snapped, "I certainly didn't!" Jerking free, Stephanie sat up and shot Huntley a sullen glare as she rubbed her wrists.

"Come on, lady," Huntley said, yanking her up with one hand under her arm, "I've got plans for you . . ."

Moments later, Stephanie was being propelled forward around the base of the butte. Loaded down with rifles and pistols, Huntley and Bates kept a wary watch for Ryan or Julian, half expecting them to be hidden in ambush behind a pile of rocks or boulders.

"I don' think Cordell's anywhar 'round here," Bates finally whined. He dropped to the hard comfort of a rock and swept off his hat, fanning himself with it. "'Least if he is, I ain't seen no sign of him."

Huntley shot Bates a disgusted glance. "I told you—look down on the ground where the tracks are gonna be, not up in the air! You wouldn't see any sign of an entire war party of Apaches, Alvie. Your head's always in the clouds instead of down to earth where it should be."

"Now, that ain't true," Bates protested, but his glance strayed up the face of the sheer rock wall in front of him. "I jus' mentioned seein' a pretty bird a while ago, an' you got all mad 'cause you think I'm not lookin' hard." A flap of white caught his eye, and he paused, staring hard. "Hey, Huntley," he muttered, flapping a hand toward his partner, "looka thar . . ."

"What now, Alvie? Another pretty bird?" Huntley flashed Bates an impatient glare, glanced to where he was pointing, then back at the scuffed tracks on the ground. Then, freezing, his head snapped back around to take another look at the alien object on the cliff-side. Huntley realized immediately what Bates had found, and exclaimed excitedly, "Dammit, Alvie! You found something!"

"I did?" Bates's expression reflected his surprise, then he said, "Yeah-h, I did find something! See, Huntley, I knew I'd find it!"

Staring up, Stephanie realized what had excited Huntley even as she heard Bates's puzzled query, "But . . . what'd I find, Huntley?"

"An entrance to th' burial ground," Huntley answered patiently. "That's Cordell's shirt hangin' from that rock . . ."

The short climb up was rough but possible, and Stephanie helped Huntley half pull, half shove Bates's round body up the steep side.

"Buffalo-blubber," Huntley muttered under his breath when Bates was finally over the lip of the wide ledge. "You are going on a diet as soon as we get back to Flagstaff, Alvie," he warned.

Bates gave him a wounded stare as he puffed for breath, and Stephanie shook her head. How on earth had these two ever managed to follow her this far? she wondered. They were the most bungling oafs she'd ever seen.

"You two are not my idea of outlaws," she told Huntley. "In fact, you are the most maladroit pair of blundering boors I've ever been so unfortunate as to meet. It's a wonder my father ever hired you."

"Mebbe that's why he fired us," Bates remarked gloomily.

"Shaddup, Alvie!" Huntley snarled.

"He fired you?" Stephanie stared at both of them. "But I thought Ryan was the reason you left the fort."

"Oh, he was," Bates said, "but yer pa had already give us our pay an' let us go. Found him another guide, he did, an' ruined all our plans. That's why we didn' send that telegram tellin' you not to come, see. We thought that once ya got here, yer pa would be glad enuf ta give us some money fer takin' ya to him. An' of course, we planned on takin' a lil' extra fer . . ."

"Alvie," Huntley growled, climbing over Stephanie to get to Bates. Reaching, he lifted Bates by his shirt collar, muttering, "You've said enough! The girl don't need to know too much, you hear?"

"Yeah. Sure." Bates shrugged free. "Didn' mean no harm," he murmured softly. "She jus' asked me a question, that's all."

"Well, you ain't no damned book of answers, so shut up! We got to see where this goes, and I'm willing to bet it leads right to Cordell and Ashworth."

It took a while for Huntley to put together three decent torches to light their way, but finally he was ready to go. He sent Bates back one more time for some waterskins, then they climbed the cliff side to the tunnel entrance.

Wrinkling her nose, Stephanie hung back. It was dark and dank in the tunnel, and she didn't trust Huntley to know what he was doing. She had visions of being lost forever inside the butte.

"No," she said stubbornly when Huntley gave her a shove. "I don't want to go in there with you. We

440

may never see daylight again . . ."

"You don't have much choice. I ain't leavin' you here, and I intend to give Cordell and your pa a little surprise. You can go willingly, or with your hands tied behind you. Which is it?"

Preferring limited freedom to none at all, Stephanie capitulated. Feeling very much like a martyr about to be thrown to the lions, she entered the pitch-black void of the tunnel. The torches threw weird shadows against sheer rock walls that seemed to rise in a V high above their heads. Fascinated by the petroglyphs carved at eye level, Stephanie let her fingers run across the etchings as they passed, wondering what they meant.

Several times she almost slipped on the slick path, and Bates seemed to have the same trouble. She could hear him panting and puffing behind her, his labored breathing marking each steep climb. Even Huntley was beginning to tire, and once he slid on loose pebbles, grabbing Stephanie's arm to keep from falling to the shale path.

It was cool inside the butte in spite of the fact there was no breeze. Stephanie was reminded of an ancient cavern she had explored in Greece with her father, and she worried that this might be an endless maze instead of a tunnel leading straight to the top.

"Did you ever stop to think that this tunnel might have several different paths?" she asked Huntley when they stopped for a water break. "We've passed one or two little offshoots that could be another path—"

"Naw. Couldn't be," Huntley decided. "They was too small, where this is wider. This has to be the main

441

tunnel to the top."

Stephanie tried again. "If the Indians who discovered this tunnel were clever enough to put a burial ground on top and disguise the entrance, don't you think they might have been smart enough to have different corridors leading to nowhere? When I was in Egypt, we had an opportunity to explore an ancient pyramid. There were many false tunnels, most of them having some sort of trap that would kill any trespassers."

"Sounds like you're making it up," Huntley said suspicously. "'Sides, if this ain't the right way, why are there still them little writings on the wall? No, you just want to waste enough time so Cordell can get away. There ain't no way down from the top but this way, lady, so you can quit wasting your breath and my time."

Shrugging, Stephanie conceded temporary defeat, but managed to lag behind Huntley and just ahead of Bates. At least she would be covered from both ends if her worst fears should prove true.

"Huntley," Bates said when they'd gone a bit farther, "my torch is dyin' out."

Glancing back, Stephanie saw his torch sputtering weakly. How would they get back down? she wondered with a trace of panic. There were only three torches, and hers wasn't going to last until they reached the top unless it was only a few feet away.

"We better use just one," she advised Huntley. "If we don't, we won't be able to get back down. You only brought three torches," she reminded him.

"Yeah, but we should be able to use Cordell's on the way back down . . ."

"What if we can't? What if he's not up there, or his torch is useless also?" Stephanie argued. "Let's save ours until we really need it."

Reluctantly, Huntley agreed, and Bates and Stepanie doused their torches. Now the light was even dimmer as they made their way along in a tight little knot. Several times Bates stepped on Stephanie's heels because he was following so close behind, and she finally gave him an exasperated push to the front.

"For heaven's sake, Bates, try not to walk so close! And you don't have to be so melodramatic about it, either," she added crossly as he dropped to his knees with a wail of terror. When Bates's pale, round face disappeared from view she frowned. "Hold up the torch, Huntley," she ordered, "I think maybe he fell into a hole."

The torch flickered across a yawning pit and Stephanie gasped. Teetering on the very edge, she fought a sudden wave of dizziness.

"Bates?" Her voice quavered, and she cleared her throat to try again. "Bates? Are you all right?" she asked at the same time Huntley was saying, "Alvie! Talk to me! Where are you?"

"Here."

Huntley and Stephanie exchanged glances. The clipped tone was barely recognizable as belonging to Bates.

"Where?" they chorused.

"Here."

Leaning forward as far as they dared, they held the torch high. It flickered across Bates's white face a few feet below them.

"He must have landed on a ledge!" Stephanie

exclaimed. "See how he's holding on to the edge?"

"Hold on, Alvie," Huntley was saying. "I'll pull you up."

Stephanie's brows rose. "He's rather heavy," she said. "Do you think you can do it?"

"I have to." Handing her the torch, Huntley lay on his belly and held out a hand to Bates, but he was too terrified to take it. "Take my hand, Alvie," he encouraged, "I'll pull you up."

"No."

Huntley slanted Stephanie a frustrated glance. "He's too scared to even talk. How am I gonna get him to let go of the ledge long enough to grab my hand?"

Sighing, Stephanie offered, "Slide forward far enough, and I'll hold your ankles. That way you can pull him up."

Huntley stared at her suspiciously. "Yeah, I believe that! You'll send me over the side with Bates, is what you'll do."

"Look. As tempted as I may be, I am not a murderer," Stephanie said firmly.

"Tell you what, *you* grab Bates, and I'll pull you both up," Huntley said. When Stephanie hesitated, he rolled to his feet and pulled the torch from her hands. "Do it," he said, "or I'll put you over the side with him."

Anger sparked Stephanie's eyes, but she crouched on the gritty floor and held out a hand to Bates. At Huntley's insistence, she stretched out on her stomach and put out both arms, grabbing Bates by his wrists. When she nodded that she was ready,

444

Huntley began pulling Stephanie backward by her ankles, until Bates was safely back on the tunnel floor.

In spite of the cool, musty air in the tunnel, Bates was dripping with sweat. His eyes still held a stunned, terrified expression, and his lips were pulled back in a fixed grimace.

"Bates?" Stephanie waved a hand in front of his eyes, but he still stared blankly ahead.

Huntley gripped Bates by both arms and gave him a hard shake. "Alvie! Talk to me, Alvie, it's me— Hezikiah Huntley, your ole buddy."

"Hezikiah?" Stephanie echoed in a disbelieving tone.

"My daddy was a preacher," Huntley snapped. "And I don't wanna hear no smart-ass comments from you, neither! Alvie, talk to me," he begged, turning back to Bates. "Talk to me . . ."

"Huntley?" Bates quavered. He blinked once, then twice as he focused on his friend. Shivering, Bates buried his face in his palms. "I thought I wuz a goner," he said in a muffled voice. "My whole life flashed in front of my eyes, Huntley." He looked up, his expression beseeching. "Let's git outta here— please!"

"We are. And we're gonna be rich, Alvie. Come on, we're almost at the top."

In spite of Bates's faint but frequent protests, the trio trudged slowly and cautiously through the dark, winding corridors of the tunnel. By the time they reached the twisting turn that held a light at the far end, Stephanie was half panting with exhaustion.

She felt as if she had walked the entire width of Arizona Territory.

They paused, the end of their struggle within sight. To Stephanie, the light meant more than just her father, or gold, or even the approaching conflict with Huntley and Bates. It meant that she would be able to confront Ryan with his final betrayal.

Chapter Thirty-Eight

Kneeling, Ryan held the waterskin up for Julian to drink from it. They were in the shade of a huge boulder on the crater's rim, where the full effect of the sun's rays couldn't reach them. He glanced around the top of the butte, noting the disarranged stones and newly dug potholes. It appeared that Julian had found what he was looking for . . .

"However did you manage to find me?" Julian croaked through dry lips. "You look vaguely familiar, but I don't quite recall your name. What did you say your name was?"

"Cordell. Ryan Cordell. I met you very briefly at Fort Defiance about a month or six weeks ago. I'll explain later how I came to be here, Mr. Ashworth. Now, tell me again what happened," Ryan said when Julian's thirst had been slaked and he pushed the water away. "And where's your guide?"

"Indians," Julian said hoarsely, "and Bingo's gone for help." He flashed a weak smile. "I thought maybe you were the help when you first leaped over

447

that barricade."

"Yeah, what's that barricade for? And how'd you get hurt?"

Putting out his tongue to moisten his parched lips, Julian answered, "The barricade was to hold back any more of those raging Indians who'd taken offense at our desecration of their burial grounds. I got hurt defending myself from them. A particularly savage blow from a lance seems to have created havoc with my leg . . ."

Ryan glanced at Julian's leg. "It looks pretty bad," he admitted. "Can you walk at all?"

"No. That's why—after we'd managed to drive back the attack—Bingo went for assistance. I can't put my weight on my leg."

"Broken," Ryan diagnosed after unwrapping and examining Julian's clumsily bandaged leg. "How'd you two ever manage to win a skirmish with a war party?"

"Fortunately, it was a burial party of Yavapais, not a war party. I think they were as surprised by our presence here as we were by their arrival." Julian winced as he tried to shift his leg to a more comfortable position. "Anyway," he continued, "we were better prepared with our rifles than they were with their bows and lances. I suppose that after seeing our camp below, they came up ready for murder." He smiled wryly. "They almost succeeded."

"That one of them over there?" Ryan inclined his head in the direction of a blanket-covered form stretched on the ground.

A frown creased Julian's face as he sighed, "No. That's our unfortunate Papago guide. I still can't understand what happened to him. He was dead before the burial party of Yavapai Indians arrived."

"When did all this happen?" Ryan scanned the area, only half listening to Julian's answer. A huge crater dipped down in the center of the butte as if the stone floor had been depressed with a giant hand. In the middle of the hollow was a large, pock-marked rock. His eyes narrowed on several bleached skeletons near the rock.

"It happened day before yesterday," Julian was saying when Ryan interrupted.

"Did your guide go near that rock in the center?" Ryan asked sharply.

"Inadvertently, yes. He slipped and rolled down the slope right up to the rock. Poor Hakiwuh. He wasn't hurt by the fall that we could see . . ."

"Magic Rock, remember?" Ryan said. "Maybe there's something to that legend after all."

"Yes, I thought of that. It reminds me of the voodoo tribes in the Caribbean. The natives are so superstitious that just the suggestion they are marked for death will actually kill them. Perhaps that's what happened to Hakiwuh."

"Yeah. Maybe." Ryan stood up, glancing around the flat top of the butte. "We can't wait on your guide to return, Mr. Ashworth," he said. "Those Yavapais probably went back for help after you managed to fight them off, and they could get back a lot quicker than Bingo can make it back here with help." Ryan didn't mention the fact that Stephanie was tied up

449

below, or that Julian's former guides had planned to ambush him. That could wait.

"How am I going to navigate the tunnel?" Julian asked, gesturing to his leg with the broken bone exposed. "I'm afraid I will be more of a hindrance than you realize. Just rebandage my leg, leave me some water, and go on. At least one of us should make it back."

"No. I was hired to see you get safely back with all your . . . souvenirs . . . and that's what I intend to do." Ignoring Julian's surprised question as to who hired him, Ryan continued determinedly. "You can lean on me, Ashworth. We'll manage to get down somehow. I know you're in pain, but let me see what I can rig up to help."

Ryan ransacked the packs Julian and Bingo had brought to the top. There was very little that would be of any use to him. He snatched up one of the blankets, a shovel, and a long, sharp knife.

"What are you going to do with those?" Julian asked, eyeing Ryan with trepidation.

Flashing Julian a faint smile, Ryan answered, "Don't worry. I don't intend to bury you yet. If I rip up this blanket and use the shovel handle, I can fashion a makeshift splint for your leg. Then we can use the rest of the blanket as a sort of sling, see? Using me as a crutch, we can get back down the tunnel easy enough."

Crouching, Ryan bent over Julian and pulled the knife from his belt. The point ripped up the length of Julian's trouser leg to further expose the broken bone.

"This should have been set," Ryan said. "Why didn't Bingo do it?"

A sheepish smile curved Julian's mouth in a grim caricature. "I wouldn't let him. I told him to bring back enough whiskey to dull the pain, then I'd let him."

"I'm going to have to set it," Ryan said with a quick glance at Julian's strained, white face. "Grit your teeth, now . . ."

Julian's hands clenched and he ground his teeth as Ryan gripped his leg with both hands. He couldn't help the strangled cry of agony that escaped when Ryan yanked, then, mercifully, Julian blacked out.

Ryan quickly finished setting it, then picked up the knife to cut strips from the blanket. Bending over Julian, he never heard the scuffling footsteps behind him as Huntley and Bates leaped the flimsy barricade at the tunnel exit.

"Hold it, Cordell!"

Stiffening, Ryan slowly turned to see the two men who were holding Stephanie in front of them like a shield.

"You two," he growled, half rising. The knife slipped from his fingers to the dusty ground as he faced them.

"Ah ah—any quick moves and she's as dead as you'll be," Huntley warned. "Keep your hands away from that pistol yer packin'. I'm serious, Cordell."

"I didn't doubt that. I do doubt your ability to shoot that straight, though, Huntley. Care to try outdrawing me?"

"Why should I do that when I've got you in my

sights now?" Huntley asked with a laugh. "And it looks like I caught you fixin' to murder poor old Ashworth, don't it? You double-crossed me," Huntley spat over Ryan's short denial, "and I can't stand a damn, dirty double-crosser! Now back away from him with yer hands in the air, while Alvie gets yer gun. Get his gun, Alvie!" Huntley prompted the nervous Bates.

Eyeing Cordell warily, Bates edged forward, finally gathering enough courage to lean over and snatch Ryan's gun from its holster. He scurried backward with the same clumsy motions as a crab, bumping blindly into Huntley.

"Dammit, Alvie! Watch out!" Huntley snarled impatiently, pushing at his partner as he was knocked off balance.

Stephanie, standing slightly aside, took the opportunity to dive to the ground in a belly-slide. Skidding over rocks and dirt, she slammed into the still-open pack lying near her unconscious father. Scooping up the Winchester poking from the pack, she rolled and pumped the lever all in the same motion. It had happened so quickly, it caught Huntley totally by surprise, and his reflexes were slow.

Both Huntley and Bates found themselves looking into the deadly eye of a Winchester .44-40 as Stephanie aimed it at them from her prone position on the ground.

"Now," she said sweetly, "it's *my* turn to give the orders! You," she barked at Ryan, "get over there with the other outlaws!"

"Now look, Stephanie," Ryan began, taking a step

452

forward as his hands lowered. A single shot from the Winchester swept his hat from his head.

"The next bullet will be six inches lower, Cordell," she said quietly. The rifle barrel motioned the direction, and Ryan, glaring at her, joined Huntley and Bates. At her orders, Huntley and Bates tossed their pistols and rifles to the ground not far from where she sat, then backed slowly away. The Winchester waggled again, and all three men stood with their hands in the air while Stephanie edged toward her unconscious father.

"Father," she whispered huskily, "what did he do to you?" All she could see was Julian's broken leg and pain-lined face. Her anger against Ryan flared even higher. Everything Huntley and Bates had said about Ryan was true! He'd betrayed all of them, and now he'd even tried to kill her helpless father.

When she dared a glance at Julian, Ryan shifted slightly. Noting his movement from the corner of her eye, Stephanie whipped the Winchester and snapped, "I wouldn't try it, Cordell! I might not take the trouble to aim right this time . . ."

"Look, Stephanie," Ryan began, but she cut him off short.

"No, *you* look! We are going down this mountain, all of us together, and then I don't care what you do once you get me back to a town with a doctor for my father. I have no intention of listening to your lies, Cordell, so don't waste your breath." Stephanie paused and glared at her still unconscious father. "Huntley and Bates may not be right about many things, but they have certainly been right about

453

you," she added, ignoring Bates's faint protest.

Pushing at the hair in her eyes, Stephanie fought the urge to cry. That wouldn't do at all, but she was sorely tempted. How could he? How could Ryan have done this? Especially knowing how she felt about him . . .

Stephanie straightened her shoulders and jerked the rifle barrel toward the tunnel entrance.

"Ryan and Huntley, you carry my father. Bates, you bring the packs," she ordered. "I'll bring along the guns. Now!" she said when Ryan hesitated.

Furious, Ryan stalked over to Julian. He felt like slamming his fist into a solid rock wall to release his frustration and anger, but couldn't risk Stephanie's reaction. She seemed to have only a tenuous hold on her self-control, and might start shooting at the slightest provocation.

"So, how am I expected to carry him?" Ryan asked coldly as he gazed down at Julian. "By his legs? That ought to feel good . . ."

"Shut up!" Stephanie's voice rose and she controlled it with an effort. "I don't know how you should carry him," she said more calmly. "Just do it the best you can—and hurry!"

Ryan's jaw clenched, and a muscle leaped in the hard line of his jaw as he bent beside Julian. Moving swiftly, he fashioned a sling for Julian from a blanket and two shovel handles, telling Huntley to carry one end while he carried the other.

"Will this do?" he asked Stephanie sarcastically when she gave the sling a doubtful glance. "Or should I call an eagle to fly him down . . ."

"That will do fine," Stephanie cut in. The Winchester pointed the way toward the tunnel. "Let's go."

"Do we have water? Torches? What about extra ammunition in case we're attacked?"

Ryan's mocking questions made Stephanie pause. She arched a brow at him and answered, "We have water. We have torches. We have all my father's artifacts the packs will hold, and *I'm* carrying guns and ammunition."

"Oh, well, *that's* comforting. I suppose you're going to take on an entire war party single-handed? I admire your spirit if not your intelligence, Miss Ashworth!"

"Cordell, I doubt very seriously that a war party will find their way up here . . ."

"Do you?" Ryan jerked his head toward the blanket-covered corpse lying in the shade of a boulder. "Tell that to him. Yavapais killed him," he lied.

Stephanie hesitated uncertainly. "I thought you . . . you killed him," she said.

"Thanks for your high opinion. No, he was dead before I got up here." Ryan's eyes narrowed icily. "That's how your father got hurt. Didn't you stop to wonder why there was a barricade erected at the exit of the tunnel? A burial party of Yavapai Indians stumbled across Julian and his guide while they were uncovering statues and vases. Your father got hurt in the fight . . ."

"Enough. I don't need to hear any more of your lies, Ryan. I saw what you were doing when we arrived. And my father's not awake to contradict you. Wait until later when I talk to him; then I may believe you."

"Forget it, Princess." Ryan shrugged carelessly and lifted his end of the makeshift litter for Julian. "I don't really care if you believe me or not. It's your party—you call the shots."

Biting her lower lip to keep from bursting into tears, Stephanie said, "Let's go, Cordell. Grab your end of my father's sling, Huntley. Bates, clear away the barricade."

The brush cleared, the small procession made its way through the ridged arch of the tunnel entrance. Bates led the way, holding a torch high. At the tail end, a rifle-hung Stephanie followed with a torch and pistols.

If she fell, Stephanie reflected, she'd never be able to get back up. Ryan's rifle was slung over one shoulder and Huntley's over the other, while she wore two crossed gunbelts around her slim hips and carried a loaded pistol. She looked like a Mexican bandit.

Anxious to get down from the butte, Stephanie hurried the men as fast as she was able. She hated the dark, dank tunnel corridors that wound around so steeply, and dreaded the descent. But Julian had to be gotten to a physician as soon as possible. Stephanie had seen his bandaged leg, and wondered if her father might have other injuries as well.

Midway down, they paused for a rest. Ryan and Huntley gently lowered a still unconscious Julian to the ground. He moaned faintly, and Stephanie stepped forward with an anxious expression creasing her face.

"What's the matter with him?"

"Don' worry none," Huntley sneered, "we didn' hurt him! He's too tough a bird ta hurt easy. Wish I was as sure about gittin' back down this damn tunnel." He indicated the flickering torches with a nod of his head.

"If they go out," Stephanie said sharply, "we'll just have to find our way in the dark."

"Yeah?" Huntley took a menacing step forward and Stephanie's rifle snapped up only inches away from his face.

"Try it," she said softly, "and I'll shoot. Bates can carry your end of my father's sling . . ."

Backing off, Huntley glared at Stephanie hotly, then glanced at Ryan. "Well, why don't we just rush her, Cordell?" he asked. "If all of us jump her at once she hasn't got a chance!"

Ryan shrugged. "I don't really give a damn now. I'll worry about who's holding the rifles when we get out of here." His smile was nasty as his gaze held Stephanie's.

Finally breaking eye contact, Stephanie motioned with the Winchester. "Enough resting. Let's go . . ."

It took longer to get down the tunnel than it had to go up, but finally they stood within sight of the exit at the base of the butte. The curved window of light beckoned temptingly to tired eyes accustomed to damp darkness.

Then everything seemed to happen at once. Wild yells and shrill whoops echoed in the tunnel and deadly arrows whizzed through the air. Dropping Julian, Ryan dove for Stephanie and the guns. Instinct made her struggle to hold on to them, and Ryan's fist crashed into her jaw with jaw-breaking force. Sprawling backward on the unyielding shale floor of the tunnel, Stephanie lay in stunned fright as bullets spat noisily and a hard-flung lance clattered against the stone wall just above her head.

Ducking, she swerved to hide her face against Julian's chest, trying to protect both of them with her arms. The dimly flickering torches sputtered and went out completely, plunging the tunnel into darkness. Stephanie could barely see her hand in front of her face. Orange and yellow bursts of light punctuated the dark as rifles and pistols fired, and she wondered how any of them knew where to aim. The noise was deafening, the gunfire echoing in resounding waves through the corridors so that Stephanie barely heard a wounded cry only a few feet from her. Immediately she thought of Ryan.

"Ryan!" she screamed, but in the general melée he either didn't hear or didn't answer. Was he hurt? Who had been wounded? Stephanie waited in agonized suspense, coughing against the acrid smell of smoke and gunpowder.

Beneath her clutching fingers, Julian remained oblivious to the chaos around him, and Stephanie caught back a strangled sob. It had all been for nothing. They would die here within sight of freedom. At least she had found her father, Stephanie thought distractedly, though it had been too late to save him.

Suddenly, it grew quiet. The rattling echoes of

gunfire ceased, and she could hear only the shuffling of feet against the tunnel floor. Who had won the conflict? No one spoke, and there was only a faint moaning sound of someone in pain. Dimly, Stephanie realized it was her father. Burying her face into Julian's chest again, she squeezed her eyes tightly shut as a huge shadow loomed over them.

Chapter Thirty-Nine

"Stephanie." A boot nudged her in the ribs. "Stephanie," the familiar voice said again, and she lifted her head to stare up at Ryan's shadowed face. His offered hand was barely visible in the faint light from the exit and a relit torch, and she automatically reached to take it. Then, pausing, she withdrew her hand, pressing the backs of her fingers against her mouth.

"Is it over?" she asked in a muffled voice.

She couldn't see Ryan's faint, wry smile in the shadows. "Yes," he answered coolly, "it's over. For now. We can't afford to waste much time, Stephanie, so come on."

Rubbing her bruised jaw, Stephanie accused, "You hit me!"

"I had to in order to get the guns. Or did you intend to fight them off alone?"

"But you didn't even ask . . ."

"There wasn't time for polite inquiries," Ryan answered impatiently. "And there isn't time now for discussion. Either stay or come, but don't stand in my way."

Bending, he brusquely shoved her aside and lifted one end of Julian's litter.

"Get the other end, Huntley," Ryan ordered.

Stephanie's gaze swerved to Huntley. Her eyes widened as she saw the blood streaming down his arm, and she looked past him for Bates.

"Where . . . ?" she began, but Huntley cut her short.

"Don't ask. They got him . . ."

Stephanie glanced back at Ryan's grim face. She hadn't liked Bates, and had hoped to see him brought to justice for all the trouble he and Huntley had caused her, but in spite of that, she'd never wanted him dead.

"Oh, Huntley, I'm sorry . . ."

"So am I. Them Injuns will probably torture him afore they kill him . . ." Huntley's voice broke off.

"Oh, you mean he's been captured? I thought he'd been killed."

"It would have been better fer him if he had!" Huntley answered fiercely. "Yavapais can be devils when it comes to inventin' ways for a man to die, an' . . ."

"Enough," Ryan interrupted. "We've still got to run the gauntlet of hostile tribes before we're safe somewhere, and there's no point in giving her more to worry us about. See if she's capable of holding the torch while we take her father out of here, Huntley."

Ignoring Stephanie's stricken expression, the torch was shoved into her hands and Ryan lifted Julian's makeshift sling to his shoulder, balancing it

461

carefully between him and Huntley. When he paused, staring at her coolly, Stephanie stepped out of his way. She stomped behind them as Julian was borne to the tunnel exit and out onto the ledge.

Blinding sunlight hurt her eyes, and Stephanie raised a hand to shield her face from the glare. Fresh air was a relief, and she sucked in deep breaths that smelled of heat and dust and open space instead of the closed, clammy smell of darkness.

By the time they got Julian down from the ledge, he had regained consciousness. As soon as Ryan and Huntley lowered him to the ground, Stephanie was bending over him.

"Don't try to talk," she urged when Julian's eyes fluttered open and he licked his parched lips. "Here, drink this . . ."

Julian pushed it away after a moment, and smiled faintly up at Stephanie. His hand flopped weakly and she took it between both her palms, pressing tightly.

"Stephanie? Daughter . . . ?" His voice was gravelly and hoarse, and Stephanie laid her fingers over his lips.

"No. Later. We can talk later." She smiled encouragingly. "You need to rest . . ."

"What . . . are . . . you doing here? Thought . . . you were . . . in New York." He grimaced with pain. "My statues . . . did you get any of them . . . ?"

"We brought some of your artifacts with us, and when we get back to New York they will be prominently displayed, Father. Rest for now."

Obeying the soft command in her voice, Julian shut his eyes. His lined face relaxed slightly as he drifted into restless, exhausted sleep.

"Feel better?" Ryan's voice held a tinge of sarcasm that did not escape Stephanie's notice.

"No thanks to you—yes!" She stood up, facing Ryan with both hands on her hips. "You wouldn't care if he was still up there, would you!"

"No? Then why do you think I went up there? To sunbathe?" Ryan's patience grew thin as he stared at her through narrowed eyes.

"Don't start trying to tell me any more of your lies, Ryan Cordell. Just get us out of here before my father's leg grows even worse." Wheeling, Stephanie stalked in the direction of the horses Huntley had managed to catch.

"There's only three of 'em," Huntley said dolefully. "Them damn Yavapais ran off with th' rest, I guess."

Stephanie grabbed one of the bridles and patted the animal's lathered neck soothingly. For some reason she couldn't help but feel sympathy for Huntley, he looked so downcast and sad, and Bates's capture had put a pall on their successful descent from the butte.

"Huntley, I'm sorry about Bates, truly I am. I know he was your friend," Stephanie said.

"Yeah. Me and Alvie grew up together. He was th' only friend I ever had." Huntley shook his head. "Sure hate to think of what's happenin' to th' little fella now."

Shuddering, Stephanie forced back images of possible fates. "Can you think of a way to get my father back?" she asked in an effort to change the subject. "He's not able to ride one of the horses."

Ryan stood behind them, startling Stephanie who

hadn't known he was there when he suggested, "A travois."

"A what?" Half turning, Stephanie slid him a questioning glance. "What is a . . . trellis?"

"Travois. It's a sort of primitive sled with two poles as shafts, and an animal skin for the bed. Indians use it for carrying loads and also their sick or elderly. I've even seen babies ride in them with a basket of willow limbs forming a cage over the top."

"Can we make one for my father?"

"All we need are long enough poles."

"The shovel handles . . . ?"

"No. Too short. These have to be long enough to fit from the back of a horse to the ground." Ryan shoved back his hat, looking at the barren plain stretching around them. "I could go look . . ."

"Oh, I see! And forget to return?" Stephanie snapped. "That's predictable!"

Stepping close, Ryan glared into Stephanie's eyes. She was very conscious of his proximity, of the smell of sweat and tobacco, that—on Ryan—was not displeasing. Steeling herself, Stephanie faced him boldly, refusing to move an inch. He would not back her down again. Particularly since she knew what an utter cad and scoundrel he was . . .

"You are a suspicious bitch, as usual," Ryan observed harshly. "Don't you ever give anyone credit?"

"Only when deserved, Mr. Cordell."

"I see. You're just as arrogant when I have all the ammunition as you are when you do. At least you're consistent."

Angered by her adamant refusal to even consider

that he might be innocent of the accusations Huntley had charged him with, Ryan reached out to snare Stephanie by one arm as she started to walk away. He was suddenly determined that she would listen to him. Giving her a rough shake, he pulled her around.

"Listen, Princess, I'm sick and damned tired of . . ." Ryan paused, seeing Stephanie's eyes widen as she stared beyond him. "What is it?" he asked, turning to see.

A dust cloud rose above the distant horizon. It was small—two, maybe three riders, Ryan estimated. The point riders of a war party, perhaps?

"Get the rifles," Ryan ordered tersely, and Stephanie obeyed without question or comment.

Huntley, Ryan, and Stephanie positioned themselves behind a pile of boulders to wait, cradling rifles and all their extra ammunition. The dust cloud grew larger, coming across the flat plain slashed with zigzagging arroyos and gullies. By the time the cloud reached the nearest gully, it could be identified as only two riders, and they were riding hell-for-leather.

"Who is it?" Stephanie dared to ask, the first words she'd spoken since spotting the dust cloud. "Indians?"

"Can't tell with all the dust, but it looks like if it was Yavapai, there would be a lot more of them." Ryan cocked his hat to the back of his head and squinted into the distance.

"Then who?" Huntley wondered aloud. He covered his eyes with one hand, peering intently at the approaching cloud. "Look—" Pointing, he swore softly under his breath. Behind the two riders was another cloud, this one much larger.

"Dammit!" Ryan's jaw clenched. There was no hope for them now. The war party would be too big, and they could not fight them off with only three rifles and short-ranged pistols.

But suddenly Stephanie laughed, and amazed the two men by standing up from behind the safety of the rock and waving.

"Are you crazy?" Ryan demanded, yanking her back down beside him. "There's no reason to invite it . . ."

"Oh, be quiet! Can't you see who that is in the front?" She tugged her arm from Ryan's grasp and turned slightly to smile at Huntley. "Look at the slower rider, Huntley, and tell me if you recognize him."

"Bates!" Huntley's face broke into a grin as he leaped to his feet. Then, frowning, he said, "But why'd he lead an entire war party here with him, the dimwit!"

Stephanie pointed out, "The man with him looks as if he might be Father's guide. I'd say they were bringing help."

"How can you see that far?" Ryan narrowed his eyes, straining to see.

"It's easy enough to see—and hear. Listen. Then look at that bright banner in the middle of the larger dust cloud. That tells you who they are."

A tinny challenge was being blown on a bugle—a regulation United States Army bugle. Now Ryan could see the flag waving proudly through the filmy haze; the red and white stripes, and a pattern of stars against a field of blue were barely recognizable.

466

"How on earth did Bates manage to run across a troop of soldiers?" Ryan muttered.

But it was the man with him who had found the cavalry, and he had also been the one to rescue Bates from the Yavapai.

"This here's all th' men th' cap'n could spare fer us," Bingo told Ryan. "But it'll git us back safe enuf, I reckon."

"Where'd you find Bates?" Stephanie asked. She glanced at the portly outlaw. "We thought . . ." She paused delicately.

"Thought I wuz dead?" Bates finished for her cheerfully. "Hell, they cain't kill Alvin Bates, nosirree! I'm a lil' bit cooked, but alive."

"They wuz a'roastin' him over a slow fire when I found him," Bingo said with a chuckle. "You shoulda heard th' squallin' an' bawlin', jus' like a baby hog! An' th' fire hadn' even caught yet! Lord, I heard him fer ten miles a'fore I found him, an' smelled him fer three!"

"You rescued him by yourself?" Stephanie asked.

"Naw, me an' them calv'ry boys I'd stumbled acrost gave them Yavapai what-fer!" Bingo chuckled again. "It wuz a good thing fer Bates that he wuz as much trouble fer them poor Injuns as he wuz, or they woulda waited until they got back ta camp ta roast him. He hollered so much, an' plumb wore out one of their horses with all his blubber, that they decided ta git rid of him early."

Affronted by Bingo's reference to his portly frame, Bates said, "Ennyway, it worked, didn't it? If I hadn' made 'em stop to kill me, you wouldn' have found me."

467

Scratching his head, Bingo agreed, adding, "An if ya hadn' of gotten yerself caught, ya wouldn' of needed findin'."

The calvary troop rode close, slowing their horses to a walk as they saw no sign of distress, and Ryan walked out to meet them. Watching him, Stephanie felt a familiar tug at her heart. The time was near for them to go their own ways, and even though Ryan had lied and betrayed her, she couldn't help the wave of grief that was enveloping her like a dark cloud. Once they reached a railroad, she would go back to New York, and Ryan—Ryan would continue with his life. Without her.

Tears stung Stephanie's eyes and rolled down her cheeks as she realized she might never see Ryan Cordell again.

Chapter Forty

Stephanie stood on the low wooden porch of the commanding officer's quarters in Camp Verde, staring at the horizon of red spires and buttes. The wagon would be there any moment to take her and Julian to Flagstaff to catch a train east. A qualified physician would be accompanying them from Flagstaff in order to tend Julian, and they were to meet Claudia in Gallup, New Mexico. The little party would then travel together back to New York.

Sighing, Stephanie thought of the long ride to Camp Verde from what she now thought of as Magic Rock. The calvary had accompanied them back to the fort, a long, hot, dusty ride that had seemed to stretch endlessly yet end too soon.

Glumly, Stephanie recalled Ryan's coldness during the ride, and his avoidance of her since they'd arrived at the fort. While plodding along on an army mule, Stephanie had had plenty of time to think things over on the way to Camp Verde. Though Julian was still unconscious most of the way, she had

469

gleaned enough information to understand that she'd once again misjudged Ryan. Bingo had been a cheerful informant without even realizing it, confirming a large part of what Ryan had already told her.

Debating on the right approach, Stephanie had finally decided to bluntly apologize. She waited for an opportunity to speak to Ryan alone, and found it just before they rode into Camp Verde. Angling her mule alongside Ryan's, Stephanie had quietly apologized for her earlier behavior.

"That's not necessary, Miss Ashworth," he'd said with an indifferent shrug when she began to stammer her apology, "I understand."

"No," Stephanie had said desperately. "You don't! I . . . I said some things that were unnecessary and unkind, even when I didn't really mean them, Ryan, and . . ."

Wearily, he waved a hand to stop her flow of words. "I said it wasn't necessary to explain, Stephanie. We're just from two entirely different worlds, that's all. You have your way of looking at things, and I have mine." He bent a smile in her direction without really looking at her. "I have to admit, I prefer mine. I may judge people at times, but at least I wait until I've heard their side of it."

Stephanie's temper flared. "Oh, is that right? Then maybe you can explain why you decided on my character before you even met me properly? One meeting—under strained circumstances, I might add—and you decided I was a spoiled, rich heiress who toyed with men's affections then tossed them aside. Isn't that what you told me?"

470

"Isn't that how you acted?" Ryan defended himself. "You got off that stage like God-almighty, Miss Hoity-toity come to visit the uncivilized savages in Arizona, and proceeded to berate some poor guy who'd driven your stage for two hundred miles! Then you sail past the scraps of humanity who'd gathered just to look at a pretty woman who wasn't a dance hall girl or Indian squaw, twitching your long, elegant skirts aside as if afraid of getting them dirty!"

"I did not!" Stephanie glared at him indignantly. "I was only angry because you made sneering references to my height, and . . . and I reacted in the only way I knew!" Her fingers tightened around the leather reins and she jerked at the mule's head to edge him closer to Ryan's stallion. "All my life, Ryan, I've watched other girls who are small and dainty, mincing coyly along and making men's eyes pop and tongues hang out. When I walk into a room, they stare at me like I'm some sort of freak! I know I'm tall, and I refuse to slump over or wear flat, ugly shoes just because of that. Most men seem to regard my height as a deficiency of some sort, and are easily intimidated. My defense has always been to retreat behind a sharp tongue."

"It works well," Ryan observed. He forestalled her next comment with an uplifted hand. "No, don't say it. It doesn't matter. I was wrong, Princess. We don't have as much in common as I thought we did, and all this self-exoneration we're doing won't change that. Let's just say we learned something from this, and go our separate ways. I'll bill you for my guide services when you've returned to New York. You still owe me a hundred dollars, remember," he said when she narrowed her eyes, "and I want to tear up that agreement I signed."

"Fine," Stephanie answered coolly. "It's been a very enjoyable lesson, Mr. Cordell. I'm certain that you have no shortage of pupils, so I won't waste any more of your valuable—and expensive—time." She kicked her mule into a lethargic trot that wouldn't have outdistanced Aesop's tortoise, silently cursing the lazy beast as Ryan rode past at a humiliatingly fast pace. Stephanie coughed on Ryan's dust, and wished for a bridle on her tongue. Perhaps it would have averted this ever-widening chasm between them, if she had not been so quick to speak out without really listening to all the facts. Her tendency to throw up an immediate shield of animosity as a defense against rejection, had cost her the man she now knew she loved above everything.

She forced an indifferent expression as another rider came up beside her, half turning to see the animal-skin clad man who was her father's guide. A faint smile lifted her lips at the unusual hat on his head, and the tiny gold earring he wore. This was definitely a very distinctive individual, she thought.

"What'sa matter, gal?" Bingo asked, nudging his lop-eared mule beside Stephanie. Following the direction of Stephanie's gaze, he glanced toward Ryan. Noting the stiff back and squared shoulders as Ryan cantered to the front of the troops, Bingo commented, "Man trouble?"

"Not really, Mr. Bingo," Stephanie said calmly. "He's only my guide . . ."

"If ya will pardon me fer inter'uptin', I think thar's

472

a heap more ta it than that," Bingo said. "I seen th' way th' two of ya act, lookin' at each other when ya think yer both not lookin', an' if Cordell means no more ta ya than jus' a guide, I'll eat my hat, wolf fangs an' all!"

"There's no need for that," Stephanie had admitted with a wry smile, "you're correct. But I'm afraid there's a rift between us that cannot be bridged."

Bingo guffawed and spat a stream of tobacco juice to the dusty trail. Wiping his mouth with the back of one hand, he'd observed shrewdly, "Even th' Grand Canyon can be bridged if'n ya want it bad enough, little lady. 'Member that."

"Oh, you don't understand," Stephanie began, but he cut her off once more.

"Do ya think I ain't never loved some fine woman, missy? Yeah, an' I found ta my sorrow that I wuz too old an' set in my ways ta change, but that one ain't." He indicated Ryan with a nod of his head.

"No, Ryan Cordell has rejected my apology, and I won't offer another one. I'd rather die!" she added bitterly.

"Pride makes an awfully cold bed, missy, an' love kin keep ya warm in a blizzard." He winked at her. "Think on that a spell."

Bingo's words were to haunt Stephanie all the way to Flagstaff. She waited on the porch for what seemed hours, smiling woodenly at the soldiers crowded around her, answering questions about her father's health and the artifacts he'd collected, until she

473

thought she would scream. Still no Ryan.

Bingo trudged across the dawn-lit parade grounds to bid her farewell, and even Huntley and Bates appeared to shyly offer apologies and good-byes, but not Ryan. By the time Julian was loaded on a mattress in the back of the wagon and the escort was mounted and ready, Stephanie's smile seemed frozen to her face.

"Well," Bingo said to her as she was helped to the wide front seat of the half-covered wagon, "tell yer father he wuz' th' best damn time I've had in a long while, missy . . ."

"Tell me yourself, you poor excuse for a worthless, no-count guide," a weak voice interjected. "Don't talk around me like I'm an invalid, or already dead, dammit!"

Chortling, Bingo stepped to the back of the wagon and peered inside at Julian.

"Pilgrim, ya look like ya been dead a week," he said cheerfully. "An' ya don' smell much better. Next time I see ya, ya lazy, good-fer-nothin' dude, ya better be standin' on both them feet."

Grinning, Julian promised, "I will. And when you come to New York, it will be my turn to guide you."

"Ah, that won' never happen! I ain't comfor'ble-like in them big, smelly cities where ya cain't see th' sky. A man should be able ta breathe fresh air that sumbody else ain't already walked on, Pilgrim." Bingo rocked back on his heels and smiled. "Now, if'n ya git tired of breathin' that stale air in Noo Yawk, come on up ta Iddy-ho. I plan on huntin' griz up thar', an' makin' me a necklace of bear claws. Not much griz down here in Arizona, but Cordell tells me

474

they're thick as fleas on a hound dog up on his place."

"Grizzlies, huh?" Julian said with piqued interest. "Like the one who removed part of your hairline? I hear those are fierce, dangerous beasts to hunt."

"Ya hear right, Pilgrim. They's a man's kind of hunt, big as a oak tree an' cunnin' as kit-foxes. If'n ya kin outfox a griz, yer pretty damn good!"

"Sold! When can I join you?" Julian asked. "I should be healed in a few months . . ."

"Father," Stephanie interrupted, "it will be quite a while before you're well enough to go on a hunt. You're not well, and will probably be convalescing for some time. Besides, you're getting too old for this! Look at what's happened to you, and . . ."

"Daughter, I'm not mortally wounded, and I'm not about to spend the rest of my life sitting in a cushioned chair and getting fat!" Julian smiled feebly, but his voice was strong as he added, "I will be there in the springtime, Mr. Bingo, to hunt grizzly bear."

"Ah, yer gonna love it, Pilgrim! Why, th' mountains up thar make th' Alps look like hills fer chil'ren ta climb!"

"Say good-bye, Mr. Bingo," Stephanie said stiffly. "I believe we're ready to leave."

Crinkling his face into a smile, Bingo tugged at the wolf-head hat he wore. Early morning light glinted from the gold earring on his earlobe as he looked up at her.

"Missy, I shore hope ya find whut yer lookin' fer, or yer gonna be a dried-up old prune with no sense of humor an' no love in yer heart fer anything," he said.

"But sumhow, I think yer gonna make it. Yer a purty smart gal once ya fergit that silly pride. Th' Bible tells ya that pride goeth before destruction, an' a haughty spirit a'fore a fall. I think mebbe Cordell needs ta learn that Bible verse, too."

"Perhaps you can tutor him, Mr. Bingo." Stephanie smiled when the old man said he intended to do that very thing. Leaning forward, she whispered so only Bingo could hear, "And tell Ryan that I hope he finds where the fair wind blows. He'll understand what I mean."

Bingo nodded and stepped back away from the wagon.

Glancing at Huntley and Bates standing forlornly on the porch, Stephanie hesitated, then waved goodbye.

"I hope you two stay out of trouble now that your sins have been pardoned," she said sternly. "We didn't file charges in the hopes that you will get honest employment."

Nodding, Bates's round face creased into a smile. "Oh, we will, Miss Ashworth! Why, I'm thinkin' 'bout ranchin', mebbe, or capturin' an' sellin' wild mustangs ta th' government. Th' cap'n here says th' Army's alway needin' good horses."

"That's honest work," Stephanie approved. She smiled at Huntley's disgruntled expression and the sour glance he gave his garrulous friend.

"It's hard work, is what it is," Huntley grumbled. "I think that Injun fire scorched yer brains, Alvie."

Bates dug an elbow into Huntley's ribs and said, "This time, *I've* got a plan, Huntley."

Bingo stepped back from the wagon side as the

476

driver mounted and took up his whip, and the wide wooden wagon lurched forward with a creaky rumble. Half turning, Stephanie glanced at the row of adobe and wood buildings, hoping for some sign of Ryan, but there was none. He'd obviously forgotten her existence.

Spitting into the dust, Bingo walked back into the shade of the suttler's as Stephanie's wagon rounded a curve and disappeared from sight. Huntley and Bates were the only two still standing in the bright sunlight of the parade ground.

Glancing at Bates, Huntley said acidly, "A ranch? Have you lost yer mind, Alvie? I don' want to work on no damned ranch! And who in th' hell wants to fight those crazy mustangs just fer a few dollars a head?" He snorted derisively.

"Mebbe we should buy our own ranch, Huntley."

"Oh, now I know yer touched in th' head, Alvie! Buy our own ranch? With what? We got two dollars between us . . ." Pausing, his eyes narrowed at Bates's serene expression, and was gripped with apprehension. "What have you done, Alvie . . . ?"

A beatific smile stretched Bates's mouth as he thumped a forefinger on the ragged pack over his shoulder.

"I collected, Huntley. That's all."

"Collected? I'll show you a collection—of yer broken bones, you idiot! I thought you really had sumthin' there fer a minute."

"I do." Bates's voice was so assured that he caught his partner's attention again. "While the rest of you were givin' orders an' plannin' on how ta git down from th' butte, I picked up a lil' memento that wuz

477

lyin' aroun'. I stuck it in my shirt, so's nobody'd see. Seein' as how Ashworth don' really need *all* them things he wuz collectin', old bones an' broken vases an' stuff, I helped myself. He won' never miss it, with all th' goods he had crammed in them packs." Shrugging at Huntley's exasperated snort of disgust, Bates continued calmly. "I didn' even lose it when all them damned yellin' pack of Yavapai got me, an' so I brung it back with me . . ."

"What in the hell is it, Alvie?" Huntley interrupted. "I'm gettin' bored with all this groundwork yer layin', and I ain't particularly interested in old bones . . ."

"How 'bout this?" Bates dug into the corner of his pack and lifted out one of his shirts. While Huntley watched with impatiently tapping toes, Bates slowly unwrapped the filthy shirt, neatly peeling back the sleeves to reveal his prize.

"Holy Mary!" Huntley breathed softly. His eyes moved to Alvie in awe.

Holding up the small statue, Bates frowned at the speck of dust that marred the smooth countenance of some ancient god. He flicked it away with one finger, turning it slightly, and sunlight reflected in blinding rays from its surface.

"Yep," Bates said. "Pure gold, an' worth a fortune . . ."

Chapter Forty-One

Rain pattered softly against the windowpanes of her bedroom as Stephanie paced the carpeted floor restlessly. Her long dressing gown dragged across the floor, and she was suddenly reminded of that feathered dressing gown she'd worn at Fancy Lil's. Quickly, she thrust the thought away, not wanting to remember.

She hadn't been able to concentrate on anything in the six months since they'd been back in New York, even Christmas. Somehow, she couldn't seem to get in the spirit of the festive season, though Julian had tried his best to buoy her spirits.

"That rain will turn to snow before nightfall, mark my words," Claudia predicted, setting down a silver tray with its teapot and cups. "The muffins are piping hot and dripping with butter, just the way you like them," she added with an anxious glance at Stephanie's pale face. "And there are some of your favorite cakes."

"Thank you, but I'm not hungry, Claudie. Just tea will be fine," Stephanie said listlessly. "Is Father home yet?"

"Yes. He's in his study with a curator from the museum. Those pieces he brought back have attracted the attention of museums and scholars from around the world. I heard a man from the Washington museum say it was a find unequaled in archaeological circles, and that your father should be awarded honors from the society."

Stephanie smiled faintly. "I'm certain Father's chest puffed up with pride at that! And I know he regaled them for hours with his adventures."

"Of course." Claudia paused, wondering if she should mention the subject that usually brought a cold stare from Stephanie. At her request, no one was allowed to mention Ryan Cordell in her presence.

It had been six months, and the poor child had not heard a word from him, not even the threatened bill for his services. It had been a mistake not to insist Stephanie stay with her at the fort, Claudia supposed, instead of encouraging her to search for Julian. But Stephanie had always been such an unapproachable, level-headed young lady where men were concerned, that it hadn't occurred to Claudia that she would fall in love with Ryan Cordell. Indeed, it had seemed as if they hated each other on sight.

Sighing, Claudia decided against mentioning him. It would only plunge Stephanie further into depression if she wasn't already thinking about him. She hesitated, debating on whether she should make

480

casual conversation, but Stephanie was staring out the long window again, lost in thought. Lately, she often retreated into that private world where no one else was allowed to follow. Claudia stood there uncertainly, then quietly left the room and shut the door.

Stephanie was, as usual, thinking about Ryan. He was in her thoughts daily, no matter how fervently she threw herself into activities. She fluctuated between hope and despair with a rapidity that was frightening. She had even descended far enough into melancholy to contemplate sending him a telegram, but that brief sojourn into insanity was swiftly quelled. Where would she send it? She had no idea where Ryan was, or what he was doing.

Was he still in Arizona? Had he returned to Idaho, or gone back to Colorado or New Mexico to work as a guide? Was he even alive?

Stephanie pressed her nose against the cold glass of her window, staring out as the rain turned into snow. She truly felt like the "ice maiden" now. Any normal response to a man was frozen inside, locked up as if surrounded by an iceberg of gargantuan proportions.

Gray light slowly faded into night, and Stephanie turned away from the window. Her tea had cooled, and the little cakes and muffins Claudie had lovingly placed on a plate were stale and dry. She was surprised to see the wall lamps lit, and realized she hadn't even heard the maid come in to light them. Stephanie gazed dully at the garland-hung tree Claudia had insisted she have in her room, "to

481

remind you of Christmas joy," she'd said.

A rueful smile curved her mouth as she turned away from the gaily decorated tree. This would never do, Stephanie told herself sternly. She had to snap out of her daze and go on with life. After all, Ryan certainly didn't seem to be missing her!

Wandering to her bookshelves, Stephanie took down a thick volume and curled up on the chaise to read. A fire popped and crackled in the grate, and her bedchamber smelled of cedar and Christmas. She tried hard to concentrate, but nothing made sense and she finally shut the book with a snap.

Stephanie was staring into space when a knock sounded on her door.

"Miss, your father would like to see you in his study," the upstairs maid informed her, and Stephanie nodded.

"Thank you, Molly. Tell him I will be right down as soon as I've dressed," she said.

Not really caring how she looked, Stephanie yanked a plain blouse and skirt from the heavy oak armoire in the corner, and drew a perfunctory brush through her hair. On impulse, she didn't twist the long silver strands into their customary tight knot on her head, but bound them with a bright, festive red ribbon. That should please Julian a bit, she thought. He worried so about her. Especially since her violent quarrel with Reginald Farrington.

Even though pleased about her refusal to marry the man he considered a "blithering idiot," Julian disliked the apathetic state into which his daughter had fallen.

"You've been dumped, young man," he'd told Farrington unsympathetically. "Accept it." Should he say the same to Stephanie?

Now Julian tapped his fingers impatiently on his desk, giving the visitor sitting in a high-backed chair across from him an occasional searching glance. This should be an interesting and very enlightening confrontation, Julian mused pleasantly. He did so enjoy surprises.

"Mr. Ashworth," his visitor was saying, "this is my list of expenses for delivery of your goods, as you requested. Will there be anything else? It's almost Christmas, and I'd . . ."

"Did you deliver to the museum those pieces I wired you about?" Julian interrupted. "They were particularly anxious to see them, and I'd hate for them to be disappointed this close to Christmas."

"Yes. I stopped there first. You are my last stop before I catch my train home."

"Home? Didn't you live in New York once?"

"Yes. A long time ago."

"Where did you meet Allan Pinkerton?" Not waiting for an answer, Julian continued. "He never did tell me, except to say that I was a bloody fool for going to Arizona without asking his assistance for a guide. If it hadn't been for my strong-willed, stubborn daughter, he wouldn't have discovered my plans at all. I'm not certain whether she did me a favor or not." He slid his visitor a sharp glance, and picked up pen and paper. "I must say, I was most surprised when I was told that Allan hired you to guide and protect me and my daughter. Too bad we missed connections at Fort Defiance."

"Yes," the man agreed blandly. "But everything turned out well in spite of the bad start. How's your leg?"

"Changing the subject, huh? The leg's fine. I'll walk with a limp for a while, but other than that, it's healing nicely." He grinned. "I had an excellent bone surgeon set it for me . . ."

There was a long silence as Julian scratched figures on his pad of paper, then drew out his leather-bound ledger to write out a draft on his bank.

"Here you are, sir," he said, handing the paper to his visitor.

As a fire burned merrily in the dark-paneled study, flickering light playing over the leather chair in which he was seated, the visitor studied the draft he'd been handed.

"This is not quite what I was expecting," he said finally, glancing up at Julian sitting behind his large carved desk.

"No? You want more?"

A faint smile, then, "No, I was under the impression that a portion of the pieces donated to the museum were to be mine."

"Oh, they are. But I took the liberty of marketing them for you, as I'm familiar with their value. They brought much more than I'd ever dreamed. You are a wealthy young man, sir." Smiling, Julian formed a steeple with his fingers, staring across his wide desk. "Would you rather market them yourself? I can give you a list of several reputable dealers here in New York . . ."

"No, no. This . . . is . . . fine. I'm just surprised by the value, that's all. I didn't expect this . . ."

"So it seems," Julian commented dryly. "Would you care for some brandy? I have an excellently stocked wine cellar, which I sorely missed during my sojourn in Arizona. Did I tell you about all my experiences out there? I know that you are probably accustomed to hearing such tales, but I miss that arid region more than I thought possible when I first got off the train. It was quite an experience . . ."

He broke off, glancing up when a light tap sounded on his closed doors.

"Ah," Julian said, scraping back his chair and bunching the fine Oriental rug, "I've been expecting you, my dear!" He limped forward to embrace Stephanie who had paused just inside the double doors, then drew her with him. As they approached, Julian's visitor rose from the high-backed chair and turned to face them.

Stephanie halted abruptly and gave her father an accusing glare that silently said, "How could you!" and wished she'd put on her deep blue velvet instead of her everyday clothes. Recovering her aplomb, Stephanie held out her hand and said, "What a surprise! How have you been, Ryan?"

She'd been right, Stephanie decided, when she'd once thought that Ryan would look splendid in a suit. He was garbed in a rich brown wool, with a tapered vest that fit his broad chest snugly. And he'd had a haircut, Stephanie noted in amazement. It wasn't short, but the ends had been trimmed to barely brush his collar, and he was clean-shaven instead of

485

wearing a familiar shadow on the strong line of his jaw. How could she have forgotten the brilliance of his eyes—and how they could pierce her to the core?

"Stephanie, you're as beautiful as ever," Ryan answered, and she surprised them both by blushing.

The air tingled with tension as they stood facing each other, and neither Ryan nor Stephanie noticed when Julian discreetly withdrew and shut the study doors behind him.

"So, how have you been?" they chorused at the same time, then laughed awkwardly.

"The last time I saw you, you were riding in a buckboard and wearing a hat and guns," Ryan said after a moment. "When you left Camp Verde," he explained at the puzzled look on her face.

"Oh. I . . . didn't recall your coming to say good-bye."

"I didn't. But I watched you leave."

She couldn't think of anything to say that would not sound like an accusation, so Stephanie asked, "How's Bingo? And Huntley and Bates?"

Ryan grinned. "Bingo is happily dug into an Idaho mountainside, plotting for springtime and grizzlies. And this is going to sound like a tall tale, but Huntley and Bates are ranchers now."

"Ranchers?" Stephanie laughed, shaking her head in amazement. "How did they get the money to buy a ranch—rob a bank?"

"That's what I wondered until I stopped by to see them about two months ago. They still like their whiskey, and it wasn't at all difficult to find out their little secret. Do you remember the confusion on the

486

butte?" When Stephanie, her eyes darkening, nodded, Ryan continued. "It seems that clumsy, bungling Bates managed to stuff a statue in his shirt when no one was looking. How he held on to it even while being burned at the stake by Yavapais defies anyone's imagination!"

"How did he find a buyer for his statue in Arizona?" Stephanie asked in surprise. "Those artifacts will bring much more in a reputable museum in New York than they would . . ."

"Solid gold," Ryan cut in. "That will sell anywhere."

"Yes," Stephanie agreed. "It will."

Noting for the first time that her father had deserted her, Stephanie silently denounced him for a traitor and crossed self-consciously to the liquor cabinet.

Watching her, Ryan recalled the Stephanie he was accustomed to seeing, dressed in men's trousers and a baggy shirt, wearing a dusty, floppy hat and a gunbelt. The slim skirt she wore now emphasized her trim hips and long legs, and the high-necked blouse with lace-edged collar and sleeves accented her feminine attributes. Which were considerable, he admitted to himself. God, he'd missed her! He hadn't realized just how much until he'd turned around and seen her standing a few feet from him, with her darkly glistening eyes wide with surprise, and the faint blush staining her still-tanned cheeks.

"Ryan?" Stephanie's voice prompted. "I asked if you would care for a drink."

"Yes. Whiskey, neat."

Pouring a liberal amount in a cut-crystal glass, Stephanie said, "It was a vintage year for rotgut, I'm told." She held out the glass, and as his fingers brushed against hers, she was suddenly reminded of a battered tin cup, a mesquite fire, and thousands of stars peppering a dark velvet sky.

Hearing the echo of his own words, Ryan's smile was soft and tender, and his eyes crinkled at the corners with amusement.

"You took a shot at me that time," he said softly, and they were both suddenly transported back to Arizona as the study walls melded into arid, dusty plains and towering red spires.

"I didn't want to take any chances," she said lightly.

"What about now, Princess? Do you dare take a chance on me now?"

Stephanie paused, unable to answer. She stared at Ryan, memorizing every line and curve of his face, the eyes, the nose, mouth and chin, so that she would always have this mental picture to carry in her heart. Her throat constricted when Ryan, his mouth set in a grim line of resignation, set his untouched whiskey on her father's desk and turned as if to leave.

"Ryan!" Bingo's words still haunted her, and Stephanie suddenly knew that pride didn't matter now. Ryan mattered, and if she didn't say something, didn't stop him, he would walk out of her father's study and her life. "Wait," she said as he started toward the double doors.

But when he turned back around, raising his dark brows to stare at her questioningly, Stephanie didn't know what to say. The right words were so important, and none would come to mind. When he shrugged after a few moments, and it seemed as if he would take those last few steps out the door, she remembered how good it had felt to fall into his arms all the other times, and Stephanie blurted, "Yes! Yes, I want to take a chance, Ryan . . ."

Chapter Forty-Two

Snuggling happily beneath the heavy wool lap robe, Stephanie watched fat snowflakes drift in a white blanket over Central Park. Carriage wheels crunched in the new-fallen snow and white clouds formed in front of the horse's nostrils as he pranced down the park lane.

"Happy, Princess?" Ryan asked, curving his arm to bring her even closer.

"Umm—I have a feeling I'm not going to miss New York at all," Stephanie said. "And Father has already made plans to visit us in spring. He said something about hunting griz with Bingo." She sat up suddenly, exclaiming, "Did you know that Father has actually taken up the habit of chewing tobacco? You should have seen the expression on Mr. Fairchild's face when Father hit a spittoon from six feet away, then announced that he'd become quite proficient in hitting lizards in Arizona! They all think he's become rather 'rustic,' Mrs. Eubanks informed me one evening at the opera."

Ryan laughed, then said, "We'll wait until spring to go to my ranch, love. The weather will be beautiful then."

"Does it snow a lot in Idaho?" she asked Ryan dreamily, leaning back and pressing her cheek against his shoulder.

"Don't you like snow?"

"Yes. But I like you better."

"That's comforting to know," Ryan said dryly, "since you have agreed to marry me. A wife should always like her husband better than snow . . ."

"And plum pudding? That's my favorite . . ."

"That's negotiable. I can be reasonable."

Laughing, Stephanie took Ryan's cold face between her gloved palms and kissed him on the tip of his nose. When she would have sat back against the thick cushions of the carriage, he pulled her half over him, his arms circling her and holding her across his lap.

"Ryan," she scolded, "what if someone sees us?"

"There isn't anyone else crazy enough to be out in this snow . . ."

"Those two men over there on the park bench," Stephanie pointed out with a wicked smile. "What if they're watching?"

Ryan considered it gravely for a moment, then said, "I think they're dead drunk. And if they can see, they'll be jealous. I can't blame them—I have the most beautiful woman in New York sitting on my lap, while they have pigeons sitting on their heads."

"Maybe they like pigeons . . ." Ryan's mouth smothered Stephanie's following words as he kissed her hard on the lips. When he finally released her, she gazed up at him with sparkling eyes. "Do that again," she breathed softly, and he willingly complied.

Finally realizing that the driver had stopped the carriage beneath a snow-frosted tree, Ryan murmured against Stephanie's lips, "I think we're melting the snow, love."

Glancing up, she agreed a little breathlessly, "Yes, but who cares?"

Ryan squeezed her tightly. "Not me. Sun or snow doesn't matter when I'm with you."

Stephanie sighed with pure pleasure. She rubbed her cheek against the rough wool of Ryan's overcoat, and slid her hands inside next to his chest.

"Ryan?" she murmured a few moments later, "Why didn't you tell me that Allan Pinkerton hired you to guide me to my father? It would have made things so much easier."

She felt his shrug as he answered, "Because he told me not to tell you. He said you'd be offended, and that your father would refuse any assistance. Pinkerton was paying me good money, so naturally I agreed."

"But after . . . after so many accusations, why didn't you tell me that you weren't a criminal, or after Father's treasures?"

"I tried," he said dryly. "Don't you remember?"

"Oh. Yes, I guess you did." She was silent for a moment, then said, "But you still charged me five hundred dollars for guiding me, even though Allan was paying you . . . !"

"Well, of course! Would you have trusted a man who'd guide you for free? I mean, you're cute,

Princess, but no man would agree to guide you through Indian territory and across mountains and deserts, just because you have a great body and beautiful face!" Pausing, Ryan amended, "Well, maybe there's *one* man who would . . . !"

Laughing, Stephanie tucked her hands even farther into Ryan's coat, wanting to get as close to him as possible. Their wedding day seemed so far away that she was tempted to suggest an elopement, but Julian would never forgive her. He was delighted with his prospective son-in-law, and loudly proclaimed his intentions to walk his daughter down the church aisles without so much as a limp.

"And then I'm heading for Idaho," Julian had said with a broad wink at Ryan, "to hunt grizzly with Bingo!"

"I'm not sure I want you along on my honeymoon," Stephanie had retorted, and Julian had laughed.

A thought struck her, and tilting her head, Stephanie asked Ryan, "What do you think of going to Arizona for a honeymoon, Ryan?"

Frowning, he looked down at her. "Are you serious?"

"I believe I really am! There's something about that desolate region that is fascinating."

"Yeah. Well . . . we could go find that map you lost when you didn't tie the packs on the horses. Julian says it would be worth a great deal to anyone who found it." Ryan scratched his jaw thoughtfully. "And I heard the most interesting story from this guy I met on the train. He was telling me about a lost city of gold somewhere down below Mexico in Peru.

Seems that these ancient Indians built an entire city with gold and silver, and when the Spaniards came they found a way to hide it. Whoever found that city would be worth a fortune . . ."

"And think of the archaeological treasures!" Stephanie added. "Oh, Ryan, do you know where it is?"

"As a matter of fact, I just happened to get the approximate location, Princess . . ."

Snow blew softly around the carriage as dusk fell in deep purple shrouds over Central Park. But the two intrepid adventurers enclosed within were already in the steaming jungles of South America . . .